THE
IMMORTALS

THE
IMMORTALS

S.E. Lister

First published in Great Britain in 2015

This paperback edition published 2016 by Old Street Publishing Ltd
c/o Parallel, 8 Hurlingham Business Park
Sulivan Road London SW6 3DU

www.oldstreetpublishing.co.uk

ISBN 978-1-910400-48-7

10 9 8 7 6 5 4 3 2 1

A CIP catalogue record for this title is available from the British Library.

Typeset by JaM

Printed and bound by CPI Group (UK) Ltd, Croydon, CR0 4YY

To the Shortman son
who is twin to this book
with love
wherever your journeys take you.

And therefore I have sailed the seas and come
To the holy city of Byzantium.

O sages standing in God's holy fire
As in the gold mosaic of a wall,
Come from the holy fire, perne in a gyre,
And be the singing-masters of my soul.
Consume my heart away; sick with desire
And fastened to a dying animal
It knows not what it is; and gather me
Into the artifice of eternity.

Once out of nature I shall never take
My bodily form from any natural thing,
But such a form as Grecian goldsmiths make
Of hammered gold and gold enamelling
To keep a drowsy Emperor awake;
Or set upon a golden bough to sing
To lords and ladies of Byzantium
Of what is past, or passing, or to come.

W. B. Yeats, *Sailing to Byzantium*

Part One

1

1945

Rosa came home after seven years, in the same year she had left. It was the beginning of the wet spring she knew so well. She found their cottage on the edge of a village, the latest Hyde home in a string of many, tucked out of the way behind a disused cattle barn. There were sandbags stacked against the steps, blackout curtains in every window. Bindweed framed the doorway. Beyond the fields a church spire rose into the dusky sky, lashed by rain, its chimes silenced.

A glossy blackbird shook its wings in a tree above her head, its liquid song filling the evening air. Everything was green, fat raindrops sliding from oak leaves and splashing onto the newly sprouted daffodils on the side of the road. There was a bicycle leaning against a silver birch. The grass at her feet was thick with snails.

She knocked, and after a few moments the door clicked open. A fair-haired girl blinked up at her politely. Rosa stared at her sister, now ten years old and tall for it, and felt the whole breadth of her own absence.

Bella ducked halfway back into the hallway. She peered out from behind her hair, plainly confused as to why this ragged stranger was familiar. Rosa's words, rehearsed across many miles and decades, caught in her throat. She had nothing to say.

"Who is it?"

Footsteps, and then Bella had been pulled aside, making way for an apron-clad woman with her hair in curlers. She had a tea-towel in one hand and a mug in the other. Her mouth grew small and tight. The mug began to shake, spilling a slick of coffee onto the floor.

"Come in. Hurry! Come in…" Her mother's hands did not touch her, but beckoned urgently. The door was pulled closed. In the hallway Rosa looked at Harriet Hyde, who had grown thinner, her face lined and her fiery hair dulled with grey. The softness around her edges had been replaced by a strained, brittle look. She bent to dab at the stain on the floor, shooing Rosa away when she tried to help. Bella clung to her apron.

"Did you walk through the village dressed like that?" Harriet asked at last, straightening up. Rosa nodded. "Were you seen by anyone?"

"I don't think so. It's dark, mother."

"Yes, yes, I know. But busybodies at their windows…" Harriet's eyes were bulging.

"Nobody looks out of their window at this hour." Rosa lowered the pack from her shoulders. She peeled off her raincoat, and untied the scarf from around her hair.

"You might at least have changed your clothes."

Rosa felt her jaw clench. "That wouldn't have been easy."

The whitewashed hallway was lit by a single bulb, umbrellas stacked beside the door, shoes in a neat line. No pictures on the walls, no peg for visitors' coats. She had forgotten that they always had this feel, the Hyde homes, this stale, unloved impermanence. The carpets were worn only by other peoples' footsteps, the pencil-scratches by the door marking the heights of other peoples' children. Occupants long-gone, each place a borrowed shell.

Harriet gestured as though it was the only movement she could remember, and Rosa tugged away her boots, wiping their muddy undersides on the mat. "You missed tea," Harriet said, as though

Rosa had merely been for an afternoon walk, lost track of the time. "We had potato dumplings. I can put together some leftovers if you'd like."

"Thank you."

Bella peered at Rosa from behind their mother's apron, biting the end of her thumb. She looked pale, as though she rarely saw sunlight. When Rosa tried smiling at her, she hid herself again.

"She was only three," Harriet said. "You can hardly expect her to remember you." The words pierced Rosa's numbness. Eyes filling, she turned away towards the wall, but then felt a hand against her cheek. For all her journeying, she had never seen anything so awful or so wonderful as the look her mother now wore. There was a ferocity and force in it she could not comprehend. Nothing on earth could have pulled her away from that terrifying gaze.

"*Rosa*," said Harriet, with a weight of longing. Bella burrowed even deeper beneath her apron. "*Rosa.*"

The room splintered and blurred. A deep ache filled Rosa's throat, breaking out into a sob even as she tried to fight it. Her name spoken in her mother's voice, the rawness of that sound. Over Harriet's shoulder, she saw somebody come to the top of the stairs. Her father towered, a faceless silhouette. Harriet pulled Bella back, and Robert Hyde came slowly, jerkily down the steps.

"I didn't hear," he said. "I was in the attic. With the trains."

Fair, like Bella, Robert had aged even more noticeably than his wife. Rosa remembered him as a tall man, but his back was now bent. There were deep lines around his eyes and mouth. He looked dazed, as though he had just been shaken awake.

"Has it been…?" His hand made to cover his eyes, but Rosa quickly shook her head to reassure him.

"Seven years for me, too. You can look. I made sure of it, that I came back to the right place."

"How old…?" he asked. His eyes, crinkled against the light of the bare bulb, darted to and fro as he attempted to work it out. He flinched when she provided the answer.

"I'm twenty-four."

Like Harriet, he offered no embrace. In fact he did not reach out to touch her at all. He stopped several paces shy of where she stood, and simply stared. The moment stretched. After a while, he said weakly, "We didn't expect you."

Harriet made an odd, inhuman noise from the corner. Rosa brushed her tears away with the back of her hand. She knew that she ought to fill the silence, to attempt some kind of explanation as to where she had been, what had brought her back after so long. But it was all mired in confusion. She could barely untangle it in her own head, let alone put it into words for these barely familiar people. There was the humiliation of it, to come knocking at their door like this, after the way she had left. If she had imagined a return at all, it was the triumphant kind that would leave them chastened. Awed by all she had built without them.

"Do you have space for me?" she asked, as evenly as she could.

Robert gestured upstairs. "We've a spare room."

"*Daddy!*" began Bella. Harriet hushed her with a stern finger.

Rosa hooked one hand around the strap of her bag. "I'll go there now, if it's all right. I'm terribly tired. I came a long way."

"*Daddy. Who -*"

"It's your sister, Ladybug." Robert did not meet Rosa's eyes. "Do you remember?"

"She doesn't," put in Harriet. Another sharp tug in Rosa's throat, and Bella retreated behind the apron again.

Robert came forward. "I'll help you with your things."

"No need." Rosa pulled the heavy pack back on, tucking her raincoat beneath her arm. Her parents were looking at her as

8

though she had risen from the grave. Harriet's hands were clasped over her reddening chest. Robert was clinging to the banister.

"Are you hungry?" asked Harriet. And then, again, "You missed tea."

*

She found that she was trembling. Moving into the spare room, she sat down on the edge of the bed. A blackout curtain covered the window, and all was quiet. The mattress creaked beneath her, and she put her hands on her knees. The space between the walls felt suffocatingly small.

Isn't this necessary, Rosa? Isn't it why you found them again? To be back in a place which helps you hold your shape. Better to be pressed in on all sides, compacted and diminished. The alternative was to drift apart from herself. She had sensed it beginning to happen on the frozen beach, and the horror of it had not yet left her. The only thing worse than being back among the Hydes was to be too far from them, to have forgotten her own name altogether.

She had pictured this moment of return so many times along the journey that, now it had finally come, she had no feeling left to spare for it. Lately she could hardly bear company, and yet grew fretful when alone. To occupy her hands, she began to unpack her bag, heaping filthy clothes and worn-through shoes onto the floor. At the bottom, wrapped in newspapers from ten different decades, were her trinkets. She did not collect anywhere near as prodigiously as others she'd met, but was unable to resist the odd trophy. She lined them up on the windowsill.

A battery-operated watch with a face that had once lit up at the press of a button. A tin train painted postbox-red. From the court of a long dead lord, a small dagger in a snake-shaped sheath. And then a square gold coin and a carnival mask, from cities and years she could barely recall. A conch shell from the shore of the frozen sea. Smuggled out of the Museum's cretaceous hall, a flat stone bearing the fossilized imprint of a feathered wing.

The door creaked, and she glimpsed a shape which ducked back into the shadow. A slippered foot slid across the carpet.

"Bella?" said Rosa softly.

Brown eyes blinked back at her. The girl moved into the doorway, wearing too-short striped pyjamas. Her hair had been plaited, and she carried a toothbrush in her hand. She squirmed shyly.

"It's all right. You can come in."

Bella was looking at the objects arranged on the sill. "What's that?"

"Which one?"

Bella pointed indistinctly again, and Rosa stepped aside to give her a better view. She shuffled across the carpet and stood on tiptoe. One fingertip gingerly prodded the spiked conch, and a palm tested the weight of the stone. She didn't know what to do with the watch until Rosa showed her, slipping it around her wrist. "It's broken now. But that used to work the light."

Soberly the little girl pressed the button, pressed it again. Rosa watched her face, but saw little curiosity there. Bella turned to her with the same passive expression, and Rosa wondered whether anything in her sister's world made the remotest bit of sense.

"It's an electric watch, Bella. From the twenty-first. The numbers would appear there, so you could see what the time was, in the dark."

It was impossible to know whether she had understood. Bella put the watch down again, and fixed Rosa with her blank-eyed look. "I'm not allowed to tell you," she said.

"Tell me what?"

"Where we've been. Or where we're going next. It's a secret. I shan't tell you if you ask me."

"I won't ask," said Rosa. She remembered Bella at three, round-cheeked, not quite yet steady on her feet. "But it's all right. Ask Mother. It's all right for me to know."

Bella chewed at the head of her toothbrush. This idea seemed new to her. Rosa had a brief flash of how the last seven years might have played out for her sister: an unending succession of cautions and closed doors. Feet kicking through empty rooms, elbows on the windowsill, chin in her hands as the world went by outside. Rosa suppressed a shudder. And then there was something else, something unexpected and unwelcome; the creeping beginnings of guilt.

"Come on, now. I said bed." Harriet had appeared in the doorway, wrapped in a dressing gown and with smudges of cold cream above her eyes. She beckoned sharply to Bella, who pattered away without protest. Rosa heard her thumping down the stairs, one at a time, to brush her teeth at the kitchen sink.

Harriet was carrying a tray which bore a steaming bowl and a slice of bread. She pushed the door closed with her foot, and Rosa's stomach sank.

"I warmed this from the larder for you. Make sure you blow on it first, it's very hot. And try not to spill on the bedclothes."

Rosa balanced the tray on her knees. Harriet hovered while she ate – potato dumplings in a thick soup. More than the sight of her family's faces, the familiar flavours told her she was back. Hungrier than she had realised, she crammed the bread into the sides of her mouth, pausing only when she saw the look on her mother's face. She wiped her sleeve defensively across her mouth.

Harriet folded and then unfolded the nightdress she had been carrying under the tray. Her knuckles were white, and the skin of her chest still mottled pink. Either of these things could forecast tears. In the end she said, "You look thin."

Rosa lowered her head over the plate, and almost returned the remark. Her mother's gown hung too loosely. Harriet looked somehow as though she had lost weight from the inside out, as though something deeper than her bones had shrivelled. Yet Rosa's impulse was contempt, not concern. Unconcealed weakness, more than anything, tried her patience.

"You'll have to use some of my clothes, for now," said Harriet, laying the nightdress down on the bed. "If you're staying. Are you...?" Her voice cracked. "Are you staying?"

"Yes, Mother." Rosa chewed resolutely.

"For long?"

"I can't know that."

"Because you can't choose, you mean?" Harriet's fingers worried at a loose thread on the bed-cover. "How bad has it been?" She sat down on the edge of the bed, as far from Rosa as was possible. The silence stretched until Rosa felt ill with dread, everything she'd just eaten rising to the back of her throat. Staring at the carpet, she searched for a reply which would close down questions instead of inviting more. Harriet pressed her again. "Did you have to travel far to come back here?"

"From further ahead than you can probably imagine." The words were supposed to be dismissive, but they landed heavily, and Harriet seemed to grow yet greyer as she absorbed them. Rosa felt distant from herself, as though she was watching the scene from above. Two red-headed figures sat hunched upon the bed in the small, clean room, blackout curtains holding back the night.

"I might imagine it," ventured Harriet. "If you..."

Rosa lifted the tray from her lap onto the bedside table. "Mother, it's late. I'm *tired*. Three months, if you want to know, by air and train and on foot and every other which way."

"From where?"

"I was about fifteen years ahead, the wrong side of Russia, and I had to come back through Kiev and Berne and Amiens. Where the right tides were, if that means anything to you. I haven't slept in a bed in weeks. Let's not talk now."

Harriet's eyes grew wider. She had not stopped staring at Rosa, as though she might read every answer from her daughter's unkempt hair, patched clothes, weather-worn face. "I hope to goodness you didn't cross those miles in nineteen and forty-five."

Rosa shook her head, and could not resist adding, "They don't say nineteen *and* forty-five, Mother. Just nineteen forty-five, if you remember from when you were one of them. Eighteen sixty-one. Fifteen thirty-nine."

"Oh, they do, do they?"

"Yes. It's not difficult, and it makes you sound simple when you get it wrong." Rosa pounded the pillow with her fist.

"Have you seen yourself?" said Harriet. "I shall have to cut your hair."

"I'll cut it."

"Well, you've always done just as you wish. Just make sure you don't draw any attention. You can't leave the house again looking like that. We're hoping to stay here until the end of the year."

"And then where?"

Harriet met her gaze. "Some other town," she said. "Some other house, and the same months all over again. What did you expect? Our war goes on." Her eyes ranged over her daughter's face, and Rosa realised that behind all her questioning, she was starving for reassurance. No rest for the mother of the runaway, not even now that she was returned alive. Harriet wanted to hear that the fears of her night hours had been groundless: that the world beyond nineteen forty-five had surprised with its kindness. Rosa let the silence limp on. Even if she had wanted to, she could have offered no such comfort.

She could perhaps have lied, but Rosa found that her anger against the Hydes had not yet burned out. Being angry with her father was useless; it simply slid over him. Harriet, less to blame, had always attracted more of Rosa's anger because she understood it. If her mother had not chosen to resist, Rosa was sure, Harriet's anger might have eclipsed her own.

You chose wrong, Mother, she thought. *You should have cut your losses long ago, and left him. You might have been set back on a more ordinary path. Bella and I would never have been born, and no great tragedy for us.*

Harriet stood and picked up the tray from the bedside table. "I'll let you sleep."

Rosa gave a brusque nod.

"I'll leave the landing light on. There won't be any raids, we checked before we chose this town. The latrine's at the end of the garden." She made for the door, but hesitated, turning back again. She was holding the tray too rigidly, the bowl and plate rattling as her hands shook. Her look was bare as winter ground.

"I do not know what you mean by coming back to us. But please understand – we *grieved* you, Rosa. We already grieved you."

Rosa wrapped her arms around her chest. Harriet's mouth was tight, her eyes damp.

"We had to, in the end. We have done our grieving."

*

Without turning out the bedroom light or changing into the nightdress, she curled up on top of the covers. They were rough against her face, and smelled of washing powder. She drifted almost at once into an uneasy doze, waking several hours later with a sour taste in her mouth, woozy and disorientated. The clock on the wall told her that it was two in the morning. Her whole body was stiff and aching from her journey.

Downstairs in the kitchen, Rosa turned the groaning tap to splash cold water onto her face. She peeled back the blackout curtain and looked for a moment at her dim reflection on the window, freckled and frowning, features hard as her calloused hands. Her hair straggled to her waist, first grown that way for her time in the fifteenth, when she had coiled and fastened it with jewelled pins. The memory brought a wave of pride and sadness and longing. She found a pair of scissors in the drawer and, without much care, hacked off everything below her shoulders.

She stuffed the cuttings into the bin and then stood at the window, holding back the curtain again so that she could look out into the moonlit garden. Bella's hula-hoop and skipping rope had both been abandoned on the lawn. Wind blew through the cornfields beyond the hedgerow, the silent church tower on the hill. Not a soul to be seen, and the rain still falling.

Instinctively Rosa scoured the shrubbery for the sight of a pale face. Branches blew to and fro, and there could be somebody hiding in that patch of darkness, beneath the weeping leaves of that tree. As a small girl, in a different home, she had once been terrified by the sight of a man who appeared from nowhere at the bottom of the garden. He had pointed a gun at her, flicked back the safety, and then vanished without trace. She had never spoken of this to her parents, or indeed anybody except Harris Black, who claimed still stranger sightings.

The thought of the stranger from the garden sometimes caught her off-guard, and set her shivering. Had she really seen him again that time in Reims, in the deep of the cathedral? She was not sure that her mind hadn't conjured him. It was impossible to reason away the fear that his appearances, real or imagined, awakened in her.

A noise from above caught her attention, pulling her back to the present. She moved to the bottom of the stairs, and saw a ladder hanging down from the brightly illuminated attic hatchway. The sound of mechanical whirring floated down. She climbed to the upstairs landing and ducked back into the spare room to pick up the tin train from the windowsill, before ascending the ladder.

She entered through the hatch without knocking. Her father knelt in the centre of a miniature train track, which had been laid out around the room. As well as the trains, there were lines of tiny trees, matchstick houses, model sheep and cows. Everything had been painstakingly hand-painted. Robert looked up when she entered, his spectacles balanced near the end of his nose, caught in the midst of assembling another section of track.

"Does it work?" asked Rosa.

Robert pushed his glasses up the bridge of his nose. "One of the trains is just for show. The other's got a steam engine, though. I had her going full speed yesterday."

Rosa moved away from the ladder, and crouched at the edge of the room. A clock ticked dryly upon the wall. The space was lit by a single bare bulb, suspended from the beams overhead. Her childhood had been full of such places, of her father's glue-smelling workshops, his perfect little towns and villages. At the end of every year, they were demolished, to be doggedly re-built somewhere new.

"Here. Watch." Concentrating intensely now, he pulled a box of matches from his pocket and struck one. He held it inside the mechanism of the larger train, which after a few moments began to emit clicking noises and puffs of grey smoke. Robert held it steady as it began to strain forward, shaking out the match with his other hand. Then, with an eager squeal, the steam train headed off on a rapid loop of the floor, taking the curve so quickly that it almost overbalanced.

Despite herself, Rosa laughed, sitting back to admire the engine's progress. But as it completed a circuit of the track and continued to another, looping around again and again with blind urgency, she was aware of her smile fading. As the train stuttered to a halt, she tasted the old bitterness .

"You'll find us very much the same," Robert said. He picked up the spent engine, and dusted it off. He was nervous as a schoolboy.

"I got you a present." She leaned over the track and held out the tin train, which he took carefully. "It runs by clockwork. You wind the lever, here –"

He wore a small smile, now, as he prised the back of the train apart to admire the interlocking cogs and gears. "This isn't quite like any other I have. A little more primitive. Beautifully crafted, though." Rosa waited for him to ask where she had got it, but the question did not seem to have occurred to him. It had never been so plain to her that he could not think himself outside the year, outside the familiar sphere of the world he had made.

She had wanted to slap Harriet to silence her interrogation, but now she felt the urge to shake Robert until he came awake. Until he could *see* her. The frustration of it was so overwhelming that it made her numb rather than furious. She wanted to say, can't you try? Can't you reach a little for just the nearest, the most mundane of the places I have been?

Her tongue felt thick. "Don't you want to know how I found you?" she asked.

Her father didn't look at her. Unsteadily, he adjusted his glasses on his nose.

"I had help," said Rosa. "There's a place where they know all about us. People like us. You're in their records."

"I see, I see." Robert was blinking very rapidly, and looking at him, she was surprised by a pang of something resembling pity. If he could not react even to that, perhaps nothing should be expected of him. It was merely that he seemed so old to her, his fair hair thinning, his shoulders hunched. He looked shrunken and small. Somewhere in her hardened heart, she lost another scrap of certainty.

"When are we at, Daddy?" she said softly.

"Let me see... March eighteenth. The Yanks almost have it at Iwo Jima. Heavy bombing on Japan, poor devils, though they've seen nothing yet. They've not had it so bad here, far enough out of London." He rubbed his hands together vaguely, and a small smile drifted across his face again. "Still a month and a half until my red-letter day."

"Yes, I suppose it must be." Her dinner now sat heavy in her stomach. Nausea came over her, and she no longer wanted to be even under the same roof as her father. The tenderness which had almost blossomed in her moments before withered and died.

Preoccupied once more with the mechanism of the tin train, Robert began to hum tunelessly. Rosa watched him, and resignation folded in upon her. *You'll find us very much the same.* She hugged her legs to herself, resting her chin on her knees, as the clock on the wall parcelled out the seconds. She left him, before long, for her bed.

*

She slept at last to the distant, uneasy sound of planes droning overhead. Her newly cut hair scratching at her neck, she tossed and turned, waking frequently in the unfamiliar room. Her dreams were filled with skaters who whirled and danced among snow-heaped pines, with the squeals of speared hogs, with city streets which dissolved like sand. With the great fish that had swum in the deepest waters, before the world was old.

2

Arline

Nineteen forty-five had first fallen away from her like an unbuttoned dress. She had discarded that year at her feet, stepped out of it and felt fresh air upon her skin. It had happened when she was seventeen, on the night of the awful row, when she had done what she'd so long threatened to do and gone running from her parents' house into the night.

Harriet's voice still screaming downstairs, Robert's lower, helpless tones. Still sobbing, Rosa had taken little time to pack. A satchel stuffed with a few necessaries, underclothes and skirts and blouses all haphazard and inside-out. A toothbrush and a bar of soap. Her father's precious fob-watch in her pocket, because it felt good to take it. She slammed the front door as hard as she could, and then her footsteps were clattering along the Shoreditch lanes where they had lived, that time around.

The night was thick with chimney-smoke. The streets in that place were still cratered and scarred; washing was strung between the windows; boys on bicycles teetered past her. Outside the Mission, an old woman hunched on the steps, drinking from a brown paper bag. People heading into the pictures for *Blithe Spirit*. Rosa wiped her eyes on the backs of her hands, but her tears would not stop.

She could barely see where she was going. Past a huddle of wardens and across the path of a swerving motor-car, past a row of allotments and within sight of St. Paul's. A stitch forced her to slow, gasping. Along the river, Big Ben was visible through the falling darkness, its face illuminated. It was past the end of April, and the blackout was ended.

Rosa kept running, and as she ran it seemed to her that the air had changed, or that her body had become painfully sensitive to the hardness of the ground and the beat of her own heart. She tried to stop, grabbing hold of a street-lamp, but dizziness carried her to her knees.

Her whole baffling lifetime rose up in her. Her throat burned, still, with the hot words she had flung at her mother and father. *I won't forgive you. I hope that you die here.* There on the pavement, with the city spread out on every side, she came loose from all that she had ever known. A wave swept her forward, stomach dropping into free-fall and limbs flying, the buildings on the darkened street dissolving like so much sand.

*

And re-forming again. She had journeyed before, of course, but never like this. It was daylight. She tasted the new century before her other senses had caught up, rolling it to the back of her tongue. Everywhere the noise of engines, car horns, musical tones, a ceaseless hum and roar which seemed to be carried on the air. She understood at once what had happened, but the shock of it kept her pinned to the ground.

She was still on the pavement, still on a street near the bank of the river beside a grassy verge. She fought the shaking in her knees to stand up, hugging the overflowing satchel tightly to herself. The place was the same, and it was all altered. It was like hearing a familiar song played on a broken record, verses skipped, the melody distorted. As to how far she had come, she could not begin to guess. Bruised, every part of her body trembling from the fall,

Rosa cast about for some clue. Pulling a newspaper from a bin to glance at the date, she was overcome by dizziness again, and sank down again by the side of the road. She let out a hoarse laugh.

Not one passer-by spared her a glance. She drank the sight of them in greedily. The brightness of their clothes, the women with their exposed legs, so purposeful and swift, their faces made up so radiantly. Some of the men had long hair, too, or loose shirt collars, and none wore hats. They spoke not to one another but to devices held in the palms of their hands.

The road was so full of motorcars that they were barely moving. Signal-lights flashed, and people on bicycles wove their way between the traffic. Some of the buses were plastered with posters showing beautiful faces or exotic scenes. Television screens half as tall as buildings flashed moving advertisements for perfume and beer and who could tell what else. On the opposite bank of the river, a slowly turning white wheel dominated the skyline. After the drabness of nineteen forty-five, it was too much to take in.

Rosa waited until the century had solidified beneath her before standing up again, clinging to a rail for support. It was then that she noticed the dome of St. Paul's, serene and unchanged amongst all the towering, gleaming new structures. She laughed aloud again. Her father kept a cut-out newspaper picture of that dome surrounded by clouds of black smoke, lit in a glorious white blaze as though heaven itself had preserved it from the bombs. During the Shoreditch year, and in the Camberwell year when she was twelve, she had crept inside several times. Played hopscotch on the chessboard floor. Lingered among stone statues of saints in the fusty quiet.

She looked down at herself, brushing off her clothes with new self-consciousness. She was wearing a brown coat over her dress, stockings and patent leather shoes, all plain enough to draw no glances. If she was sharp enough, bold enough, nobody need know

21

where she had come from. She needed only to stay safe, to watch until she was ready to become one of them.

*

She had no clear plan. It had never been possible to make one, with no clear idea of what lay beyond nineteen forty-five. Now, caught up in the bustle of this miraculous new London, she knew that she wanted to go wherever these people were going: to wear what they were wearing, to be swept along in the flow of the age.

But first she must pursue more immediate needs. She found a pawn shop, and without looking to the left or right approached the counter and took the fob watch from her pocket. It was examined by a slow-moving man who grunted and shuffled across to the till. Rosa stood on tip-toe to look at the display in the cabinet - diamond earrings, a rack of gold rings, an array of items which were completely mysterious to her. Were those cameras? They were small enough to be slipped into a pocket. She misted the glass with trying to stare more closely. When paper was handed over and clutched in her clammy hand, she exited quickly. She paused on the threshold to look over her spoils. Two red notes, printed with the head of a curly-haired queen.

Making a quick list in her mind, she squeezed in and out of shops until she had bought sturdy waterproof shoes, a thick coat and small supply of food. When darkness fell, she found a doorway. She stayed awake, chewing hungrily at a chocolate bar, the hood of her new coat pulled up. Turning her head to follow the progress of every passer-by, her eyelids began to droop. It was not until the pavements had emptied that it occurred to her to be afraid.

Rosa had lived in many places, but she had never slept a night anywhere that was not a Hyde home. She huddled as far back into the shadows as she could, turning her head at every sign of movement beneath the street-lamps. *Don't be a baby*, she told herself. A trio of drunken figures lurched too near after a distant clock had struck three, leering, too loud. One of them urinated in the corner of her doorway.

The next morning, stiff with cold and tiredness, she bought a small knife and kept it tucked into her belt.

She used it, in the nights which followed, to threaten a man who trailed her in her search for a sleeping place, a too-curious dog, and a stringy woman who approached her with an aggressive tirade she couldn't understand. She witnessed many thefts – some furtive, purses snatched from handbags, others ending with fists raised and blood on the pavement – and held her precious satchel all the closer. *Not much longer*, she promised herself, and when her money ran out, put out a cardboard carton to collect coins. She washed in public bathrooms and drank from the fountain in the park. *Soon, I will find my feet*.

Sitting in the corner of a cafe, she listened, rapt, to the conversations on every side. A group of girls talked about their boyfriends, whispers punctuated by gales of laughter. Two businessmen blew on cups of black coffee; a young boy bent his head over a flickering screen. A lone woman in green sat wholly absorbed in her book, marking pages with the pen in her hand. Rosa did not have a very clear idea how such people occupied themselves, and as she watched them, she attempted to imagine how their days might be arranged. They must have houses which they left in the morning and returned to at night, homes which remained theirs, year after year. They might have families who were waiting for them there. They might have studies or work or pastimes which filled their hours and their minds.

She settled arbitrarily on the thought of her mother's profession. Harriet had been a teacher before her fateful encounter with Robert, dress tucked between her knees as she bicycled to school along the lanes, arriving in the classroom to put frogs in jars and scratch Latin grammar onto the blackboard. I could do that, thought Rosa, once I'm accustomed to this place. Her heart lightened.

She balanced along the narrow safety of this idea as though walking a tightrope. There will be more, things will be better. It was autumn, and as she strode through the streets to St Paul's, brown leaves whirled about her feet. Head down, shoulders hunched, hands tucked in the coat's deep pockets. Approaching the pillars around the cathedral door, she saw a crowd of people with cameras and leaflets. They formed an orderly queue inside the entrance hall, and Rosa saw them handing over money to a man in a booth.

She sat on the steps and watched the bustling streets below, chin resting on her hand. The noises and the smells of the city crowded her senses, this place that had changed almost beyond all knowing. She welcomed every alteration as a bracing gasp of air.

Sixty years, she thought, barely more than sixty years forward. I would have lived this long, in a lifetime like one of theirs. I might have still been here, a silver-haired old woman shuffling down the street with my shopping. Mumbling memories of our last year at war, of our red-letter day.

*

She discovered that she was merely one of many in London without possessions to her name or papers to prove her existence. There were rooms behind boarded-up windows where they slept packed in like tinned sardines. At first she looked hopefully into each face, wondering which years and decades they might have come here from. But it did not take long to realise that they had made journeys of a different sort.

The city's secret citizens spoke in foreign tongues, or not at all. They were grey-faced men who had crossed borders clinging beneath trucks, women whose hands were red and thickened from hard labour. Girls Rosa's age hid their hair beneath scarves and slept with one eye open, and she began to do likewise. Sometimes one or a pair would vanish overnight, and it was not long before Rosa found herself in a state of constant watchfulness. When approached, even with the friendliest gestures, she shook her head violently and brandished the knife. She stopped sleeping outside, and in whatever shelter she took, she kept her back to the wall. *You'd never have credited me with this, Mother, Father – with such a keen instinct for survival.* Her pride in this new-found freedom burned more fiercely than her fear.

She took a job where no papers were signed and no questions were asked, vacuuming carpets along the long corridors of an apartment block. She did not ask how to work the device, but discovered for herself how to plug it in and flip the switch. The noise made her teeth rattle. When she was let into the flats to scrub ovens and spray bathroom tiles, she drank in every detail. Coloured televisions with screens a yard long, lamps which dimmed and brightened at the lightest touch, showers which jetted powerful streams of hot water. Her heart turned enviously in her chest and she began to store up thoughts of having such a home herself. She stood in the corners of their rooms, dustpan in her hand, and trembled with hope and desire.

The inhabitants of these places came and went – women in smart suits, men with leather briefcases. If any of them addressed her she pressed her lips together and shook her head. Better to pretend she had no English than to use the wrong words, not to know words which were commonplace here. Alone, she opened cupboards and desk drawers, furtively shook food out of packets. Once she fell asleep curled on a mattress so soft that it moulded to fit her body's shape.

Her favourite was on the fifth floor. Its rooms were large and its walls hung with photographs. These showed a man and a woman, both fair-haired and smiling, holding a young girl and a baby. The curtains were patterned with red and cream flowers, and light poured in all through the shortening hours of the day. Rosa would complete her work as quickly as she could, then sit at the kitchen table in a shifting patch of sun, eyes closed.

She made sure to leave before they came home, but several times she passed them in the corridors on her way out. The baby was now a pudgy toddler in a woollen hat, the girl – clinging to her mother's hand – about Bella's age. Rosa turned to look over her shoulder as the family vanished into the lift, and felt an unexpected tug in her stomach. She had not thought to wake her sister, the night she fled the Shoreditch house. Perhaps Bella had come to her room later in the night, when the planes were droning overhead, and found the bed empty when she crept under the covers in the darkness.

The children here shared a bedroom with a shelf of picture books and a cupboard full of toys. Once she had vacuumed, Rosa sat on the edge of the girl's bed, twisting the electric cord around her finger. She leaned into the little one's cot and pulled the tab which brought the musical mobile to life. It played a tinkling lullaby while rotating gently in circles.

She stripped the parents' bed to launder their sheets, which she sometimes smelled furtively, inhaling sweat and perfume combined in a musk which seemed mysterious, and deeply private. Like the home itself, the scent unlocked a longing in her which she had never known existed. Her heart pounded faster with it. Before the bathroom mirror, she smeared scarlet lipstick on her mouth, smoky powder on her eyelids. Throwing open the curtains in the darkening afternoon, she saw London laid out before her, lights glinting in the window of each office-block and all along the winding river.

In a moment of sudden joy, she tugged the scarf from her hair and flicked the switch on the radio. Eyes closed, heedless of any outside gaze or the chance that a key might click in the lock, she jumped and wriggled to the unfamiliar music. She stretched her arms and held up her palms as though to embrace this strange age; as though to bask in the wide-open space of a year which would flow outward and onward.

*

Winter sank down over the city, muting everything. Rosa slept behind the machines in the laundry room at the tower block, where heat from the boiler next door kept the frost from her eyelashes. The machines rattled and juddered until long past midnight. To prevent doubt from blowing in under the door along with the chill wind, she replayed the scene of the row over and over in her head, and kept her anger alight. Anywhere but there, anywhere but nineteen forty-five. Here, at least, she could breathe.

There will be more, things will be better. Details of this bright future eluded her, but it didn't matter. When her rummaging through bins yielded only scraped-out tins or overripe fruit, she took food instead from the shelves and cupboards of the rooms she cleaned. A little here, a little there. With Christmas around the corner, she licked her fingers and dipped them into jars of mincemeat, pocketed fresh-baked biscuits cooling on wire racks. She cleared away the crumbs carefully afterwards.

When she had finished work for the day she wandered the lamp-lit streets, breath misting the dark air, moon on the rise. Bright bulbs and plastic snowflakes hung in strings between the shops. Behind the curtains of every home, glowing yellow light. Rosa watched the shadow shapes behind these windows as they moved and merged. She saw a sign, *Room for Rent,* and counted the money in the brown envelope she kept in her coat.

Everything seemed so simple for the strangers who resided warmly behind those walls. There was nothing they could possibly want. Late one afternoon she sat back, suddenly dizzy, from scrubbing bathroom tiles in her favourite apartment. As she wiped her sleeve across her forehead, she thought that she smelled pine needles. A waft of something smoky. Standing and pulling off her gloves, she moved into the kitchen, then the darkened bedroom to search out the source of the smell. It was gone, but her head was still spinning.

Rosa sat down slowly on the bed. Her fingers smoothed the covers on each side, lingering on the soft cloth. She picked up a watch left on the father's bedside table and gave it a careless shake, wondering whether the light inside would be extinguished. It wasn't, and she busied herself for a few minutes fiddling with the dials. No doubt Robert would have understood the mechanism. She pocketed the watch without any intrusion of conscience and proceeded to rummage in the mother's drawer, which contained an engraved bracelet in a wooden box. It was silver, and supposing it might be worth something, she pulled it out of its case.

Rosa placed her cleaning things on the kitchen table, and stood still for a moment in the empty room. Faces looked down at her from the photographs on the wall. Then she let out a laugh and left without bothering to lock the door, descending the steps two at a time. Out in the blustery afternoon her feet carried her with new, buoyant purpose. *Where would you like to live, Rosa?* Somewhere small at first, of course, but perhaps later... perhaps in days to come...

She had barely made it three streets away, towards the twilit Thames, before the city began to crumble at the corners of her vision. With a lonely, echoing rumble, towers receded to nothing and roads retreated like measuring tape.

Her body bent backwards. The smell of pine-needles, of fish-flesh and woodsmoke. It was still dark. She had journeyed again.

*

How far, this time? Forward again, or back? Thin though her schooling had been, she could hazard a fair guess. There were wrought lamps with gas flames, cobbled streets that teemed with carriages, passers-by in long coats and caps. Like a book illustration, like a postcard. She gasped for breath on a pavement that was thick with straw and stinking dirt, and pulled herself quickly upright.

Greyish fog swirled and thickened on every side, and the people of this age swam through it like fish through the element they had been born into. London lay deep in flickering shadow, dark almost as a blackout night, while white ash floated up from the firepits in side-alleys and a man turned a marble-eyed pig on a glowing spit. Blinkered horses flared their lips about the bit, and snatches of music drifted from tavern windows. This city, with the towers of glass and steel felled from its skyline, seemed more familiar.

She bent to tie her bootlaces. Feeling the brown envelope in her pocket, she was furious with herself. What use were those silvery slips of paper with their curly-haired queen, here where the woman on the throne was straight-locked, po-faced? All her work, the scrubbing and the vacuuming, had been useless. Now she would have to begin again. She felt tired and disorientated, and could not bring herself to remove the anachronistic coat, or the scarf from her hair.

Bags of hot chestnuts hung from carts, and holly wreaths were nailed to each door. With a feeling of brittle unreality, she followed the drill which had served her last time. "Might you point me to a pawn shop?" she asked one of the chestnut-vendors. "Or a jeweller's?"

He looked her up and down. "In carnival costume, miss?"

"I'm a performer in a festive play."

"Stores near here'll be closing now, save on Straight Street, where some keep later hours. You might try there. What is it you're dressed as, may I ask?" When she fumbled for an answer, he pressed her. "What manner of play is it?"

She raised her chin as she looked back at him. "A comical one."

The silver bracelet fetched enough for a long dress, which she purchased from the first open store she passed, and pulled on hastily in an alleyway. It fit badly, trailing on the ground. Together with the coat and the satchel, she knew it only made her look more peculiar. There seemed more cause to be frightened here than in the London of the twenty-first. The night was thicker, its sounds more chaotic.

And there was something else, too, inside her. A deeper sense of panic and bewilderment. *Did I plan for this? Did I know that this would happen? That I would journey again?* She could not remember. In her head she tried to re-assemble the life that had started to take shape in the twenty-first, to imagine how it might look here. The substance of the imagined thing seemed frighteningly thin.

The night was bitter. Desperate for warmth Rosa peered into the windows of several nearby taverns, and stood for a while warming her hands by a baked potato vendor's fire, until the proprietor shooed her away. Eventually she ducked inside a theatre, slipping easily past the ticket-men and into the uppermost circle, where she slept curled on a seat in the back row. She woke in confusion during the second act of an opera whose name she'd paid no heed to. The hairs on the back of her neck were standing on end. A shiver worked its way down her back, and she sat up as a high and otherworldly melody rose to the theatre's rafters.

I dreamt I dwelt in marble halls
With vassals and serfs at my side.
And of all who assembled within those walls
That I was the hope and the pride.

I had riches too great to count, could boast
Of a high ancestral name.
But I also dreamt, which pleased me most
That you lov'd me still the same,
That you lov'd me, You lov'd me still the same,
That you lov'd me, You lov'd me still the same.

In the centre of the stage stood a girl about her own age, cheeks rouged and hair curled, hand laid over her heart. Below her feet the gas-lamps flickered, and the audience sat rapt. And as the girl sang, without knowing why, Rosa found that tears had begun to stream down her face. She wiped them fiercely away, but they continued to flow, and from the corner of her eye she saw a man at the end of the row lean forward to watch her.

I dreamt that suitors sought my hand.
That knights upon bended knee,
And with vows no maiden's heart could withstand,
They pledg'd their faith to me.

And I dreamt that one of that noble host
Came forth my hand to claim.
But I also dreamt, which charmed me most
That you lov'd me still the same,
That you lov'd me, you lov'd me still the same,
That you lov'd me, you lov'd me still the same.

As soon as the aria had finished, she slipped from her seat and back out into the frozen night, stopping behind the theatre to support herself against the wall. Her breathing was hard and ragged, moisture prickling on her cheeks and eyelashes. Below her ribcage was a plummeting emptiness for which she sensed there could be no comfort.

"You know, they say that song is cursed."

She flinched, hands flying up to dry her eyes once again. Beneath the nearest gas-lamp, hands tucked comfortably into his waistcoat pockets, stood the man who had leaned forward in his seat at the end of the row. He wore a threadbare top hat, a loose cravat, and a look of lively interest. When she turned towards him, he tipped her a nod.

"So much as whistle the tune near any theatre folk, they'll have you out on your ear."

"I don't believe in such things," said Rosa flatly. She glanced over her shoulder, to where light spilt out onto the cobbles from the tavern across the road. She wondered if she should back away. He whistled a few bars between his teeth.

"You enjoy the opera, did you, miss? Only it came to my notice that you seemed to be sleeping through the first act. Shame, seeing as you'd paid for a ticket, and it's a fine story."

Rosa pulled her coat close about her shoulders and adjusted her satchel. But as she made to turn and leave, he took a step towards her.

"No matter. I'll tell it to you."

"I don't wish to hear it," she said. Her hand found the knife that was now tucked into the outer lining of her dress. Rosa knew that she would do it if he came too close: that she was fully reckless enough to hurt him. She would aim for the shoulder. Thrust it in deep, then run as fast as she could

"The girl is Arline, born to a noble family, and rescued when she is a child from beneath the hooves of a fearsome stag. Her saviour is pure-hearted Thaddeus, but his companion Devilshoof steals her away. She lives among his gypsy people, never certain of any home, far from her family."

He made a careful, deliberate pause. During the little silence Rosa's heart missed a beat in her chest and rose suddenly into her throat. A kind of blizzard seemed to have risen about her in the still night.

"She hardly knows herself, this wanderer, or the shapes she dreams of. It's a sad thing, I'll grant you." The man shook his head, and delved into his greatcoat pocket, pulling out a pipe. He lit it with nimble fingers, and continued to watch Rosa as he inhaled thoughtfully. "A sad thing."

Terrified now, she met his gaze. It was very possible that the strength of her own wishes were clouding her mind: but no, there was something odd about him, something *off*. He did not carry himself like the men of this age, but seemed too much at his ease, like one watching a race that he knows he will not have to run. Beneath his hat he wore his hair long, tied back in a ponytail. A copper watch on a chain swung from his pocket.

In her confusion she fell back on what she had always been taught. She raised a trembling hand, fingers together and thumb pointed upwards, to hide her eyes.

And heard him laughing. "Come on, sweetheart," he said, and she realised he had stepped closer. She felt him cover her hand with his.

"Come with me."

3

To the Journeys

A great, rangy grey dog raised itself from the hearth when they
entered his rooms, sweeping the flagstones with its tail. It
licked its master's hands appreciatively, then moved on to Rosa,
sticking its nose inside the pockets of her coat. She hesitated, and
then when it showed no signs of aggression, scratched the base of its
ears. The man, who bent to stoke the fire and then carried a match
about the room to light the wall-lamps, muttered affectionately to
the animal.

"Here, Wolf, leave her be. I wouldn't have' left you by yourself,
but you know you don't like the theatre." When the dog continued
in its overtures towards Rosa, he shunted it aside with his foot.
"Leave our guest be, won't you? You'll frighten her away."

As the space brightened, Rosa took a better look at him. He was
perhaps five or six years her senior, his hair and trimmed beard
strawberry-blond. He was tall and well-built, easy within his own
skin and in her presence. He removed his hat and coat and rolled
up his shirt-sleeves. His green waistcoat was patched and faded,
but his shoes shone as though brand new, and were not at all in
the style of the age. Without a care, he was whistling the unlucky
tune from the theatre. Somehow the pieces of him did not quite
fit together.

"Tea?" he asked. She nodded, and he disappeared into the next
room, dog close at his heels. There did not seem to have been any
choice other than to follow him here. She kept her coat on, hugging
it tightly to her body as she moved towards the fire. He did not

appear to have many possessions, and nor did his rooms, on the third floor of an ordinary town house, look as though they had been inhabited long. The space was almost bare of furnishings, save for two lumpy armchairs in front of the fire and a table with three legs. Odd socks hung along a string in front of the hearth, and a heap of folded newspapers teetered by the door. The space looked as though it had not been dusted in months. The umbrellas in the stand by the door had gathered cobwebs. She was fleetingly reminded of the temporariness which haunted her parents' homes.

The mantelpiece was crammed with an array of objects which Rosa moved closer to examine. A tarnished silver cup with engravings she could not decipher. A selection of coins in different shapes, sizes, metals. A stone pipe carved to resemble an otter. A sepia photograph showing two identical men on a porch, arms around each other. She picked up a miniature electronic device which she guessed belonged at least two centuries away. No, there was no doubting what he was.

"Many of us become magpies," said her host, from behind her. "After a while. Terribly hard to ignore the shine that things have once your interest's been caught." She put the object down, taking the cup that he offered her and grasping it between her numb fingers. "I take it you're newly arrived. No need for tears. It's all kinds of fun here once you learn your way around."

"I wasn't crying," said Rosa.

"No?"

"And you had no business watching me, if I was."

"I wouldn't worry. Theatre here is supposed to have that effect." She did not know what to say, and looked down, suddenly shy. "Their plays are sentimental, their laws are stringent, and their parties are elaborate. The food is variable. The cities have an unhealthy climate and are full of glorious goings-on." He grinned. "Like every age before them, they think that they have reached the end of all meaningful progress. They're particularly self-important about it."

Rosa took a mouthful of scalding tea. There were so many things she wanted to ask him but they all seemed to cancel each other out, leaving her speechless. Her father's warnings about such encounters had always been vague and ominous. It was in conscious defiance of Robert that she had followed this stranger home, that she now sat before his hearth, defenceless save for the knife in her dress. She watched him scratch the squirming hound beneath its chin, and did not feel that he posed any physical threat. Nevertheless he struck her, though she did not know why, as some kind of dangerous man.

"Where did you come from?" he asked. He was looking at her expectantly, and she hunched her shoulders, trying to decide whether to tell him. The dog had deposited itself in front of the fire again, chin resting on its paws. Its melted brown eyes stared up into Rosa's face, tail arcing encouragingly from side to side.

"Early twenty-first," she mumbled. On reckless impulse, she added, "And before that, for a long time, nineteen and forty-five."

"They don't say *and*, you know. Just nineteen forty-five. Eighteen forty-three. It makes you sound strange when you get it wrong."

"I'll get it right, from now." The words came out too quickly, too sharply. But he only laughed, a wide grin flashing across his face.

"I'm sure you're learning fast. Did you find the twenty-first to your taste? I go there often. Early, and mid." He was leaning against the mantelpiece now, stood above her as he poured his own drink. Rosa was conscious that he was leading their encounter, that he seemed to be reading her with little trouble.

"I liked it there," she said, trying to match his easy tone. She rubbed her thumbs around the rim of the teacup, and was casting about for some clever remark when he spoke again.

36

"Nineteen forty-five, you said. That year has a powerful pull – from certain cities in particular. I've always imagined it must be uniquely exciting."

She let out an involuntary bark of laughter. He raised a curious eyebrow. "How long is a long time?"

Rosa looked at the stranger who was like her, yet whose life seemed to be unlike hers in every enviable way. Blood pounded in her ears. Something violent and powerful was bubbling behind her throat – the anger which had driven her from the Shoreditch house into the night. She looked up, and met his gaze. "All my life."

He looked momentarily puzzled, then taken aback. She watched his expression shift with satisfaction. It was good to have surprised him; to be relaying her grievance, at long last, to a sympathetic ear. "Dear God, in one place? How did – ? But wait, I think I've heard… I never gave any more thought to it." He scanned over the items on his mantelpiece as though he could hear them murmuring, then turned back to her with intense interest. "There was a story going around that a man got stuck there. Slipping back to the beginning again at the end of each year."

"My father," she said.

He laughed, as he seemed to do easily, and often. It had never before occurred to Rosa that there might be anything remotely amusing about Robert Hyde's circumstances, but she joined in, and found that it released something inside her. It did what even running away had not entirely done, and cut a cord between her and the Hydes. The more she laughed, the smaller they seemed to become.

Her host was shaking his head, still grinning broadly. "I'd only heard rumours."

"Oh, it's true. His father died in the fighting and he couldn't move on from it." Only five minutes ago the words would have been too heavy and terrible to utter. Now, it was a relief to be rid of them. "By the time I was born, he'd lived the year fourteen times. Thirty-one, now."

"*Thirty-one times!* And you…?"

"We were carried with him." She leaned closer to the fire, and as the flames blazed, blood finally began to flow in her fingers. "Every time. My mother, my sister and I. It would happen each New Year, and we'd move to another town, another house. Go through the year all over again."

He exhaled wonderingly.

"I hated it – I *hated* them." She took another hot gulp of tea, and added shakily, "I told them, too. That they were cowards and I couldn't bear to be a part of it any more." *His face, her father's pale stunned face, the awful ringing silence in the room.* Rosa felt a surge of triumph. "I told them. I ran away. I'm not ever going back."

"Why on earth did you settle for tea? This calls for something – a great deal – *stronger*…" He leapt up and crossed the room, pulling out a half-empty bottle from behind the curtain, along with a pair of glasses. Rosa, who had never tasted alcohol except for a few furtive swigs of her mother's gin, put down the teacup and held out her hand.

The fire had begun to take hold again, and she removed her coat, curled up deep in the soft cushions. Her host sat down in the armchair opposite, tugging apart the knot in his cravat and undoing his shirt collar. He poured a generous measure of amber liquid into each glass. The dog had rolled over onto its back, eyes closed and front paws tucked over its chest, twitching sporadically.

"To the journeys we've yet to make."

"To the journeys," Rosa echoed nervously, and clinked her glass against his before emptying it in one. The breath in her throat ignited. Taut muscles in her neck and shoulders relaxed, and she realised for how long she must have been poised and watchful.

Her host watched her with enjoyment, taking his own drink more slowly, "Now you won't mind me saying, I'm sure, that it's a little too plain you're new to this. There are some things you could —"

"I survived the twenty-first." The drink had made her flushed, fierce. She had lost her shyness. "I was on my own, and it was winter, but I survived. You don't have to talk to me like a child."

"I wouldn't dream of it. Just giving you the same friendly advice I'd give anyone." He pointed at the coat she had hung over the back of her chair. "That's not even close to a good match. I know others who don't especially care, but personally I make some effort to look the part. You don't want the bother you'll get otherwise."

"I didn't have money for a new one."

"That's another thing. Don't take currency on your journeys, unless it's just a memento. You want gold, diamonds, something that won't lose its value."

"I already worked that out." Pride swelled in her chest, and eagerness along with it. The questions began to tumble out one by one. "Will I always take what I'm carrying with me?"

"Yes, usually. What you're wearing, what you're carrying. Who you're with, if you're lucky."

"And how far can I go?"

His laugh rang out again, and he sat up, delighted. The dog twitched and snuffled at the sound of his voice. "However far you like," he said.

He filled her glass again. "Can I choose?" she continued breathlessly, before she drank. "Where to…? Which way…?"

"Oh, not especially. It may be a while before you can get more than a hundred years forward of where you first came from. Travelling forward, that takes more out of you. You'll need to loosen up. And even then…" He waved a hand. "We're subject to winds blowing this way and that. That's half the fun. You'll go where you go, and you can make of it what you want."

Rosa felt her cheeks glow as the pleasurable burning which had begun in her throat spread through the rest of her. She tugged the scarf from her hair. A golden glow was cast across the stranger's face as the firelight shone against his half-filled glass. His expression at rest was a teasing look. "So what is it," he asked, "that you want?"

Nobody had ever asked her such a thing before. She pictured herself slamming the door of her parents' house, falling half a century forward, landing on her knees. To her surprise, she answered frankly. "I only ever wanted to be free from that year. To live like one of *them*, always going in the same direction. To have what they had. That's all I knew to think of."

Even as she said it, the half-shaped desires which had driven her in the twenty-first showed themselves to be dusty and dull. Now grander hopes came creeping in from the cold.

The man leaned towards her. His lively eyes were dancing. "Listen," he said conspiratorially, and a hot shiver ran down her spine. "I've seen Rome built stone-by-stone and I've seen it in flames. You know what they call us, those who know we exist?" She shook her head. "Well, I shan't tell you, as you're sure to find out for yourself. But they are *mayflies*, even the best of them. Burning brightly for no longer than a day."

"And what are we?"

The grin returned. There was something vulpine about him, something a little sly. He gave her no answer.

A log dropped from the heap below the chimney, scattering ash onto the hearth. The dog woke with a start, huffing and whining, and ran to bury its head in its master's lap. Rosa turned to look out of the window behind her, where through the half-closed curtain she could see a light snowfall drifting to the street below. She had almost forgotten that London continued below them, bustling with life in the smog and the darkness.

"There are thin places," he said. "Maybe you already know. Certain cities at certain times, places where it's easier to come through. London's a rabbit warren." He scratched behind the dog's ears. "You can always be sure of finding a few of us here, in the years when the tides bring us together."

She could not think yet of *us,* in the plural. He was already too much. "Did you never know," he asked, "that there were more of us?"

"Of course I knew." Robert's warnings still rang in her ears. *Raise your hand, Rosa, hide your gaze.* "I just never had a chance to... to..."

She tailed off, realising that her host's attention had been withdrawn from her suddenly, and entirely. Their conversation, it seemed, had run its course. He rose from his chair, dislodging the dog, and strode towards the window. He stretched, arms raised in silhouette above his head. Snow drifted past beyond the grey glass.

"There's ice six inches thick on the Serpentine, and skaters on the water, like the Frost Fairs of old," he said. "There are bowls of Thames oysters, and hot wine, and spice-cakes. There are women in ermine shawls, and bull-baiting, and puppet plays."

He had picked up his greatcoat from the chair and swathed a scarf around his neck before she realised that he was issuing an invitation. She stood, not wanting him to see her hesitate, and pulled her own coat back on as she moved to stand with him by the door. The dog looked eagerly between them.

"Come on then, Wolf." He slapped his leg, and turned the handle. The dog had already dashed out into the stairwell before Rosa found her tongue.

"*Wait...*"

He turned and answered her question before she could utter it. "If you like, I go by Tommy Rust. Though I shan't mind whatever else you wish to call me."

"I'm Rosa." Unsure what was expected, she held out her hand, which instead of shaking he bent courteously to kiss. She did not pull away. She wondered whether, if she had not volunteered her name, he would have thought to ask.

*

It was late, but London was not yet sleeping. They walked together through the snow-strewn streets, past imposing town houses with wrought iron gates, towards the park. Cabs rattled past in both directions, sending up spray from puddles near the pavement. A man strode by, bearing a bundle of documents, tapping his cane impatiently against the kerb. A woman in a heavy coat called after two small girls who were running hand-in-hand across the road, heads tilted back and braids swinging.

The dog darted back and forward, one minute treading over fresh snowfall delicate as a dancer, the next scrabbling and shaking out its wet paws. Rosa buried her hands deep in her pockets and raised her nose to catch the scent of the night. Woodsmoke and pine needles. Warm spices, and something salty from the nearby river. She scanned the skyline for a sign of St Paul's, but in the misted darkness and the snow, could see no further than the rooftops of the next street.

Tommy Rust strode comfortably beside her, sure-footed on the ice. He had changed into a pair of sharp-toed, tan-coloured boots, and put his top hat back on. At the corner of the park he caught her by the arm, and stopped at a stall to buy hot wine, chestnuts, oranges. Rosa watched her own breath mist white on the air beneath the lamplight, and peeled back the orange-skin with cold fingers. The fruit was sweet on her tongue. The wine, swimming with black cloves, thick and heady. Warmth crept into her cheeks.

The path to the lake had been lined with potted pines, each decorated with bells and ribbons, walnuts and golden apples. Beyond these trees, on the banks of the Serpentine, a bonfire blazed surrounded by colourful tents. The sound of violins and drums drifted in and out of earshot, caught and carried by the same wind which blew in the snow. As they approached, Rosa watched silhouettes passing between the stands, melting into the gloom beyond the flames, gliding away onto the frozen water.

Between the tents, a juggler tossed white pins between his hands, then knelt to prop one on his chin. In a pen around which a small crowd had gathered, two trick riders circled one another, their white horses high-stepping elegantly. The crowd gasped as the two jumped to exchange mounts, turning a somersault in the air. A stocky man crouched atop a podium and twirled a flaming stick before thrusting it into his throat. The stick emerged doused, and after a moment the man blew out the swallowed fire in one billowing breath. Rosa leapt back, alarmed, and the fire-eater caught her eye with a wink and a grin. His lips and teeth were blackened by soot.

All around were costumed men with painted faces. Rosa wished she could look in every direction at once, that each part of the scene was a page in a book she could open, savour, open again. She moved nearer to Tommy Rust and threaded her arm through his. He glanced across at her, firelight and shadow shifting over his face.

"You want to go on the lake?" She nodded, and he led her through the crowds, the dog padding two paces ahead of them. A man on stilts teetered overhead. Children were bunched around his feet, laughing and scurrying back whenever he wavered.

There were more potted pines along the edges of the water, these undecorated save for the snow which was beginning to settle in their branches. Heart lifting in excitement, Rosa sat beside Tommy Rust on an upturned crate, and pulled a pair of hired skates onto her feet. The blades were silver steel and sharp as knives. She had skated before, when she was fourteen, in the Withernsea year, when the Hydes had lived in a remote cottage on the cliffs. Her father had taken her out on the frozen pond behind their house, holding her carefully by the elbow. Harriet had stood watching from the kitchen window, hands resting on her swelling stomach.

"Ready?"

She gave a last forceful tug at the laces and nodded. Torches had been lit between the trees, reflected gold on the thick ice. The shadowy skaters whirled and danced like music-box figures. Standing, she found she had gained several inches on her usual height, and stepped out onto the water with stilt-walker strides.

Tommy Rust arced around her, hands tucked behind his back. He offered her no assistance, and she was glad, slowly finding her own feet. There was nothing to hold on to, and she found herself shuffling at first, eyes on the ice. As her confidence came she stood straighter. Her skates formed smoother tracks, sweeping in unbroken half-circles. Men in black coats and tall hats wove past, women wearing luxuriant mink, their skirts lifted from the ground. She turned her head to watch them, elegant in shades of russet and rose, navy and cream.

She wondered whether there were still any creatures alive beneath the ice. How much this surface might bear before it began to bend and break. Then the snowfall slowed and all doubtful thoughts melted away with the last flakes, leaving only the vigorous breath in her lungs, the air rushing against her face.

When the torches had begun to die and the crowd on the banks to diminish, she found that she stood face-to-face with Tommy Rust. His cheeks were pink with cold above his beard, his eyes alight.

"Do you see?" he asked.

Behind him, the scene blurred to embers beneath the night sky. For a moment Rosa felt that the two of them might be anywhere: perhaps upon a frozen sea in the ancient world, or in a space between the skyscrapers, in the London that was still to come. Stars glinted through a break in the clouds.

"Yes. Yes, I see."

*

They hung their coats before the fire to dry, and dozed opposite one another in the twin armchairs. It was past midnight. Rosa was aware of the soft ticking of the clock, the drip-drip of melted snow onto the hearthstones. On the street below, a cab rattled noisily past, bringing her back to wakefulness. She pressed her palms against her cheeks, which were glowing from the fire's warmth. There was a satisfying tired ache in her feet and legs.

Her own shape and presence in the world had a new feeling to it. This place, this moment, was not an island but an archipelago, with submerged connections branching out on every side. And she was welcome to it all. Better still, she thought, I know now that there was never anything wrong with me. Anything amiss. It was all *them*, all Robert and Harriet, all their fear and folly.

"We could wake up," she said aloud, "and be a hundred years away." Though Tommy Rust's eyes were closed, she could see that he was awake, one hand lazily stroking the belly of the dog which lay sprawled across his lap. His boots were propped before the hearth, steaming.

"You afraid?" he murmured.

"Not the slightest bit."

A grin climbed up the side of his face. "I'll take you to meet the others, when the winds blow that way. I often see the Brothers Black. And Amber. You'll like her, she's the cleverest of us. Perhaps the Hares, or Marta Mosel. You can find them for yourself, if we get separated."

Her heart sped again. To hear them spoken of so casually, the others who were like her. Maybe one day they would all utter her name with the same ease, the same familiarity, as though she were a friend with a key to the house or a character in a shared fairy tale. "I'll know these people, then, in cities of millions?"

His eyes opened. He regarded her across the narrow space between them, still smiling slightly. "You will know. You'll learn to know from a second's shared glance, the glimpse of a face in the crowd. There's a look that we have."

Rosa was about to ask whether she yet had this look. But without warning her thoughts turned to the man who had once emerged from the dark undergrowth in her back garden. Pointed his gun at her chest, features grim in the moonlight and pale as death. As ever he brought with him a sudden cold chill. His breath had misted white in the night air.

She was tempted to confess the peculiar power that this visitation still held over her. But in Tommy Rust's presence, the notion seemed foolish. He was as far as could be imagined from the anxious realm of her childhood, the dark corners in each Hyde home, the hushed voices of her parents behind closed doors. The dread in the pit of her stomach as the last days of December drew in.

Resentment curdled within her and took on a new clarity. Rosa sat up in her chair, filled with a need to unload the details. She was still one part in a doze, her tongue loosened. "My mother," she said, "wasn't yet one of us, when she met my father. But it changed her. She fell in love, and from then on he dragged her along with him."

The clock on the wall chimed the first hour of the new day. The dog awoke suddenly, sliding to the floor with a clatter of claws and padding away into the kitchen. Tommy Rust sat up too, trousers rolled to his shins and bare feet on the flagstones. His long hair, which he had let loose to dry, hung tousled about his face.

"Sometimes I think, at least she had those years before she knew him. She was twenty-five. She had friends who grew older with her, and… she had an occupation, and went to the pictures with boys, and…"

"How old are you, Rosa?" he asked.

"Seventeen."

"And you've never been to the pictures with a boy?"

"I never had the chance." She found herself flushing angrily. "I suppose you've had a different woman in every year you went to."

His laugh was loud and wholehearted, the corners of his eyes creasing with good humour. "If I told you, you'd probably think it a sin."

"There's no greater sin than naivety," she said, and was surprised how bitter the words were to her. To be rid of the taste, she leaned forward and kissed him on the mouth.

4

Old Acquaintance

Frank Hyde of the Glider Pilot Regiment had been shot down over Arnhem in the bitter month of November, nineteen forty-four. His wife had passed away years before, and he left behind only his son, to whom he had been both mother and father. Robert had lived out the war years alone save for the servants, who were poor company to a young man in a great country house. He whiled away the days in waiting for Frank's return. For the coming of peace. He was fifteen years old.

Instead of peace came the ring of the doorbell, the uniformed man with a face longer than a Sunday afternoon, the fob watch in a brown envelope. Robert Hyde had sat on the staircase for many hours, the chain of his father's watch swinging between his fingers, the cook's oblivious singing drifting along the corridor. *Time waits for no one, it passes you by... it rolls on forever, like the clouds in the sky...*

Inside his head, a spinning like an empty record-player turntable. On his face, the look of vague detachment which he would wear for the rest of his days. Rosa, who had pieced together this tale from tired confessions and overheard snippets through her childhood, often imagined the dawning of that look. The hook sunk into her father's heart.

Robert had been too young to be alone in the world, but there was nobody to notice or care. Unlike so many men barely older than him, he had his life – and he had money, the house sold and his bank account full to bursting. Dazed, numb, he tried and failed to be grateful. When dust sheets had been laid over the furniture of his father's house, the servants departed and the doors locked up, Robert took solitary London lodgings and made no friends. As hopes rose around him for the end of the war, for victory, he held only to the nonsense of it all, his father tumbling from the sky over Arnhem for no tangible purpose. The outside world only grew fainter, and Frank Hyde kept on falling.

May eighth. He was not ready for the day to move him so. As he opened his curtains to investigate the noise and bustle below, he saw trestle tables being carried out into the street, bunting strung between the drainpipes. Union Jacks hung from every window. Children in paper hats chased each other between the chairs, and a man wheeled a piano out of his front door, setting it on the street corner and sitting down to play.

Robert Hyde had descended into the crowds and allowed himself to be swept through the streets, past trucks loaded with young men waving their caps in the air, girls dancing with rosettes pinned to their blouses, bus-drivers merrily saluting passers-by. The windows of every home were open and the door of every shop was shut. From a wireless propped on a windowsill, the declaiming voice of Churchill, the rapturous cheering of the hordes at Westminster.

As he stumbled into Oxford Street, with people pressing on every side and music swelling in his ears, Robert Hyde felt laughter and tears lodge in his tight throat. The heart behind his ribcage, which had beat out of mere passionless obedience for months, pounded giddily. He swept off his cap and clutched it to his chest.

Something brushed against his cheek. He tilted back his head to see confetti fluttering from the sky, dancing like a thousand snowflakes, landing in his hair and eyelashes. Rosa pictured her father standing this way, stock-still amid the celebrating crowd, paper flakes settling in his fair hair. Now she knew what had changed within him then: the flame of joy which had ignited, the breathless sense of all things coming perfectly together. Gone, gone with the dying of the day, gone with the sweeping of the tangled strings of bunting from the streets. Inside the head of Robert Hyde all grew hazy once again. On the wireless he heard that a bomb had fallen on Hiroshima in a light-flash bright as the end of the world.

He retreated back inside, drew the curtains of his solitary room. Rosa imagined that the memory of his most precious day had made a nest inside him like a mouse in a skirting-board. And so when it came to the end of nineteen forty-five he did not cross the line of midnight into the New Year, but instead looked over his shoulder, and tumbled backwards to the beginning.

*

How old, before she had known? It was impossible to say. Children do not know anything all at once, but dwell in grey territory, where things are and are not. It was in her sixth year that she first began to dread the journeys, because they frightened her, and because she loved each new home a little less than the last. As usual, Harriet was helping her to pack her few belongings into a bag on the last night of December. As her mother was pulling her arms into her warmest coat, Rosa said, "I don't want to go."

"Is that so, madam?"

"I like this house. I'm going to stay."

"On your own, Rosa? What would you eat? Who would put you to bed?"

She squirmed and sighed. Her mother pulled mittens onto her hands. She had knitted Rosa a thick pair of socks and an extra vest. "May we live somewhere with a garden?"

"Perhaps. Keep still, now. You will remember to hold on tightly, won't you, when it comes."

Rosa remembered something she had heard a woman say in the grocery shop. "I don't care for it!"

"What's that?"

Rosa's lip began to shake, and her forehead creased in a scowl. She tried to wriggle free from her mother, who knelt in front of her and held her firmly by both hands.

"This is what we do," said Harriet. There was a tone in her voice Rosa had never heard before, which cowed her into stillness. Her mother had seemed endlessly strong to her then. "This is how we are."

Her six-year-old heart wavered. Harriet's sharp gaze did not let up until she shuffled her feet and swallowed her protests.

Her father was pacing the hallway, bag on his back. He grew this way at the end of the year, feverish and focused. The hook in his heart was causing him pain. From behind her mother's legs, she stared up into his face. There was a lost look in his eyes.

"Ready?" he asked. Harriet nodded without a word.

They followed him out of the door, Harriet carrying Rosa by the arms, and as they set off along the street she turned to look over her shoulder. Her boots scraped the pavement. The night wind lifted her hair. The neighbour, bringing in the washing, cast an unfriendly look after them. Another house sat darkened and silent, empty and closed-up once again.

They were on the village green when the church bells chimed midnight. Singing spilt out of a nearby pub. *Should old acquaintance be forgot, and never brought to mind...* The Hydes grasped hold of one another in the night, Robert and Harriet's arms wrapped around Rosa's back and their hands clasping hers. Her father's ragged breathing in her ear. She was tumbling backwards, pulled through nothingness after the quick violent motion of his body.

The landing took the skin from her knees. Harriet pulled Rosa quickly to her feet and straightened her knitted hat. The journey always left her bruised, pulled her outside of herself. Left her hollow.

It was now daylight, afternoon, some early day in January. When the air had settled around them they took a bus and a train and trudged along pavements. Looking for an out-of-the-way place or a nondescript street where they might arrive and leave unremarked. Build and dismantle once again. This is what we do, the Hydes. This is how we are.

*

Rosa often wondered where other families went, where their December journeys took them. She was not allowed to go out into the street. She did not go to school, but was taught reading, writing and arithmetic by Harriet at the kitchen table. In the mornings, and again in the middle of the afternoon, she would scramble up onto a chair and rest her elbows on the windowsill, watching other children as they passed in their uniforms. Grey shorts and knee socks, straight skirts and neck-ties and Mary Jane shoes. Older sisters holding hands with younger, friends swapping marbles. Boys kicking footballs back and forth. Rosa was not sure whether she would like to go and play with them, since this would mean sharing her toys.

She lay on her stomach building card-towers and then struck them down with some pleasure, humming along to her favourite songs when the news was over. The year was marked by the usual events, ebbing and flowing like the turn of the seasons. Rosa hardly yet understood the words she heard from the wireless, but their rhythm was familiar. Victory at the Bulge, then at Iwo Jima. Our boys crossing the Rhine in their Buffalos, as they always did when the snowdrops came up and the hard frost turned to soft showers of rain. The liberation of a place called Belsen Camp.

The red-letter day. When Rosa turned eight, Robert agreed for the first time that she might go with him to the celebrations. Harriet plaited her hair and helped her into her best coat. Then Rosa held Robert's hand and skipped all the way to the bus stop, where he gave her a little flag on a stick, and told her she could wave it once they reached London. The streets there were so busy that her father lifted her onto his shoulders, and she wrapped her arms around the circumference of his forehead, elated. She was high enough to reach up and grab the strings of flags which hung between the houses. The rest of the revellers were a sea below her, all in red, white and blue. Streamers flying. She was not sure what they were so happy about, but she wanted to be one of them.

Robert bought her a sticky bun and they stayed until it was almost dark, until Rosa's head began to feel heavy and she had to be carried in her father's arms, nodding off on his shoulder as he carried her back to the bus.

"Rosie," he whispered into her hair. "Should you like to come with me again next year?"

He was never this way with her; he never held her so close. If he was different on this day she wanted to always spend it with him. Rosa nestled into his coat, and nodded.

"Did you understand it, Rosie? What happened today?" She nodded again, because she thought it would please him. He pulled out his handkerchief to wipe her sticky face. "We won. It was all worth it, in the end."

"We won," she repeated.

"History will never be the same." She could actually feel the quickened beating of his heart. "They're going to look back, every year after, and remember this day."

There was an oddness about the phrase which she could not grasp. There was a splinter somewhere below her skin which was beginning to sting. If she could only find it, dig it out. "We won," she muttered, and eight months later found herself lying awake in the night, listening to the planes fly overhead. The war went on, and was won – and was being fought again the next year. She went with Robert to his red-letter day, and watched people cry tears of victory.

She knew, then, and did not know. She saw through a darkened glass.

*

For as long as she could remember there had been a word which sent a shiver from the base of her spine to the roots of her hair. *Hiroshima*. The bomb called Little Boy always fell in the hot part of the year. A bumblebee buzzed in through an open window, and on the wireless, a solemn voice broke through the afternoon broadcast. *We interrupt our program to take you to Washington. The world will note that the first atomic bomb was dropped on Hiroshima, a military base. We won the race of discovery, and have used it to shorten the agony of war.*

This was the light which burned bright as the end of the world. It dissolved a hole in everything. Rosa listened to the news too long and too keenly, and when she went to bed dreamed of an explosion which obliterated everything in its path. She woke crying out as her own body dissolved in the white-hot heat. Limbs tangled in the sheets. Her mother brought her warm milk and sat with her until she slept again.

"Don't worry, Rosa. Don't fret. Nothing can reach you here."

Hiroshima seeped into the corners of her world. For a time she was anxious about everything, fretting about aches in her body, dangers from outside. She jumped at sudden noises and made her father double-check the locks. The cloud that had risen from the bomb seemed to hang overhead, casting a shadow over every thought.

The next time Little Boy fell, she crawled into bed between Robert and Harriet in the light evening, and fell asleep with a hand resting on the back of her head. The sweet smell of cut grass drifting in from outside.

*

They lived through her tenth year in a great old house in Lambeth, where the walls were hung with crooked landscapes and the bomb-damaged attic was packed with bric-a-brac. Rosa sat cross-legged in a shaft of dusty light and delved into the mess. There were dolls and wooden soldiers, a set of pots and pans, envelopes full of antique stamps. The previous occupants must have left in a hurry, forced on by the war's chaos. She rummaged through the detritus of their lives.

In a box in the corner she found a set of seven books with plain-coloured covers and a musty smell. "*A History of Britain,*" she read aloud, and pulled out the fifth volume: *The Age of Reason.* At first she flipped idly through the pages, looking at pictures. Soon she tipped the rest of the books out too, and lined them up, side by side. *The Tudors. The Age of Empire. World War.* A sequence.

There was a fuzzy sensation in the very centre of her head, as though her eyes were trying unsuccessfully to focus on something. She spent hours reading pages at random, stumbling over unfamiliar words and concepts. When she came back to look for the books a few days later, they had gone, cleared out to make way for Robert's trains.

Like everywhere the Hydes had lived, the Lambeth house was cold and full of whispering. When she was very small Rosa had supposed these sounds to be other, invisible occupants, perhaps ghosts in the cellar, or scurrying goblins under the floorboards. Now she realised that her parents argued under their breath when they thought she could not hear. Harriet's tone reasoned, Robert's defensive. Rosa would crouch outside the doorway to their bedroom, sucking on jelly buttons she had sneaked to the sweet shop to buy, and catch snatches of their exchange.

"… grow up so peculiar, surely there couldn't be any harm in…"

"… what we agreed, Harriet. You can see how she manages to…"

"It's not enough. If you don't know that now, you'll see it in a few years."

"… any reason why she shouldn't be perfectly happy. I'm sorry, but –"

Somebody moved towards the door, and Rosa ducked out of the way, back into her own room. Without knowing why, she drove a fist silently into her pillow, once, twice. That afternoon she left the house without permission and walked the streets alone, kicking pebbles into drains and playing hopscotch on the pavement slabs. Everything was drab and grey. When darkness came she jumped between the squares of light which shone dimly from every window, until the curtains were drawn.

"Where have you *been?*" A pale, horrified Harriet opened the door just before midnight. Rosa shrugged. Her mother pulled her inside and hit her twice on the backside, hard. She didn't cry, then, or later when she was sent upstairs without supper. She sat on her bed-covers with her arms around her knees.

Harriet entered in her dressing gown and curlers. She had not brought food, but she no longer looked angry. She perched at the foot of the bed. "Listen," she said. "I asked your father whether you might go to school. Just for a few months, so you would know what it's like. But he said no."

"Didn't say I wanted to," mumbled Rosa, turning aside. Her mother did not leave.

"He's cautious, Rosa. I'm sorry. Perhaps he's right. It wouldn't do, if you arrived in a classroom from nowhere and someone took too much of an interest. We need to be left alone."

A moment of cold clarity. They do not make journeys as we do, those children in their knee-socks and smart shoes who pass by the window. It is impossible to imagine the kind of lives which they might lead. It was not a new realisation, but nonetheless Rosa felt foolish for not being sure until now, and found herself blushing. "You do understand, don't you? That we mustn't draw attention?"

"I don't want to go to school," she said. "I want to go to..." – and there it was, at last, on the tip of her tongue – "... nineteen forty-*six*."

Harriet's face tightened. The skin of her chest, Rosa noticed, had begun to redden. "Things are as they are,' she said. 'You're better off than millions, do you see? Her voice rose in volume, and she took Rosa's wrist for a moment in a hard, painful grip. "Think of all the children who lost their parents in this war. At least you have us. We've got to make the best, as we've always done."

*

On the eve of her eleventh birthday, Rosa was coming in from the privy in the garden when something made her pause in the back doorway. It was a blustery dusk in early spring, branches casting strange shadows, bluebells and crocuses bending in the flower beds. A robin hopped about among the broken pots. Something had caught her eye – the movement of a shape in the undergrowth beside the back fence.

She was about to close the door when there was a rustle, and a man emerged onto the grass in the moonlight. He was wearing a mud-stained, tattered coat which hung on his thin frame. His features were grim, chalk-pale, his breath misting on the chilly air. Hair slicked flat to his skull. He was pointing a gun at her.

She froze. For a fraction of an instant she met his gaze and knew that his presence here was not natural. He seemed to trail terror and grief and loss in his wake, as the back of his coat trailed in the soil. He clicked back the safety, and before she could even draw breath to scream, he had vanished.

Rosa said nothing to her parents. In part this was because she was sure the visitation had been meant for her alone, but it was also because nothing made sense now, in any case. Why shouldn't a stranger appear from the air and disappear again? Why shouldn't the Hydes be rolled around nineteen forty-five like butter in a churn, while history marched on behind and beyond them? Ration coupons expertly forged, Robert's inheritance carefully parcelled out. Each new home checked against old news reports, to make sure no bombs would fall there. The noose of the year's events tightened around her with every year, crushing the breath from her chest.

She had heard all of the songs on the wireless two hundred times, knew every joke on *It's That Man Again* before it was made. In the back row of the pictures, by herself on Saturday afternoons, she had seen every film enough times to mouth along with the actors as they spoke. On either side of her sweethearts held hands and kissed surreptitiously. Rosa threw chocolate drops in the air and caught them in her mouth, glancing sideways at the lovers in the flickering penumbra.

The Hydes never befriended anyone. They made only the most cursory conversation with the neighbours, with shopkeepers, with vicars and doctors and passing postmen. Robert and Harriet deflected questions with stiff, rehearsed answers, and kept their door closed even on warm days. Rosa sat on the garden wall and watched the butcher's boy, who was sixteen with broad shoulders and brylcreem hair, as he rode past on his bicycle. She knew that it was pointless to smile, to meet his eye.

Robert dampened her every enthusiasm with caution. As painstakingly, as delicately as he built his toy towns, he took it upon himself to furnish her with warnings. "There might come a time," he told her, "when you meet someone else who's like us. They don't just go back or forward, some of these people, but all over the place. And if that happens, you have to watch out for yourself. You're a step away from chaos. Don't get pulled in."

He showed her a gesture, and she copied him with some reluctance, raising her fingers above her eyes with her thumb pointed upwards. "Why must I do it?" she asked.

"In case you look upon an old friend you have not yet met. Can you imagine the mess that might make? You must always proceed slowly, always ask questions, and back away at the first sign of danger ..." He lowered his hand, voice wavering. "There is always the danger you will... you have... encountered *yourself*..."

The idea struck Rosa darkly, impressively. In case you look into your own horrified eyes, wrinkled and clouded with age. She played at it, jumping in front of mirrors and concealing her eyes from her reflection. "Where have you been?" she asked Rosa-of-the-future, who replied, *To another year. To years beyond this.* This imagined Rosa was taller, her freckles faded, her red hair longer and more lustrous. *Into new happenings you can't imagine, when the war is over. Come and see, come and see.*

*

"Mother," she asked Harriet, as the year after Lambeth, in Camberwell, drew to a close. "What if I stayed to see forty-six?"

Her mother, mixing starch for wash day, looked up. "Rosa…"

"I mean it. If I could hold on here, after you left. Maybe it will happen, if I want it to."

"It won't," said Harriet quickly. "You're our daughter. You're tied to us. Just as I'm tied to my husband." Her hair was pinned beneath a rag to keep it clean. Her face looked pinched.

Harriet had once taught classrooms of girls, Rosa knew, before meeting Robert Hyde in the reading-room of a London library. He, in search for some clue as to the distressing turn his life had taken. For a book that might tell him why time had bent back on itself. She, in search of Hemingway's *For Whom the Bell Tolls,* which her friends had spoken of so eagerly. Robert had spied her between the shelves, her red hair and coat vivid in the dull room. Rosa imagined that Harriet had turned to find his eyes on her, this scruffy wide-eyed boy. She should never have looked up from her book: she should never have smiled.

"Well then, how old must I be before I'm not tied to you any more?" With a little thrill, Rosa saw her mother wince.

"Don't think about things like that," said Harriet in a low voice.

"I could run away," said Rosa. "I could leave. Maybe I will."

She was too young, not yet sure enough. And so she was still swept back with them, though she held more loosely to their hands now, and wriggled from the shelter of their arms. She was pulled along despite herself. The tale of Frank Hyde falling out of the sky over Arnhem was by now fully known to her, and she picked it over and over in her mind, ever more impatient and angry. It was ludicrous that Robert should expend all of his feeling on a man long dead – and on that solitary day of victory, where he could feel alive for a few passing hours. It was unjust that his grief, which marked out the orbit of his world, should mark out hers and Harriet's too.

He's a fool, thought Rosa, and she's a fool for ever following him. Once she had drawn this conclusion there was no going back from it. Yet she journeyed with them, still, as they were flung back to January, as they relocated to Windermere and then Withernsea. She knew that after spending so long in London Robert must be afraid of encountering himself one day, of accidentally walking some street he'd walked before, catching the gaze of a familiar fair-haired man. Raising his hand too late to hide his eyes.

Rosa was certain she saw her father for all that he was. She supposed Harriet must tell herself there was a beautiful tragedy about him. How could she love him, otherwise? But the truth was that he never grew tired of the year because he was too fascinated by his own loss, the reliving of it, and the relieving of it. He was feeble-minded. Rosa spoke none of this aloud, and the wild cold of the lake and coast country ate away what remained of her childhood. When Robert made the long journey down to London for his red-letter day in May, she did not join him.

She was fourteen, soaked in resentment but not yet sparked alight, when her parents came to her with odd smiles and inexplicable looks between them. Harriet was flushed, bashful even. Robert moved his hands around and mumbled, as he always did, but for once looked straight at her as he spoke. "We didn't mean for this to happen. We weren't even sure… but in any case…"

"Sit down, Rosa," said Harriet.

*

The baby grew in Harriet's belly, and Rosa's anger grew with it. Her unborn sibling could not know what it was being born into. It could not choose. And her parents had chosen, through sheer colossal thoughtlessness, to create another Hyde.

She might have run then, had they not lived that year in such a remote place. Outside the town, above the sea, which shifted from green to grey as the seasons turned. Winter waves gnawed away at the cliffs. The wireless crackled and stuttered until they switched it off altogether and were left adrift from the events which usually marked time. Rosa knew them by heart, anyway.

Robert, oblivious to her silent seething, became cheerful as the baby's arrival neared. The pond in the yard froze over and he picked up two pairs of ice-skates whilst in town buying his newspaper, chivvying her to put them on and wrap up in her warmest hat and coat. Rosa moved onto the pond, watching her father as he shuffled round, chuckling to himself. There was barely enough room to manoeuvre, and she wobbled half-heartedly back and forth, arms clasped round her middle to stay warm. The bitter wind troubled the sea below.

A gust carried Rosa's hat from her head, and she turned to snatch it back. She glimpsed Harriet stood at the kitchen window, one hand resting on her stomach, staring out into the distance. In the unguarded moment her features had fallen from their usual firm resolve, and she looked younger than her years, dazed, scared.

Bella was born soon after their next journey, in a London hospital. Robert had been unable to resist the city's lure for long. Rosa peered through the cot bars at the wrinkled little creature who was her sister, the clenched hands, the duckling fuzz of hair. She sensed her mother's gaze on her back. Harriet was curled on her side, wan-faced on the hospital bed.

"Still going to leave us?" she asked.

*

Not now, not yet. Not before the baby can smile, before she can sit up, before she can crawl. Rosa spent much of her time in daydreams, imagining what it might be like to live past the strike of midnight on the last day of the year. How the sun would rise on the first morning of nineteen forty-six. "What will they say on the wireless?" she whispered to Bella, when she was called to brush her sister's teeth or run her bath. "What will Sinatra sing next? What'll be new at the pictures?"

She held Bella on her knee in front of the living room window and watched her sister's eyes follow every passer-by. The duckling hair had stayed fair, the arms and legs growing less chubby by the day as the little girl learned to walk. Words followed soon after, accompanied by a laugh which seemed to bubble up from deep inside her. Rosa could not remember anybody ever laughing like that, in any Hyde house.

But even before Bella was two, the laugh had quietened. When the planes whined too loudly overhead she pushed her way into Rosa's room in the dead of night, her bear trailing behind her, face pink with tears. Rosa let her under the covers and lay with her sister curled against her chest. She whispered all the comforting words she could find, made up stories which went nowhere. She drifted into sleep, always, before they were finished.

"Was I a mistake?" Rosa asked, sixteen now, coming to her parents' bedroom doorway late one evening when Robert was in the attic and Bella had been put to bed. Her mother was mending one of Robert's shirts, sewing kit laid out upon her knee, needle held between her teeth as she threaded it. At the sound of Rosa's voice, her head drooped momentarily, as though she had failed to find the strength to answer.

"I suppose I must have been. There's no other explanation. Why could you have thought it was a good idea to bring me into the world, otherwise?"

"You're trying to upset me."

"There's no excuse for it," Rosa threw at her. "It's *miserable*, mother, it's so *miserable*."

Harriet turned. "To love your father, is miserable? To be loyal to him?"

She must preach this to herself, thought Rosa, every morning when she wakes up, and every night when she goes to bed. Don't look to the right or the left, don't dwell on what's been lost.

"Who says that I love him?" Rosa set her jaw and drew herself up. Harriet stood, and she realised that they were now exactly the same height. Her mother did not look enraged, as she had hoped; neither did she seem distressed. She did not shout and she did not cry.

"You weren't a mistake, Rosa. I hoped that it might not last, that he'd come out of it after a few years. We were happy. We wanted a family. It was… perhaps you don't see this. It's the most ordinary thing."

"I'll never forgive you," said Rosa.

They looked at each other, and Rosa had the sense of something unravelling from her insides, so fast and so final now that it had begun. When Harriet spoke it was with dreadful quietness.

"You hear about so many deaths," she said. "I used to worry because you heard about so many deaths on the wireless every day, and you'd sit there listening… and I'd think, what must this be doing to her? All these battles, all of these bombs, day in and out, over and over again. But then I thought, shouldn't it make her grateful? All those deaths, happening not so very far away, and she's safe here. She's always been safe and she always will be. And she gets the red-letter day, too. She gets to see every year how it ends. Think of all those poor soldiers who were buried never knowing. Think of her grandfather, thrown in an unmarked grave."

Harriet sat back down upon the bed. She picked up her sewing. "For my daughter, I decided, there could be worse things."

'I'll never forgive you,' said Rosa, again.

*

The Shoreditch year. She was seventeen and certain of herself. Her restless feet took her from the house at night, leaving Bella alone in the bed as she walked the dim streets. The daily news was known so intimately to her, now, that the rhythm of falling bombs played in her head like a familiar waltz.

This night, this bomb – a V2 sailing in silence through the sky from across the ocean. Destined for the corner of Hyde Park. Rosa's feet carried her there and she sat on a bench in the stillness. She felt clear-headed. She hoped that her parents would wake and find her missing. A light flicked on in the window of a house opposite the park, and Rosa thought of the bomb now hurtling towards them. She scuffed at the dirt with her shoes. *Eeny, meeny, miney, mo. Stay or go.*

She took delight in imagining Robert and Harriet's faces if she was caught in the blast. But even better, perhaps, to see their anger first-hand. When the V2 blew apart Speaker's Corner Rosa was two streets away, raising her face, eyes closed, to the shower of cinders and dust. The blast rang in her ears, rendering her half-deaf to the screams and the wailing of sirens as she picked her way out through the rubble.

It was nearly morning by the time she got back to Shoreditch. She had climbed out by her bedroom window, into the garden, but now she gave a firm and deliberate knock at the front door. Her ears were still ringing, and she still felt giddy with adrenaline. When Harriet appeared in dressing gown and slippers, Rosa stood deaf to her cries of fury and alarm. She watched the ugly twisting of her mother's reddened face, and felt satisfied.

She slept the day away and woke, her hearing restored, to the sound of her mother's voice calling her from the kitchen. She came down the stairs with her fists balled, with a burning sensation inside her chest. Robert and Harriet were stood either side of the table, the sun setting outside the window behind them, blazing in Harriet's vivid hair.

Robert was looking at the floor, scraping at something with his shoe. He glanced up to give Rosa a weak smile, which quickly died.

"What are we going to do with you?" asked Harriet.

"It was the V2," said Rosa. "In case you hadn't guessed. By the park. I felt like a little excitement."

Harriet's face and body were rigid. "Did you mean for..." She choked. "No. You only meant to mock us. What do you want from us? Why do you have to be so cruel?"

"Cruel? *Cruel?*" Rosa heard her own voice rise dramatically in volume, and Harriet crossed the room quickly to close the kitchen door.

"Quiet! Bella —"

"I told you, I won't forgive you because you don't deserve it! I don't owe you anything! All either of you ever cared about was him!" She jabbed a finger at Robert , and saw him recoil in shock. She felt the blood rushing to her cheeks, and shouted all the more loudly, exhilarated. *"What* he *wanted, what* he *needed..."*

"You'll wake your sister!"

"I don't care! I hope the neighbours hear too! I hope they hear out in the street!" Rosa pounded at the wall with her fist. *"Oi! The Hydes have me in here! Will somebody come and rescue me?"*

"Grow up, Rosa." Her mother's tone was frosty, scornful.

She was momentarily lost for words. When she found her voice again, she could barely spit out a sentence. "But that's — that's exactly —" She was breathless, shaking all over. *"Because of you, because of him, I could never..."*

There was something wet trickling down her face. Rosa did not want to cry in front of them, not now, but there was no stopping it. Whatever happened now, nothing could be the same again.

"Why won't you look at me?" she demanded of her father. He was hunched behind the table, as though an opportunity might come to edge out of the room unnoticed. He was too pathetic even to fight his own fight. "Don't you know this is all because of you? I hope you're still here in twenty years, and that you die here knowing you've wasted your life! *And that nobody visits your grave!"* Very slowly, Robert raised his eyes, and Rosa barely registered his look of stunned disbelief. A laugh of triumph bubbled up to mingle with her tears. *"She'll* never tell you this, but you're a coward."

There was an awful silence. Then without warning, Harriet cracked. *"HOW DARE YOU!"* she screamed, starting towards Rosa. *"How dare you speak to your father like that! How dare you —"*

Rosa stood still and held Robert's gaze. Over his shoulder, outside the window, the night beckoned.

"I hate you," she said. "You won't see me again."

5

The Fabulist

"Watch me," said Tommy Rust. "Do as I do. Speak as I speak. And stay close."

Rosa wore his shirts and grew accustomed to his habits. He rose early, ate plentifully, never cleaned his rooms. Talked to his dog as though at any minute it might answer, kept a fire always blazing in the grate. Gave a loud, full laugh at every satirical picture in *Punch*. Out in the city she took his arm and kept in step with him, enamoured with the way her bell-shaped skirts swept the ground.

She watched Tommy, and imitated him in everything. He strode with confidence, eyes always at street level, because only visitors look up. His hands in their threadbare gloves were quick to lift things from stalls and shop counters, apples, newspapers, diamond necklaces. There was a thrill in it, she discovered, the moment of taking not only what was needed but what was wanted – that cameo brooch, that china ornament. Her fingertips traced lightly over each curiosity, and objects found their way into her bag. She quickly picked up the shape of the city in that century.

He showed her Shoreditch, which at that time was home to narrow streets where the shoemakers worked, and the stinking sprawl of the Old Nichol slum. She was not much interested in seeing the place she had run from more than a hundred years later, nor any of the other streets where the Hydes would live. Of all Tommy's favourite places she preferred the docks at Blackwell on the bend of the Thames, the East and West India where the spice-boats came in, mist coiled about their sails. Warehouses measured in miles, whirling with activity from sunrise until nightfall, when throngs of labourers continued their work by lamplight.

Tommy held the dog's collar to stop it going wild with excitement, and they walked along the bank above the river, watching the cargo of an Indiaman brought to shore. Rosa could feel the warmth of his arm through his coat. "Where do they all come from?"

"The furthest parts of the world," he said, the corners of his eyes creasing. One of the workers caught sight of him from the dock below and waved, cap in hand.

"Mr Rust! Back from the Americas, I see!"

"Indeed I am, Mr Arkow! How's business?"

"Tolerable, sir, tolerable. Come for a drink with us when the day's done, won't you?"

"I was in this year before, oh, perhaps three years ago," Tommy explained to Rosa later, in the corner of a crowded table. She scratched Wolf's ears under the table, and the dog licked her hands. The inn was swelteringly hot despite the chill night outside, the ale watery. "They think I'm a trading gentleman with an interest in cotton..."

She enjoyed watching him in lively talk with the dockworkers, the group's mirth growing noisier with every drink, until the men bade him goodnight and he sunk back into his seat. Wolf laid his head in Tommy's lap and dozed there, while the room began gradually to empty around them.

"The sun never sets on the empire," said Tommy. He flicked a finger through the flame of the candle on the table. "So they're fond of claiming. And it'll last a good while longer. Until your time, at least."

"Not *my* time," said Rosa. "Don't call it that."

"But of course! You're no citizen of that year or any other, now."

He looked up to meet her gaze, and Rosa returned his smile. She was aware that she had nobody with whom to compare Tommy, and did not want to be more impressed with him than he deserved. But everything about their encounter had been lucky for her. At first her skin had flushed under her clothes when he was near, but all shyness was now gone. She had never so much as kissed a boy until the night that Arline sang at the theatre, but she had shrugged off her innocence gladly and kicked it under his bed.

They did not stay long in London, in that bitter winter at the midpoint of the bustling nineteenth. There were no plans made, no belongings packed. Only a walk one full-moon night down a foggy lane on their way back from the penny gaffs in Blackfriars, a shifting in the earth beneath their feet. Rosa's insides lurched forward and she immediately seized Tommy's hand, clinging to him as they tumbled into nothingness and the city groaned and crumbled about them. She cried out and fell uncomfortably on her knees. She was catching her breath in gasps, feeling herself for bruises, when Tommy pulled her to her feet.

For a moment she was surprised to find him still beside her. He looked at her quizzically. "All right?"

"Yes, yes..." They had come forward, and it was still night. Rosa pulled back from him and brushed herself off.

"Did you hurt yourself?" He must have landed on his feet.

"I'm fine. What about your things?"

"My – oh, those bits and pieces. I'll collect new ones. Don't worry, I'm always prepared." He showed her a flash of gold in his pocket and sniffed the air with relish, untying his cravat so that it hung loosely around his neck. The journey, which had knocked the wind from her, seemed to have imbued him with fresh energy. "Fifty years or so, I'd say! That monarch, she's a fat old lady in black by now. What do you say we call on her for tea?"

When Rosa didn't answer, he tugged playfully at her arm. "You know that you can travel light, don't you?"

"I don't have anything with me."

"I mean…" Tommy made to move off and she followed him, trying not to stare at her surroundings. "It doesn't have to hurt."

"I *said*, I'm all right."

Tommy held up his hands, and within minutes, the pain had receded. Her knees ceased their shaking. It was not until some time afterwards that she remembered his dog, and hoped that somebody would feed it.

*

Every few weeks there was another journey. They chased down the thin places where they might pass through, hitching rides in fast cars and hay-carts, traipsed between towns with their belongings on their backs, hung from the windows of steam-trains. The skin on Rosa's feet grew tough.

She woke with him again in some city and some year she could not recall, and rising, tied back her hair beneath a scarf. She padded bare-legged across the dim hotel room to draw back the curtains. Cars sped along the road below, and an aeroplane climbed slowly into the sky above the dawn-lit rooftops. She watched its progress towards the clouds, trail alight behind it.

"Don't tell me where we are," she said. Tommy turned beneath the covers and opened his eyes. He stretched, propping himself on the pillows, and regarded her with half a smile. The light from between the curtains fell across the bed.

"Shall we make it a guessing-game?"

"No. I mean, it's almost better, not knowing."

She pushed open the window and breathed the morning air.

Tommy yawned widely, languid as a cat. "A fine spirit to begin in."

She looked over her shoulder at him, and everything seemed exactly in its right place. Anyone could shipwreck themselves against him so easily, she thought, if they were foolish enough to come in too close. Steer wisely, ride the current alongside, and he can be just as you need him to be. One morning, one journey at a time.

"Now you look thoughtful," he said.

"I was wondering whether they're all like you. Our kind."

"None quite alike." In jest he spread his arms, wing-wide, against the pillows. "History couldn't hold us all. Do you know, I was once venerated as a divine being by a mountain tribe in the thirteenth? We'll always know more, we'll always be more than they are. They built statues, and brought me the best of their crops."

Rosa gave a snort of laughter, and turned back to the window. "I hope you were good to them."

"Oh, most benevolent." She heard him getting out of bed, busying about the room as he found his clothes. A flock of pigeons rose into the air from a nearby rooftop and circled noisily, a flurry of white and grey. She rested her chin on her hand, as she had done so often at so many windows, and her smile grew broader. Soon they would be going outside.

Tommy drew alongside her, and she buttoned his shirt, tucking his watch into the pocket of his waistcoat. The city below was warmed by the morning sun.

"Come on then," he said. "The day awaits."

*

She woke in two dozen different beds with her forehead pressed into his broad back, her hands folded across her chest. Sleeping, he

72

seemed safe, almost tame. It reassured her that he had never once tried to put his arms around her while she slept. Any such sign of attachment would soon have driven her away.

She occasionally wondered where his own journeys had begun, which place in history had made him, but she did not really want to know. He was better this way, free from such ordinary detail. They walked together in the evenings, down wet pavements, through streets lit with neon strips or gas-flames. One century bled into the next.

They celebrated her eighteenth year with oysters and champagne, in a roof-garden beside the sea. It was the middle of the twenty-first, and wind-turbines populated the waves, white blades whirling fiercely below the wide sky. Rosa rolled the expensive flavours around her tongue and felt that she could taste her own adulthood, the being she was becoming. No previous birthday had ever held this delicious anticipation.

"One day," said Tommy, eloquent with drink, "I shall go to Hiroshima. Or some other such city, where the fabric of the place has been torn."

"Hiroshima?" she repeated, jolted for a moment from her reverie.

"One of the cities where they dropped –"

"You think I haven't heard of it?"

"I thought you must have. Well, an event like that, it makes a mark in time. It stirs things up. They say that for our kind, it's like walking on a glass floor at five hundred feet."

His eyes were narrowed, the shadows of long clouds trailing across his face. He looked at her. "And where should you like to go, gypsy girl? What should you like to see?"

Lately she had begun to shuffle the possibilities in her head, recalling the set of books she had once found in the attic of the

Lambeth house – history spread before her. "Perhaps somewhere in the far future. Or this country, in older times. Long before the war. When there were still wolves in the woods."

"We'll catch the tide there, when we can." His coat collar was turned up against the wind. He pulled a pack of cigarettes from his pocket and attempted to light one, shielding it with his hand. "But remember, it'll be harder the further back we go. For you, I mean – to speak and be heard, to move freely and safely, unless you're with me.

"Why?"

"Isn't it obvious? Amber tells me that she travels as a man when she goes back further than the nineteenth."

Rosa let this sink in, then raised her face, inhaling Tommy's smoke. "And if I lose you?"

He tucked the hand that was not holding the cigarette into the small of her back. He blew a grey stream towards the sky. "We'll meet again, sweetheart. If that's what you want. You'll be surprised how soon you find me."

*

When his hand slipped from hers for the first time, as they journeyed from the very middle of England in the seventeenth, she was ready.

She reached out for him but he was already gone in the darkness, and the buildings all about were tumbling like sandcastles, the shadows of pine trees sprouting into being. The breath was knocked from her lungs. When she landed she was thrown back on her heels and the flats of her hands, bruised again, but exhilarated.

Rosa did not cry for Tommy Rust, or even search for him. She took her bearings just as he would have done, lifting her nose to sniff the air, mud and straw and the ripe stench of livestock. She moved quickly from the place where she had landed, along a dirt road which led around a squat huddle of buildings. These were thatch-roofed, rudimentary. Two men were leading a horse along the path some way ahead of her, their language strange to her ears. Another wave of excitement rolled over her. You can do this, she told herself. You know how.

She was carrying only what could be kept in her coat pockets – the flick-knife from the twenty-first, a bag of gold jewellery, a few worthless odds and ends she'd grown fond of. Kneeling beside a ditch, she emptied out anything that wouldn't be of use into the mud. She pushed open the unwatched door of a nearby home, having silenced the dog outside with gentle muttering and ear-scratches. Though the crooked little rooms within were mostly bare, they yielded a few essentials.

Chickens scratched about the straw-strewn floor at her feet as she snatched a loaf of bread and a flask of milk from the table. Her coat, which she had acquired in the twentieth, was quite plain and too warm to relinquish. Beneath it she changed into a too-large tunic which had been left on the bed, and hid her long hair beneath a cap as Tommy had advised. She rubbed dirt into her cheeks. There was little chance that her hard face, hard hands, hoarse voice would give her away.

Rosa slept the afternoon in an empty barn and then ventured into a tavern, intrigued by the half-familiar language being spoken all around her. She dug her knife into a bowl of stewed mutton and vegetable pottage, and listened. After travelling with Tommy it was tedious having nobody to converse with. Days later, riding on the back of a hay-cart with a couple of the right coins in her pocket, shelled walnuts in her palm and sunlight on her face, she climbed up to sit beside the driver, a toothless old man with dirt etched into every line of his features.

75

"I know you can't understand me," she said to him, "but it makes no odds. Even if you could, you wouldn't be able to grasp the first thing about where I've come from."

The man glanced at her, hardly alert enough to be curious. Rosa tossed a walnut into the air and caught it in her mouth. She pointed to the thick forest which covered the side of the hill. "This will all be flattened, I can tell you for certain. Bricks and concrete and glass where those pigsties are."

She watched others pass by with their pack-horses, their market-day errands, and felt vindicated. She wanted to stand and wave her hat in the air, and shout. Men of this age! What do you know of steam-trains, and factories, and motor-cars? Of aeroplanes lifted on steel wings? What will you ever know of the things I've seen, the things I've yet to see? You were born and will die in your blinkers. In the box of your given years, only just large enough for you to shuffle round in, if you're lucky, like a dog in a kennel.

Rosa thought of Tommy, dancing so lightly across the surface of each year he passed through, and wondered why he was content to remain in corners. She did not want to spend more nights in dilapidated hotel rooms or cattle-sheds, or days climbing furtively through strangers' windows. This earthbound struggle for food and shelter didn't interest her. Surely it needn't be so. Not when we are what we are. Not knowing all that we know.

As though it had been biding its time before making an entrance, the idea came fully-formed to her mind.

*

The journeys still snatched her breath away, but now she leaned back into them, letting her body go limp. She went further, and faster. She dropped from the brink of each year as though slipping from a cliff-edge, arms outstretched, plummeting. Her heart thundered so hard it might burst, and she did not know whether it was terror, or the greatest thrill she had ever known.

She began to read everything she could. In Oxford, the seventeenth, she holed up between the shelves of the great library there as it took shape, passing beneath the Tower of the Five Orders and running her finger along countless leather-bound spines. Books from the Orient, from the ancient world, from the collections of kings. Rosa soaked in their pages as though reclining in a scented bath. No more scrabbling in dusty attics for knowledge, no more gaping in ignorance at each new age she encountered. She thought in passing of Harriet Hyde, searching out Hemingway in a London reading-room, studious and sharp with youth.

Where there were no libraries she simply watched and listened, taking copious notes in her smallest writing. She sketched the skyline of Birmingham as the chimneys rose in the late eighteenth, of London in sixteen sixty-six as the famous fire raged. She traced out the inner workings of the machines which powered the age of steam, the engines which had turned the word's wheels, their pressure-valves and cylinders and pistons. The Mohammedan astrolabe caught her eye when it was brought west, the quaint mechanics of Irish tide-mills, the powder-cannons which blasted apart the old order in the Hundred Years War. She tore pictures from leaflets and newspapers in the twenty-first, cut out maps and photographs.

Everything recorded in pencil and in bright-coloured inks, everything folded and tucked into the bags which she carried on her back. Nothing will surprise you now. Pass among men and women as they go about their everyday business, mimic their movements and their speech. Don't mind it if they turn to look at you as though you are something out of the ordinary – because that, after all, is what you are. Try out their strain of the language on your tongue.

Rosa realised too late that she hadn't marked the commencement of her nineteenth year. She wondered whether Tommy might be close, perhaps even in the same age, following the same tide. She couldn't deny that the thought pleased her: but between the journeys it turned out that there were other men, other beds to wake in. Bodies with faces she paid little heed to. She rarely stayed even to exchange names.

In the pages of her notebooks she drew a figure, trailing long embroidered skirts, high collar decorated with lace and pearls. Jewels in her hair. Twirling her pencil, Rosa added a sheaf of paper tucked beneath the arm, a golden band across the forehead. She smiled.

*

It was in the chaotic twelfth that she tried it first.

Veil covering her face, robed in simple dark cloth, she strode beneath stone arches into the heart of a north-country monastery. As she passed the monks looked up from their labour in the gardens, where physic herbs grew in shivering bunches. The damp air fragrant with yarrow, with wormwood and bay. In the cloisters, rainwater went trickling down the mossy walls and over every floor, into the crypt.

The monks gathered around her in the chapter-house, earth upon their hands and feet. One reached out tentatively to touch the fabric of her cloak, and she let him do so, hiding a laugh as he exclaimed at its softness. She stretched out her arms so that the others could creep forward and do likewise. They spoke to her in sentences she barely understood, words which she supposed would later change beyond recognising, or simply die out, like the wolves in the woods.

They took her to the abbot, a frail-looking man who regarded her with sunken, puzzled eyes. She laid her books upon his table, and by the light of evensong candles, pointed to herself. "I am to be born eight hundred years from now," she said.

The monks stood back, mute. Each syllable reverberated around them, a singing hum which might have come out of another realm. They were already hanging upon her words.

"I have lived through many ages. I have seen things beyond the furthest limits of your knowledge. And I have come to tell you of your fate."

She let the largest book fall open. They gathered near, muttering to one another. Their nervous breath upon her neck. Their fingertips traced the map on the page before them, the complex crossing lines of the London underground. Overleaf, a drawing of a five-needle telegraph. A newspaper photograph of a satellite, its arms spread against the backdrop of blackest space.

The monks' eyes grew wider, their voices more animated. They jostled one another for a better look until the abbot broke between them, fear and wonder mingled in his face. His veined hands shook as he looked up at this otherworldly visitor.

Rosa closed the book and adjusted her veil. The silence was delicious to her. "I will take a bed for the night," she said. "And wine. *Wine*, do you hear me? I know you understand. Think of the wrath that will fall upon you if turn a prophetess away."

*

Soon she sailed away from that country which now seemed too small to hold her, and walked the streets of Milan in the feverish late fifteenth. Below the turrets and red rooftops, tradesmen haggled over silver going out to the ships at Genoa and timber coming in from Flanders. Rosa wore a gown in richest blue, pointed shoes and a mask over the upper half of her face. Passers-by pointed after her in her wake, this curiously dressed figure with her head held high and a paid porter struggling under the weight of her bags. Lizards scuttled over the warm stone walls of workshops where musicians, artisans, architects, painters and poets were bringing a new age to birth.

It seemed more than probable that other travellers were close, but Rosa had no interest in meeting them yet. It was satisfying to be so admired by those who received her, as though she was the only being of her kind to walk the world. Presenting herself at the court of the duke, she was afforded rooms overlooking the city, with silken sheets and goose-down pillows. Ladies fanned themselves in the shade as she knelt among them, spreading out her best sketches and explaining things in mime, with small snatches of the language. To them she was a new entertainment, better than any jester or harpist, and they plied her with sweetmeats and jewels.

After most of the court had gone to bed she stayed up with the duke's favoured artists and learned men, watching them debate with one another and appraising their work by candlelight. The warm breeze blew in through the *Palazzo*, and Rosa regarded them from below her mask. These men were at the centre of this changing age, and yet they were in awe of her. They marvelled over her pictures of impossibly intricate mechanisms, of cities unlike any place which could be built or imagined. Proudly, they showed her their best scientific diagrams and conceptual inventions. She was charmed by an automaton which had the shape of a devil, a wicked thing in metal and wood which could spit fire.

This, she thought, is the way to move through history: not as faceless vagrant, but as honoured guest. Her own ingenuity delighted her. This way, she could walk with confidence into places where no stranger – and certainly no woman – might otherwise walk. She could travel freely to wherever took her fancy, taste the finest food of every century.

The tides took her again. Back, still further back, to days before that city's stones had been laid – the days of druids and the first hammered swords, the smoke of sacrifices and the gods in every wood and valley. Hulking shadows between the trees. The land smelled different, was wracked by wilder storms. On an island built far out in a misted lake, where offerings were dropped from the platform into the black water below, she sat wrapped to the shoulders in a bear-pelt. The priests of that place came to pay their tribute, to sit at her feet as she spoke in a tongue they did not know of sights they would never see.

They knew that she was a thing from another world because she wore cloths that had been woven by no human hand, dipped in dyes found nowhere in nature that they knew. Precious stones glimmered at her collar and sleeves. The pictures in her book were like dream-visions. When the fancy took her she journeyed to the city which Tommy Rust had once seen rise from its foundations, now in its prime.

Where in history books Rome's buildings had all been white, all spotless alabaster pillars and statues, the reality was in colour: Tyrian purple, Egyptian blue, yellow saffron and red cinnabar. The sense of daring, here, of being at the stretched limit of the familiar. The blood on the steps of every temple. Rosa gazed with appraising eyes over criminals hung spluttering from trees, over the crowds who flooded the amphitheatres, the processions led before them to battle and die. Turning into the marketplaces, she smelled perfumes made with myrrh and styrax, helped herself to the finest earrings and bracelets and cloths. She ate fat figs and olives straight from the vine.

Before returning to the land where she had begun, she travelled south and across the water to another city. To that underground sanctuary where the future curls and rises with the scented smoke from out of fissures in the earth.

*

Your name, they tried to ask her in that smoke-filled cave in tongues she barely recognised, and later in parlours and castle chambers, in her own country and across the sea. *Your name, woman whose years have no end. Foreseer of such strange visions.*

A veil concealed her satisfied smiles. She closed her books and gathered them to herself. She departed, always, when the fancy took her, and without farewells.

"There is a title," she told them, "by which I am known."

6
Seysair

The Fabulist walked into Seysair Tower in the reign of Henry the last Lancastrian, in the middle of the fifteenth. From the battlements flew the flag of the resident border lord, depicting a twin-headed ram. The crest flapped and strained in the high wind.

They saw her coming from the windows, and unbolted every door before her. Heads turned, lords and servants and ladies and knights, to watch her pass. She wore embroidered skirts which trailed in her wake, a high collar of pearls and lace. A gold band encircled her forehead, and her long, fire-coloured hair was held to her head with jewelled pins. Her face was powdered porcelain-white.

The Lord of Seysair sat upon his chair on the dais of the hall, and in this high state watched her approach. He was a round-bellied man, advancing in years, his huge furred mantle making him appear yet larger. A chained hawk shuffled its wings on a post beside him. The Fabulist did not lower her head, or even cast her eyes towards the floor. Her skirts whispered against the stone.

In silence, she laid out her books on the table before him. Sunlight poured in through the frayed tapestries hung overhead, dust dancing in the air. His household gathered about the edges of the room, muttering to one another behind their hands, bright as garden insects.

"They say that you hail from a far country," said the Lord of Seysair. His accent was thick, but not beyond her comprehension.

"Indeed. From further away than you can imagine."

"It is our honour to receive you. They say that you have appeared before princes. I hope that our comforts here will be sufficient for you."

The Fabulist was careful to keep her porcelain face composed. The Lord of Seysair stood and offered a small scrap of meat to the hawk, stroking its hooded head with his thumb. He came sideways down the steps, heavy mantle dragging after him, and approached the table. Inquisitive, he indicated the largest of the books.

"These are your prophecies? Of the ages to come?"

"Not prophecies," she said. "Visions. I have seen these things before me, clear as day." With practised confidence she peeled apart the book's pages, and watched him lean forward. Photographs from the twenty-first of cars and cafés and pouting film stars. She shook her head as he reached out to run a finger across the glossy surface of the page, and he withdrew at once, chastened. "Please. You must consider these as sacred."

"How were they handed down to you?" he asked breathlessly.

"I cannot speak of it. Now come. I will show you marvels you have never dreamed of."

*

The man was so entranced by the pictures in her pages that he sat her at the head of his table that night, before piled plates of saffron eggs, pheasants with gilded beaks and claws, gingered fish and pig-trotter jellies. The timbers groaned beneath the weight of thirty different dishes. She sampled everything, capons and stuffed squabs, salted hare and songbird pie. In imitation of the Lord on his carven chair, and his long-faced wife beside him, she cast the bones to the floor for the dogs to squabble over. She licked the fat from her fingers.

As the heaped plates diminished, servants stoked the roaring fires at either end of the hall, and the air grew thick with sweat and smoke and the aroma of roasting flesh. A great roar of voices, punctuated by the blowing of horns and the barking of dogs, came drifting in from outside. The Lord of Seysair stood to his feet.

"The hunt!" he cried, above the din of the diners. "The hunt is returned!"

There was much cheering and hammering of the tables. The knights of the hunt burst in with their hounds at their heels, red-faced and riotous with victory, braces of rabbits and partridges hung from their hands. The greatest prize, a red stag with velvet antlers and a lolling tongue, was draped over the shoulders of the knight who led the party. At the urging of the others, he leapt onto the table and let the slain creature slide from his back. It landed with a room-shuddering thud.

"To the men of Seysair, the spoils!" he cried, to deafening cheers, and was at once pressed with ale on every side. Fist raised above his head, he gulped down one tall flagon after another.

The Fabulist watched him, and as he finally took a seat, turned to the nobleman beside her. "What is the name of that knight, and from where does he hail?"

"I believe him to be one Thomas Rymer, journeyed lately from the south, so he says."

"The south."

"Yes. Though we know little of his ancestry, or his deeds before coming to our court."

She kept her eyes upon him as the servants brought out rosewater plums, sweet creams, glazed pastries and honeyed figs. The knight ate ravenously, making loud and animated talk with those beside him. Reaching for something on the far side of the table, he looked up and met her gaze for a moment. The room was too dim to read his look. Briefly, mockingly, he raised his hand to cover his eyes.

When the meal was ended, a servant led the Fabulist through the torch-lit hallways towards her chamber. They were about to ascend a flight of spiral stairs when there came the sound of footsteps behind them, and the Lady of Seysair hurried around the corner. A lantern swung from her hand, and she was breathing hard.

"Celandre," she said to the maid, "go and prepare the chamber. I will speak with…"

Her speech was more deeply accented than her husband's, her movements nervous and quick. She wore a cape lined with grebe and marten-fur, a green gown embroidered with leaping fish, and a thin veil. She clutched her lantern close. The servant gave a nod and disappeared up the stairs, leaving the Lady and the Fabulist alone in the quiet corridor.

"May I speak with you," asked the Lady of Seysair, "of a personal matter?"

The Fabulist glanced over her shoulder. She was sleepy with rich food and good wine, more than ready to lay her head down. She was not sure that this woman could have much to say that would interest her, but gave a cursory nod.

"I have three sons, of fighting age. You understand?"

"Yes."

"Two nephews, lost already to the border wars. Reivers kill and pillage without care, unless we ride out against them. Nightly with tears I pray to Our Lady and to Saint Monica for the keeping of my sons." Her trembling hands made the lantern-light unsteady, shadows quivering across her face. "If only I could know, if only I could be assured that they will live!"

The Fabulist could hear the howl of the wind outside the tower, the crackle of the torches upon the wall. She felt a strange compulsion to turn her back, to climb the stairs without another word. But it would have been discourteous. She had not felt uncomfortable within her own skin for a long time, but here it was – an unexpected doubt. The sense that these robes, this painted face, were fraudulent.

The Lady of Seysair took a tentative step towards her.

"Have you not seen what is to come?"

The Fabulist looked up, and not wanting to appear as though she had been caught off guard, clasped her hands tranquilly. "Yes, my lady. But matters of this kind…"

"I know it is such a small thing to you. Forgive me." The woman bowed her head stiffly. She was clearly pained, but she did not move away.

The Fabulist drew a long, awkward breath. "The secrets of the future, the things which are revealed to me… please understand, they are not… I cannot…" Her hands gestured of their own accord, indicating a grand sweep, a far-off vista beyond her purview.

Still the woman did not leave. Her expression was so desperate, so delicate still with hope, that the Fabulist fumbled for something to offer. "Do you have daughters?" she asked, after a while.

"Five."

The Fabulist tucked her hands behind her back.

"My Lady. I cannot tell you what will become of your sons. But your daughters…" She looked as unflinchingly as she could at the woman before her. "Your valiant daughters will be the glories of your life."

The cloud did not entirely clear from the Lady's face, but she flushed in gratitude. She curtseyed, backed away. The Fabulist stood for a moment in the corridor, surprised at herself. She wondered whether her own words had been meant as a kindness, though she owed none to anybody.

*

In the darkened chamber, the servant Celandre unlaced the Fabulist's dress, and helped her into her nightgown. Left alone, she wiped the white powder from her face. She arched her shoulders back, glad to be free of the constricting costume. Glimpsing the side of her face in the mirror, she paused a moment, contemplative. Perhaps it would have been better to give no reply. It had been a foolish request, and she didn't want all of Seysair's court coming to ask their own fortune.

There came a sudden tapping at the door. She moved nearer and inclined her ear, but the noise was not repeated. She turned the handle.

She looked her visitor up and down. "If you're seen here…"

He was grinning from ear to ear. His shoulders were broader, his beard fuller, but she would have recognised his lively eyes anywhere. He was still wearing his hunting clothes, boots caked in earth and leaves caught in his hair. A little intoxicated, but sharply aware of himself nonetheless. Before he could move across her threshold, she stilled him with a stern finger on his chest. "How long for you?" she asked.

"Three years. You?"

"Two. I lost you when we were passing from the twentieth."

"Yes. We can't have been too far apart in the meantime."

"And you haven't seen me since?"

"I haven't seen you since."

She let him pass, and pulled the door closed behind him. He was staring at her, she was pleased to note, in undisguised delight. "Madam Fabulist," he said, only half in jest, and made a little bow. She lingered on the gratifying thought of how changed she must seem to him, even without the attire – her skin browned by hot climates, face and shoulders sugared with freckles. Her back straighter, eyes clearer, presence as imposing here as in the hall before the lord of the tower, if she wanted it to be. She looked back at him fearlessly, skin prickling as though the air between them had become charged.

"I nearly spat out what I was eating. You know who you look like, in all your finery? And you know she won't be born for nearly a hundred years?"

She glanced at the wardrobe, where the servant had hung her embroidered dress with its magnificent pearl collar. Her face broke into a teasing smile in reflection of his own. She made a flawless curtsy, bare foot sweeping the stone.

"You've come a long way, gypsy girl," he said quietly.

"And what of you? I suppose Thomas Rymer is your real name?"

He took a step towards her, taking off his hat. He spun it around on his finger, then hung it upon the bedpost. "Oh, I carry several. I forget which of them I first owned."

She laughed, and in doing so realised that she was truly happy to have him close again. Once she might have resented the feeling as weakness, but now it didn't seem to matter. To want him was a small crime, now that she no longer needed him.

One night, one journey at a time. She moved towards the mirror, and behind her heard the pad of his boots across the stone. Warm hands resting on her hips, his breath on her bare shoulder.

Back still to him, she began to pull the jewelled pins from her hair.

"Blow out the candle, will you, Tom?"

*

They rose early and walked together through the gardens. It was spring, and everything was coming alive. They passed through the walled gardens, dew-soaked and tranquil, every flowerbed tended and every shrub neatly trimmed. Seysair was set upon a low hill, woods and moorland stretching out on either side. The tower was covered in climbing creepers, grey stone and green leaves reflected in the lake below. A group of men were visible in the field on the hill opposite, small as Robert's model-town figures, harnessing an ox to the plough.

A long-legged dog came loping down the slope to great Tommy on the lakeside path, and Rosa watched him tug its ears affectionately. It was strange to be wearing her heavy dress once more, face powdered and hair pinned, in this fresh morning. She would rather have gone barefoot, perhaps in her nightgown and coat, but it would not do to have them see her so.

She clasped her hands behind her back and stepped lightly, letting her arm brush against his. "You've been here long?"

"A month, or thereabouts. You like it?"

"Yes," she said. The sun had just risen over the moor, and its light warmed her face. "Very much."

"It's been a lively time, I'll tell you. They know how to keep a guest." He kissed his palm and held his hand to the air, a gesture she hadn't seen before. "Bless the tide that brought me here. Hunting and hawking and swordplay, and feasting every night. I've got my own chamber with a feather mattress."

"Luxury indeed," she said.

He looked sideways at her, eyes glittering. "Your own fortune has been yet better, I see."

It was on the tip of her tongue to tell him about silk sheets in Milan, about druids who had chanted in her honour in a forest clearing, about monastery wine which had been a century underground. But she realised that he had not asked, and changed her mind without missing a beat. It was not done, it seemed, to fill in the ellipsis between encounters with too many details. It leaves us free, thought Rosa. Not bound to one another, but new and unknowable each time.

"As you see," she said, "I have been able to make my way."

"You were well-taught."

"But this was my own invention."

He looked at her, arms folded across his chest, and grinned broadly. "It is," he said, "*ingenious*."

"And I am?"

"Extraordinary, Rosa. Extraordinary."

The dog trotted on ahead of them, sticking its nose into every bush, chasing a string of ducklings which had strayed from the water. At a distance, behind the bulrushes, a group of the court ladies could be seen emerging from the chapel after mass. As they came down the hill, they caught sight of the knight Rymer walking with the Fabulist in the morning mist.

"Stay close to me," said Tommy in a low voice. "And talk, all the while. They will think you're telling secrets of my future."

The ladies of Seysair whispered behind their hands. Rosa leaned in close to his shoulder, and murmured to him.

"Your future, Tommy Rust, is blinding in its brightness. I see a hundred new ages ready for your taking. Roads await your feet. I see cities in the sky. I see a horizon filled with lights."

On the lake behind them, a flock of brown geese came in to land, droplets showering from beneath their webs and wide-spread wings. A solitary coot stepped across lily-leaves near the bank, bobbing its black head, out-sized toes splayed.

"Speak further," said Tommy. He was looking straight ahead, eyes narrowed as though straining to spy out the very things which she described.

"I see a life like no other, blazing across the pages of history like a comet. Never coming to an end."

He gave a bark of laughter, and the ladies turned to stare over their shoulders. He took Rosa's arm, leading her along the bank, out of sight of the tower. They paused on the far side of the lake to take in the picture, Tommy leaning against a tree-trunk and tucking his hands behind his head.

"What do you think to that?" he asked.

Blossoming willows trailed their branches in the water. Beyond, the hills were moss-green and patched purple with heather, smoke rising from a hamlet across the valley, mist on the distant mountaintops. There were no skies like this, Rosa thought, in later centuries. This vaulted height and depth, this rich deep blue.

"I think that I should be content to stay here for some time."

*

She grew to know the little nooks where one might draw a curtain and read undisturbed for hours, the hidden courtyards with their dovecotes and stew-ponds. She wandered at her will, and the folk of Seysair grew accustomed to having the Fabulist among them. The days became warm, and bees swarmed around a cluster of hives on the hill, spinning sweetness from the heather.

The Lord of the tower sent for her from time to time, and she sat with him in the hall or in his private chambers. Her fluency in the dialect had improved and she was able to converse with him at greater length, outlining designs which made his eyes widen like a child's. I might as well be telling tales of sea-monsters, she thought, phoenixes, wyrms, satyrs, fiery salamanders. He clapped in delight over the concept of the camera, the box which painted portraits, and refused to believe that towers built by human hands would one day rise so high. Once he had seen all of the pictures in her books, he demanded that she be brought paper, and she drew more.

"And this is not a living creature."

"No, sir. A mechanism, a machine."

"But with resemblance to beasts in nature."

"These wings, they don't move. Not like bird wings. When the machine moves forward, air travels under the wings and creates a lifting force. Then it can float in the sky like a boat on water."

"And it doesn't fall?"

"A stone sinks in water. A boat does not, although the boat is heavier. This works by the self-same principle."

"I understand."

He did not, and Rosa hid her smile as she watched him nodding seriously, attentive to her every word. Like most of the men in this place he was gruff, grease-smelling, a being of body rather than mind. But he was keen to show his curiosity, and clearly proud of her presence in his halls. While he consulted her, the Lady of Seysair hovered about the edges of the hall then drifted away, aloof. Rosa was pleased one day to spy her seated in a shaded arbour with her daughters about her, the gathering lively with talk and with mirth.

"Madam Fabulist!" called one of the girls, an excitable creature of fourteen or so, with a long yellow braid wrapped around her head. "Won't you come and praise our skill at needlepoint?"

They were all six of them tangled up in wool, working upon different corners of the same large tapestry. Drawing close, Rosa saw that this depicted the hunt in full cry, in pursuit of a bear which had been set upon by a dozen dogs, red thread denoting the blood which flowed from its hide. Men on horseback brandished long spears, while women in elegant gowns trussed the carcasses of swans. The younger daughters were busy embroidering the detail at the top and bottom of the tapestry, a rushing river filled with fish, wild woods where deer darted away between the trees.

They were all looking up at Rosa. The eldest girl, who had thick dark brows and a serious air, said, "It bears no comparison, I am sure, to beauty you have beheld elsewhere."

It was true that the work was rudimentary when set next to paintings she had seen in Milan, less than fifty years forward from here. But she was charmed by its details – the bear's doleful eyes, the tower sigil on the men's tunics. "It's beautiful work," she said, and meant it.

The girl's forbidding face brightened, as did her mother's. The Lady of Seysair put down her needle and tucked her hands into her lap, saying with an almost boastful air, "Heloise, Idla, Ingrede, Anice, Maria." She pointed to them one at a time, eldest to youngest.

"Shall we make a gift to the Fabulist, when we are done?" blurted out Idla, who had been putting finishing touches to the bear.

There seemed no need, yet, to talk of tides, to tell them that she would not be able to carry such a thing. Seysair seemed to exist in a sheltered dip in a valley, solidly within its own time, a place which one might fasten to for as long as was wished. She allowed them all to assent eagerly, to proclaim that there was still space to add the Fabulist herself to the tapestry, to have her riding with the men upon a white horse or standing beneath that tall oak.

"Sit with us, Madam Fabulist!" cried yellow-haired Ingrede.

It was a fine day. Rosa realised for the first time that, though she had conversed with great lords and ladies, with philosophers and poets and priests, she had never in her life sat down among girls her own age. She lowered herself to join them, spreading her skirts upon the grass.

*

"They're interesting, the people of this time," she told Tommy later, as he was falling asleep. "Not as crude as I expected. They have some imagination."

"Just a little light is enough," he said drowsily.

"What?"

"We're still half stuck in the Dark Ages, here. All those stirrings in Italy haven't really reached them yet. Just a little light is enough to get them excited."

Most nights he came knocking at her chamber door, and most often, she let him in. He grew verbose sometimes in the small candlelit hours, and propped against the pillows spoke of places he had known: of the little ice age which had frozen the Thames to its heart, of foreign towns where he had vanished into festival crowds, of the floating city which would drift in seven hundred years upon the South China Sea. Before dawn he would check the time and date upon the pocket-watch he kept hidden inside his shirt, and slip back to his own quarters.

"I had far less to see by, back in forty-five." She was sitting up with the blankets drawn around her, one arm about her knees, tracing the text of a *chanson*. "I'd have killed for it, to be told what came next."

On the wall somewhere beyond the chamber window, a watchman called the top of the hour. She liked the way that time moved in Seysair, not tightly tied to clocks or radio pips but fluid, barely tamed. Marked by the shadows on sundials or the dripping of wax from tapers, receding and expanding with the earth as it breathed in and out, as spring was overtaken by summer and daylight lingered deep into the evenings. The guard on the north side of the tower called in response, and quiet fell once again.

"What do you suppose they think I am, Tom?" she asked quietly. "Where do you suppose they think I come from?"

He's asleep, she thought. She closed her book and cupped the flame of the candle in one hand, leaning over to blow it out. For a moment she seemed to hold the fire between her fingers, as though she had conjured it by the power of a force coursing through her skin. She toyed with the feeling, smiling slightly, before snuffing the light with a quick breath.

7

Your Ain Countrie

The people of Seysair believed that the world would end in flame. On the walls of the chapel, paintings depicted many-headed dragons and lion-beasts with horns and sceptres, angels bearing scrolls and trumpets, stars dropping from the sky like hailstones. A city with shining walls. They believed that the thread upon their wheel had almost spun out its full course, that the future she spoke of must be close at hand, or otherwise from an eternity beyond the present order.

Rosa had encountered variations on this sentiment before, and knew that it was nothing so simple as fear. In truth it must gratify people such as these, to think themselves the last generation of the living – to think that it was they and they alone who might look back across the course of history and summarise its moral. Even to believe that the trespasses of their age were uniquely wicked, enough at last to shock the heavens from their long patience. All this the exercise of beings who would be snuffed out in a few short seasons, whose own worlds would turn dark without the earth pausing its motion to mourn them.

Poor mayflies. While Tommy and I, while those like us are leaping light-footed between the centuries. How could we imagine the extinguishing of our light?

Rosa found Seysair's ghoulish imaginings amusing and pitiable in equal measure. A pair of women, the Lady's widowed cousins, came to her trembling, with tales of unsettling dreams and ill-luck omens. Two children had been born in the village on the second

Monday in August, an evil day. A snake with a second head had been found in the woods across the valley.

"In your visions, Madam Fabulist, what has been revealed to you of the end times? Are they not to come soon?"

"Not soon, Golde, Gunnhilde. I assure you, with all my wisdom, that it's a foolish matter to waste worry on."

They would not be reassured. "Should floods or famines, earthquakes or betrayals or fire in the heavens be our sign? Or all of these together?"

"None of these things, dear ladies. Do not spend your hours on such anxious thoughts." Their world was yet smaller, if possible, than Robert Hyde's. She allowed the women to clasp her hands, and to kiss them as though they were relic bones. Added mischievously, knowing that it might unsettle as much as comfort them, "This earth will endure far beyond your lifetime."

*

Neighbouring lords were invited to come and marvel at this honoured guest, to attend feasts where mummers performed battles between black-clad and white-clad figures, dances of day and night, death and rising. They brought out the old gods, who had the heads of rabbit and asses and wolves, trooping hand-in-hand across the hall. By the light of the fire in the hearth the eyes of these creatures looked too alive, and Rosa shivered pleasurably, seated at the top of the dais with a dignitary at each hand and a pile of warm dogs dozing at her feet.

The Lord of Seysair served his freshest venison and finest wine. When called upon, the Fabulist obliged with visions of things to come. She drew slender turbines rising from the ocean waves, recited verses from poems which would not be composed until the Romantics set pen to paper in the eighteenth. The air of the room changed. She sensed each body leaning forward, every pair of eyes upon her, every ear attentive. Only Tommy reclined, low in his seat and limbs sprawled lazily. When nobody else was looking, he raised his cup to toast her.

In thanks for her services and in praise of all that she was, they gave her comb-honey, cases of silk cloth, a pendant stamped with the tower sigil. During quiet afternoons when she walked through the tower's rooms, Rosa ran her fingertips over the finer things displayed on shelves and mantels – ornate rings and goblets set with sapphires, embossed pewter plates and gilt mounts of the saints. Most of these were too large to secret away, but she lifted a little dagger with a snake-shaped sheath, slipping it into her sleeve.

"You can't carry all that," said Tommy, indicating the growing pile of cases in her chamber. "Not half of it."

"I know. None of it's sentimental. I'll take what's to hand, when the time comes, and not think twice about the rest."

"When will that be, do you think?" He was leaning against the door, picking a tooth with the tip of his knife. She glanced over at him, and paused before answering. She kept her voice light.

"I'm in no hurry. When the tide takes us."

"Unlikely to happen here. This place is all wrapped up in itself, you must feel that. We'll need to break out ourselves."

"Do you want to?" she asked. She watched him carefully as he pocketed the knife and stretched. It would not do, to appear any more eager to remain than he did.

If he sensed that the moment was a delicate one, he did not show it. The teasing, lopsided grin made another appearance. "You devil," he said. "You're eating up their admiration. "

As the dark hours lengthened again and the air gained a chillier bite, she thought that she caught flickers of a different mood in him. The watch seemed to sit always in the palm of his hand, and he glanced at it frequently, flicking the case open and closed. In the middle of the night Rosa turned over to find him perched on the edge of the bed, hands clasped beneath his chin and eyes fixed upon the wall.

"Careful not to lay your head too long on the same pillow, gypsy girl," he murmured. "Don't look for too many days upon the same set of faces. Or *ye'll ne'er get back to your ain countrie.*"

"What are you talking about?"

"Let's not stay too much longer."

He turned. Still half asleep, she squinted at him through the darkness. "A little while longer?"

"A little while." He was squirming, she noticed, like a dog with an itch. She lay back down, and lost consciousness so quickly that the exchange was all but forgotten by morning.

*

The sons came and went with their retinue, and since the borders were quiet, hunted beasts instead of men. From the woods Rosa heard the shrill squeals of boars being pierced through the hide to the heart. The slain pigs were borne back upon the shoulders of the men, dog pack a mass of excitable noise, muzzles stained with blood. At the evening's feasts the fruits of the hunt took pride of place, the meat stewed with ale and juniper berries, head severed, boiled, basted and stuffed. Both in the coursing and the eating, the knight Thomas Rymer was fastest and merriest.

He never wanted for company. She saw him wrestling with stable-hands and deep in conversation with the lord's falconer, an old freeman who was handsomely paid to train up birds for the master: those tame from hatching, those captive from the wild.

Tommy had not, as far as she knew, composed any elaborate tale for them as to what his former home had been or how he had come to be among them. She supposed that he had simply knocked at the tower's great oak door one rainy night, soaked to the skin and too congenial to be denied, so quickly established in their number that they forgot he had not always been there. This was the way he had, of seeming to occupy the present so entirely that it belonged more to him than to its natives.

It could not be painted on like powder, this knack, or slipped over the body like a costume-gown. *There's a look*, he had once said, and she wondered if this was it. A form of attention that was full, alive, sincere even, but which could be withdrawn as easily as it was offered. She practised her expression alone before the mirror, in the company of the lady and her daughters. Always a slight turn of the head to one side, a smile which knew more than it divulged. She did not tell them her name.

"Won't you walk to the village with us, Madam Fabulist? Won't you play tric-trac with Anice, since she is asking for you? Won't you advise our right worshipful mother as to the purchase of these twenty ewes, which are to be kept in the lower pasture?"

She noticed that the older girls had changed their style, decorating their braids with jewelled pins, gold bands fastened across their foreheads. Ingrede had seamstresses embroider pearls onto a wide lace collar, and even mixed madder root and vinegar to colour her fair hair red. Little Maria, all of eight, coated her face in flour and chalk, much to her sisters' amusement. They often accompanied their mother to the village whenever she needed to inspect tenants' houses or hear disputes, and Rosa went with them, enjoying the muddy bustle of the place, the smell of fresh bread from the bakery. The people here were even more in thrall of her than those at the tower, stepping aside to let her pass and invoking the names of saints. She wore a fur-lined cloak, with a servant following behind to lift the train of her dress from the dirt.

The grain grew high and ripe, plots cut one by one, chequering the hills about the tower. Mountain mists returned, veiling the low round sun. At Mell-Supper, after the last sheaf was cut, the farrier's son was named lord of the harvest and paraded about on the hay-cart, garlanded with ears of wheat. Bread was broken and music played. Idla and Ingrede knelt either side of Rosa and, dismissing her protests, replaced the gold band on her head with a woven crown of corn.

"There, Madam Fabulist." They hung to her sleeves, laughing. "Now you are queen of the fields."

*

They went hawking in the amber-lit afternoon before the first frost, when fallen leaves covered the surface of the lake. Fat fish splashed in the water below. The women of the tower were helped into the saddle by their attendants, horses' hot breath rising in clouds as the animals snorted and stamped, dogs nipping at their heels. Rosa, who could now ride a little, stroked the mane of her own mount and looked around at the colourful company. Bridles, saddle-blankets and cold-weather gowns edged with russet and blue, even the hawks themselves in gold-embroidered hoods.

The falconer brought out the snowy gyr, favoured by the lady herself; the merlin, for Heloise, and lanner-hawks for the rest. Rosa herself declined, preferring to ride alongside as the women pulled on their gloves and set off down the hill. The smell of earth, of horse-sweat and leather. Passing a newly harvested field she saw a solitary hare crouched among the stubble, orange eyes unblinking.

The sight of the bold animal took her so much by surprise that she didn't call out its presence.

Then the birds were released from the hunters' hands and shot out like arrows from a bowstring, gliding low over the treetops and the corn-stubble. The riders fanned out to follow their path, and Rosa followed Heloise, whose brown mare nimbly navigated the rocky hillside and took them into open country. Strands of the girl's dark hair blew loose from her braids, whipping about her face as she turned her mount around, looking for a sign of the merlin.

"You see him?" she called to Rosa.

"There!"

The speckled bird was winging across the landscape at speed, and Heloise let out a delighted cry, kicking her horse and speeding up in pursuit. "Hurry! We'll be the first to spill blood!"

Rosa kept pace with her, and for a moment they were neck and neck, breathless and laughing, cheeks flushed and wind in their hair. The hawk hovered tantalisingly at the horizon. It seemed to have spotted something on the ground below, wings a sharp black dash against the grey clouds. Then it was gliding again, over a patch of woodland now, letting out a shrill cry. As the bird plummeted, Heloise swung her lure and whistled sharply between her teeth. In the thunderous dash between the trees, branches lashing her face and dappled shadows flickering, Rosa fell behind.

Her horse stumbled over thick roots, snorting indignantly. Rosa patted it on the neck, then dismounted with stiff legs. She could still hear hooves pounding, Heloise whistling. The other noise, that hard gasping for breath, was her own. Her knees shook slightly, as though she had just landed from one of the gentler journeys. Rosa gave a hoarse laugh, for her own benefit. Her skirts were torn and stained with mud. Alone amid the trees she felt a sudden consciousness of herself. Madam Fabulist, you were not raised to hunt or ride. You were tamed and tethered to that tedious year for too long, if you remember. Best return quietly to the tower, and powder your face again before they see you so dishevelled.

A rustle in the undergrowth, some way ahead. Wondering whether the merlin might have lighted upon its prey there, perhaps a rabbit or squirrel, she left her horse and moved towards the sound. Something moved in the shadow of the trees. A shape far larger than she had been expecting. Rosa pushed between the hanging ivy, deeper into the wood, all sound hushed now and the sunlight muted. The animal eluded her, moving quietly away, nothing visible of its form save the high branches of its antlers. She stood alone in the green darkness.

When that night's feasting was done, the lady and the daughters of Seysair presented her with the finished tapestry. They had indeed woven her into it, a small resplendent figure in the right-hand corner, real pearls embroidered upon the gown. The woman in the fine dress seemed a strange addition to the scene, curiously inactive while all the flurry of the hunt went on around her. Rosa hung it above her bed and in her dreams drifted into tangles of thread, trying to follow a solitary red strand which, woven among too many others, slipped from her fingertips.

*

"Rosa."

"What?"

"Rosa. Wake up."

Somebody was shaking her shoulder. For a moment she was eight years old again, being roused before the dawn chorus for her father's red-letter day. Tommy was bending over her, and though the room was too dark to make out his expression, she could tell that he was fully dressed. She rummaged around for flint to light the candle, but he grabbed her wrist.

"Just get dressed. I'll get your things."

"What hour is it?"

"Still night."

"Tom, what –?"

"You won't want to carry these silks, will you? Or any of those cases." He was throwing things haphazardly into a bag, jewels, purses, food. She jumped from the bed, naked, and grasped instinctively at the most treasured of her books. He gestured urgently. "Put some clothes on. Not the Fabulist gown. Something you can run in."

She hurried into the mud-spattered dress she had worn hunting, and made from months of habit to pin her hair, paint her face. But Tommy pulled her away. "You've no time for that."

Away from the chamber without time for a backward glance at the pile of cases and the tapestry still hung above the bedstead, down two flights of stone steps and out of a small side door. Tommy led her through the gardens towards the slope of the hill, gesturing for her to tread quietly, to stay close to the hedgerows. Rosa clutched her remaining sack of belongings close to her chest. Baffled, she looked from Tommy Rust's expressionless face to Seysair, which stood shadowed and silent in the near-darkness. "*Tom*," she whispered urgently, "what on earth–?"

A flock of grouse rose from behind the tower. Their shrieks cut through the still air, and Rosa glimpsed a flicker of movement in the heather on the hill. The echoing snort of a pony. A faint gleam of moonlight upon plate-armour.

She halted, shaking Tommy off as he tugged at her arm. One by one, riders were emerging from the undergrowth, picking their way along the river and gathering at the base of the hill. Longbows hung over their shoulders, lances in their hands. As she watched, a fiery torch was lit and raised high in the air, illuminating the full length and breadth of the raiding-party.

"Border-reivers!" she breathed. Blank with panic, she snatched at his arm. "We have to run back, we have to warn —"

"I thought you would have learnt." There was something like pity in his voice. He was breathing unusually hard. "Read history, Rosa. The day has come for Seysair to be razed and these fields sown with salt." He took hold of her, forcefully this time. "Read the right pages. And never look for too many days…"

Watchmen's cries were drowned beneath the rumble and roar as the raiding party started forward, and lights were struck too late along the walls of the tower. Rosa felt herself go limp, and Tommy released her. She felt curiously detached from the spectacle now, as though she might still be asleep and dreaming. I ought to have taken the tapestry, she thought. It will burn to ashes in no time.

As the sun rose scarlet above the mountains, they stumbled away through the turned earth and corn-stubble. It was only when they had gained more than a mile on Seysair that she dared to pause mid-flight, to look over her shoulder. The tower was shrouded in smoke, flames billowing at its windows, a mass of dark figures locked in combat on the ground below.

She bent her body forward and clutched her skirts above her knees. Her thinly-shod feet seemed to beat out a rhythm as she ran. *And ye'll neer get back, ye'll neer get back to your ain countrie.*

Part Two

8

All in Gold

But it cannot be that you care, Rosa. Not for the folk of Seysair, nor for the heart of Tommy Rust, since you don't rebuke him, or try to lead him into any other kind of life. It cannot be that there is any need to mourn. You have become more than you could have hoped for on that first night with him in the London winter, when you needed the warm proof of your hands on his skin, since he seemed almost too wondrous a thing to touch.

In the first days of travelling after the tower fell, she looked at Tommy and thought, *we are the same*. Rosa found that she was strong enough in body to keep pace with him and his journeys, strong enough in mind to put Seysair entirely aside. To see Rome built-stone by stone and then to see it in flames, to barely blink at the sight, to leave without glancing over your shoulder. If our ways seem far above theirs, then that is our nature. It is foolish to forget, to fall into anything less magnificent.

"Tom. Did we bring only one of my books?"

"We were in a hurry. Didn't you pack them?"

She rummaged through her bags. "Not the rest. I thought you had them already." The pages she had laboured over must have curled and crumbled in the flames.

"We'll make new ones, Madam Fabulist."

There will be new books and new belongings, new clothes and new names. There will be new tides to follow, new cities to wake in. She recalled how, on the night she had met Tommy, his attention had fixed so fiercely upon her and then darted away, like the beam of a searchlight. He does not hold on to you, she reminded herself. He does not hold you down. A little wave of confusion rippled out softly, silently inside her.

*

Plunging forward to the turn of the twentieth they took a steamboat to Calais, and she stood on the back deck, hair whipping about her head and salt stinging her face. Tommy was inside, deep in conversation with a friendly émigré, and she was glad to be alone for a moment. Rosa drew the cold sea air into her lungs, watched the white crests of foam which formed in the boat's wake. She pulled the pendant bearing the Seysair crest from around her neck and trailed it playfully along the rail, before letting it drop.

She turned away before it hit the surface, pulling up the collar of her coat against the spray. The last time she had crossed this water it had been on a Spanish caravel in the late fifteenth. The Fabulist would live again, Rosa resolved, as soon as she could be put back together.

Paris, forward another decade, and the world was changed again. The city was intoxicated with itself, caught in the wild head-spin of relief that had followed after the Great War. After the fury, after the wound which had opened in the surface of the world and swallowed all sense into itself, this giddy respite. The women were boyish in short straight dresses and the men wore cream suits and pinstripes in place of uniforms. The streets bustled with carriages and busy shoppers. Tommy could hardly keep still, riding high on excitement and absinthe and the husky music which spilt from every street-corner café.

"Just think," he said, "of all that has flooded here, from across the world. Of all that will come to be written of this place, in this time."

Rosa felt it, too; the powerful coming together of tides in the city and the year, the energy which hummed beneath the air. She had known nowhere else like it. She began to scrutinise faces, that man with lined eyes sipping a coffee, that couple passing by in the peculiar clothes, that young woman lingering in the shadows of a doorway. *There's a look that we have.* Here of all places, others must surely be close.

In a side-street market, she noticed an elegant woman who was running her fingertips over the trinkets on one of the stalls. She was wearing a grey velvet dress beneath a long coat with a luxuriant fur collar, lace gloves and a wide-brimmed hat. As she turned her attention from the stall her eyes fell upon Tommy, and Rosa saw her stop. Long fingers discreetly tucked objects deeper into her handbag. Below the brim of her hat, her mouth curled.

"Why," she said, with curious emphasis, "I believe I have Seen You Before."

At the sound of her voice Tommy looked around, and at once he was laughing, cap swept from his head. He bent to kiss her hand, but she tucked her fingertips under his chin and drew him up to face her. "No, darling. As they do it here."

She kissed him, twice on each cheek. Stationary, the two of them seemed nonetheless to circle each other. Rosa's eyes were drawn first not to their faces but to the dust upon their shoes.

"How long?"

"Five years, Amber Lakshmi."

"Six, for me." A sleek black bob framed her features, her eyes elongated with smoky lines of powder. "It was in Moorish Andalusia, in the early part of the twelfth."

"So it was. And you don't look a day older. Your journeys must have been good to you."

"They always are." Her voice was deep, rich as cream. "And to you too, I see." Amber's eyes ranged over his shoulder to where Rosa stood. She resisted the urge, so very strong, still, to shield her eyes with her hand. *In case you look upon an old friend you have not yet met. In case by some unfortunate chance...*

"This is Rosa." He did not add her surname, and it occurred to her that there was no reason why he should know it. "You haven't met?"

"No. Though I have heard you spoken of." Amber removed her hand from Tommy's grasp and held it out. Still puzzled by her words, Rosa shook it.

"Amongst us," Amber explained, "there are few secrets. We hear things on our own roads, and then grow garrulous when we are together." Bracelets rattled on her brown arms. She squeezed Rosa's fingers as though testing the ripeness of a piece of fruit. "Whisper into any listening ear, and it'll reach us in the end."

*

"I take it you haven't been here long, Thomas. You both look as though you travelled from an age before mirrors. You shall have to tidy yourselves up. We have a loft in Montparnasse, which suits me quite perfectly, though the boys are losing patience with my odds and ends."

"Who else is with you?"

"Oh, just the Brothers. They have been eating me out of house and home, and keeping me amused. I'm sure there are others around, but nobody I care for. You will stay, of course?"

"For as long as I stay," said Tommy. "Of course."

It was a bright day, wisps of cloud reflected in the surface of the Seine. The black spine of the tower rising into the sky behind them, they walked through leafy parks and onto the Boulevard St-Germain, where wine-barrels were stacked high in passageways, wrought lamps and bed-frames displayed outside the iron-works. They passed a tinsmith's and a bookbinder's, a butcher singing as he strung up his wares in the window. Montparnasse was a place of narrow streets, plaster crumbling from the sand-coloured buildings, washing strung between crooked windows and placards hanging on walls. *Atelier d'Artiste á Louer.* The smells of turpentine and strong coffee hung on the air.

Along an alley on a sharp hill, Amber turned into a doorway, and led the way up a seemingly endless series of stairs. Rosa, bringing up the rear behind Tommy, was panting from the climb by the time they reached the top floor. When the door into the loft apartment was pushed open, she barely had the breath to gasp.

An Arabian cave of treasures lay before her, objects crammed onto every table and chair, piled in corners and stacked against walls. Books and china vases and framed paintings and mannequins and sculptures in wood and bronze. Boxes overflowing with golden jewellery, vinyl records tied together with string, sketches and autographs and photographs pinned to boards. The ceiling was low and sloped, shutters open wide onto the street below, letting in the fractured daylight. It was not immediately clear how anybody could live, or was living, in such a space.

"Boys!" called Amber, removing her gloves. Rosa noticed a mattress on the floor at the far end of the room, surrounded by a sea of rolled canvases. Another poked through the door of what appeared to be a cupboard. "Boys, come and see!"

Two heads peered out from behind a half-wrecked partition wall. Two pairs of eyes blinked, glanced at one another, glanced back to the doorway. Two men rose slowly and silently, moved closer with one accord.

They were not entirely identical, Rosa saw, as one hung back and the other flew forward to embrace Tommy. The hesitant twin was slighter, smooth-faced where his brother was moustached. When the larger man let go of Tommy, Rosa saw him in full profile, his muscular frame and savage's grin. He looked as though he ought to be kept outdoors.

"Four years, Nate Black!"

"Two, Tommy Rust, two." His voice was a cud-chewing drawl. "You're laggin'. Where you been? We lost you in the Seventeenth."

"Here and there. You know I've never been lost in my life."

Nate Black laughed and slapped him on the chest. "I know it, brother. Bless those tides, we'll have a time of it, now you've come."

"You haven't been enjoying yourselves without me, have you?" Tommy asked the quiet twin, who squirmed happily and shook his head. His shy smile had a vacant quality.

"Glad to hear it. Now, this is Rosa. Unless you've already—"

"No," said Nate. His eyes flicked in her direction, and they exchanged nods. She did not offer her hand. "We made eggs. Do you want some?"

"We been makin' eggs," echoed the other brother.

"Have you now, Harris?" Amber laid a hand upon his head as she passed by, picking her way nimbly through the chaos of objects. Rosa would not have thought it possible, but within minutes a space had been cleared upon the table, chairs unearthed from beneath draped sheets and sheaves of paper. She perched upon the same stool as Tommy, one eye upon the narrow balcony beyond the window, where a cat was balancing along the rail.

"Eat, eat," urged Amber, indicating the pan of eggs, bread and cheese wrapped in brown paper. Nate sat with his legs apart, food in his fists. His brother leaned so close to his shoulder that it was hard to tell whose arms were whose. Tommy basked in a patch of sun, eyes half-closed, more contented than Rosa had ever seen him.

"You know," he said, "I had been thinking lately of our time in Andalusia."

"I heard Sonny Brevik ain't so far away, now." Nate broke the neck of a bottle of wine without attempting to uncork it. "And Marta got in trouble with the law, over in the twentieth. Always needed someone to give her half a head of sense."

"The way the sun bakes the cold from your bones. I missed that, in London."

"Oh, I came across some beautiful treasures there," muttered Amber.

"You seen anyone else, Tom?" asked Nate. "In the meantime?"

"I have been positively solitary. You would not have known me."

"Not quite solitary," said Amber. The Brothers' heads turned at once towards Rosa as though fixed to the same body, and she returned their look with curiosity. She wished that she could have grown up alongside these people, wherever it was the tides had taken them in years gone by, instead of listening to the wireless play the same old songs in nineteen forty-five. "Have you tolerated him long, Rosa?"

"Some while. On and off."

"You're familiar with the twentieth, I take it." Amber's gaze was even and shrewd. Rosa could not tell whether she knew – had heard, perhaps, of Robert Hyde and Rosa's connection to him – or was simply being polite. Or maybe it was possible, with experience, to know at a glance which century had shaped a travelling stranger.

"Very much so. Not this decade, though."

"There are few like it," said Amber.

Nate gave a grunt of assent through his mouthful of food, and Tommy thumped the table approvingly. It was strange finally to be in such company. Since Tommy had first spoken of others, a small part of Rosa's mind had been busy spinning the legends of these unknown beings. It was no disappointment, to meet them in the flesh.

Where did you spring from? she wondered. Did your fathers' or your mothers' folly tear you from your first homes? Or did you begin your journeys through your own error, or choice? She knew better, by now, than to ask directly, just as she knew not to share her own tale too readily. The possibilities of their stories were dazzling. Between them they must have laid eyes on every great city in every age of man.

In the bright, broken light there was something unreal about the four of them, Tommy Rust and Amber Lakshmi, Nate and Harris Black. As though they were figures fixed in a varnished painting, beyond the touch of air or dust. Rosa thought that they looked everlastingly beautiful.

*

Nate stood barefoot in his braces and shirtsleeves, blade in one hand and brush in the other. Before him sat Tommy, face and neck a mess of white lather, tablecloth tucked into his collar. Amber pulled his long hair back over his shoulders and examined his profile.

"Short back, short sides," she said decisively. "And take most of the beard. Don't fuss."

"You tell this amateur to be careful," said Tommy.

"Ain't I always?" Nate twirled the blade with a forceful motion more that of butcher than barber, whistling through one side of his mouth. Rosa watched as the Tommy she had first met outside Drury Lane Theatre began to emerge, the unruly knight vanishing snip by snip. Harris darted round the chair, ducking under his brother's elbows to pick up the clippings.

"Same service for *madame?*" Nate asked, not unthreateningly, when Tommy had risen to examine his fresh face in the mirror propped next to the window. Rosa felt the weight of her waist-length hair, so very out of place here. Something held her back – just the sharpness of that blade, perhaps, in Nate's large hands. She shook her head.

Later she coiled her hair into braids and tied it tightly beneath a scarf, as she had done in London in the twenty-first. The jewelled pins of the Fabulist had been left behind at Seysair.

When evening came Tommy and Nate put on waistcoats and neckties, and slipped from the loft. Tommy looked over his shoulder as he passed through the door, offering just the flash of a grin and the tip of a hat in Rosa's direction. She watched from the window as they headed down the hill to the cobbled street beyond, hands in pockets, Nate still whistling. Lamps were being lit as tables filled outside cafés, the moonlit tower rising above the rooftops.

"Where are they going?" she asked Amber, who was emptying the bag she had earlier carried in the market. Harris perched on the stool beside her, weighing each new object carefully in his palms.

"Carousing." Amber rolled the word around her mouth, seeming to enjoy its taste. "As they always do. One can carouse in Montparnasse in these years perhaps better than anywhere else I know. They'll be back in high spirits past midnight – if they're back at all before dawn." When Rosa looked once more to the window, she added with a touch of sympathy, "Oh, you're not in love with him, are you?"

Harris emitted a laugh. At first Rosa was taken aback, but then said proudly, "*No*."

"Others have been more foolish." Amber's eyebrows arched and lowered like shifting dunes as she watched Rosa's face.

A heavy notebook open before her, Amber carefully catalogued each of the objects on the table, murmuring to Harris, who fetched ink and lit the candles. Rosa joined them when the sky had grown dark beyond the window, and the shadows of Amber's treasures crept up the walls.

"What will happen to all of this?" Rosa asked. "When you journey on?"

Harris rested his arms on the table and his head in his arms, eyes large and liquid in the dimness. Amber's long fingers teased the edges of a photograph from its frame, flipped it over to read what was written on the back. "What's worthless will be left behind. But what's precious – what will be precious, in ages to come…"

Rosa sat up straight, beginning to catch on. "How do you carry it with you?"

Amber looked infinitely pleased to have been asked.

"It goes in the ground," volunteered Harris. "Deep, deep under the ground."

"I have vaults," said Amber. "In every city where our tides have ever flowed. There are hiding-places where my hoards stay undiscovered and undisturbed for centuries." She closed her notebook with care. "I have hunted down treasures in caves, and king's tombs, and tunnels below far-off mountains. When I attended the Pharaoh Hatshepsut I took a single brooch from her robe, and carried it in my pocket across two millennia, until a collector gave his millions for it."

Rosa imagined the troves tucked out of sight in every corner of the world, below the feet of the ignorant, of those who trod only upon ordinary earth. Something thrilled in her, and she looked at Amber with new eagerness. The older woman seemed to brighten further in the light of her admiration, like an opal stone showing the shimmering depth of its colours. She laid out her hands on the table, and Rosa saw that each finger bore a different ring, some already antique, others of such strange design that they had to come from future ages.

"Mesopotamia," she said, pointing to her right index. "The first. Tenochtitlan, the fourteenth. Rajput Surashtra, the ninth. China, Black Province, the twenty-first. Each of them priceless, out of its own time. It's just a matter of knowing where they will be valued most highly."

"And getting there, I suppose," said Rosa.

"Oh, I have never had any great trouble with that." Amber drew back her hands with a small smile. Rosa leaned forward.

"You can choose where you go?"

"None of us choose every journey. But often I go where I please, or thereabouts. Thomas has so little control, he probably told you it's not possible."

Rosa tucked the words away, close to herself, and sat back. It was impossible to tell from Amber's expression whether she was in earnest. This woman was inscrutable as the sphinx beneath whose shadow she had once walked.

"I suppose you must have amassed a fortune," said Rosa. "Though I can't imagine how you would spend it."

Amber handed the book to Harris, who slipped obediently from his seat and carried it back to the shelf across the room. "One day when I am tired of these travels, I shall take what's mine from below the ground, and live out the rest of my days in high style." Her crescent smile widened. "It's all in gold, Rosa, my wealth. Think of that! All of it gold."

*

When Amber was draped sleeping over one of the mattresses, Rosa woke restless on the other. The shutters were open, letting in a cool breeze from outside, and she could see by the faint moonlight that Nate and Tommy were not yet back. She rose, and crossed the room to the wide window. A pair of passers-by were arguing animatedly, the tinkling of piano keys echoing across the cobbles from a nearby café. The sounding of a motorcar horn, an outburst of laugher.

Sitting cross-legged on the floor, she lifted her face to the fresh night air. The sky above the city was clear, stars sharp as gems.

She remembered when she had looked out over London in the same manner, then flung open her arms and danced with the joy of possibility. At the time no dream had seemed greater than that of keeping her feet on the same ground. How small, how simple-minded the thought appeared now. *I see a hundred new ages ready for your taking. Roads await your feet.*

Didn't you know, Robert Hyde, of any place greater than your precious red-letter day? Couldn't you conceive, Harriet, of any place worthier than your husband's side? Rosa almost laughed at the far-off thought of them. She rested her chin on her hands, and her mind wandered to pyramids and sand dunes, to blazing horizons, to cities in the sky. You will not know me, she thought. I will pass through nineteen forty-five one day in my Fabulist's robe with the light of undreamed centuries in my eyes, and you will not know your daughter.

The realisation that she was not alone there, sat before the starry window, came upon her so gradually that it did not alarm. What she had taken for one of Amber's statues, tucked against the wall, shifted to scratch its back.

"You're awake?"

Harris Black nodded his head. In the half-dark the pupils of his brown eyes were unusually large, as though he took in too much of the world, or looked on it in too much wonder.

"Do you see 'em?" he asked.

"Who?"

"There, in the trees." He pointed. There was a blanket wrapped around his shoulders, and beneath it he looked like a nocturnal creature poking a curious head from its burrow. The leaves of the line of birches in the street below were silver with starlight. Puzzled, Rosa leaned forward to try and see what he was talking about.

"Sitting in the trees," said Harris Black. "On 'most every branch, some with their wings unfolded, and bright as day."

He smiled. Something about the openness of his manner, a lack of the practised self-possession of Tommy and Amber, made her anxious for him. She wondered whether she should indulge this pretence of angels, as one would with a young child.

"I'm sorry, Harris. I don't see."

"Did you ever see one?" he asked.

From nowhere a chill touched the back of Rosa's neck. All thoughts of her Fabulist's robes, of Amber's buried gold, wavered and crumbled.

"You mustn't tell." Rosa's heart was pounding. She imagined that she was telling him a story, like the stories she had once whispered to Bella beneath the bed-covers as the planes whined overhead. A nothingness which would be swept away and forgotten by morning. "You mustn't tell, Harris. But I think... I think I once saw the Angel of Death."

He nodded. She cleared her tightening throat.

"He appeared in the garden, when I was a child. Just for a moment. He was holding a gun. His skin was so pale, and his face..."

His face, she wanted to say, was terrible with grief. *And I knew even then that it was the grief of my own ending.* She had not thought of him in so long that the memory was a cold shock to her, and she quickly pushed it aside. Her heart slowed again as she took in the rooftops of Montparnasse, the reassuring glow of the street-lamps.

"He's one I ain't seen," said Harris Black. "Not yet. Though it's as well to be ready."

The reflections of stars wheeled within his oversized eyes, as though they took in all of the universe, as though he had swallowed it whole.

9

The Holy Fool

In idle moments Rosa pictured herself tiptoeing back across the carpets of some Hyde home or other, leaning over her younger self as she slept, and whispering in her ear. It will be all right, you in your knitted bed-socks, you with your face-full of freckles and your ever-growing fury. It will be all right. When the time comes, and it will come, nineteen forty-five will fall away. No need to pound your fists into your pillow or drag your feet on the last night of the year, no cause to scream at your mother until your throat burns, because your future is all in gold.

You will wake for a series of sunlit mornings in a Montparnasse loft, sometimes with Tommy Rust tucked beside you on the narrow mattress, sometimes with the space to stretch your legs. There will be the smell of fried potatoes and brewing coffee, the fall of feet upon the stairs as Harris brings in a newspaper and a fresh loaf, the *thump-thump* of your downstairs neighbour beating his rug out of the window. Canaries are singing in their cage on the sill of the apartment opposite. A milk-cart is rattling down the street, the rhythmic swish of the gutter-sweeper's brush.

And there is Amber Lakshmi in her peach silk dressing gown, sat beside the window with a narrow cigarette between her fingers, talking with Nate, who is still in his best waistcoat and drinking ginger-root to calm his raging headache.

And Montparnasse, Rosa, Montparnasse after the turn of the twentieth! In that place you can glance through windows at night and glimpse men sat half-stripped at their typewriters, women appraising their easels by candlelight, groups gathered about tables with their voices raised in intense disagreement. Strolling musicians fill the streets with the strumming of mandolin strings, and crowds spill from theatres and night-clubs long past midnight. The lights never go out. The stakes at the card-table can never be too high and the orchestra can never play too fast. Why would anyone waste more than a little time upon sleep, why would anyone will these ceaseless songs into quiet?

You will hope to hold on as long as you can, to that city in that year. You will forget all cares there, Rosa. You will be surprised how quickly, how utterly you forget.

*

In a grimy corner of the loudest cabaret in the district, the Brothers Black played gin rummy with such uncanny speed and co-ordination that they drew a crowd. Hats askew and sleeves rolled to their elbows, they dealt and shuffled and flipped cards in near-silence, offering each other the occasional nod or grunt to signify their intentions. Nate's brows were knitted together, chew-tobacco poised between his teeth. Harris, flushed and breathless, moved his hands in a fluttering blur.

"Aha!" he laid down his final hand with a flourish, and the men gathered about the table broke into laughter and cheers. Nate leaned over slowly to check the cards. His jaw began its customary chewing motion once again, and Rosa saw a good-humoured look pass between the brothers as he conceded victory with a tip of his hat

"Somebody buy these men a drink!" demanded Tommy, who was perched on the arm of Nate's chair, blowing out cigar-smoke. He slapped his fingers theatrically against the back of the other hand, before shaking Harris by the shoulder. The winning player beamed at him, bright-eyed. "You're divinely gifted, dear boy, and I never bet money against you. Speaking of which —"

He snapped his fingers to garner the attention of the gathered huddle of men, who rolled their eyes and dug into their pockets. Smiling, Amber moved away from the table, her eye apparently caught by a series of pencil drawings pinned to the wall. The room was perfumed and packed, lit by gas burners which were reflected in a hanging mirror. Women and waiters flitted between the tables like night-birds. Rosa stretched out her arms and inhaled Tommy's drifting smoke, enjoying the light-headed sensation it gave her.

When the rush of curiosity and congratulation died down, Nate slouched back in his seat, gaze wandering to the platform where a slender young woman was moistening her lips from her liqueur-glass. Appreciative cries and applause passed across the room as the piano started up, and she stepped to the front of the stage, all soft smiles and lowered lashes. Nate elbowed Tommy in the ribs until he turned in her direction, and the two reclined, lighting fresh cigars from the same flame.

Rosa watched Harris shuffle his deck of cards again and again, each time with the same rapt attention he had given to the game. He seemed so oblivious to all else that she was surprised when he looked up and asked below the sighing of the singer, "Do you play?"

"Just solitaire. And whist, a little." Solitaire, for solitary hours in all those Hyde homes. She shook off the memory with a small shudder. "I taught myself."

"We'd play with our pa, every night on the porch, as dark was comin' in," said Harris.

Rosa looked at him, and then at Nate, who was smoothing his moustache and muttering something to Tommy with a coarse curl of the lip. An image came to her of the brothers tumbling together through time, an island of two in a sea of chaos. There was something reassuring, even enviable, about the picture.

A new doubt, a quiet-voiced thing, tapped tentatively at her shoulder. She hardly thought of the Hydes now, except to feel relief at having left them so far behind. Years had flown by since she'd slammed the door on her parents after the Shoreditch row. There had barely been time to pause and wonder about the fourth person in the house that night. *But what if*, said the doubt, *what if*. Bella was so little, she told the quiet voice. There's no way I could have taken her with me. Think how she would have held me back, think how she would have cried for our mother. Rosa imagined a small hand clutching her own as she journeyed the space between the years, a pair of brown eyes blinking trustingly up at her.

She swallowed an unexpected tightness in her throat, and felt a rush of protective warmth towards Harris Black. He had begun to lay the deck out on the table again, one at a time, completely absorbed in the task. Rosa touched his wrist. "Harris, were you ever parted? You and Nate?"

"Never." His smile was serene. "I don't think I should much like it."

She wondered what it was which kept them close, just as the Hyde family had for so long been kept close. Curiosity rose up in her. "Can I ask you -" She hesitated, lowering her voice almost to a whisper. "Where was it, Harris? That you used to play cards on the porch?"

From the corner of her eye she saw Nate's head turn a fraction.

"Back home," Harris said without hesitation.

The song ended, and the room became a riot of whoops and whistles. Tommy rose, stretching, and began to weave through the crowd towards the counter. Harris flipped a joker between his fingers, his expression fond. "The nights are longer out there," he said. "And blacker. But in the day you can hardly see nothin' but sky."

The piano started up again, a free-run of notes from the top to the bottom of the register, and the singer sighed her way into a new melody. *Pack up all my care and woe, here I go, singing low…* Harris closed his eyes, somewhere else entirely. Rosa tried to place herself where he might be, to imagine the little hole in history where the brothers must once have slotted in. "Tell me," she said.

"Walls of timber, I remember, and a stove in the corner. A hayloft where we slept." His fingertips brushed the air, as though he might reach across decades and miles to touch the place once more. "We built fires out under the stars. The steers grazed all summer in the high pasture, and got fat while we cut and baled. We would ride up there, Nate and Pa and me, to bring 'em in before the winter come. 'Til me and Nate was old enough to go alone, and that was when we fell the first time, since we were ridin' in such a strange light and my mind was not upon the earth."

"What do you mean, Harris?"

His eyes snapped open. Rosa realised that Nate was now craning around to look at them. *Make my bed and light the light*, crooned the singer. *I'll be home late tonight…*

"I was thinkin' of empty spaces, and how much of 'em there is, and how little of us. I was thinkin' how God might let a few slip through his fingers, if he did not watch 'em close enough."

Nate rose. As he opened his mouth, leaning over to place a heavy hand on Harris's shoulder, Amber slipped back into her seat. Reverently, she laid on the table a scrap of paper which looked as though it had been torn from the display on the wall.

There was an odd pause. Nate looked at it uncomprehendingly as Amber's smile grew and grew.

"It's a Picasso," she said.

*

Later, when the room had grown hotter with the press of bodies and the piano louder to be heard above the din, Nate cornered Rosa beside the counter. He had been drinking since the afternoon and was scarlet-faced, unsteady on his feet. Taking her by surprise as he pushed her against the wall, he squared up to her, absinthe sloshing over the rim of his glass.

"You don't much care for me, do you?"

She turned her face in distaste at the smell of his breath. Her first impression of him, as a dog too wild for the hearth, had not altered, and she wondered that Amber let him live among her treasures. His large boots and rough hands seemed always about to break something. "No. I can't say that I do."

"It's neither here nor there to me. But you will... refrain... from..." He attempted to jab her in the chest, and almost lost his balance.

"Tommy's been with you all day, and he can still stand straight," she said.

"You don't care for him out roisterin' with me." Nate's lip curled, and he tried clumsily to wipe his moustache. "You'd rather he came back to your bed."

Rosa laughed. "He can do as he pleases. We've no kind of understanding."

Nate did not seem to hear her. "So taken with him, ain't you? Think his appetites are any more refined than mine?" He jerked a thumb at Amber, sat beside Harris at the table with an affectionate hand on his arm, still poring delightedly over her drawing. "Think hers are?"

"Go and lie down somewhere, Nate." She tried to move away, but his body blocked her in.

127

"You will refrain," he said heavily, "from *prov-o-cation* of my brother. From mockery. He's been ridiculed since we were boys, and there are those still say he ain't sound in the head, but I shan't hear it. He talks no more foolishness than most."

Faintly catching his drift, Rosa shoved him away, then clasped the top of his arm to keep him from falling. "I wasn't mocking Harris. I wouldn't do that."

"You would have him recall what sent us off," growled Nate. "He shouldn't talk of it. He'll grow restive, and it's me will have to calm him. "

"All right. All right, Nate, I'm sorry. I wasn't mocking him."

He regarded her through bloodshot eyes, and wiped a sleeve across his sweating face. The apology seemed to have stymied him in the midst of his rage.

"I'd never once have journeyed," he said baldly. "If it weren't for him. Never did feel the tides the way he does. But where he goes, I go, since he needs watchin' over. Always been that way, and always will."

Rosa's stomach tightened with a quick, passing cramp. She clenched hands which felt hot, too conscious of their emptiness. With a shake of the head she silenced that same tap at her shoulder, that quiet voice. As Nate moved away, she could hear him still muttering below his breath.

"If he is a fool, then he is a holy fool. I shan't hear any say otherwise."

*

Rosa had suspected, even before Nate's taunts, that Tommy sought other company on nights when the two went out together into the city. She had done so herself in her first days as the Fabulist, and did not see that he should need either permission or forgiveness.

A tide might come at any time and wash one of them away; they might meet again in a hundred years and decide that they wanted one another again, for that time, for that place. She wished she had explained this better to Amber and to Nate, laid out the nature of their involvement in clearer terms. She did not like to seem foolish.

Besides, the arrangements in the loft did not lend themselves to intimacy, and Rosa found she hardly missed it. It suited her to have him near, still, and she liked to watch the animated movements of his face when he told stories in the small hours. He had so many faces, had lived so many lives.

"They do begin to run together somewhat," he said to the ceiling in the dark of the night. "The places where we go. Sometimes I have dreams within dreams within dreams. I can wash and dress and walk around for half the day before I recall where I am."

"You don't stop, Tommy Rust."

He was in earnest, stripped of any daytime artfulness. His eyes were wide. "It's never lessened, for me, the thrill of waking somewhere new. Not in all these years. The smells of some fresh city in the morning, the sights of another century...my heart's beating faster just thinking of it. Here, feel." She smiled, let him lay her hand briefly against his chest. He simply has more blood in his veins, she thought, than anyone else. "I can't imagine having my fill, not in twelve mayfly lifetimes."

Amber was breathing deeply on the mattress behind the partition wall, Harris curled under the table like a cat. Nate was still out somewhere in the night. Rosa leaned her head back on her arm, watching a patch of moonlight as it brightened and faded on the ceiling. "When I was little," she said, "I used to think that every other family went back to the beginning of the year too, like mine. Every other child."

"It's endearing, the small thoughts you had," said Tommy.

"It was hard to have any other kind."

A gaggle of men passed by on the street below the apartment, arguing loudly in French. One of them began singing at the top of his lungs, and was hushed ineffectively by his companions, who broke into gales of laughter. Rosa looked sideways at Tommy. In the dark it felt almost safe to wonder what kind of child he had been.

"How do they feel to you?" he asked her with uncharacteristic seriousness. "The journeys themselves?"

In the dark it seemed almost safe to say it. "Like falling, Tom."

"Never, to me. They always feel like flying."

Harris murmured something in his sleep. Rosa turned over onto her stomach, and regarded Tommy from above. She was aware of checking the tone of her voice, of taking care to keep it light. "Amber says that you have no control. She said that most often she can choose where she goes."

Tommy snorted, scratching lazily at his bare chest. "She's exaggerating. Amber does well, better than most of us, and it's gone to her head. Where's the fun in forcing your path, anyway? I suppose," he added in a whisper, "she does it by thinking so hard and so often of her treasure-troves."

Rosa smiled, though she felt the expression waver. "So I could go back to nineteen forty-five? If I wanted to?"

"I thought you despised that year."

"I do. I do. But if for any reason I wanted to go back?"

"It might be easier," he said slowly, "in your case." He was frowning, and she realised that she ought not to have asked. She lay back down, giving a deliberate yawn. The men in the street had passed by, and the night was quiet at last.

"But who can really say *why* our journeys are what they are?" Tommy breathed into the dark. "Who would wish to know? Isn't that... to spectacularly miss the point?"

*

Don't lay your head too long on the same pillow, and don't grow too accustomed to the company of your own kind. This constellation has moved into place only for a short season, the way that bodies in the heavens slip into one another's orbits. Every ten years, every ten thousand, each hurtling along in its own remote course. Rosa loved the thought of pattern and light made beautiful in brevity. We five luminaries from the remote corners of history, aligning for a matter of months in a Montparnasse loft.

She wandered at Amber's side through the latest exhibition at the Salon d'Automne, the walls hung with still-wet paintings that would be admired for decades to come. Cubes and crescents of colour like stained-glass windows, figures in vivid geometric landscapes. Patrons murmured their appreciation and sipped champagne. Amber was the most exquisite thing in the room, shimmering in a peacock-green turban and white mink shawl, pearls wrapped about her throat. A diamond on each finger. She had taken off her gloves to scrawl in a small notebook, eyes moving with a calculating gaze from one canvas to the next.

"I will buy that one there. And the Gleizes in the corner." Amber clicked her tongue. "I'm considering the Picabia."

She drew Rosa closer, her hands moving expressively. "Look at the arrangement of the forms. They represent this cup, this figure perceived simultaneously from every angle. The plane of a fourth dimension, made visible." Her long, Kohl-lined eyes narrowed in pleasure. "The whole of the world happening at once."

Rosa thought of the shapes that passed before her eyes when she moved from one century to the next, how cities blurred into abstraction then formed themselves again. "What does that mean?"

Amber gave a reverent sigh. "They paint time itself."

As the hum of the Salon continued around them, Rosa hesitated, and then leaned forward to ask Tommy's question. "How do the journeys feel to you?"

Amber took Rosa's arm, and they moved slowly through into the final room of the exhibition. Women fanned themselves and men haggled over a block-ish plaster bust. "They feel to me," Amber said, in a low voice, "like following a silken rope with my fingers, through a great fog and darkness, towards daylight."

"And you always find your way?"

"There is nothing so very difficult about it. Nothing to fear – so long as you have your wits about you."

"Oh, I'm not afraid," said Rosa. "Not in the slightest bit."

When Amber had agreed her price with the curator and arranged for delivery to the loft, they headed out into the foggy evening. The sun was going down over the Seine, the street-lights flickering into life as the pair crossed over the Pont des Invalides. Rosa wrapped a shawl around her shoulders, listening to the water lap below, and wondered what her next journey would be.

Soon, she told herself, I'll start to assemble all I need to be the Fabulist again. Whatever that might mean in this time. She had never tried it so far forward, and was not sure how it would go. People here would not be so easily impressed, perhaps not even greatly interested. As they passed along a series of narrow streets Rosa watched lamps being lit outside cafés, painters and poets and musicians emerging from the day's isolation. They had made their own wonders. They had created for themselves an ever-unfolding *now*, a bright bubble of noise and laughter, floating away above the century.

I'll be something else, thought Rosa, and vague possibilities danced before her like the spots of light reflected from Amber's diamonds. I made the Fabulist out of nothing; if I need to, I'll make myself from nothing again. As she looked sideways at Amber, she wondered whether even this supremely confident traveller might be outdone.

"Oh, darling," said Amber. "I know how you have been dying to ask. But it's terribly bad manners."

"What?"

"I heard you already winkled it out of Harris. He barely knows any better, poor boy." They walked beneath arching lines of trees, their first russet leaves beginning to fall. "He would tell the tale of where he came from to any inquisitive stranger. But we, Rosa! Those of us who make an art of this life – we might consider it crude."

"I didn't ask you," Rosa said. She felt a flash of the prickly indignation that had animated her every word and move in her first meeting with Tommy, years before. She would not allow Amber to make her feel like a beginner. "Don't flatter yourself that I'm so curious. I have never asked Tommy, either, in all the time we've spent together."

"There's that, too."

Rosa turned to Amber, ready to laugh off her advice.

"Take whatever lovers you like," said Amber. "Even grow fond of them, if it suits you. But if you're wise..."

"Of course, I won't know how to live unless you instruct me!"

Her sharpness did not seem to pierce in the slightest, and it dawned on Rosa that she was not being admonished at all. To be teased in this way was to be made part of Amber's circle, to be invited to the table.

"... if you're wise, you'll stick to the other kind."

"Is that what you do?" Rosa asked, more congenially.

"I grew very fond of one, the writer, in this decade. But she did have such terrible moods." Amber's eyes glittered slyly as she rearranged her mink wrap. "If you stick to the other kind, you can leave them where they belong. You won't have to encounter them again at some inconvenient moment. That's the way most of us play it."

Rosa watched the people of the city pass by in their September hats and coats. It had been raining for most of the afternoon, and many carried umbrellas, picking their way carefully around the puddles. The cobbles were sleek with a skin of water. Motorcars rolled noisily by, and as the sky darkened, their headlamps shone narrow beams through the gloom.

They walked in comfortable silence all of the way up the slope to Montparnasse. Rainwater trickled from the mouths of stone gargoyles along the tops of the walls. Rosa returned to the thought of how she might leave this place. Alone or in company? Back perhaps to be the Fabulist again, or forward into the unknown? There was nothing left to fear. At last the girl who had once sobbed her heart out in a theatre on Drury Lane felt like a stranger.

They approached the doorway that led to the loft, and Rosa realised that Amber was watching her. She wanted to tell her how she had spent most of her life starved of this feeling – of the sense that she was safely above water, captaining her own course.

"Now you have a look in your eye, just like the one he gets," said Amber, tilting her head to one side as she unlocked the door.

"Tommy?"

"Yes." Amber smiled her Pharaoh's smile. "I think he believes in his heart of hearts that he is going to live forever."

10

Come Away

"I should like to see Berlin, in this decade," said Tommy. "It's supposed to be full of disreputable libertines. Even more than here."

"Your kind," said Rosa. He winked at her.

"I feel one ought to take in a little Berlin after Paris, like dessert after dinner."

Amber raised an eyebrow. "But would you like where the tides are headed? Less than ten years forward, and that city won't be so friendly to strangers."

They were sitting out on the balcony in the late afternoon, sipping hot coffee, coats about their shoulders. The autumn sunlight cast a rosy glow over the rooftops and the cobbled street below, where a flower-seller pushed her cart down the hill. In the loft behind them the Brothers Black were clattering pans as they prepared stew. A strong savoury smell drifted out through the shutters.

Tommy arched his back as he stretched. "Perhaps not. Istanbul, then. Or any place with its face set ahead. I have not gone far enough *forward* in some while."

"We all know where you are itching to go, Thomas." Amber blew on her coffee. "Hiroshima is a long way from here, in any decade."

"That can wait," said Tommy.

"I haven't felt much movement in the tides here," said Rosa. "At least, not in this part of the city. We might have to go looking."

Amber inclined her head. "Then go looking we shall. If you're both amenable to us remaining together, for the time being?"

Rosa nodded. In the room behind Harris had begun to sing, words indistinguishable and tune unsteady. Nate laughed before joining in.

"For as long as we are together," said Tommy, "of course."

In the weeks that followed, they gathered rumours like scraps of fleece from a hedgerow. Rosa watched Tommy and Amber pausing to speak with figures who slept in doorways, with the limping man who prowled back and forth outside the disused paint factory in the hours of night. There must be more, she realised, in the city, among the city. More than she had first imagined, landing here upon their knees and then walking as though they knew the streets. *There is a look that we have.*

Rosa peered into the faces of passers-by, at their clothes, the bags they carried. Searching for that almost indefinable oddness which had marked Tommy out to her at their first meeting. She exchanged a furtive smile with a woman who was sat alone in an emptying cafe, eyes devouring her surroundings. A long-haired man grabbed Rosa's elbow on the tram and tried to greet her in a language she did not recognise, hand hovering courteously over his eyes. They were none of them old, no older than thirty or so. It must be that they grew more adept over the years at deflecting attention; or otherwise that this city in this time was simply the haunt of the young.

Perhaps someday she would meet one as ill-prepared as she had been, wearing a look of panic and a coat from the wrong century, darting from shelter to shelter like a rabbit between burrow-holes. They would look at her in tentative recognition, in fear and in hope. She would pause, Rosa thought, and smile, and reach out in invitation. *Come away, traveller, and see what awaits. Come with me.*

Amber's treasures began to disappear from the loft, to be stowed, Rosa supposed, in places only she knew. Her pockets rattled with jewels, since she was preparing for a journey that might come without warning. Rosa watched as she packed only what would fit into a single battered valise, the rest of her many outfits left hanging in the wardrobe, her countless lotions and perfume bottles lined up on the sill for the loft's next occupant to find.

By now Rosa knew Tommy's preparations almost as well as she knew her own. He jettisoned most of the odds and ends he had collected, keeping only those that could be easily tucked inside his coat. He became possessed of a sharp, voltaic energy. She fed off it, ready to feel the shifting of the air as the present peeled back and gave way to something new. She packed her bags and waited for the wave to break.

"We hear talk of Venice," Amber told Rosa and the Brothers across the table one morning, as she idly flipped the front page of the newspaper. "A way has opened up there to the twenty-first. How should you like to see the twenty-first, Harris?"

"Shall we all go together?" he asked.

"If we can. And I will sell Titians to every gallery that will take them."

They bought tickets for the train to Milan. The day before they left, Rosa agreed to take Harris on the bus to Reims, since he had long wanted to see the cathedral's famous smiling angel and his brother would not indulge him. He was restive, as Nate had predicted, and she was not sure how to reassure him.

"Let's count the cars, Harris. Or I brought playing-cards."

"I don't want to play."

"But you're so clever with it. You'll beat me in no time."

137

He pressed his forehead against the bus window and blew mist onto the glass. "Shall we all be going together?" he asked again. "Me 'n Nate? And you, and Amber, and Tom?"

"We'll try to. But you know it doesn't always work that way."

"How far do you think we shall go?" he asked, in a sing-song tone. "How far away?"

Rosa laid a hand on his hair and let it rest there, watching his gaze flick from side to side as he followed the cars which passed them, the horses grazing in fields and kestrels hovering at the roadside. "I suppose we have been here for quite some months," she said. "One shouldn't rest one's head too long on the same pillow, after all."

The day was clouded and chilly, the first bite of winter in the air. The towering walls of the old church were marred by scaffolding, workers still tending to the wounds the structure had sustained in the last war. Rosa craned her neck, trying to keep up with Harris as he darted between visitors in search of his angel. When he found her he stopped stock-still below the statue, staring upwards, unmindful of those in whose path he stood.

Rosa caught up with him and took hold of his shoulder. The angel was carved in sand-coloured stone above the archway at the entrance, her head tilted and her hand raised, her look filled with benign warmth. Given the damage that bombs had done to the surroundings stones, her smile seemed unaccountably tranquil.

"Is she as you hoped she would be?"

"Oh, I have met with her before," he said.

"Where was that, Harris?"

"She comes to see me." His eyes remained fixed on the statue. "Brings others with her. I see 'em all the time."

Rosa left him and wandered into the darkened belly of the building. A row of red candles glimmered in the vestry. A handful of other visitors were scattered about, whispering beside the organ or admiring the tapestries upon the walls. She made her way down the central aisle towards the altar on its raised stage, dwarfed into smallness by the great pillars on either side. The sound of her own slow breath echoed back to her as she trod further from the daylight.

Shadows yawned in the vaulted ceiling, fingers of stained light filtering through the windows. She remembered the grand, heavy stillness of St Paul's, the way it had arrested her as a small girl. The hush seemed to hang huge overhead, a weight more like water than air. Carved into the walls on every side, she glimpsed old friends; the stone things immortalising fishermen, and whores, and kings.

For some reason Rosa thought of the Brothers Black riding out towards the endless horizon of their childhood, the dissolving of time all around them, the terror of too much empty space.

And then she saw him. The back of his head was enough. The slightest turn of his pale face. He was sitting alone in the foremost pew, before the flickering candles. He was gaunt and grim as she remembered from her first glimpse of him, that night years ago in the darkening garden. He wore the uniform of the war that was still to come.

Her breath caught in her chest. Rosa stepped back, and the Angel of Death did not see her. His hands were clasped in his lap, his head bowed. He was the shadow of the end.

She tore her eyes away and stumbled back towards the door, blood pounding in her ears, half-certain now that she had imagined him. But before she reached the daylight and cold fresh air, there it was all of a sudden. That pain, that hook in her heart. Rosa felt her body bend beneath it. The distant strain of a once-known home.

In the languid Venetian night a carnival crowd flooded the streets and put out gondolas onto the water, white-masked and robed in glittering azure, in tangerine and gold. Rosa and Tommy Rust moved among them, she a magpie in black and white, he a tragic hero, the mouth of his mask curved mournfully downwards. They broke open a bottle below a bridge and kissed in the darkness, masks askew, hands beneath each others' clothes. The smell of frying pastries, smoky air and sweet wine, the familiar taste of him.

They climbed the steps to the bridge and pushed through to the front of the crowd, leaning elbow-to-elbow on the railing. A flaming torch lit the front of each barge, the whole procession reflected in the canal below. Somewhere close at hand, a drum pounded with a rhythm like a racing heartbeat. Figures wove and dived about them, men with three faces, players dressed as plague-doctors with protuberant beaks. An *odalisque* danced in scarlet silk.

Rosa let the night flood her senses. Painted eyes darted sideways in the shadows. In her ear the sound of Tommy laughing below his false face, his hand in hers.

Sometimes I have dreams within dreams within dreams. Air distorted in the corner of her vision like a curtain blown by a breeze. Her head snapped sharply around. For a moment she thought that she saw a man in a soldier's uniform, vanishing from view as soon as she turned to look. Was that him again, unmasked and sombre in the heart of the crowd, that pale face, those hollow eyes? Nowhere to be seen. Rosa's breath would not slow. He might be merely in her mind, but he was here, and cracks slithered outward from him across the surface of everything.

The sting of champagne upon her tongue. Her insides heaved

involuntarily as the world spun around her. She awoke later in a strange bed still in her harlequin mask, feathers in her hair.

*

When they travelled to the twenty-first it was together, the five of them swept from the same Venetian street as they wandered below the archways. Harris let out a cry, drowned under the roaring rush of the air and the groan of the crumbling skyline. Stones tumbled and skittered. A flurry of limbs, hands clasping hands. Rosa clung tightly to her bag of possessions, and landed on her knees.

The journey was too rough, the arrival sending a shock of pain through her legs and hips into her whole body. Bruised, annoyed, she brushed herself off. *You have outgrown this, Rosa*, she thought. She was aware that she had begun to turn her head constantly, certain that she had caught sight of something out of the corner of her vision. She rubbed her eyes until they were sore, but it would not go away. The distraction was maddening.

She did not ask Tommy or Amber whether they had ever experienced this. It was a head-cold, a disruption in her rhythm which would surely right itself soon. But the thing that had altered persisted into their next journey, which took all of them even further forward, to the time when the sea had finally claimed the city and the streets were built on stilts. In this place and time Rosa felt that she too had been submerged, water trickling in to block her ears. It took too much energy to remain present. With conscious effort she smiled at amusements, admired the beauty of the dripping architecture. She fought not to look over her shoulder.

Then came the next journey, still in Venice, five years back. Just a gentle tug and her body seized in mid-fall. Before she knew it she had let go of Tommy's hand on one side, Amber's on the other. She cursed the painful landing, but what was to be done? Though she might not have chosen this moment to go on alone, it would have happened in the end. Better not to have used time over goodbyes. She only felt sorry that Harris might miss her. Rosa gathered her belongings and left the city.

Bag upon her back, road beneath her feet. She tried to laugh at her own continued unease, shadow-boxed around it until it retreated. *Do not let panic rule you. Didn't you flourish alone, when you lost Tommy Rust that first time and painted yourself as the Fabulist? Didn't you feel your back straightening and your head lifting, your whole self singing in your long-sought freedom?*

She knew that there was so much more to be, so much to take hold of – a hundred different tides waiting to carry her off. The next thing, Rosa, the next thing is on its way. When the tale of her life was told, this direction-less chapter would be omitted. She smoked hashish in a tiny Istanbul cafe, buried amongst cushions in a threadbare couch, blowing out receding rings towards the ceiling. The world blurred in a cloud of white while a wasp buzzed in the café's window. She closed her eyes and felt her body succumb to the smoke from the blue-glass pipe. Lethargy washed through her blood and eased the tension away.

You can learn the lay of the twenty-first, just as you have learnt the centuries that came before it. You can follow the whispers to the next city, the next country along, where they say the winds are blowing forward.

Istanbul. Cairo. Jaipur. The same century. Before she knew it she had traversed so many miles that she could not point to her whereabouts on any map. And what was there to do but go yet further? She caught so many trains east that she began to wonder whether she was trying to reach the city where Tommy had spoken of heading one day. The city with a name like a sigh, the city of that light flash bright as the end of the world. Perhaps Tommy would be there when she reached it, Amber still at his side, the Brothers Black following close behind. Or perhaps they had already gone their separate ways, four bodies spinning off into space.

You could find them if you wanted to, Rosa reminded herself. You will find them again if you only catch the right current, in the right place. There is no call for panic, gypsy girl, much less grief. After all, you never belonged to one another.

*

She made mistakes. She asked the question of people who looked at her as though she had gone mad. *Can you tell me of the tides? Can you tell me where I am?*

Nothing prepared Rosa for the fall which came one day in a town on the shore of a cold sea. She was snatched by a violent jolt as she stood gazing at the wild waters. Her body plummeted backwards as though she had tripped over a stone. It was too sudden, too fast, and she cried out as she fell through layers of air, but there was no end to it. She spun screaming through dissolving centuries.

"Tommy!" she shrieked, and as she hit the ground at long last with a crippling *thud* his name echoed above a forest of frozen pines. She heard the sound ripple back to her, no longer a call for help, but a livid accusation.

She rose groaning from the bruising of her bones. Something red dripped onto the snowy ground, and she touched a hand to her face. A stream of blood trickled from her nose.

"*Tommy!*" she bellowed again, with all the air left in her lungs, and flung a stone in her fury as she turned around.

Only snow, and silence. Only the icy ocean stretching out to the horizon, as far as the eye could see.

11

Black Wave

For as long as the daylight lasted Rosa walked parallel to the water, wrapped in every item of clothing she had in her possession, scanning the snowy landscape. The fall had skinned her knees, left grit embedded deep in her palms, but she did not stop to clean them. She called out until her throat grew too sore. The place where she had been was an old fishing-town, but here there were no trawlers moored between the rocks, no ramshackle shingle-roofed houses built atop the cliff-line. No aeroplane-trails crossing the sky, no rumble of a distant road.

She had never known a silence so complete. As twilight fell, constellations blinked into being, diamond-white and far more vivid than she had ever seen them.

The darkness was beginning to deepen. Rosa caught sight of a thin line of smoke rising into the sky about a mile ahead. She almost cried out in jubilation, and despite her exhaustion ran towards it, snow spraying up beneath her boots, bag rattling noisily. The smoke wound upwards from a cluster of tree-strewn rocks above the beach, and as she drew closer she saw that the snow had melted on the surrounding ground.

She bent double, gasping for breath, and limped the final yards at a painfully slow pace. As she rounded the rocks she realised that the smell was not smoky, but sulphurous. There was no fire, nor anybody to tend one, only a crack in the rocks through which steam coiled out.

Rosa swore uselessly at the sky, and sunk to her knees. Her pack of possessions clattered behind her. She had fallen very far. She tried to push aside her panic. Without the few degrees of warmth within these rocks, she might well have been dead by morning.

She inched up her skirt to examine the bruises which were blossoming all along her legs, touching them with shivering hands. With a small clump of moss, she cleaned the blood from her knees and hands. She spat into the wounds, wincing. Her cheeks grew hot where she faced the rising vapour, her back cold where the wind blew into the dip from across the beach. Her bag made a hard and lumpy pillow. She wrapped the cloak she had worn in the Venice carnival over her head, and drew her arms in through her sleeves so that they hugged her bare skin.

*

She was sore when she woke, the exposed skin of her face raw with cold. Daylight revealed deep cracks between the rocks, and she found a space large enough to stretch her limbs in. Digging in her bag, she unearthed the dagger with the snake-shaped sheath. She pulled the rest of her belongings into the cave, and from the outside piled pine branches to cover the entrance. She walked half a mile and looked back to see the thread of vapour winding its way into the chill sky.

The roaring silence of the beach became terrible to her. She combed the edge of the water for any debris that was not shell or stone, anything that might have been touched by human hands. Patches of frozen sand cracked below her boots. She turned over driftwood and weed, as though some message might be hidden beneath them. Her mind felt numb and sluggish as her body.

In search of the exact spot where she had passed through, Rosa trod back the way she had come the previous day, but it all looked the same. White sky, grey sand, black water. No shifting of the scenery in the corner of her eye, no movement in the currents behind the air. She flung stones towards the ocean again, yelling and screaming into the emptiness until the echoes of her distress had faded.

There was a little food in her bag, and a flask. She returned to the crack between the rocks and huddled close to the spring of hot vapour, tearing at a handful of bread with her teeth. The sustenance and warmth brought some clarity. There must be people living beyond the cliffs, cities or at least small settlements beyond her line of sight from here below, perhaps miles to the west where the sun went down. You will find them, Rosa, and you will find favour there. You always do.

She breathed out onto her stiff hands and rubbed them together. Her fingers would not unbend.

*

Rosa walked through the woods, shaking snow from the branches and hungrily picking unfamiliar berries. She spat out those which were too sour to swallow, fearing poison. She followed scattered tracks and found tufts of white fur caught upon low-hanging branches, patches of nibbled bark. Using the dagger she cut off strips for herself, and chewed it grimly as she climbed upwards between the trees, away from the ocean.

She had found her way to the cliff-top via a perilous series of ledges, pocketing birds' eggs from nests and clinging to outcrops. Beneath the trees, sheltered from the bitter wind, the air felt a little warmer. She remembered following Heloise's hawk into the forest at Seysair, the animal from the shadows which had disappeared into the green quiet. Here was no first-hand sight of any living creature, only signs and the dimmest sounds. Something flapped and disturbed the branches far overhead.

Snow covered the world. Only the hardiest of greenery had forced itself through, and the sky above was featureless. The highest visible ground was a craggy shelf of rock, perhaps a mile or two away. She dragged her unwilling legs through the snow towards it, head bowed, lips moving as she urged herself on. *From up there, from up there you will see.* A line of smoke from a distant chimney, a road winding through the landscape, a huddle of primitive huts.

She climbed as best she could, numb fingers struggling to keep their grip. The cliffs had already taken almost all she had, and she was already weak with hunger, and panting for fresh water. When she reached the top she could only slump, gasping, tears streaming from her wind-shocked eyes. It was several minutes before she could even find the strength to stand.

When she finally rose to her feet it was with shaking knees. She held up her arms against the force of the wind, and made another fruitless attempt to muffle her ears and mouth with a scarf meant for warmer climates. Her body, which until that terrible fall had rarely reminded her of its limits, seemed suddenly frail as a hollow eggshell. Snow, for mile after hard-frozen mile, scattered with belts of pine and scraggy grasses. At her back, the heaving iron sea.

For a long time all was silent and white. Empty of life. Then in the distance, a solitary shape loped across the scene. A moving thing, a warm breathing thing. Not a human. Not even a wolf, but perhaps resembling one, long of leg and sharp of snout. Rosa felt fresh tears sting her cheeks, freezing instantly as they met the air. How many millennia would pass before this creature assumed the form she knew? Just how far, how unthinkably, impossibly far, had she come?

Its tail swept the snow. Pausing in its course, it raised its dark head, ears laid flat and tongue lolling red. It was wild and strange and belonged to this world as she never would.

The not-yet-wolf let out a cry to the laden clouds. Rosa joined with the sound, howling from the knot in her guts, from the wrenching ache in her chest.

*

Each day became a new notch in a pine branch. When her dagger grew blunt she sharpened it against a rock and tested the edge with her thumb. Ten days. Fifteen. A month. Rosa swallowed each new dawn like a pill. It would be worse, to have ceased to count. The worst has not come until the chaos takes you, and time itself becomes a wilderness.

It was for this reason that her eyes still searched out cooking-fires, human footprints in the snow, though she had relinquished any hope of it in her heart. Better for the hours to have some shape, however purposeless. She walked from her cave in wider and wider arcs, mapping the landscape, holding the shape of it in her head, since the pages of her notebooks had dampened and disintegrated. All she saw only confirmed her fears. There was something wrong not only in the low bodies of the wolves which ran in the woods, but in the look of the rocks above the sea, the sulphurous smell of the air.

She had come too far back. The surface of everything had begun to peel away like paint. Why were you never warned, Rosa? Did Tommy Rust not think to tell you of such rip-tides – that a violent current could come from nowhere and snatch you to icy exile? Perhaps he did not believe in such things.

Anger kept her warm, as it had done years ago, millions of years away, in the boiler room of a London apartment block. Rosa took out her rage on the unsuspecting almost-hares which came to sniff among the grasses, slitting their white throats and skinning them with clumsy strokes of her knife. As a child she had often helped Harriet prepare rabbits snared in the hedgerows, unmoved, for the most part, by their tender eyes. Who can spare mercy for the small, in wartime?

She padded her coat with the furs, but for a time had no way to cook the flesh, since she could build no fire. After a hundred bad starts, she ate raw from sheer hunger. The first and second times she vomited the meat straight back up again, and spent painful nights clutching at her stomach. The third she kept it down, and many times after that until the trick of fire came. She had seen it done at Seysair with a spinning flint in a bundle of kindling, but learning the motion for herself – and with such poor tools – was another matter.

This was not supposed to happen. She flung blunt pieces of flint down the beach and screamed incoherently. With growing fear she ran her fingertips down the jutting bones of her spine. *This was not supposed to be.*

At last she succeeded. With a hoarse yell she sprung back from the spark, the little dancing flame. She fed it with dried pine-branches, guano cut from the nests along the cliff, afraid even to breathe on it in case it was extinguished. She squatted behind the fire, stinking smoke seeping through every layer of her clothes. She had not washed in weeks.

Rosa kept a fire burning each night in the dip between the rocks, which soon became stained with grease and soot. Bones were littered all around. The not-yet-wolves sniffed cautiously about the borders of the light until she bellowed at them and threw stones. They had never seen such an animal. She watched her own shadow flickering upon the cave wall, and traced the contours of the stone with her fingertips. Fancifully, she scratched out forms with berry-juice, sticks of charcoal. Towers tall as the clouds, figures on horseback, Harris's smiling angel. The shapes seemed nonsensical here, so far out of their time. She stood back from her creations, shoulders hunched and hands stained red, and felt something collapse in her chest like a tower of cards.

She curled her body around her bag of possessions, fearful that she might journey in her sleep and leave it behind. All day, so long as she was not hunting hares, she carried it with her.

Another tide will come, she told herself. It must come, because otherwise there would be nothing to do other than lie down on the frozen ground in defeat. I will build up my hope and my courage again, and the tide will come and carry me away.

Yet she feared the journey now, the memory still fresh in her bones of that awful, plummeting fall. She could not sleep without dreaming of it, waking with a cry and a jolt, blood trickling from her nose.

*

Was the earth groaning? Rosa thought that she heard it, the far-off rumble of rocks, the roll and crack of colliding stone. Along the coast, she saw pieces of the continent crumble away and plunge into the ocean. New fissures opened between the boulders on the edge of the beach, belching steam. She did not feel that she ought to be seeing these sights, hearing these sounds. It was like watching an acquaintance get dressed at the beginning of the day. The world was awakening slowly, stretching in the early light. It had yet to put on its face.

Rosa willed the rumbling planet beneath her to move faster as she squatted atop the rocks with her knife in hand, scouting for hares. The snow lay thick and undisturbed. Hurry up and change. Grow more life.

She passed her tongue across her bleeding lips. Slowly but surely, the chill was cracking her flesh. Each day she tried to speak, to the tools in her hands, to the prey she killed, to her own shadow, but she knew that silence was coming for her. Her voice sounded ever more swollen and strange. Her stiff fingers had begun to fumble the pine branch which counted her days here, leaving the notches uneven, crossing over one another until she could no longer count them. Two months? Three? It was no longer possible to know.

She found she could not look directly into it. *This is not the dream: this is the waking. The chaos which is beneath everything, which you thought you could walk upon without sinking.* For the first time she allowed herself to truly wonder what might happen to a body at the mercy of the merciless cold. Where its breath might go.

Huge and dreadful questions circled around the edges of her firelight, along with the wolves. The anger which had sustained her had no fuel left to burn. Rosa had never before been without it, or otherwise the thrill of triumph which was its mirror image. She felt her shoulders slump Her feet no longer carried her in wide determined paths, but limped back and forth along the same familiar stretch of beach. She turned stones and shells with the toe of her boot and stared at them for hours, unmoving.

The hiss of the waves across the frozen sand, the clattering of small icebergs washed close to the shore. She crouched at the edge of the water, her thoughts turning to fish, and how deep she would have to go to find them. She fashioned a spear, lashing the knife to a sturdy stripped branch. Poised knee-deep in the sea for as long as she could bear it, her eyes learnt to find the flickering shadows beneath the surface. Yet her hands seemed to strike always a little too late.

When a huge shape broke the surface of the waves, not half a mile out, her spear dropped to her side and her mouth gaped open. The monster's never-ending back arched out of the depths and then vanished vertebra by vertebra, tapering to a flattened tail. The water resounded with its moaning call. Rosa stood transfixed, hardly noticing the water as it lapped against her bluish skin. She had never seen anything so far beyond her understanding, anything less concerned with her being.

After this she saw the great fish many times, and would sometimes sit cross-legged on the sand wrapped in her furs as the sun sunk low in the sky, listening to the clicks and creaks of its song. The presence of the creature – or creatures, for surely there were many – was somehow comforting to her. She imagined it as it rolled its huge body in the deepest waters, wrapped in its own unknowable thoughts. For what other thoughts are there, so far from anywhere? With what other thinking being do you now share this world?

The stars winked overhead, fires set alight still longer ago, when the universe first moved into motion.

*

Air began to blur in the corners of her vision. In the dip among the rocks her nights grew all the more fitful. Days of dizzy spells and nosebleeds. Her thoughts whispered that a journey might be close. But Rosa, Rosa, could these not be the ordinary pains of a protesting body before life leaves it? Its floors being swept and its windows bolted shut, like a Hyde house on the last night of the year? Her stomach cramped and the blood would not return to her numb fingertips. She sat on the icy beach and wept.

She no longer had the strength to hunt, to climb up to the woods and gather moss and berries, or even to melt snow for drinking. When the last of her supplies in the cave were gone, Rosa lay down on her side and rested her head. Her eyes ranged over the paintings she had made upon the wall. She felt a dim smile haunt her mouth. Her eyelids slid closed.

In her faint state, her mind slipped. She imagined that Tommy stood before her, the form of him fading slowly until only his grin was left behind. "Come on, Rosa," the grin said. "Surely these are matters for the mayflies. Not for the likes of us."

In his light, shadows seemed such a childish thing to have imagined. "I know," she said. "But I want to be sure…"

"I feel it in my heart of hearts," said the grin, "I can assure you."

"But Tom. I think I have to know it for myself."

Rosa awoke, and raised her body with the last of her strength. In the thin first light of dawn, shivering from head to foot, she packed every one of her belongings back into her bag. A tin train, postbox-red, which she had taken in the nineteenth; a glowing watch, a gold coin, a dagger. A harlequin mask. She left the dip in the rocks and headed slowly back down the beach, pausing along the way to pick up a stray shell which lay upon the sand. It was cone-shaped, smoothed by the sea, coloured coral and cream. She blew gently into its hollow to clean out the sand. Pressed the side of it against her cheek.

She set her face towards the iron sea and walked without hesitation, biting down a gasp as the water covered her knees, hips, stomach. Her clothes grew heavy and her skin screamed. Muscles in her limbs seized and she forced herself deeper, struggling to move as her bag and fur-lined coat became saturated. Submerged, she spread her arms wide.

A black wave fell over everything.

12

The Museum

Light splintering. Her heavy body pulled upside-down and side-to-side. She closed her eyes, and heard from somewhere in the deep the moaning, echoing call of the monstrous fish. Her lungs flooded with ice. She was spinning forwards through nothingness, water roaring in her ears.

Then, newly formed below her, dry land. Sun on her back. Rosa dropped to her knees, heaving salt water out of her stomach. The light was different: the snow had given way to ochre-coloured pits. A series of jagged hills rose overhead. The sea was nowhere to be seen.

Pushing the tangled, streaming hair from her face, she raised her head to look around. There was greenery. Grass beneath her, which she seized in her fists. Trees overhead. She turned onto her back, and felt tears streaming from her eyes and running down her cheeks. Above the branches, which swum in and out of focus, an unmistakable line of smoke rose into the sky. She closed her eyes again and felt her body shuddering with uncontrollable sobs.

*

"She's here."

"She's *here*!"

"Can it truly be?"

"Look, she weeps!"

"Will she stand?"

"Let me..."

"Stand back, stand back, give her air..."

Hands on Rosa's hair, her face. Hands upon her shoulders and elbows. Faces filling her vision. She fought their hold fiercely, kicking and biting until she drew blood.

"Let me go! Let go, let me—"

"We understand that you are distressed. We are not going to hurt you."

"Where's Tommy, where's Tommy? I'll kill him! I want Amber, I want Harris..."

"These people are not here. Please, calm yourself."

It took five of them to subdue her. She lay panting, wild with rage, as disconnected pictures flashed across her mind. The blinding sight of snow. The broken body of a small creature in her hands, blood spilling from its split skin.

"My things!" she croaked.

"You brought them with you. Look there, on the grass. You have been very far away."

"Faraway..."

They shushed her and stroked her hair, her forehead. She dropped to her knees. The men and women sank down with her. She realised that some of them were singing softly. Others had their eyes closed, hands raised to the heavens. Their expressions were blissful. She found herself staring at them, fascinated.

They carried her reverently through the misted trees, around the side of the hill to a rough-built timber and tent settlement. She was laid in a hammock and covered with blankets. A fire was lit in a grill beside her and its warmth gradually filled the space inside the canvas, bringing blood burning into her fingers and face. Rosa cried again with the pain of it, and the strangers huddled around, singing over her. Somebody tried to spoon sweet water into her mouth.

She turned her head away. In the dim light she saw glass cases on the other side of the tent, containing several large, flat pieces of stone. Something was daubed upon these in dull colours. Skyscrapers and smiling angels. There were more objects too, books and papers and monochrome photographs, but she could not make these out.

"Your paintings. They were sealed by a rock-fall for millions of years," whispered one of the women at her bedside. "Found by those who came before us. We knew that you had been here. We have been waiting."

"They are the jewels of our collection," said another.

Their smiling faces swam and blurred. Rosa felt a tug behind her ribs, and even in the midst of her confusion, knew that she was already slipping from this place. Somebody had lit a scented taper, and its thick smell filled her nostrils. She thought that she saw a wide blue sky overhead. A rhythm like the beat of a drum was pounding in her head.

"We have been waiting for you," said the woman again. Her voice shook. "We are here because of you. We have this honour..."

A man with a thick beard and an intense look bent over her. His eyes were at once too full and too vacant. "When you are strong, we will hear your wisdom. You will give us your blessing."

"Wanderer of many paths," whispered another.

"*Fabulist.*"

Rosa lurched up and forward from the tangle of blankets as though she was about to vomit, but the motion did not stop. She fell from the grip of the hands that held her, and kept on falling.

*

A dusty road wound across the empty horizon, a motor-car rolling along in the sunlight. Blue sky and clear air. The hills had all been levelled save one, on which stood a magnificent building, new-cut pale stone topped with burnished golden domes. A long staircase had been cut into the turf of the hill, leading up to the arched entrance. A tower on the far side looked half-finished, still surrounded by scaffold.

In the shadow of the hill lay a town of tents and trailers. A biplane was parked at the end of a short runway. The whole encampment was fenced around with posts and wire. Rosa's mind could make no sense of it. Her body gave out. She felt her head hit the dirt, and with blurred sideways vision saw a line of dark-suited figures running out from the compound towards her.

*

She was lying on clean sheets in some kind of infirmary, patches of sun on the pillow. They had carried her, she recalled, these dark-suited strangers, up the many steps and through the archway to the cool hush within. Hadn't this happened twice? Had she dreamed another arrival, dim and misty, filled with strange songs?

Slowly, stiffly, she sat up. There were people around her bed. They had come and gone many times through the days she had lain here. A woman in a white coat bandaging her sores, washing the filth from her skin. They were not those from before, but more sedate, more drab. Even now that she was more fully awake, they seemed indistinguishable from one another, these neatly-clothed men and women whose expressions gave little away.

"Are you in pain?" asked one.

She became aware of aching limbs and the heaviness in her head, insides that felt twisted. Her skin felt as though it had been stretched too tightly over her bones. "Some pain."

"Do you know where you are?"

She did not answer. There was no room in her mind for it. She licked her lips. "Water," she said.

It was brought to her, and she drank in cautious sips. The skin of her throat felt like sandpaper. The doctor was taking notes in a paper pad.

"Do you know in which direction you have come?"

"Forward," she said.

They were all looking at her. She felt the weight of their attention, and wanted to shrink back from it, to cower beneath the covers. She did not want any more questions. There was only one thing she felt strong enough to claim, one corner of ground to stand upon. She said it quickly, only to be certain that she still could.

"I am —" She swallowed. Her voice strained and cracked from lack of use. "I am Rosa Hyde."

"We know who you are. Lie down, Miss Hyde. Sleep until you are stronger."

*

Their presence discomforted her, yet she did not like to be alone. She lay staring at the ceiling, trying to think of nothing. She had called after Tommy and the others upon that first arrival, but now she could hardly recall why. Montparnasse and everything before it felt frozen out of her.

It was several days before she was able to get out of bed, shuffle a few steps across the room. After a week or so the woman in the white coat led her by the arm into a sun-drenched courtyard, seating her upon a bench and leaving her to breathe the fresh air. It was apparent that she was at the centre of the great building, in a hexagonal space with high walls rising steeply on either side.

The light splintered through arched windows on every side. A fountain splashed peaceably.

For the first time she wondered about her surroundings. She thought back to the encampment in the misted wood, and tried to remember the clothes they had worn, the way they had spoken. It had not been so very far, from there to here: and here, odd though it was, definitely appeared to be the twentieth. They were a long way from England, but everyone was speaking English. She seemed to remember from her outside glimpse of the building that it was unfinished – and sure enough, the noise of construction continued all through the hours of daylight.

In a moment of panicked clarity she realised that she had not brought her bag when she made the second journey. But then it was brought to her in the infirmary, dust-covered and musty-smelling, each object within still present and correct. She handled her things in astonishment, unable to comprehend what had happened.

"Our predecessors were disappointed that you left them so soon," she was told. "But they kept your belongings safe, these last nine decades."

Rosa could only nod in thanks.

"Is there anything you wish to donate to the Museum?"

"The Museum…?"

"Many have already come here. Great treasures have been left to our keeping."

She turned the coral-coloured conch over in her hands. Her thumb polished the face of the electric watch from the twenty-first. She shook her head, gathering her things close to her chest. If I can hold them for long enough, she thought, the places where they came from might not seem so far away. Her skin prickled uneasily.

There was a mirrored panel along the wall opposite her bed, and Rosa knew that she was monitored even whilst sleeping.

When the sores and bruises on her body had begun to heal and she could eat and walk unaided, when she no longer needed their hourly care, they still watched her. She had only ever been the observer, not the observed. Even as the Fabulist she had drawn only as much attention as she desired, absorbing it from behind her painted mask.

A few of them told her their names, but she barely listened. They were of the other kind, and yet they knew what she was. Nothing in all her travels had prepared her for this. She had no idea what they might want.

*

"Would you feel well enough to come and talk with us, Miss Hyde? Perhaps for an hour or so?"

"I suppose."

She was seated in the courtyard in her white medical gown, watching the afternoon shadows slide across the stones. A man had appeared at one of the doors, removing his hat. Like all of them, he seemed to want to look at her intently, but not to be caught doing so.

"You are not too tired?"

"I've rested long enough."

"If you are sure. Would you like to —" He indicated her gown, suggesting that she change. She shrugged, dismissive, and shuffled after him as she was.

They passed through a sloping, low-ceilinged chamber, lined with glass cabinets. Some were empty, while others had been half-filled with clay pots and slender-necked vases. Each had been meticulously labelled. *Bull-leapers, Crete, 1700 BC. Yushan Porcelain, 14th Century.* A collection of feathered spears and curved scimitars was fixed to the wall. Boxes and crates were stacked everywhere, some still sealed, others unpacked and spilling crumpled newspaper.

"This way." He led her down a flight of stairs and through a door into a room where five of the others were sat along one side of a long table. Each had a pile of files and papers before them. The wall behind was covered by an enormous board, to which were pinned countless notes, newspaper clippings and photographs. Rosa's eyes flickered over the display. Her heart had begun to pound.

She was seated at a solitary chair on the other side of the table. The man who had fetched her sat down. The figures before her were all in shadow, straight-backed and still as stone.

"You look a great deal better, Miss Hyde."

She was still staring past them, to that ominous wall. There were no windows in the room, only a buzzing strip-light. A watch ticked on somebody's wrist. It did not occur to her to thank them for their care.

"They were very concerned for you, our predecessors. You were very distressed when you vanished from their midst, and they could only hope you had gone forward. That you would be back."

"The Museum," said another, "has been waiting."

"It must have taken moments, for you? Here, nearly a hundred years have passed."

"Think of it! In the blink of an eye."

This last said not with wonder, but squeamishly. Rosa could not tell whether they were fascinated or repelled, or both. An unfamiliar feeling came over her, as though she were standing in the doorway watching herself. She did not know what to say, and tried to disguise the shaking of her hands by clinging to the seat of her chair.

A throat was cleared. They muttered amongst themselves. The man who had fetched her from the courtyard lit a cigarette, and leaned across the table to offer her one.

She accepted, rolling up the sleeve of her white gown and taking a deep drag. It helped, to hold something. Rosa looked at the ceiling, and remembered Tommy smoking on a rooftop beside the ocean, the salt wind in her hair. Her eighteenth birthday. She blinked dry eyes, and exhaled slowly.

"Where am I?"

"You are at the Museum, Miss Hyde."

"This is a place of pilgrimage. The most precious relics of civilization will forever be preserved here, far from man's destructive reach."

"Perhaps you require some explanation. There has been a settlement on this site for a very long time, since your paintings were found preserved in the rocks. There were already those who venerated your kind, and they gathered here. They began this work."

"No, I meant…" She struggled to re-frame the question. "*When*." The word felt wrong on her tongue.

There was a pause, and in it she felt the depth of the chasm between her and these people. A shiver ran through her, as though she could still feel the bitter wind of that ancient beach.

"Of course. We ought to have told you. The year is nineteen sixty-two."

A mere seventeen years off from Robert, Harriet and Bella. She had come so far, and not thought of them in so long. With one hand, Rosa raised the cigarette carefully to her lips. With the other she clung to her chair. Could she be glad to hear it? That nineteen forty-five was so near? She tried to steady herself. "Nineteen sixty-two," she repeated. "I suppose you think the world's coming to an end?"

An uncertain silence.

"We know history must continue, in some form or another. This is a place of pilgrimage. Your kind come here. Some, we believe, from future years."

"And what do they tell you?"

"Nothing, of the future. We do not ask."

She gave a laugh which turned into a cough, and stubbed out her cigarette.

"Miss Hyde? We will not keep you long today, if you are feeling unwell."

"What do you want?"

"We are compiling records. To begin with, there are some points we are hoping you can confirm for us."

She nodded. A vivid memory, suddenly, of sitting opposite Tommy in a threadbare armchair, whisky in her hand. The fire it had lit in her. His dancing eyes, his bewitching certainty. Whatever was woven that night, she thought, it is now being unpicked.

"You are Rosa Beatrice Hyde."

"Yes."

"When were you born?"

"In nineteen-forty five. London.

"To Robert Frank Hyde and Harriet Elizabeth Hyde?"

"Yes."

"And you remained there until you were seventeen."

"In nineteen forty-five. Not in London. Yes." The scribbling of pens upon paper. Rosa adjusted her gown, wishing now that she had dressed. She was aware of her exposed legs and shoulders. "How –"

Through the fug of smoke, in the darkened room, the six of them stirred in unison. "You always leave a mark, you people. Whether you intend to or not."

"You leave a trail."

"When one begins to look into the right corners of history, one comes across some fascinating things."

Rosa breathed out slowly. She did not want to hear what pieces she had been leaving in her wake for these people to pick up. It made her journeys seem somehow tarnished.

There was a dry shuffle of papers and snapping of pen-lids. Then: "How old are you, Miss Hyde?"

"Twenty... twenty-three?" She did not know how many months had slipped between her fingers at the frozen beach.

"How old are your parents, were your parents, when you last saw them?"

"I... I don't know. My mother... was in her early forties, when I left. My father a few years older."

"And this was the Shoreditch year."

A tug of surprise at this intimate detail. Rosa looked across the table, lost for words. She nodded.

More scribbling. "Were your parents susceptible to illnesses, Miss Hyde? Did they ever complain of aches or pains, blurred vision, faints, nosebleeds?"

"I do not wish to discuss my mother and father."

She had spoken too quickly, too curtly. There was a silence. Then, in the same neutral tone: "Which year did you go to after Shoreditch?"

She rubbed her forehead, an ache beginning to spread from her temples. She wanted to be back in bed.

"Somewhere in the early twenty-first. The middle of the nineteenth. Then... a little further forward. Then further back. I'm sorry, I can't..."

One of the women had stood up and was examining a thread pinned to the board on the wall, a strand in a web of many. Rosa trailed off in fascination as she watched.

"You can't confirm for us specific years? It would be helpful. We have references from several centuries, but little that's concrete."

She was leaning away from them, her spine pressed painfully into the back of her chair. It was too much to see it all laid out like that, her whole life a matter of someone else's record in this basement room. There was something terrible about the tone of their interest, at once greedy and probing, cautious and cold. Rosa wished she could stand before them in full Fabulist regalia, straight-backed and bejewelled, and see them bend. But this is not who you are to them. She pulled her thin gown over her knees.

"Our research indicates that you travelled for some time with a man who calls himself Tommy Rust."

"What can you tell us of him, Miss Hyde?"

"In the course of your travels, have you met any other men or women who are like you?"

It was too much. It was too close to that awful plunging fall. Rosa withdrew her hands from under the chair and forced herself to lay them on the table, clasped together. She shook her head. "No more," she said.

"You have never crossed your own path, met yourself?"

She winced. "No more. Please."

"And this journey you have lately made. This is not the usual way for your kind. To go so far, alone, against the tides."

Rosa did not even know whether they expected an answer. Her heart hammered in her throat, her whole body hunched defensively. She looked along the line of shadowed faces.

"Who are you?"

"We are historians, Miss Hyde." The insistent ticking of the watch in the dry air. Six pairs of eyes upon her. "Historians. That is all."

13

God's-Eye

The Historians tried to cut away her matted hair, but she would not let them. They brought her hot meals twice a day, but she did not want anything except the plainest bread and biscuits. She wished that the infirmary room had windows. Without daylight, time seemed to lurch and stutter. Rosa felt brittle as a dry leaf, ready to be washed away by the first and weakest tide which came along.

Though they still kept close watch on her, the Historians stopped short of locking her in the room, assuming perhaps that she was still too weak to wander. Waking restless one night and rising to check that there was nobody behind the mirror, she walked barefoot up the stairs and into the halls of the Museum, white gown trailing the floor. For the most part the rooms were still empty, awaiting their exhibits. Each was labelled by century and by decade, by continent and by country. Vacant glass cases reflected the moonlight shining in through high windows.

On the third floor she found the case she had glimpsed in the tent – the stone slabs cut from the cave where she had daubed charcoal and berry-juice. The images were now reduced to stains of faint colour. She wondered who had discovered them. The lives and passions of the other kind had never occupied much of her thought, but now she found herself imagining them as they descended into the dark cave with lamps held aloft, gasping at what they beheld there. Torn for a moment from the dim narrow channel of their own passage.

What did it mean for them, to know that I am in the world? Suddenly uncomfortable, she drew back from the glass and turned to find a pair of Historians watching her from the doorway. The two men nodded silently to her. One flicked on a torch which sent a beam of white light across the long floor.

"You can't keep me down there," said Rosa. "You can't forbid me to see this place."

"We never forbade you."

"So I can go where I like?"

"Our only concern is for your well being."

The beam of torchlight found her feet and rose to blind her. Rosa shielded her eyes, and the light was diverted to the case behind her.

"How long are you going to keep me here?"

"We are not in the business of keeping you. You may go where you please. When you please."

They always sound the same, she thought, always the same flat, careful tone. As though they are holding me with gloves, the way old things are handled. Crumbling things.

*

The Historians unnerved her, and she already wanted to be gone. As soon as she was strong enough she descended the hundred steps into the encampment below, trying to get her bearings. It would be difficult to slip from the Museum unnoticed. Cars came and went upon the long, dusty road that disappeared over the horizon, only a few rocks marking the landscape.

She noticed a newly-landed biplane being unloaded in a flurry of activity. Rosa stood to one side as crates were passed from hand to hand. The new exhibits were borne ceremonially up the hill, like sacrifices to a temple. It seemed that the Museum did not merely wait for travellers to bring their treasures, but collected its own from all corners of the world.

The warm wind blew over the hills, and Rosa wondered about a departure by air. She was distracted by the sight of men at work within the nearby craters behind the wire fence. They burrowed into the ochre earth with shovels and picks. Below their tools ancient bones lay pale and exposed. She squinted into the distance, to where the sea had once been.

Was it her imagination, or was a great fish laid bare out of the ground there, ribs arched like the pillars of a cathedral, spine longer than a double-decker bus? Rosa walked to the excavation site and leaned on the fence, the better to see what was being dug from the earth. She remembered the rolling of its body below the waves, the flick and spray of its flat tail. The bubbling moan of its song. The millennia that she had passed through like a butter-knife had calcified it, turning flesh to dust and bone to stone.

She had shared the world with it, once. They don't know about that world, fish; only you and I knew it, before the continents were formed or the birds and beasts had found their shape. You used to sing to me under the night sky. There is no one else alive who remembers. These mayflies, they have only the evidence of objects to tell them of the ages that have passed. No memory from their own senses; no smell of sulphur from below the rocks, no still-pulsing leg of hare, blood between their teeth. This is history to them, and history is fleshless bones.

They say that others like me have been here, great fish, but there are none here now. And are there any who went where I did, back before the light of civilisation was lit? Who would really hear, if I told them? Not the Brothers Black, who do not know what it is to travel alone. Not Amber, who is far above the thought of being lost. Not Tommy Rust, since he thinks it is the same as being free.

Perhaps he is right, Rosa, but you are too weak to see it. The question is not how you are to leave this place, but where you are to go. She felt ashamed. Somewhere in the spaces between the years you have fallen and lost your place, and now you are afraid to try and find it again. They say go where you want, when you want, but all you want is to crawl back to a time before such choices were required of you.

A time before you ever dreamed of greatness, or fell short in trying to grasp it. Rosa looked over her shoulder. High above, at the windows of the Museum, faces were watching her.

*

Can you describe for us the sensation of travelling? The Historians sat in a line before her once again, and each new question left her more shaken. *Can you explain to us the circumstances under which it most often occurs?*

"It feels like falling through infinite nothing." Pens skating and hissing across paper. "Backwards, sideways, in all directions. It feels..." Rosa swallowed and closed her eyes. "As though there will never be ground again – until your knees meet the ground."

She barely knew whether she was speaking these things aloud. "The journeys come because of the tides from outside of ourselves. They come because... when... something turns our eyes from the time we are in... when something inside is restless..."

At the Museum, she felt how tides stirred the surface of the air, but none carried her away. She was afraid of where she might be taken, above all still afraid of the pain of landing. She wondered in dismay how long it would be before she could journey as she'd done before that fall.

What do you see? What passes before your eyes when you are between one year and another?

169

"I see cities dissolve and remake themselves. I see mountains fall and seas retreat."

Mountains, cities, seas, centuries. Geometric shapes, perceived simultaneously from every angle. Don't you know that the world looks this way, beneath the thin fabric of its surface? They requested that she draw it for them, but the pencil sat uselessly in her hand. The Historians offered no help or encouragement, but merely watched, keen-eyed. Rosa told them how streets would begin to blur in the corner of her vision, how her head would start to spin as though there was not enough air to breathe. She had little desire to do as they asked, but the more she spoke, the more seemed to spill out of her. With every word she seemed to move further away from herself, drawing up and back, until she looked down at the top of her own head from a giddying height.

She wondered why they were so curious, what purpose their questions might serve. When they became too much she retreated to her room in the medical bay and drew the curtains around her bed. She sat cross-legged and straight-backed upon the mattress, facing the wall.

She imagined Tommy Rust's disembodied grin, hanging over her shoulder once more. "To me," it said, "they always felt like flying."

*

The emptiness of those cavernous round rooms and low-ceilinged corridors. The unceasing quiet splash of the fountains in each courtyard. Staircases led out to scaffold in the starry night where towers and upper rooms were as yet unfinished. In the small hours Rosa moved through these expectant spaces, knowing that half the time she was followed. A Historian or two with a dimmed torch padding at twenty paces behind.

The room where they questioned her was below ground level. She entered it alone for the first time, and quietly flicked on the light. Making her way around the long table, she approached the pin-board on the wall. It had nagged at her thoughts since she had first glimpsed it.

Her heart began to hammer. She recognised her own photograph first, close to the centre, her blurry black-and-white face circled in the centre of a crowd. It could have been London, on a red letter day. Who had taken it, and how had it come to be here? It was hard to tell from the picture how old she was. Eleven, perhaps, or twelve, just beginning to scratch at that splinter beneath her skin.

Following the thread, she found her father and mother – a copy of a familiar picture taken on their wedding day. February fifteenth, nineteen forty-five. Harriet had once told her about the empty pews and the second-hand dress, the puzzled vicar who had been the only witness. A marriage made in secrecy and rooted in sadness. For a long time Rosa stared at the photograph as though hoping it might yield answers. She had not laid eyes on them in more than six years. They looked so young here, so full of resolve. *You must have known by then*, she thought, looking into her mother's sepia face. *What he was. What this would mean for you.* Harriet was smiling, one hand clasped around Robert's where it rested on her waist. You knew what you were tying yourself to, by then, and did it willingly. Her parents' familiarity brought her a kind of relief, but there was distress too. How could more than six years have passed by? And there was envy, because the two people in the picture had one another to hold.

There was no sign of Bella on the board. Higher up, she was not surprised to find Tommy – an older, formal portrait perhaps taken in the nineteenth. His gaze was fixed past the photographer, thumbs tucked into the pockets of his waistcoat. She traced her fingertips across the picture, which was surrounded by indecipherable notes, dates with question marks. *1830? 1843?* Tucked underneath were more photographs of him, eight or nine at least, each taken in a different year, showing him in a different guise.

Amber was pictured in a faded newspaper cutting on the far left of the wall, which looked to be from the same year in which Rosa had first met her. She was posed at the back of a group standing around a painting, long cigarette between her fingers, neat black bob framing her face. She too had been circled in red pen, and plastered liberally in notes.

Rosa's eyes flicked from one image to the next as she looked for the Brothers Black. She could not see them, and as her gaze passed across the sea of unfamiliar faces she found herself stepping back. In her eagerness to find those she knew, she had not paused to take in the whole picture. She grew still. The size of the display imposed itself gradually.

There are so many of us. So very many of us. A web of hundreds, scattered to the centuries, linked by thin strands of thread. How strange this possibility had seemed, that night in the nineteenth before Tommy's fire, how miraculous. Where is that thrill now? Why does the sight of all those unknown faces make you want to lift a hand and hide your eyes like a frightened child?

Rosa's sense of herself shivered, somehow, and shrunk. She sank onto a chair, still staring upwards at the wall of nameless travellers. The clock on the wall bit deeper and deeper into the night.

*

"Have you nothing to ask of us?

She was still too numb to offer much resistance. The Historians measured the proportions of her limbs and around her skull.

They monitored her temperature and heart rate whilst running and at rest. They tested her with picture cards, with word games and wooden puzzles which she toyed with apathetically. They questioned her, at last, into silence.

"Do you not wish to know what we are building here? What else we have uncovered about you, about others like you?"

They seemed baffled by her indifference. It is as though, she considered saying to them, someone had displayed a sudden interest in why you choose to exhale after inhaling, or why you go to sleep one day and wake up the next. But there was no sense in explaining, in expecting them to understand.

So where do you want to be, gypsy girl? What remains now of the hopes you held when you left the Hydes behind? She could barely remember a time before Tommy, a time when she had dreamed of different, earthbound things. All she really wanted was to sleep, but sleep no longer came. When a plane arrived bearing crates of fossils wrapped in delicate tissue, she crept into the cretaceous hall at midnight to look at them. Imprinted on each piece of stone, fern fronds, spiral shells. The little finger-bones of frogs.

What did she want? Rosa opened a cabinet and slipped out the thinnest, lightest slab, which bore the image of a feathered wing. Turned it over in her hands. The only possible answer came as she was tucking the object into her bag back in her room, where it nestled amongst her other possessions as though it had always been there. There was only one place where the cold wind of the too-wide world might not reach her.

She sat down in the middle of the floor in the dark room, arms wrapped around her knees. She laughed, a dry helpless sound, and kept on laughing.

*

Where might Robert and Harriet be, in the seventh year after she had left them? The Historians' passing mention of *the Shoreditch year* suggested the existence of a record, or map. A god's-eye view.

Next to the basement room with the pinboard display were several storerooms, a kitchen, and what appeared to be a small library or catalogue system. One night when she was certain that she was not being followed, Rosa descended the stairs and rattled every drawer until she found the one which contained the keys. She opened cupboards and stood on tiptoe to see what was on the highest shelves. There was much paperwork relating to the construction of the Museum, the assembly of its collections. Files on each of the Historians, which she flipped through and discarded without interest.

At last she found a heavy box of files with surname tabs sticking out of the top. One of them was her own. Heart in her throat, she heaved it out onto a nearby table, and then stood hesitant. Her hand moved of its own accord to cover her eyes. Between her fingers she read the label on the box, and felt an odd shiver run from the base of her back to the nape of her neck. *You know what they call us,* Tommy had said, *those who know we exist?* Now she had found out, and wished she had not.

Rosa drew a deep breath. She only wanted the smallest fragment of the knowledge which might now be at her fingertips. A slip of the fingers, the wandering of an undisciplined eye, and she might learn more than she could bear to know. Just Robert and Harriet. Just 'forty-five. Nothing else.

She ignored the tab, near the back of the box, labelled *Rymer*. Her fingers trembled as she flipped through countless others – *Eischer, Ekwu, Fei, Harding, Hare* – until she reached *Hyde*.

All she wanted was to know where they were living, seven years after Shoreditch. Weariness filled her body. To know how to get back.

Rosa did not want the Historians to see her go. Whatever they claimed, she felt sure they would try to stop her. She watched the coming and going of the cars and planes until she had a sense of their routine. She waited until the Historians had ceased to peer down from the windows each time she went outside. Each night she unpacked and re-packed her bag. She did not feel ready, but she knew she never would.

She left the Museum on a bright, cloudless morning. From the top of the Museum steps, she could see the sun reflected in blinding beams from the biplane's wings. With a glance up at the windows she made a dash for it, descending the stone stairs as quickly as she could and hiding behind a parked motorcar. When the crates had been unloaded from the back of the plane and the pilot had disappeared into one of the trailers to refresh himself, she heaved herself and her bag onto the plane's back seat, covering her head with the tarpaulin. She had never flown before. When the craft took off with a series of violent bumps, she almost yelled in panic.

They had been airborne for an hour before she dared to peer out. Spread in the midday haze, a flat landscape of burnt brown and lush green, the plane's shadow rippling over rocks. No sign of human habitation came into sight until dusk, when the moon sat low on the clouds like a pearl upon a pillow, and city lights winked into being far below.

Somewhere down there would be a tide that was flowing gently into the past. That would carry her to the place she least wanted to go; the only place that was left to her. Back to nineteen forty-five.

Part Three

14

Red Letter

Rosa was not sure she had ever loved her parents. In fact she was not certain that she loved anyone, apart from Harris Black, and then only because he was so easy to love. For the most part, she felt that she was empty of real human feeling.

Only two things seemed to offer evidence to the contrary. First, that she had once sat at the back of a theatre on Drury Lane and wept as the gypsy girl Arline sang of marble halls. Second, that the simple sight of lit windows at night had begun to tear her heart out. She would be walking along an unknown street, head down, bag upon her back, when suddenly some stranger's parlour or bedroom would catch her eye beyond the glass. They stopped her short, these intimate little tableaux, these snatches of mayfly lives. They dredged something up from out of the depths of her.

When she woke in a bare little bedroom, it was to the now-familiar numbness. She lay staring at the whitewashed ceiling, caring little where she was or who she was with. She turned over and found herself alone in the bed. Then she heard the sound of voices from downstairs, and sat up.

Nineteen forty-five. The pillow was strewn with strands of her newly-cut hair. A blackout curtain covered the window. In her dreams, she recalled dimly, skaters had whirled and danced on a frozen lake. The smell of pine needles. She swung her legs over the side of the bed and sat for a moment with her head in her hands, breathing slowly. She felt a passing wave of anger at Tommy Rust, for being somewhere that she wasn't, decades away.

But you came back, Rosa. You *chose* to come back. This place has pulled you back in the way the moon lures water. You do not want to be here, but have crossed decades and continents to be here. She was ashamed by the strength of her relief.

The village below lay quiet, and not a soul passed by on the road outside. The days had seemed short when she was a child, but now she wondered how she had ever filled them. She went with Bella into the field behind the house and watched her sister steer a bike between the sprouting lines of corn. The earth was weighed with the previous night's rain, the sky still hung with clouds. Rosa ran her fingers along the tips of the long grass-blades, her hair tucked beneath her mother's woollen hat.

Bella wobbled and shouted, and Rosa ran ahead to help her, taking hold of the handle-bars. The two made slow progress towards the far hedgerow, beyond which stood the village church. Bella's face was puckered in concentration, her legs pumping hard. When they reached the gate she stopped and dismounted, pulling the bike away from Rosa and then forward through a hole in the hedge.

Rosa followed. They emerged into a dip below the hill on which the church stood. Gravestones were scattered in the shadow of a broad yew tree, whose twisted roots delved into the soil. Everywhere was a creeping green moss. Bella wheeled her bike towards the tree and left it leaning against the trunk, jumping between the flat graves as though they were rocks in a river.

After a few minutes absorbed in this she looked suddenly over her shoulder at Rosa and said, "You know how Granddad died? Daddy told me. He got shot out of the sky over Belgium."

A robin landed on a nearby headstone and tilted its head. Rosa wondered how much her sister had pieced together. Perhaps she did not even see enough yet for the world to seem mysterious. "Father told you that?"

"Yes." Bella hopped sideways. "Granddad doesn't have a proper coffin, even. Daddy thinks the Germans just put him in a pit with a hundred others."

She hopped onto the next stone. Rosa watched her, captivated by the change in her, the stringy limbs and the guileless face that was a miniature of Robert's. Where was I, she tried to recall, at ten? Not angry then – not quite. Not as wise as I wanted to be. Acquainted with the terror of Hiroshima, though not yet with the stranger from the garden.

Bella now spoke in sentences, had fully-formed thoughts, and Rosa did not know what to say to her. Absurdly, she was discomforted by this tangible proof that the Hydes had gone on existing in her absence. It threatened to steal away the very familiarity for which she had returned. If forty-five was not a constant, a fixed point in the wheeling, expanding universe, what was she doing here?

Bella had known her own forty-five, her own afternoons beside the wireless, and rushed December journeys and ration-coupon dinners. Her own clashes, perhaps, with Harriet and Robert. Rosa felt at once repelled and intrigued. A part of her fervently hoped that her sister hadn't found a way to love them.

"Does Mother ever talk about me?" she asked. "Does Father?"

No reply. Bella only blinked at her, and Rosa covered the moment with an uneasy laugh. "I don't suppose they do. Does he ever play with you, Bella? Has he taken you with him, to London, on his special day?"

"Two times. I didn't like it. I couldn't see anything and there were too many people."

If her small life did not yet orbit around the pull of that day, there was still hope. Rosa attempted a smile for her.

Then Bella said, "When you're dead you can't see anything, or hear anything, or think anything any more. You forget how to be sad or angry about dying."

In the dull light of the day her sister's brown eyes looked coal-black. A gust of wind blew her hair across her face. "Sometimes," she said, "I imagine what it's like to be under the ground."

Rosa felt cold. "*Bella...*" she began, shocked, but did not know how to continue. An ache took hold of her temples and sinuses, and she raised a hand unconsciously to check for blood from her nose. Her fingers came away clean.

They regarded one another. Rosa took a step back, and remembered with a pang the duckling-haired toddler, the delighted bubbling giggle. Bouncing Bella on her knee in front of the window, brushing her hair before bed. The memories threatened to burst a dam she hadn't known was there, and she pushed them down.

"You come here a lot?" she asked. "Ladybug?"

Bella shrugged, suddenly shy. She clambered over a fallen branch and went loping between the graves, up the hill towards the church, bending to pick up daffodils and stray feathers. Rosa perched on a headstone and looked out across the neighbouring fields. There was a row of allotments, soil thick with fresh lettuces and swaying carrot-tops, dwarf peas climbing over canes. The road wound between a cluster of cottages and then past the school-house, the post office. It was an unbearably tranquil view.

She spotted a woman in a short-sleeved dress riding a bicycle, basket stuffed with brown parcels, and a man heading into the allotments with a shovel over his shoulder. The sun broke through the clouds for a passing moment. She closed her eyes and lifted her face, but little warmth had yet reached England in that month.

When her sister came back down the hill, arms loaded with yellow flowers, Rosa pushed the bicycle and they walked back through the cornfield together. When they were nearly back at the house she looked at the top of the yellow head bobbing beside her and said uncertainly, "Bella."

Feather behind her ear, attention turned in obedience. "What?"

"Do you remember me?"

*

Peeling potatoes with Harriet over the sink. Thumbs cold under the water, earth in the plughole. Silence between them. Rosa glanced periodically sideways at her mother, who was trussed in a grey apron, head bent. Each new line on her face needed to be seen and seen again, until it was no longer a shock. The bones of her cheeks and nose showed different shadows now, the silver in her hair catching the light.

"Corned beef and cabbage tonight," said Harriet. "And soup for tomorrow's lunch. I might have to send you into the village for some bread."

Rosa nodded. Her mood was on a tightrope, liable to overbalance at the slightest thing. Since the beach she had been subject to these changes. Outside the kitchen window, the late afternoon sunlight flickered through budding branches.

"And suitable new things, Rosa. I don't have enough dresses for you, or shoes. We can take a bus. Your father will need to go to the bank. Perhaps on Tuesday."

"I take it the inheritance is holding out," said Rosa. Her mother did not respond, sweeping the peelings into her apron. Bella's head bobbed in and out of view as she swung from a low limb of the apple tree at the end of the garden. "You know she goes to the graveyard, don't you? I think she goes there often."

Harriet dropped the potatoes into a pan of boiling water, each in turn. She wiped her hands together. "Are you asking after her well being?"

Rosa wanted to tell her what Bella had said that morning. But it would have felt meaningless in the repetition. It was not just what she had said, after all, but her manner, her appearance. Rosa shrugged, while Harriet rummaged in the drawer for a box of matches.

"I teach her myself, as I taught you. She's just as able to stay cheerfully occupied as you were at that age. She loves to draw pictures, to be outdoors."

Something of the old anger stirred. Rosa made only the most half-hearted attempt to hold her tongue. "I'm glad you can carry on convincing yourself of that, Mother. I'll tell you what will happen in a couple of years. She'll turn out so peculiar, you won't know what to do with her."

Harriet regarded her with a clear, considered gaze, eyebrows raised. "If you think she ought to have had a companion," she said, "it's a little late."

There it was again: that jolt, that intruding realisation that the clock had not stopped the night she left the Shoreditch house. Rosa turned away to wash her hands, scrubbing too hard.

I have the measure of them, she tried to tell herself, I've had the measure of the Hydes for a long time. But there were paths she had never been down. Places where solid walls were in fact doors, leading into spaces which perhaps had always been there, unexplored. Were there things which Bella saw, which Harriet saw, which even Robert saw, that she didn't? Rosa shook her head to dispel the notion, but it would not be so easily chased away.

She looked again at Harriet, and felt a curiosity that was alien to her. If Harriet had never met Robert Hyde she would have come through the war with the other women who were finding their feet in that time. Since men were in such short supply she might never have married, might have risen to become headmistress of a town school and bought a smart apartment, lined the walls with books. The landscape of the age had changed just a little too late for Harriet.

How soon did he tell you? wondered Rosa, watching her mother bend over to light the fire in the back of the oven. On that first day, when you left the library together and took a stroll along the Thames, staying out until long after dark? Unlikely. Later perhaps, when promises had already been exchanged and your talk had turned to the life you would share. Or not until it was too late: not until you had taken his hand one winter night and found the city shifting around you, the New Year fireworks fading from the sky, the hours sweeping you back together.

Did you believe him? Harriet had straightened up again, untied her apron. Rosa watched her tucking back stray strands of hair, neatly stacking the plates from the draining rack. Or did you laugh in derision, turn your back and walk away, stare in dumb distrust?

Such questions would never have occurred to her before. But the Museum had put them in her mind. Somehow the Historians, with their strange, stilted questions, had crept into her head and rearranged the furniture. She could not yet say, though, precisely what they had moved.

She turned back towards the window. Bella had climbed into the higher branches of the apple tree, and sat with her feet dangling in mid-air.

"It would be nice if you could go with him," said Harriet, from behind her. "Next month. Bella never took to it, and you know I've been as many times as I can bear to."

Rosa scuffed her foot along the skirting-board. "Must I?"

"You used to adore it."

"When I was *eight,* Mother. Nine, maybe."

"You used to count down the days, and make me tie up your hair in ribbons."

"*Mother...*"

"He's gone alone, five years out of the last seven. See if you can't find it in yourself to spare one day for him."

There was so much to infuriate in this that Rosa could only laugh. "It ought to make him nervous, going back there time after time." She faced Harriet, whose arms were folded defensively across her chest. "It can't be long now until he runs into himself there, and then what will he do?"

He'll see an old man, she did not say, weak and endlessly foolish. He'll try to cover his eyes, but it will not be enough. She did not say, perhaps that's why he taught me to fear such moments: because he knows that if he were ever to look into his own eyes, it would be the end of everything.

*

But you chose to come back. It was alarming how quickly the familiar rhythms took hold of her again, how the raging colours of her journeys were already beginning to dim. Perhaps, Rosa, you never ran from here at all. Perhaps you only dreamed a long dream to stave away the boredom. Made an invention of the kind of people you wished more than anything to meet, had them tell you what you wanted more than anything to hear.

Listen: that song playing on the wireless. That episode of *It's That Man Again*. She sowed turnips on the allotment with her father, watching the care he took over each tiny seed-hole, hands gentle as he patted down the loose earth. While her mother seemed always to be balancing on the brink of a dozen devastating questions, Robert had retreated from them. He hummed to himself, and chattered about the day's news. He smiled benignly at her, as though she'd never been away.

"Did you hear the news this morning? They had a special report."

"I didn't." But you must have heard it many times, Father. Forgotten it, heard it all over again.

"I never cease to find the Kamikaze extraordinary. These chaps, they're volunteers, you know." He straightened up, squinting into the sun. "They call themselves warriors. The man on the wireless said he'd seen one drop from the sky quicker than a kestrel on a mouse. No hesitation."

His hand made an arc in the air. His brows furrowed. "I wonder what they think about on the descent."

"Somebody lied to them, Father. That's all." Rosa held his spade as he knelt on the earth, checking the height of the tomato-canes. "Somebody told them death was beautiful."

"And they are so young. What a terrible waste. Such brave men should have died for our side."

Snowdrops sprouted in a thick carpet from every verge, pink blossom on the apple trees. Three weeks after her return, she was beginning to feel that everything outside of nineteen forty-five was a mere fiction. This made it possible to think of the journeys without pain, to enjoy them as tales of great deeds and dangers are enjoyed from the safety of an armchair. The year wrapped its tendrils around her and lulled her down into itself.

Bella began to creep into Rosa's bed late at night, without any explanation. Rosa felt her sister's icy feet against her shins and shuffled over to make room, the two of them huddled close beneath the covers. "Do you want to know where I've been, Bella?" she whispered. "I could tell you about the twenty-first. Or Seysair Tower, in the fifteenth. Or Paris, before this war..."

Bella only looked at her blankly, and Rosa tried again. "Or I could tell you about Tommy... or Amber... or the Brothers Black..."

Bella shook her head and turned over. She slept on her back with her mouth wide open, plaits at right-angles, eyelids twitching. Rosa wondered whether she dreamed of lying deep in the dark earth, below the spring flowers. Her own sleep was flooded by a frozen sea. She heard the rumbling groan of the great fish, smelled blood and smoke, and woke gasping.

*

Harriet threw away her travelling clothes without asking – the garments stained with blood and soot and grease, stinking and riddled with holes. She had carried these things for a long time, but it seemed churlish to protest. Rosa went with her mother to the nearest town and allowed herself to be measured waist and bust, to be shuttled from one shop to the next.

She caught Harriet peering sideways through the curtains as she stripped to try on a blouse, and realised how strange it must be, losing a child and regaining a woman. Indifferent to her body, she had herself barely paused to notice the change. She looked down in a kind of trance, passed her hands down her belly and the tops of her legs. Is this the shape of who I am?

The rough cotton of the blouse was itchy against her back. They sat side-by-side on the bus on the way home, and Rosa saw how closely pursed her mother's lips were, how pink the end of her nose. For once she felt the urge to make peace.

"Mother," she said awkwardly. "It's all right."

"How can I know that?" said Harriet, too quietly.

"I'm here. Nobody… *hurt* me."

Harriet looked at her. There was a long silence as the bus rattled over a series of potholes. "Seven…" she began in a choked voice. "*Seven years,* and I've imagined every… I've lost you in every… and now you don't want to talk."

Rosa clenched her fists in her lap. Once she had imagined coming to their door in her Fabulist robes. How they would fall to their knees before her.

"You won't tell me where, and what, you've come back from."

"For goodness' sake," said Rosa, throat tight. She wished her mother would hold on to some dignity.

"It's only normal, Rosa, that I'd want to know."

"Just because I came back," she said, "it doesn't mean that you have any right to me. I didn't come back for you. You, or *him*."

As Harriet clutched the shopping bags in her lap, gaze fixed ahead, Rosa felt the fuse of her temper ignite. It had never taken much. She raised her voice. "All right. If you want to hear it so badly... I lost my virginity in eighteen forty-three, to a man I'd met four hours earlier outside a theatre. I had other lovers, after. More than I can recall. I stole things I'd no need to steal. I ate raw flesh when I was starving in —"

"Enough, *enough*." The other passengers on the bus were turning to stare. Harriet's cheeks burned, and she stared out of the window. Shaking, satisfied, Rosa sat back in her seat. Fields rolled past, woods carpeted with bluebells, blacked-out road signs.

"Don't you dare repeat any of that to your father."

"I was wondering where you would be by now, without him," said Rosa.

"You've a nerve to ask." Harriet turned around. There were tears in her eyes. "You've quite a nerve."

*

On the morning of May eighth, Harriet woke her early with a cup of tea, throwing the blackout curtain wide and perching on the end of the bed. Rosa sat up against the pillow and sipped, staring

189

into the cup to avoid looking at her mother.

"Will you go?" asked Harriet. "Put on something smart, wash your face, and don't make a fuss? I can't bear the thought of him going alone again."

When Rosa didn't answer, her mother sighed. Her hair drooped on each side of her face and trailed down the back of her neck. She looked as though she had not slept. There was a deep crease in her forehead, and she hesitated before saying heavily, "What is it that you want from us?"

Rosa looked up, caught off guard.

"On the night you returned, you said that you meant to stay. Why would that be, since you have made it plain how you despised us, still despise us? Since you won't say, I can only guess. You might think I know nothing, Rosa, but there's no mother who does not know when her child is broken-hearted."

Robert could be heard pottering in the kitchen downstairs, the whistle of the kettle, the crackle and buzz of the wireless. Rosa sat very still.

"A few years younger, I might have told you it will pass. But I think we're beyond that. You have seen enough of the world."

Outside the window, the sun had risen over the fields. Rosa closed her eyes. She wrapped her hands more tightly around her teacup, felt the steam dampening her face. Harriet's words had hardly reached her, yet. But she knew that they would be expanding inside her for days, weeks to come. Burning up all in their path, scorching old tangles away until there was room for – what? Can anything new grow, here?

"I'll go," she said.

"Thank you."

"I'll take care of him, Mother," she added on impulse. "Don't worry."

The bus into London was noisy and packed. Robert, in a clean shirt and with his hair neatly combed, shuffled in his seat, restless with excitement. He joined in heartily with the outbursts of song which broke out from time to time. He turned to smile at Rosa, and she tried to return the warmth of his look, arranging her face as best she could. She remembered, as she knew he must, the eager little girl bundled in her best overcoat, clinging to his hand. She had sat upon his shoulders staring over the heads of the throng, until she grew too tall.

They got off the bus when they began to hear music, and walked in towards Westminster from Marylebone. Rosa watched her father's face as his gaze darted about, from the brass band outside the pub, to the pair of American soldiers whooping as they raised their star-spangled flag, to the woman in a hairnet hanging out of her window to get a better view.

"To the palace?" Robert suggested.

"If you like."

His cheeks were flushed, his head held high. He was grinning like a schoolboy. Rosa remembered the last time they had done this together, when she had been twelve years old, too wrapped in her own restlessness and resentment to pay him much heed. As she watched him now, she felt as though she was seeing him for the first time. She was not at all inclined to laugh, as Tommy had once done at the very thought of Robert Hyde's predicament.

This was the centre of it all, the sun around which she had spent seventeen years in motion. For a moment Rosa wanted desperately to feel the pull of it as Robert did: to be overwhelmed and consumed by it, to the exclusion of all else. To feel so thunderingly alive, so *present*, even if it was only for a few brief hours.

Her father led the way, weaving expertly through the crowds, nimble as a much younger man. She kept up as best she could. As the noise of cheering rose to a deafening pitch, as a shaft of sunlight broke through the clouds to illuminate the boats upon the river, it was distress rather than elation that stirred her heart. She glanced about, dreading that at any moment she would spy a second Robert close at hand, the back of his fair head, little daughter hoisted onto his back. Such a sighting would be more than she could bear.

The press of people seemed suddenly suffocating. *Any moment now*. Any moment and you will see her freckled face turned over her shoulder towards you. She will blink curiously; you will raise a slow hand in greeting. There is nothing you can say to her. There is nothing worth promising her, worth warning her against. You will not even hide your eyes, because you know that Tommy Rust would laugh.

She jumped when she felt a hand upon her shoulder, but it was the Robert of now, hanging back to find where she had got to. For a moment she failed to hide the fear in her look. His broad smile wavered, and he squeezed her shoulder uncertainly.

"Are you all right?"

"Yes, yes... The crowds, I'd forgotten..."

"We can find a cafe later, if you like. Sit down somewhere quiet."

Someone jostled them from behind, knocking Robert's hand from her shoulder. But he took it again, more deliberately this time. She realised that he was staring at her without dipping his gaze, no longer glancing around her to other things that had caught his interest. His eyes widened a little.

"Rosie," he said. "You were always my best red-letter-day friend."

Her throat grew tight. She nodded. Ahead of them, a group of boys was scaling the palace fence, a police-horse turning and stamping its foot.

"It hasn't been the same, since you've been gone."

Rosa shook her head. She raised a stubborn fist to the tears speeding down from the corner of her eye. "That's not true, though."

"What?" The people surrounding them had begun to roar, straining for a view of the palace balcony, waving their hats high above their heads.

"That's not true. It's always been the same for you. Your little world, it would be the same with or without us."

She was not sure how much he had heard. His face registered puzzlement. Then in the distance two small figures emerged onto the balcony, and the noise rose still further, to a deafening pitch. A girl perched in a nearby tree tossed a handful of confetti into the air, and as it fluttered down Robert Hyde's features were transformed. He tilted his head back, all the lines etched into his skin by time and grief smoothed over. He closed his eyes, and laughed aloud.

Rosa felt no portion of his peace. *Father*, she wanted to say. Father, Frank Hyde and millions like him lie buried still beneath the foreign mud. And there will be more, in decades not yet written. There is nothing but the long fall through empty air. Wave your flag high and cheer yourself hoarse, but nothing is truly ended. Nothing is made right.

She had come here from the Museum only because there was nowhere else to go. Because she had journeyed and reached the perilous edge of herself. It had come to this. She was merely her father's daughter, treading in another blind circle as though it might bring her home.

"I don't feel well." She pulled at his sleeve. "Father, I don't feel —" And there, over the heads of the crowd, a glimpse of a chalk-pale face. Hair flat against his skull. There, gone again. She pushed her way out, nauseous now and light-headed. Faces blurred as she passed them in seemingly endless succession.

She turned sharply into an alleyway, afraid that she was going to fall, and felt something hot and wet trickling from her nose. Raising her fingers, she saw scarlet blood. She leaned against the wall, trying to stay upright as the scene flickered around her.

He was standing there among the dustbins, just yards away. Her gaze travelled upwards over his steel-capped boots, his dark uniform. The gun at his belt.

"Not yet," whispered Rosa. "Oh please, not yet."

The soldier's face was cold and white as marble. His eyes were shadowed hollows. He took a step towards her, and she felt her body lurch forward into nothingness.

15

Long Fall

O ut of place, out of time. Out of sight of any familiar face. It had come too soon. A bandage torn away before the wound had stopped bleeding. The Angel of Death had not taken her as she thought he must, but sent her falling forward.

But perhaps it was all the same. Dislocated, she was dimly aware of the place she had come to. She walked streets which were only noise and blurred movement, coloured grey. Mile after rolling mile of pavements. It was as though her ears had been plugged, leaving only dizziness and a low dull buzz. Stay awake, Rosa. Don't sink so deep into it, or you won't come up again.

She had left her belongings behind at the Hyde home when she took the bus to London with her father. A careless choice. Now she would have to begin again. The thought of Robert refused to leave her as she fought to find her feet in the London-that-had-now-come. She could not shake the image of him turning in the red letter day crowd to find her gone, eyes searching for a fox-haired head, voice raised to call for her. She imagined him staying until after sundown, checking every alleyway, grabbing the elbows of street-sweepers and off-duty policemen. *Have you seen...? Did you notice...?* Children skipping home below the street lamps, mouths sticky with the day's revelry, clasping their mothers' hands.

She thought of him sitting alone on the bus home with his hat in his lap. Walking slowly up the garden path, stepping carefully between the oblivious snails. Wordlessly meeting Harriet's gaze as she opened the door.

Their story had continued without her before, and would continue now. This was still fresh to her, still cause for a kind of wonder. She had not seen them at once from every angle, but only face-on, one plane at a time. They were not fully revealed to her, her parents; they were puzzles with missing pieces. And then there was Bella, whom she had known from a wrinkled little creature in a hospital cot. *Bella*. She could barely begin to puzzle Bella out at all.

The strange thing, the strangest thing was that she had intended to stay. She still could not believe it. If she had crept into the bedroom of her younger self and whispered it, the other Rosa would have laughed.

But that Rosa did not know about the frozen beach and the black wave. The stillness of the Museum. How the years unweave everything. If it had not been for the pale-faced soldier in the alleyway, the sudden lurch of her body into the empty void, she would have stayed.

*

The fall had taken her nearly a century forward, to a London that was a series of wide islands submerged in a dark sea. Dappled clouds passed across the mirrored panels of skyscrapers, which angled their roofs towards the sun like light-starved flowers. Through the day the surface of the city rippled and shifted, creaked and sighed. On the ground the long shadows of towers criss-crossed the streets.

The life of the city was twenty storeys up and it was subterranean, where the ceiling-screens had been calibrated to give the feel of daylight. Grass grew between curb-cracks fifty feet beneath the pavements. Grilling food smells and engine-smoke smells filled the hot, close air; every surface was damp and greasy.

Rosa moved deeper and deeper into the maze of concrete

archways. In violet-lit tunnels, mile after mile of crops swum in shallow water. Pale roots reached down into nothing. She watched the small army of white-clad figures who moved among the rows, spraying the new seedlings and harvesting what was fully grown. They wore masks over their mouths. She recalled briefly being paid to vacuum carpets and wash bed-linen in an age gone by. They had given her crumpled pound notes in a brown envelope. Down here in the half-dark, nothing would be asked of her. If she chose to, she could work until she was tired enough to sleep.

But no. London was washed through by countless tides. She would be taken again before she could so much as catch her breath, and where to? How many more years away? There was no knowing.

Her body began to shake at the thought. Better to be somewhere where the tides would not touch her. She left London with her eyes cast to the ground, glad that she had no companion to witness her cowardice.

*

Rosa took a train which flickered through the causeway below the sea, winding out onto dry land among woodlands and vineyards. Germany, perhaps, or further east? She slept with her forehead pressed against the window then disembarked to walk as though in a new dream. Steering clear of cities, she wandered far to find the places where there were still farmsteads and villages, fields and woods.

Empty barns had sufficed, after losing Tommy for the first time, before the Fabulist. They would have to do once again. Abandoned warehouses and shearing-sheds. Rosa picked berries and mushrooms, trapped rabbits and slow partridges. Pulled herbs from the earth. Lit little fires in forest clearings, licked fat and blood from her fingers. It was not such a strain here, this business of surviving. But there was a strain inside her chest, the tightness of a string stretched to its limit. There was no flavour to anything she cooked, only the taste of smoke and ash.

So far out of the way, it was impossible to gain any grasp upon the time she was in. She hardly cared to. The only people she might encounter here were those in poverty, those living in old and dying ways. No doubt the cities would spread, soon, to cover all of this. The tides would cross over one another, troubled and fast-flowing, bleeding together until there was no distinction any more.

All those days and decades and centuries, all those roads awaiting her feet, and all she wanted to do was hide in the woods. Perhaps if she searched long enough, hard enough, she might find a way back to nineteen forty-five, but she had no heart for it. Have you a heart for anything, Rosa? Have you a heart at all? All she had ever reached for dissolved in her hands like so much cloud. Perhaps there is nothing that does not go this way, that does not turn to melting mist the moment you draw close.

She lifted clothes from washing-lines, lingering after each theft, in overgrown gardens and behind walls. She did not give the act much consideration. But the windows, those windows, drew her gaze. At dusk when lights were lit behind glass Rosa crept near, barely daring to breathe. These intimate little tableaux. These snatches of lives so utterly unlike her own.

There was never much to see, but still she would watch for hours. Snatches of talk overheard in a foreign tongue. Perhaps a solitary man reading in an armchair. Children eating at a table, dog on the floor, watching them eagerly for scraps. The flickering colours of a television. Shadows moving in a bedroom behind drawn blinds. Rosa pulled up the hood of her coat, and laid a hesitant hand against the glass. A dark figure from out of the night and the rain, slipping away again without trace.

He made a ghost of me, she thought. The Angel of Death.

One evening, walking through a valley, she saw setting sun light the windows of the houses on the hillside opposite. From far away, they were brightest gold.

*

In this way she drifted for uncounted months. When it grew too cold and everything green began to die, she fell upon the pity of strangers. Knocking on their doors she practised simple words and gestures she hoped they might understand. *Traveller. Lost. Hungry. Food?* Some turned her away; some let her in.

Rosa slept amongst hay-bales in their leaking barns, ate gratefully from the tables of wary homesteaders. Their children watched her over the rims of soup-bowls, shuffled near to peer through spare-room doors, as Bella had once done. In every home, she liked to touch things. Her fingertips met the cold slate of a mantelpiece, soft bedclothes. Hearthstones still warm from the evening's fire. The arching spine of a cat. These things all solid beneath her hands; but she knew they would not remain so, if she tried to stay.

"You can lodge the winter, if you help me plant come spring." An old woman with fluent English put her up in a room which had once been a child's. Rain dripped through the ceiling into buckets, and beyond the window, the faraway lights of a city glimmered ominously.

"Thank you," said Rosa. "But I cannot."

The woman, who seemed to live alone save for a pair of snarling dogs in the yard, looked suspiciously at her. "Are you some kind of... fugitive?"

"A traveller. I told you. I can't stay."

"Where are you travelling to? I'm telling you, stay clear of that city. They live in filth – of every kind."

"I'm not going to the city."

"Where are you going?"

"I need to sleep now," said Rosa. "If you don't want me here, I'll be gone."

She had no answer to the question, and the realisation kept her awake. She didn't dare think of anything beyond the day-by-day business of food and sleep and shelter. Why come to these doorsteps with lowered eyes and empty hands? Why not enter as you once did, with a gold band about your forehead and jewelled pins in your hair, with your face painted white and the future on your lips?

Because that future is come and gone, now, and nothing is known beyond it. Whatever you dreamed or feared you would become, in nineteen forty-five or at Seysair or before Tommy Rust's fire, it was not this.

Would you even have known yourself, if in your younger years you had woken to find this Rosa beside your bed? Would you have known this shabby stranger with her hard face, hard hands, hoarse voice? She moves differently, warily, shoulders hunched and eyes watchful. She smells of far-off places, of too many nights in unsheltered doorways. The mud of millennia is caked to her boots.

*

More than a year later, on a mountainside between still pines she slipped a little way forward, carried by a quiet tide which chilled the back of her neck. The landing did not hurt, but she felt the ache of the journey in her joints. Rosa wondered whether others might have been drawn close by the same current. She caught herself longing for a mere few minutes' conversation with someone who would know her name, recognise her face.

It was some months and many miles before she began to hear

rumours of another traveller, a man who had walked out of the trees wearing peculiar clothes and speaking an unknown language. Rosa held her hopes in check, as she traced the whispers to their source. That wall at the Museum had shown so many faces.

And yet she knew him at once when she glimpsed him from behind, seated alone at the bar in a dark hostel, a whisky in his hand. Rain raged through the night outside. Rosa approached slowly and sat herself upon the stool next to him. She waited until he turned, spying her from beneath the brim of his hat. Below the fire-lit pine-wood eaves, they regarded one another in silence.

"Three, for me," she said at last. "Or thereabouts. Venice, the twenty-first…"

He gave a cursory nod, held up five fingers.

"Where's Harris?"

He rubbed his forehead. He shook his head. For a long moment he seemed unable to speak.

"I'll buy you a drink," he said.

"That's very kind."

He gave a nod to the barman, indicated her, then his own glass. "Don't say that 'til you tasted it. They got nothin' good here." The veins were standing out on his temples.

"Cheers, then."

Rosa took a small sip of the amber liquid she was handed. It was barely strong enough to warm her throat. She swirled it around in the bottom of the glass, and asked again without looking at him. "Why isn't Harris with you?"

"I lost him," said Nate, almost too quietly to be heard. "We lost each other."

A panicked flaring in the pit of her stomach. "Where?" asked Rosa.

"Passin' forward from the late twentieth. Just an ordinary journey. When I landed, he wasn't with me." Nate's whole body seemed to sink in his seat, down towards the bar. His voice slurred. "I been lookin' ever since, 'cross five or six countries, followin' tides of all kinds. You ain't seen him, have you? Or any sign?"

Rosa knew she should lay a hand on his shoulder, speak some word of comfort, but she could not do it. "I'm sorry, Nate."

He shrugged. "That's no use to me."

She drank with him, while behind them the place began to empty of its few patrons. The wind howling in the woods outside whenever the door was opened, rain spattering across the floor. Rosa tried to feel amazed by their meeting, fortunate that in all of the wide world she had stumbled upon this man. This little piece of Montparnasse, of a brighter time.

"We found each other pretty easy, huh?" he said, seeming to read her thoughts. "Though I bet you'd rather I was a certain someone else."

Remembering something Tommy had once done, she kissed her palm and held it to the air. "Bless the tide that brought me here. I'm glad to see you."

His mouth gave the smallest twitch. "Drink that slow, now. Must have already gone to your head."

He did not ask what had become of her after Venice, and she was glad. She would not have wished to put the terror and the rawness of it into words for anyone, Nate Black least of all.

Nate's dirty fingernails toyed with a stray coin on the bar, spinning it one way, then the other. She remembered the Brothers playing cards at the cabaret, their hands so fast and their heads bent together. If it was possible for the two of them to be torn apart, what else could be broken? Oh Harris, please don't be too far. Please be with someone who is looking after you, some smiling angel. Rosa emptied her glass.

"You were no longer with Amber?" she asked. "Or Tommy?"

"She went her own way, long before, in search of some precious Chi-nese idol or other. He weren't with us either, but he ain't far off, and I know where he was headed."

"Where?" Before she could stop herself.

"You know how often he's spoken of Hiroshima."

A line of white-hot light cracked the night sky in the window behind them. Nate reached the bottom of his glass and stood up from his stool, staggering a little. Pity took Rosa by surprise, just as it had when she'd sat with Robert Hyde in the attic on the night of her return to nineteen forty-five.

She stood too, stretching out her limbs. Nate, seeming to sniff her pity, looked away.

"Where are you staying?" she asked.

"Nowhere."

"Shall I come with you? We could..." Rosa trailed off. She did not know what could be done. Nate pulled down the brim of his hat so that only the lower half of his face was visible, the grim streak of his mouth.

"How is it that we find each other so easily, and fall apart the same?"

"Nate," she said in an undertone. Her heart was jumping. She did not want him to speak aloud the fears which ate at her in secret. "Don't."

"I been thinkin', there's no sense in it. It feels to me almost as though..." If she could have covered her ears without appearing foolish, she would have done so. "...as though the fonder we become of anything, the more God spits on our luck." He was very still, each word heavy as a millstone. "The tides are conscious of us. They are savage with us. As Harris and me were passin' through, you see, the harder I tried to hold him, the faster he fell away."

Reluctantly, Rosa clasped his shoulder. He turned to look at her again. His childish puzzlement, the indignity of it held incongruously in his tall strong frame, was painful.

"I cannot know," said Nate, "whether he will be all right."

16

Hiroshima

They say that it is in the *Suiren* district, the quarter of the city which never grows dark, that the travellers gather. And since you have come here looking for one of them, or at least to search out whatever he is looking for, you could do worse than to begin there.

Hiroshima and places like it, you see, have long known about the *tabibito*. Or at least that there are men and women who make pilgrimage there, for no other reason than to dance on the edge of the void. Natural tourists rub shoulders with the unnatural ones, with the young locals who have forsaken their books forever and given themselves up to the nightclubs. And since you have come such a very long way, *henro-san*, since you have come across land and sea and even risked passage through the air, you could do worse than to join them.

Hood up, bag on your back, you vanish into the crowds. It is not difficult to disappear. Breathe the air, taste its strange charge on your tongue. Wasn't this the kind of thrill that filled your heart before the coming of the black wave? When you called yourself the Fabulist? You have half-forgotten, but perhaps this is how it felt — as though the tides had poured themselves into you and flowed out beneath your skin. Your body limp and loose, ready to be washed away.

Perhaps here you will find what you were always looking for. A city to erase the need to think or to be anything. A city of pure sensation, an electric jolt to your numb bones. You feel everything, and so feel nothing at all.

*

For our kind, Tommy had once told her, *it's like walking on a glass floor at five hundred feet.* Or like walking on a tightrope with strong winds blowing on either side. Like running in the moving eye of a whirlwind. On the other side of the air gaped a chasm which drew all tides towards it, a light-flash bright as the end of the world, more than a hundred years ago. Every inch of ground, every wall remembered it. To be in the city was to be always moments from that explosion.

It would take only a lapse in concentration, a second of too-deep surrender. In that place Rosa's heartbeat was twice as hard and half as heavy. Adrenaline coursed through her blood from the moment she awoke. She'd never drunk or smoked anything so strong, never felt her knees buckle this way at any man's kiss. She raised her face to Hiroshima's neon glow. I see it now, she thought. I see why he spoke so often of this place.

The city was all blue, all white and chrome, its light matched in the dusk hour by the unbroken violet of the sky. Something was always in motion. Pixelated girls danced and eels undulated and symbols she could not read descended flashing on the sides of every tower, holograms whirling between the spires and the clouds. *Shikansen* arched overhead on elegant sky-rails, which criss-crossed one another and wove between the buildings like glittering rivers.

And by the port, where oyster-boats hauled in the day's catch and the fish-markets were crowded with haggling restaurateurs, the *Suiren* floated just offshore. A series of irregular islands linked by brightly lit bridges and densely built with nightclubs, with karaoke booths and *kabakuras*, with all-night bars and sub-aquarian saunas, the district heaved with life from sunset until dawn.

No space for the threat of silence, no need ever to be alone. Bodies were easy to find, easy to leave behind. Most mornings Rosa woke with a new stranger, men to whom – if she gave a name at all – she was Arline. At the point of waking something odd seemed to happen to time, as though it were expanding to contain every such moment from the last eight years of her life. For a few seconds she was at once in nineteen forty-five and the twelfth, in Milan and Delphi and Seysair, in Montparnasse and on the frozen beach. The shape beside her was Tommy Rust and it was any number of others, and it was nobody at all.

As she awoke further these other ages and other shapes fell away until she knew where she was. But she was not always certain enough. Some parts of her were not quite pulled back into the present. She stared at the backs of anonymous heads on pillows, sat up naked from their sheets and set her feet upon their floors. Ran her hands along the frames of their narrow beds, for the sake of touching something solid. *Hiroshima. The twenty-first.*

"Girl from far away." A bed in a dim apartment room. A businessman who woke when she did, tried to exchange unwanted words as she made ready to leave. "Tell me somewhere I can go. I want to live more than this."

She paused in peeling a T-shirt back over her skin, turned to where he sat watching her from the bed. His hair had been swept the wrong way across his forehead while he slept. He looked like a little boy.

"Why are you asking me?"

"Excuse me. You are *tabibito*."

At the edge of her vision, she thought she glimpsed a third person in the room, standing in the doorway dressed in dark clothes. Breath caught in her throat, then released. She remembered that he had insisted on hanging his suit up there so that it did not crease.

"I don't know what you're asking," said Rosa. "Go to work. Go about your city. You don't understand the price we pay."

He gave a little bow of the head. "*Sumimasen*. I am sorry if I offended you."

"It's all right. Now don't look at me any more. Turn around. I'm leaving."

*

Night in a warm glass-walled pool, sunk into the sea a mile out from the harbour and lit a deep shade of indigo. Stars covered by a dull glow in the open sky above. Rosa swam slowly back and forth with her head beneath the surface, hands stretched out in front of her. She watched her limbs move in slow-motion, ripples of brightness passing across ghostly flesh. The air and the water were black beyond the reach of the lights. She wondered how deep the water was beneath the glass.

Above the surface, the noise from the nearby islands intruded. The spinning illuminations. The deep bass beat of music could be felt in the water, a series of muffled rhythmic shocks like distant earthquakes. Rosa sank again and drifted with her arms around her knees, letting out bubbles of breath.

Something was moving out in the ocean. The indigo light caught the end of streaming tentacles, a swarm of pulsing mushroom-shaped forms. On the other side of the glass wall, jellyfish the size of grown men propelled themselves dreamily by. Rosa let go of her knees and kicked back to the surface, rising from the water and pushing her sodden hair back from her face. On the steps, she paused with her shivering body prone to the breeze as though willing herself to wake, looking out towards the neon city on the shore.

Sauna-steam flushed her skin, sent sweat trickling down her neck and back. Bodies moved around her in the hot cloud. On the bridges between islands Rosa walked between food-stalls and loud-voiced hawkers, hood still covering her head. A relief, to see once again without being seen. When she slept alone it was in a white capsule, one of hundreds stacked ten-high along the narrow shoreline streets, hired for a few yen a night by those too drunk or guilty to go back to their homes.

She learned to paint herself like the girls of that quarter, who wore their hair short and dipped at the tips in cobalt dye, who powdered their faces white and traced intricate images about their eyes: cobwebs and lizard-scales, clock-hands and octopi. In the press of bodies at midnight below the pulsating lights with the music driving all thoughts from her mind she might have been back in Venice, back in the carnival crowd among jesters and sun-queens, courtiers and phantoms.

There was no knowing one kind from another. All might have been travellers from a century before or behind, from lands near or far. In the darkness every face was blurred about its edges, ageless, every voice muted in the pounding noise. Rosa began to feel that she could no longer pick her own body from the seething mass, her own hands from the multitude raised in the air below the wheeling lights. Past midnight the mirrored walls tilted and flickered into life, transforming into towering screens which projected galaxies of stars. She threw back her head and danced in the gaping space of the universe.

A faint memory came, when she least expected it, of stripping sheets from a bed and pressing her face into their warmth. Inhaling a mysterious perfumed musk.

Partway through her twenty-sixth year, by her reckoning, with her waist encircled by the thick arm of a man who was pushing through the crowd to buy her *shochu* from the vending-bar, something caught the corner of Rosa's eye. She was not sure why she turned, following the progress of a slender woman who was moving alone between the dancers. Her hair, contrary to *Suiren* fashion, hung long and unstyled. Below the line of her black dress, inked onto her calf, was the image of a deer.

As the woman moved the creature appeared to run, flexing its delicate legs. Before she knew it Rosa had slipped free and was giving chase, weaving through the forest of dancers as the lights flickered on and off, on and off. For a moment the deer was lost, but then it reappeared again, darting away into the dark. The woman approached a man who slid a hand below the strap of her dress, and she stretched to kiss him lightly, body moving against his to the rhythm of the music.

The fury which Rosa had nursed since she first landed on her knees on the frozen beach, since she had screamed his name above the pines, dissipated in that instant. In her mind she had berated him countless times for failing to warn her of what the tides could do, but now, he was here. He was vigorously alive, vigorously himself amid the sea of strangers, as though a spotlight from the ceiling had been fixed upon him.

At the sight of him, it seemed to her that the cold upon the frozen beach could not have been as cold as she remembered it; that the road she'd taken here had not been so hard or so desperate after all. There was nothing to forgive.

"Tom." She pushed her way towards him, and saw his head half-turn as she called his name. "*Tom!*"

His features illuminated. He was laughing in extravagant delight, mouthing something she could not hear. The lights flashed green, blue, red. He let go of the woman and tried to wade through the crowd in Rosa's direction, and she felt something release in her body, as though she had long been holding her breath without realising it.

He was smooth-faced, the first time she had ever seen him so, half of his strawberry hair shaven close to his head, the rest swept in angular style across his forehead. He had sweated through his thin T-shirt. When he embraced her it was with full affectionate force, and she wrapped her arms unhesitatingly around his damp torso. They held one another too long.

"*Rosa! I can't —*" The pounding music blurred fragments of his words. "*Three for me — look so well! — find me? — in here, but —*"

"I can't hear you!" She cupped her ears and shook her head. He took her by the wrist and pulled her away. Over her shoulder Rosa saw the woman in the black dress melt back into the crowd.

Tommy pushed through the door into the men's toilets at the back of the club, tugging her after him. Lines of cubicles and urinals, violet and white under strip-lights which made her eyes stream after the dark of the dance-floor. Nobody gave the two of them a second glance. Tommy was grinning, opening his mouth to say something in the relative quiet when his body lurched suddenly and he staggered to a nearby sink. He vomited in one neat heave, and then stood back, pinching his nose.

"Are you all right?"

"I enjoy myself, gypsy girl, you know that."

"You're bleeding."

There was something red between his fingers. His smile stretched. In the brightness she saw that the skin around his lips looked dry and cracked. He must have seen her recoil, because he added teasingly, "Come, one does not traverse between the ages without a little wear and tear."

Rosa hit him on the arm, not nearly as hard as she had meant to. "I'm so angry with you, you bastard. After Venice I fell so far back I thought I was going to spend forever waiting for the dawn of man."

"You didn't!"

"I certainly did. I had to live on berries, and make conversation with my own shadow."

He laughed so hard that the blood from his nose spilled over, and he had to stem the flow with toilet tissue. But his mirth was as infectious as it had ever been, and despite herself Rosa felt the edge of her mouth twitch. She could not remember the last time she had laughed.

"You should have warned me."

"Well, you're here now, aren't you?" Tommy leaned back against the sink, balling the tissue in his fist. It was impossible to stop looking him up and down, assuring herself again that he was really present. The easy way he moved, the way his T-shirt stuck in patches to his broad chest and back. His lively eyes taking her in, in return.

To be worried for Tommy would be like worrying that the sun might go out. In the giddy space of the moment, all was well, and would be well. "I'm here now," she said.

"This city," said Tommy. "This city, Rosa! I'll take you to the bar I found, out on the fifth island, where they set everything on fire. Or the sky gardens, or the *onsen* in the north district, you won't believe…"

Something inside her was straining to catch up with him. She'd kept her own pace for so long, had barely caught herself slowing down. "I've places I could show you, too."

"I don't doubt it."

"Are there many of us here, do you think?"

"Everybody's journeying forward, it seems. I should think we'll run into more old friends, before too long."

Old friends. She felt a rush of warmth, of expectation. The memory of sunset on a Montparnasse balcony. She opened her mouth to tell him about her encounter with Nate, but the right words did not emerge. She glimpsed again the scarlet tissue balled in his fist, and her heart gave an odd stutter. She said, "Four years for me, since Venice. Or thereabouts. You?"

"Three or so. Don't worry, we're all in order."

"I wasn't worried."

They looked at one another. The door behind them swung open and banged closed on the chaos and the deafening noise beyond. Rosa wondered whether the woman in the black dress was out there waiting for him.

"Is she anybody, Tom?"

He did not break her gaze, or ask who she meant. "Yes, as a matter of fact."

Rosa nodded. Because we are free, because we are infinitely moving towards and away from one another, and it is all the same. He flushed away the blood-soaked clump of tissue, splashed water onto his face, and pulled up his T-shirt to dry it. With a crooked half-smile, he beckoned her back towards the dark.

"Come on, sweetheart. Come with me."

17

The Soldier

Tommy lived with Chiyoko Hira in a fifteenth-floor apartment close to the floating islands. Rosa was taken back there in the early hours of the morning, her ears ringing and her feet aching as they traipsed between blocks, sirens howling in the distance. Chiyoko walked with a loping stride, tilting her head to listen whenever Tommy spoke. Rosa followed the two of them up an endless spiral staircase on the outside of the building, comprised of steel mesh through which she could see the entire fall to the ground, the shimmering neon of the street below. The steps led onto a balcony, where Chiyoko clicked a key in a sliding panel which opened on the cluttered space within.

There were only three rooms – a narrow living space, with a bedroom and bathroom beyond. The former contained a sink and stove, jutting out of the wall, a low table and a futon. There were clothes everywhere, suspended in damp drying-lines from the ceiling, or otherwise scattered in crumpled heaps, underwear strewn across the floor. The table was covered in cigarette ends, food-cartons, empty bottles, unwashed plates, candle stubs, needles. Tommy threw some sheets onto the futon, and Rosa slept there until after noon.

When she woke, she lay for a while and watched Chiyoko moving about beside the stove, boiling something which smelled of sea-salt. She wore a long shirt and nothing else, hair curtaining her face, the image of the deer stark upon her bare calf. When her food was done she perched upon the arm of the futon, picking at it with chopsticks.

Rosa sat up, and the woman gave her a long, measured look. Neither of them spoke. When Chiyoko had finished she deposited her bowl in the sink and stalked away into the bedroom, emerging fully dressed, hair coiled and pinned to her head. She left via the balcony without a single word.

"Are you sure I can stay here?" Rosa asked Tommy when he emerged from the bedroom, yawning and absent-mindedly doing up his trousers.

"Of course."

"She doesn't mind?"

"What? Oh, no, don't worry." He picked up a T-shirt from under the table and sniffed it before discarding it again. "She's hardly the jealous sort."

The table had been partially cleared, Rosa noticed, the cardboard cartons thrown away and the needles – if she had not imagined them – vanished. Still shirtless, Tommy padded across the room and rummaged on the shelves, scooping out the remnants of Chiyoko's meal to start his own in the same pot. He returned with two bowls of rice-porridge, one of which he handed to Rosa before seating himself cross-legged in front of the table. He too ate with chopsticks, and she noticed that he only took a few mouthfuls before stirring the rest about disinterestedly.

"Where did she go?"

"She does trials at the university lab. They pay pretty well for subjects, and she can go in when she likes. And... there are other perks."

Rosa did not ask him to elaborate. "This place is small," she said.

"They all are, here." He yawned again and flattened his dishevelled hair, before adding, unprompted, "I met her at a party where everybody was some millionaire's son. She was going to be a doctor. Then one day she woke up and she didn't want to any more. Now she goes out on the islands every night."

She could not tell whether he thought this was strange or admirable. In daylight the loss of his beard was a little startling. He looked at once all the more handsome and somehow reduced. He was thinner. Rosa found herself watching his mouth, the angle of its curve, the deepening creases where his years had made their mark. Mapped out upon his skin, all the many places he had been.

As she finished her bowlful he pulled out a pack of cards and flipped them between his fingers. He flashed her a grinning glance. "Do you remember Nate and Harris pulling in crowds with this in Andalusia?"

"It was Montparnasse," said Rosa. "At the cabaret."

"Yes, yes, if you say so." He dealt in a quick sequence onto the table. "I swear, they were each born with half of the same mind. That would explain everything. Harris took all the brains and none of the sense."

He laughed, and when she didn't so much as smile, paused in his game.

"I saw Nate," she said, and regretted it at once. The acknowledgement hung on the air, requiring her to shape words around her formless unease.

"Me too, since Venice, but I was sometime ahead and I had to walk away. Counting their coins in a Tangiers street, the nineteenth. Still a pair of green teenagers, imagine!" One of his eyebrows slanted quizzically. "Where did you see them?"

"Just Nate," she said. Tommy gave her an odd look. "He was alone. He was searching for Harris, and I couldn't help him. We parted ways."

"You're sure he was alone?"

"Yes, Tom."

He returned to his cards, licking the dry edges of his lips. It was too late now to put the stopper back in. She waited for him to speak, but when he did not, went on, "I keep thinking... I keep wondering what he's doing. Whether he was – is – all right."

"There's no cause to be so curious."

"And Harris, too." Her voice had taken on a tone she didn't recognise. She put down her empty bowl and rested her cheek against the back of her hand. "Where do you suppose he went? What made him let go?"

Tommy did not look up. To all appearances he was merely concentrating upon his cards, but there was something studied, even pained about his disinterest. Suddenly restless, Rosa stood and made her way over to the panel which led out onto the balcony. It was transparent by daylight, and beyond it, the floating district bobbed quietly on the morning tide. In the opposite direction, silver in the haze of the city, two sky-trains hissed across the horizon.

"It's too near the edge here," she said, almost below her breath. "My heart won't slow down."

"Don't be dull."

The brief words bruised unexpectedly. She turned her back on him and wrapped her arms about her torso. There was no good reason why she should care what he said of her, why the image of Nate Black hunched alone over the bar should be seared onto her eyelids. You've grown weak, Rosa. You've grown so spineless and thin-skinned.

Part of her wanted to push further into the bruise, to make it hurt until it could not hurt any more. She drew a deep breath and let it out quickly, fiercely.

"I want to tell you where I went after Venice. Are you listening? I was caught on a riptide. You never told me. You never said that could happen." She did not look back at him. She hardly wanted to know whether or not he had paused in his game to hear her. "I fell so far back..."

"You told me." He was candidly puzzled.

"No, I didn't. I was all alone. It hurt so much when I landed. I think I was the only person in the entire world." Each breath was catching in her chest, cold and painful. There it is, that bitter chill. You did not imagine it. It can still reach you here. "Tom. There was nobody, there was nothing. I stopped hoping for any way out from it. I had to eat..." Her stomach revolted at the memory. She pressed a hand to her mouth.

"What are you saying?"

She looked back at him. He had laid down his cards, but now sat stiffly, uncomprehending. The new note in her voice, she realised, was one of pleading.

"Please listen. It felt like the end of... it felt like..."

His face was blank. She was shaking with an anger which had no direction, with grief which had no object. She could not go on.

*

Winter came to the city like another pilgrim. The tops of the towers were swallowed by shivering mist. Planes drifted silently in from out of the white sky. A woman on the overpass between Chiyoko's apartment and the western district blew huge elastic bubbles which froze when they met the air, brittle as sugar-glass, reflecting shades of red and electric blue. Rosa stopped in her tracks to watch the fragile shapes drift along on the air just above the heads of the crowd, shattering the moment they made contact with a ledge or a curious hand.

During the daylight hours she could hardly bring herself to move from the apartment, sleeping until late into the afternoon before dragging herself up to stand comatose under the shower. She closed her eyes and tilted back her head, arms limp at her sides. The Hiroshima winter sent aches into new parts of her body, slowed her mind to a sluggish crawl. The rooms were unheated, and she was warm only beneath the steaming water, and at night, when the three of them ventured out into the island district.

On every close-pressed dance-floor her eyes were drawn to Chiyoko Hira, who seemed to vanish inside the music as though her only desire was to be lost there. She moved less with grace than with abandon, a figure in free-fall. The brightest lights revealed scars along the undersides of her arms. Clothes hung from her limbs like dying leaves. Her body seemed to Rosa a surrendered battleground.

She never spoke to Rosa, who felt under her gaze too deeply known, and entirely insignificant. Who are you here, after all? Even the darkness is hardly yours to inhabit, but staked out by those who have lived there far longer. It was not that she felt unwelcome in Chiyoko's home, since that would have required attention, an acknowledgement that she was present. If she tried to explain, Tommy would only give her that baffled look, perhaps shrink the size of her pain with a smile or the wave of a hand. The thing that was wrong would recede from view, and she would feel the cold wind blow right through her as though she was not there.

The walls within the apartment, little more than paper panels, were too thin. On the futon in the small hours, Rosa covered her head with a pillow, and slept in a strange fog of night noises and half-dreamed dreams. Of all the noises which came from the bedroom, it was the sound of conversing voices which bothered her most. She wondered what Chiyoko and Tommy spoke of in the small hours: whether he was telling her about the time he had been venerated by a mountain tribe in the thirteenth; about skating on the frozen lake between snow-sprinkled pines, or hunting boars in the woods beyond Seysair tower. She wondered what Chiyoko told him in return.

A question nagged at her for months before she put it to Tommy, so irked by her own uncertainty that she didn't much care how it made him look at her: surprised, a little pitying, as though concerned for her well-being. Perhaps he is right to be, Rosa. It could be that you have slipped from the edge of sanity.

"You really need me to tell you whether she's one of us?"

She forced herself to keep his gaze. "I usually know. It's usually far clearer to me."

Tommy folded his arms and regarded her with his head tilted to one side. The edge of his mouth twitched like a line tugged by a fish. "What do you make of her, then?" he asked.

"I wouldn't have picked her out for you."

"No?"

"But that's neither here nor there, is it? She must be something, for you to have stayed with her."

"I have stayed a while," said Tommy. Rosa saw his heel begin tapping against the floor of its own accord. His gaze wandered.

"I told you once about my mother," said Rosa on impulse. "Didn't I? How she wasn't one of us, until she met my father. It was only because of him that she ever journeyed. And Nate, I think it was that way for Nate…" Carried along by the thought, by the impossible questions it begged, she fell into silence again.

There was a pause. Tommy leaned forward, hands clasped, wrists resting on his knees. "I wouldn't credit myself. She was moving that way long before we met." He flicked Rosa a quick, impassive glance. "Chiyoko's close, if that satisfies you. She's crossing over."

Rosa knew that while she slept the days away, he was imbibing the city to its dregs. He was wandering the fish-markets where no other visitor would think to go, eating steaming *udon* in tiny side-street vendors, finagling from talkative businessmen an invitation to a party above the clouds. With Chiyoko at his side he would ascend to the top of a glass-roofed tower, move among the immaculate crowd as though he'd been born to it. Crystal champagne glass in one hand, the other upon Chiyoko's waist, or clasping the shoulder of a new acquaintance. That undying grin, which Rosa now knew had a life beyond its owner, spread over his face.

His eyes were sore around their rims. She would hear him in the bathroom, long after Chiyoko had fallen asleep, vomiting his guts out.

*

Hiroshima, you were calling us all along. We were made for places like this, where the fabric of time is forever folded back on itself. In the memorial museum, long fallen into disrepair, Rosa stood fixated before a glass case which held a stopped watch. The presence of the flash and the blast, always a gaping century, a few moments away.

And then there are those other explosions, the small unregarded things which have detonated inside your chest through the years. Their devastating waves rippling outward in slow motion, so that you did not even know of it until now. The effort of not giving in to that long fall. Her body shook when she woke. She wiped blood from her nose, steadied herself against walls whenever dizziness came. Imagine, Rosa, tumbling over the edge of it, just as you tumbled down the millennia to the frozen beach. Imagine being swallowed into its white-hot heart.

On the night that Hiroshima welcomed in the New Year, lasers criss-crossed in the air above the skyscrapers and imitated showers of sparks. Thumping music shook the city to its foundations. Tommy and Chiyoko took Rosa to the old city, where girls hung charms in their hair and bought their fortunes for the coming year on slim slips of paper. Bells tolled outside shrines. The three of them made their way towards the island district eating rice-cakes and drinking *sake,* the deep reverberation of the bells still echoing in their ears.

Boats sailed out from the harbour, strung with illuminations. There was dancing on the decks, but the music they were dancing to was muted by distance. The disconnected movement of so many distant bodies made for an odd spectacle. At the shore, hundreds knelt and laid lilies on the water, mechanised lanterns lit neon

220

orange and blue and rose, which unfolded their leaves as they drifted outwards into the ocean. The glowing shoal became a stream of light a mile long, diminishing into the distance below the night sky.

Rosa crouched shivering beside the water, holding a yellow lantern in her palms. The dark sea slopped against the harbour's edge. Beside her Tommy and Chiyoko had already cast their lilies away, and stood to watch them open.

Her thoughts turned to nineteen forty-five and the way it had always ended, clinging to her mother as she was carried away from whatever home they were leaving. *Should old acquaintance be forgot.* The violent motion of her father's body pulling them away from the present. In those later years, Bella with her arms around Harriet's neck, eyes screwed tightly shut. The four of them huddled together in a tangle of panicked breathing and clammy fingers, swept back as one upon the last chime of midnight, upon the strength of Robert Hyde's misguided longing.

Rosa laid her lantern gently on the water, and looked up at the surrounding crowd. Their faces were brightened from below in unearthly shades, their eyes wide, each caught in an instant of laughter or wonder or quiet contemplation. Oblivious to all except the moment and themselves. A regret and an aching envy rose out of the depths of her.

What are your days made of? What are your mayfly hours filled with that satisfies you so? From what disparate pieces, from what places and faces and roots and branches, does one build a life? Tell me, because I cannot see it. Tell me, because I do not know.

She passed a hand across her tired eyes. Amongst the press of people, for a fraction of an instant, she thought she glimpsed something as she rose. A white-faced man with hollow eyes, dressed in a black uniform, who was looking straight at her. She blinked and he was gone.

Blood roared in her ears. Not by chance, surely, that he comes now — just when you have begun to wonder what distance remains between you and the void. One thing to wonder, another to look it fully in the face. Do not fool yourself that you don't still cling to this life, even as it disintegrates in your grasp.

Through the night's celebrations she could not shake the thought of him. She was almost certain that his shadow lingered in the corner of her gaze, following her amongst the packed crowds in the clubs, looking on as Tommy threw an arm about her shoulders at midnight and planted a drunken kiss on her lips.

The shadow followed the three of them at a distance back to the apartment through streets strewn with the debris of the night's revelry. Rosa looked over her shoulder. Above the silver mist of her breath, the screens on the side of every building flickered and danced silently.

*

She did not sleep. When a quiet knock came upon the sliding door leading out to the balcony, she rose to answer it as though in a dream.

It had begun to snow. The Soldier stood still as a statue, veiled by whiteness. Each flake caught the glare of the red neon light from the tower opposite. He was paler than a buried man. His heavy boots appeared to be the only thing weighing him to the ground.

Rosa looked on him with all the terror that accompanied the end of everything. The night air numbed her bare arms and legs.

"Please," she whispered. *"Please. Not yet. I'm not ready."*

The Angel of Death blinked, and she saw that there were snowflakes clinging to his eyelashes. There was a moment of utter stillness.

His body crumpled without warning, and before she knew it he had collapsed at her feet.

18

A Thousand Years

The Soldier was wrapped in a blanket and carried inside, then laid on the futon where he slept as though he had never known rest before. Wordless, they pulled off his boots, and cushioned his head on a rolled-up scarf. Chiyoko laid the back of her hand against his forehead, pressed firm fingers along his spin and limbs, and leaned close to listen to his chest. When he came to for a few minutes in confusion, she spooned honey and green tea into his mouth, the Soldier swallowing obediently. She wiped her hands and stood back with a sharp, appraising eye upon the prone figure.

Rosa kept vigil over him, watching every flickering movement of his eyes beneath their lids. It was too much to take in. The phantasm she had feared since childhood was four feet away, shaking fitfully and helpless as a baby. So he was flesh and blood, after all.

"He climbed the stairs, in this state?" asked Tommy.

"He must have."

"Unless he appeared from nowhere," said Chiyoko.

"Will he be all right when he wakes?" Rosa asked.

Chiyoko gave a small shrug. "He has no fever. No injury, I do not think. Hard to see."

"And he's certainly human." She was so overwhelmed that the words slipped out before she could stop them. Chiyoko did not react.

Tommy squatted beside the futon, rubbing his hands across his face. "Have you seen him before?" he asked Rosa, uncharacteristically serious.

Silence followed. Chiyoko, leaning against the frame of the bedroom door, lit a cigarette and moved out onto the balcony. Flecks of snow blew in as she pulled the panel closed, vanishing as they melted in the air. Rosa turned reluctantly to Tommy.

"I have seen him. More than once."

He did not ask her where, or under what circumstances. She counted on her fingers below the table. The bottom of the garden, nineteen forty-five. Reims cathedral, Venice, where she might have merely imagined him. Then forty-five again, for certain, in that alleyway on the red letter day. Either he had followed her or the same tides had carried them by chance, his presence stitched thinly back through her years like a solitary red thread.

Tommy rubbed the shaven half of his head. He seemed out of sorts. Side-by-side, they sat and watched for several long minutes as the Soldier stirred, groaning. Even in sleep he looked troubled, as though his dreams gave him no peace. His face contorted and he muttered incoherently.

"He's one of us," said Tommy.

"It would seem so."

Chiyoko pushed back the panel and came inside, brushing snow from her shoulders. Scarred arms folded, she flicked her eyes towards Tommy and then towards the bedroom. He rose slowly, still looking at the strange sleeper on the futon.

"Better cover your eyes then, gypsy girl, and block your ears. He might be a ghost come a-visiting from your future."

*

She dozed on the floor with her head tucked uncomfortably onto the futon, by the Soldier's feet. When she woke she found him sitting up, staring straight ahead with his hands clasped together.

She had never had a chance to look at him properly before, at close quarters. He was perhaps thirty, though it was hard to tell, with an angular peak of dark hair and skin greyed by exhaustion. He had slept in his uniform, including the long thick coat, and now looked crumpled and unkempt.

For several minutes she sat and watched him, massaging her stiff neck with her knuckles, before he turned and noticed her.

"I hope you don't mind,' he said. 'I saw you by the harbour." His voice was hoarse and faint, as though long unused.

"You followed me," said Rosa.

"I hope you don't mind," he said again.

"Are you armed?" she asked. He shook his head and turned out his empty pockets. She was not sure what she would have done, had he answered otherwise.

"I'm cold to my bones," he said.

Not wanting to wake Tommy and Chiyoko by going into their room to fetch another blanket, she boiled a pan on the stove instead, and brought him a bowl of rice-porridge. He ate it with the bowl close to his chest and the spoon clasped in his fist like a grenade, his gaze never leaving her. When he had finished he brushed the stray hair from his forehead back to his scalp in a careful movement.

"Thank you."

"It's not my food," she said. "None of it's mine."

"You don't live here?"

She shook her head, indicated the bedroom door. "I'm passing through," she said.

The Soldier watched her with focused intensity. "Please tell me," he said, "if I am mistaken. But I believe that I have seen you at least twice, before last night. Once in a garden, near Camberwell, in England. You were very small. And then in Westminster, in an alleyway beside the palace, on the festival day."

Rosa barely had time to cover her eyes in fear and amazement before she found herself uncovering them again. The Soldier seemed baffled by the gesture.

"I am not mistaken, am I? It was you?"

"Yes, it was me."

"In nineteen forty-five. You were a child, and then mere months later, you were perhaps ten years grown. I recognised your look. I could barely believe it. Until that moment I had thought…I had feared…"

His hands twitched back across his hair. They flew to the table, unconsciously aligning the card-pack, the bowl, the spoon, a series of cigarette-ends. Every object was straightened, checked, straightened again.

While he was still caught up in this ritual, the bedroom door slid open and Tommy emerged, bleary-eyed. He closed the panel carefully and then came across to the futon, shrugging a shirt over his shoulders.

"An ungodly hour to start the New Year," he said.

"Did we wake you?"

His eyes ranged from Rosa to the Soldier. The stranger's hands had retreated back into his lap. "Should you even be talking to this gentleman?" asked Tommy.

She could not answer him. He sat down on the table opposite the Soldier, legs apart. "I'm sorry, brother," he said. "But unless you've come with an especially compelling tale, we're short on space. As you can see."

The Soldier stared at him.

"Well? I take it you're some vagrant from the last century who's still learning the ropes. Maybe someone told you that the best of us head for Hiroshima. I'll show you around the city sometime, but you can't sleep here."

Tommy pointed at the man's uniform, and the Soldier looked down as though noticing himself for the first time. "I'll give you one free piece of advice, and that's to lose the look. It doesn't take much to pass unnoticed, here, but that's not even close to a good match. I don't know which army you think you're fighting for."

"Most lately," said the Soldier, as though hypnotised, "the fifteenth battalion of the North China ground corps."

Tommy opened his mouth, a frown creasing his forehead, but Rosa touched his arm to silence him. The Soldier seemed to be scrabbling around for language. He sat still and straight-backed, but his hands had a nervous life of their own, repeatedly straightening his crumpled collar.

"Can I ask you...I barely know how... you are... you are both...?"

"We are like you," said Rosa. "We are travellers. We have come here from years long past. From years yet to come."

He turned his hollow eyes upon her. She shuddered, still half-convinced despite herself that she looked upon the Angel of Death.

"I can barely believe it," he said.

Tommy leaned forward, the full burning focus of his attention suddenly fixed upon him. "Did you never know that there were more of us?"

*

He remembered little, he said, before his twelfth year, when three strangers had come in through the open back door and shot each of his parents in the head. The eyes of these intruders were at once full and empty, shining with worship and with envy. They wore grey suits and polished shoes. He had hidden behind the kitchen counter and watched as two pools of blood widened across the clean floor.

What does the boy do, then? He runs as hard and as fast as he can for as far as he can, until he falls into another decade entirely. This is nothing remarkable to him. As soon as he can figure out how and where, he gets a gun of his own. It cannot be long before they come for him too.

His name? The Soldier turned his head fretfully. He remembered too little. He thought that one half of it might be *Harding*. The rest was lost to time. Carried away like a stick tossed onto the surface of a river.

The boy teaches himself to fire the gun with accuracy, practising behind empty warehouses and in the woods at twilight. It hurts his skinny wrist and arm until he learns to hold it right. Afraid to leave London, he flits backwards and forwards through the years, constantly looking over his shoulder. One spring night he tumbles into nineteen forty-five and finds himself in an overgrown garden, filled with rustling and shifting shadows. A sudden movement startles him and he raises his gun, turning to see a red-haired girl who is frozen in terror by the door.

His eyes meet hers, and he sees that she is appalled by him. In that moment he learns something about his nature, about the way he must move through the world. You are for the outside, boy; you are not for the lights behind those windows or the warmth behind those doors. The look upon her face tells you this, and you will carry the knowledge with you wherever you go.

The tide whips him back to the cusp of the Great War, and then leaves him be. In the years before the storm-clouds break he sleeps in potting-sheds and below railway bridges, gun tucked inside the old sack which serves as his pillow. He knows nothing except how to aim and how to pull a trigger, and so when the time comes he falls into soldiering without a thought. Nobody asks the right questions. He is seventeen years old when he is handed an infantryman's uniform and a Lee Enfield rifle, and shipped to Flanders. He thinks he is ready.

Nothing could have readied him for this. Grey rain slants down on black hillsides, scarred by tangles of wire. Men wade through mud as high as their waists, merely to come within range of the enemy. Six bearers to every stretcher, battling through the treacly miasma. On his first day Private Harding sees a sentry clipped on the side of the head by a sniper's bullet, spinning weirdly in the air before he falls back into the trench, skull cracked and dribbling like a dropped egg. After dark, when the others write their letters home, Harding sits and watches slugs heave over the earth walls. Someone offers him a smoke and he fumbles it, coughing. A cold moon passes between the clouds, illuminating the sore stubble of the land below, the chaos of stumps and craters. The young soldier wraps his arms around his knees and wonders how he came to be here.

No sleep. One dim dawn follows another. The incessant searing whine of shells. The first time they go over the top he stumbles up the ladder, mind blank, vision filled to the right and the left with the scrambling figures of his comrades. At any moment he expects agony and darkness. Something flashes overhead and he flings himself down into the mud. Crawls around the rim of a pit on his hands and knees, and suddenly there before him half-mired in sticky tar is a man in the other uniform raising a gun, howling like an ape. Harding is howling too and before the trigger is pulled he thrusts his bayonet into the enemy's belly. Feels it sliding through skin into flesh.

For weeks after the young soldier finds that his ears continue to ring even in the quiet hours, and that his hands shake uncontrollably as he cleans his rifle. Brown rats gorge on dead men's eyes. He is troubled by a pain in his stomach. He can hardly bear to swallow the smallest morsel of food. The stench of sweat and shit and putrid flesh and chloride and lime. The *crunch* of lice crushed beneath his fingernails.

Harding grows calmer at the prospect of death. He volunteers for patrols, and lifts his head above the parapet to look out over no man's land. He gains a reputation as a madman. But no bullet comes for him, no well-aimed splinter of shell, no blessed gangrenous infection or bout of cholera. His body, though reduced to a rattling bag of bones, remains whole.

By the time the war is over, he is beyond any sense of surprise. His trench-coat is blood-stained and mud-hardened, moulded to his shape. His ears are filled with the echoes of old bombs. The tide picks him up again and, as though it has read his innermost heart, washes him across the years before depositing him in nineteen forty-two. He is fit for nothing else. In another uniform he finds himself at El-Alamein, flies on his eyelids and sand between his teeth, flat on his chest in the shadow of the dunes. At night the fires of burning tanks and petrol dumps light the sky above the desert.

Come for me, machine-gun fire. Come for me, bombs whistling through the air from beyond the ridge. Men fall on either side of him. Tunisia, then Sicily, and still nothing hits. The madman Private Harding listens to talk of wives and mothers, of sons and daughters and homes left tucked between English hills. He lies awake scratching his mosquito-bites in dugouts as his aloneness encroaches upon him. The strange shape of his existence is his and only his, a nether-land whose borders are still mysterious, whose weather comes without warning. The suspicion of what he is begins to take shape in the warm nights, beneath the Mediterranean stars.

Reason it out, now. He has known no other who slips between decades as though crossing the street. He knows no other who has so often walked untouched from battlefields where hundreds lie slain. Is it possible, might it be that he is some other kind of creature than these; some undying thing whose flesh is gold, not clay? Lying on his back, he raises a hand to frame those distant lights, which keep their secrets. What a solemn, what a wondrous, what a terrible burden to bear.

He shoulders it, and feels the heavy weight of it upon his spirit. At first it is shameful to him – how could it be otherwise, among so many of the dead and dying? He walks with it, fights with it, rests with it. It is as though he has ascended an uncharted mountain and now stands alone upon the summit, buffeted by cold winds on every side, with barely the courage to journey on. If there can be no home, Harding, where then will you go? If you cannot die, how then will you live?

The fearful possibility of his endless years yawns wide before him. Trying to fit them in his mind is like trying to swallow down a shape bigger than his own body. It would surely break him, to comprehend that future. Once again he lives out the war without a scratch. And then, returned to England and swept up in the victorious crowd which surges through London's streets that May day, he catches the smallest glimpse of a familiar face.

How he knows her, he does not know. At least not at first, not until he has fought his way urgently closer. Her cropped hair is fox-fur red, her features hard. He had seen her across a darkening spring garden, passing through this very year before the wars, a wide-eyed child at the back door. Mere months ago, in anybody else's time. Yet here she is, perhaps more than ten years grown, pulling away from the greying man who is gripping her shoulder.

Harding is thinking of nothing, as he follows her away into a side-street, other than his urgent need to speak with her. Hope devours all caution, all doubt. She turns, stemming a flow of blood from her nose, and the terror on her face stops him in his tracks.

She looks at him as though looking upon her own impending end. That same look. Whispers something he cannot hear. And then – she vanishes.

The girl from the garden comes often to his mind in the years that follow. She is the only sign that he is not utterly alone. Sometimes he thinks that he glimpses her in far-flung places, her bright hair, her hard face in the midst of a crowd, but perhaps he only imagines it. Because of the life he has led until now, he is taken by tides which drag him back and forth between the wars of the world. He crosses continents and ten centuries from armoured skirmishes on trampled English fields, to sweat-soaked crawls through Asiatic jungles, to sun-baked city squares which heave with revolution. He fights because he has known nothing else – and more and more, as war follows on from war, from a sense of what he owes.

He never asked to be spared. To live with the guilt and the dread of it, he must believe that he has been spared for a purpose. *Choose carefully, Harding, alongside whom you will stand. Think long and hard upon all you do, because you may never taste death and its forgetfulness.*

Still no bullet makes its home in his chest, and no landmine tears the ground from under his feet. He puts on new uniforms and new names, too, as the memory of his own grows hazy. What is he, but the colour of the coat and cap he wears? Myth or man, chosen saint or bleeding, breathing, doubting being. He knows that all these contradictions might be held within him.. He knows that his miraculous life is hardly his to keep.

Sometimes the tide snatches him from the middle of battle, and he wonders what tales he leaves in his wake. Perhaps there is a story told high in the Mongol mountains, as the tribesmen sharpen their scimitars, which surfaces again down the centuries in another shape, another tongue, another war. They say, there is a soldier who appears from nowhere and does battle as though no pain can touch him. He stays a time, solemn as a priest in all his dealings, until suddenly he is gone without trace. To see him is an omen of coming death; a mark of the favour of the gods; a sign of certain victory, or of terrible madness.

Fifteen years of his life Harding fights this way. He fights for a thousand years.

And then, heartsick and weary on leave from the Chinese Civil War in the year 2047, he hears that Hiroshima is the place to lose himself.

*

"Tom."

The Soldier lay sleeping once again. He had talked himself into exhaustion. Bruised, orange-edged clouds hung low over Hiroshima, the horizon a thin line of pale light. Rosa slid the balcony door closed behind her.

Tommy lit his cigarette and leaned on the rail. Flecks of snow settled in his strawberry hair.

"Look at me, will you?"

He threw her a glance over his shoulder, tapping ash into the air where it fluttered and danced, grey flakes among the white. She moved forward to lean on the rail beside him. The luminous city lay before them. Their breath formed clouds.

Rosa did not trust herself to speak without weeping. Not for Harding, or not only for Harding and his odd, thwarted life. But for something that his tale had wrenched from inside her. For all the things in the short course of her years and in the long relentless march of history that had been wasted, that had been lost.

She wrapped her arms around her chest and wished Tommy Rust would look at her, wished that he would wipe it all away with the flash of a grin and the wave of a hand. That he would beckon her outward as he always did into the shining city, where all thoughts of darkness could be put away.

"A thousand years," she said aloud. "We've both travelled that far. Further."

All that way. She did not say: and I do not feel wise. I do not feel whole. Silently Tommy offered her the cigarette, but she did not take it. "Which of us is going to tell him?" she asked, through a tight throat.

"Tell him what?" Tommy looked sideways at her at last, his eyes bloodshot.

Rosa stared. "That he's *wrong*, of course." The cigarette hung unfinished in his hand. She thought that she saw patches of colour forming high in his cheeks. "He thinks that he really might be, that he really is… you know. It's kept him going all this time. It's not like it has been for us, not a game, not some kind of idle boast. We've got to tell him, Tom! I can't do it, I can't bear it!"

He had turned his eyes back towards the city. He was silent for so long that she made to go back inside, shivering with cold, mortified that she had so revealed her distress. But just as she was about to tug the panel open, Tommy finally spoke again.

"Who says he's not?"

Red lettering pulsated up the side of a skyscraper behind him. One side of his face was caught in the glow, the other left to shadow. In that moment, there was nothing familiar about him.

"We are everything that the mayflies have named us," he said. "Do not doubt it."

Rosa looked bleakly back, bereft of any strength or conviction to argue.

"I'm so tired, Tom. Aren't you *tired?*"

19

Weep for Us

The spilling of the Soldier's tale seemed to light a fever in him. For days afterwards, he was unable to piece clear words together. His skin burned so hot that Chiyoko was obliged to do more than frown and shrug, instructing Tommy to help her strip him and sit him under a cold shower. Through the bathroom door Rosa glimpsed him slumped insensible beneath the flow of the water, all ribs and spine. She wondered whether they ought to have let him speak so much of himself at once. Perhaps after so many years carrying his secrets alone, his sanity had slipped out along with them.

Those secrets, knotted around his body like coils of wire, might have been the last thing holding him together. When he dreamed of sniper's bullets and the fire in the sky above the desert, yelling out and thrashing through the night, Rosa did not cover her ears. She lay flat on her back on the hard floor. There is something to cry for, Tommy Rust. And while I am learning its shape from my swallowed silence, while you are disgorging your insides in private, Harding will weep for us all.

The worst of the sickness took ten days to break. In the middle of the night, his cries quietened to a murmur. His breathing deepened. She dozed at the foot of the futon, becoming aware that he had woken when he propped himself unsteadily on his elbow, leaning over to look at her. Red and blue lights flickered and wheeled behind the translucent screen on the other side of the room.

"Rosa," said the Soldier hoarsely. "I heard them call you Rosa." One side of his face twitched while the other remained still. She watched him, repelled and fascinated. The fever had deepened the grey bruises beneath his eyes. "Do I keep you awake?"

"No."

"Was this your bed?

"No. It's all right." She made to turn over, afraid to speak to him without the others present. In the bedroom, Tommy was coughing.

"Rosa."

"What?" she whispered.

"Did they shoot your parents too? Is that how it happens?"

She looked hopelessly back at him through the half-dark. It was hard to know how to bridge the space between his understanding and her own. There was a particular sting in how the truth made her appear. "Nobody hurt my parents. I left them in nineteen forty-five, when I was seventeen." She heard her voice harden. "It was my choice."

"That was where I saw you."

"You need to sleep. It's still night."

"That man with you, in the crowd. Was he your father?"

"It was my choice. Though no sane person could have done otherwise." Rosa turned over, and doubts that had long lain dormant came poking their shoots through the soil. She curled up, arms around her knees, and tried to breathe through her growing disquiet. She heard Harding lie back down again, pulling his blankets close to his body.

That angry girl who had fled the Shoreditch house was barely even a memory now. Rosa's certainty flickered from view, darted away from her through dappled shadows. She tried calling it back. Who in the world would, who could have done otherwise?

The Soldier slept long hours then began to eat ravenously. He consumed bowls of hot porridge and soup, noodles, dumplings, boiled chicken, eggs, sweet-bread. He could not keep down anything raw or fried, but otherwise devoured what was laid before him as though it was about to be snatched away. It seemed to amuse Chiyoko to keep on feeding him, if only to see when he would stop.

Rosa avoided being alone with him as best she could. It was not only that she feared what he might ask, what she might be obliged to tell him for the sake of honesty. A lifetime of superstition could not be shaken all at once, and knowing the truth about him hardly helped. He still looked like death to her.

When at last he was strong enough to leave the apartment, Rosa and Chiyoko took him to the harbour, where the stinging breeze that blew in over the water might help to invigorate him. They sat side by side along the sea wall. Behind them fishermen were laying out their stalls for the evening market, pink bream sliding over one another, giant amberjacks swinging from hooks, stacked crates of oysters. They sharpened gutting-knives, passed Geiger-counters quickly across their catch. Home-bound locals and errand-runners sent from restaurant kitchens moved between the barrels, the air misty with sea-spray and loud with sales patter.

"On the way back," said Chiyoko, "I will buy octopus, and make *takowasa* for you." Her arms were bare despite the cold, one leg hanging either side of the wall. She twisted her wind-blown hair into a tight topknot. "All the tourists want to try it."

Harding, gaunt in Tommy's too-large clothes, worried at the edges of his borrowed scarf. Rosa watched him undo and redo its knot several times. "Do you have the stomach for it?" she asked him. The fresh air had brought some blood into his face, but he still looked pale.

237

"To *tabibito*," said Chiyoko, "everything is foreign."

Harding turned his face in the direction of the sea, eyes closed. Weak sunlight splintered the snow-laden clouds. Chiyoko glanced at the bustling market, and then at the Soldier.

"You are never curious," she said. "I notice this. Never truly curious, any of you."

Rosa bristled at once. "I don't know what you mean. We see more of the world than they ever will."

"Only scenery. You do not ask, do not care about anything more."

"That's not true," Rosa said, but she felt a sense of dull surprise. Chiyoko looked coolly back at her.

"It is true. It is because you do not stay. And because you must only think of yourselves."

She spoke without criticism, as though describing an immutable law of nature. Rosa looked down at her own hands, which were gripping the edge of the wall. She tried to think about Chiyoko's proposition. There was little she had seen in Tommy or Amber, in the Brothers Black, certainly nothing in herself, that was sufficient to prove otherwise. Only – and this was slender evidence indeed – that she had once sat at the back of a theatre on Drury Lane and wept at the gypsy girl's song.

And perhaps not even that. After all, who were your tears for that night? Only for Arline –for Rosa Hyde, sick and sad for some home that she has never known.

It had begun to snow again, and the many colours of the city behind them were muted. They helped the Soldier down from the wall, and the three walked back through the market, between barrels of wriggling eels and of spiny urchins, stallholders waving clams bigger than their own hands. Harding turned his head sharply this way and that at every raised voice. Rosa looked at him with new attention.

When Chiyoko stopped, he wandered a little way off on his own. Rosa watched him, the figure in the out-sized coat. He was still gazing out towards the quiet sea.

"Chiyoko," she said, the words tumbling out in a rush. "There is a place, I have been to a place, where they know more of us than we know of ourselves. I stayed there, for a time, but I ran away." It felt like a confession. "They asked questions of me, but I asked none in return."

Chiyoko gave no sign of having heard. Instead of replying she called to the stall-holder in her own language, and they began to haggle. Rosa looked down into the barrel. She remembered sinking her teeth into raw flesh on a frozen beach, before time.

When they walked away, a bag swung from Chiyoko's hand, the tips of eight blood-red tentacles protruding from the top.

*

I do not know you, she thought, as she watched Tommy make his barefoot tousle-haired way about the apartment, smoking half-dressed on the balcony or playing cards with Harding. The two of them bent over the low table opposite one another were a study in contrast, the fair head and the dark, the broad shoulders and the narrow. Harding's movements even at play were hesitant, painful, as though he was trying to recall a pattern of doing and being that was all but lost to him. Tommy crouched with his feet flat to the floor, flipping cards down carelessly, rising up without warning whenever the activity began to bore him.

Rosa's thoughts were just as restless. Her memories of Tommy Rust began to shift like sand, until the man she had once known seemed an impossible fiction. I have never asked, and you have never told me, where you came from. How your journeying first began. You told me once, in jest, that you could not remember the first name you owned; I am certain now that it is true.

And along with Tommy, everything else. The tale you have told yourself dies on your lips. You stare back down the years, and even nineteen forty-five is not the place that you knew.

So many times there she had heard the name of this very city spoken in grave tones on the wireless, intoned as a byword for that unspeakable flash of light. For a new kind of death. She remembered before Bella was born, hearing too much of the news and crawling into bed between Robert and Harriet on the night the bomb fell, the sweet smell of cut grass from the open window, her father's hand resting on the back of her head. The silence between them. That sighing like the exhalation of a final breath. *Hiroshima.*

And could it be, Rosa, could it be that there are worse things, that you knew even then of worse things than remaining among the Hydes in nineteen forty-five? That there was a gentleness shown towards you by Robert, and by Harriet when she brought you warm milk to help you sleep after you had dreamed of the explosion, which you have wilfully forgotten? Which you never returned? She sat cross-legged at the table and smoked Tommy's cigarettes with shaking hands in the middle of the night, while Harding dozed fretfully. A cloud of smoke drifted unheeded over his head.

She remembered the things too long unsaid and then, finally, said in anger that last evening in Shoreditch. The pallor of her parents' faces, Harriet's body held rigid with shock. Robert's disbelief as she named him *coward*. A jumble of clothes shoved into a satchel, the golden gleam of her grandfather's fob watch as she lifted it from the bedside table. She had pawned it, Rosa remembered, immediately and without a thought, on her arrival in the twenty-first.

She slipped under the sheet and onto the futon where she lay facing Harding, a gap of inches between her and his sleeping body.

She breathed in the warm smell of another human form. He became aware of her gradually, eyelids flickering in puzzlement.

Rosa's chest was rising and falling painfully fast. She was certain at last that it was more bearable to speak the worst than to carry it in silent doubt. Better to have him pass judgment than to stay in this wraith-world, beyond judgement's reach. An unseen hand constricted around her ribs.

"Do we seem so very callous?" she asked him. "Tommy and I?"

"You are the first I have known." Harding held his arms close to his body, no defence, no accusation. "You are as I find you."

"We must be a terrible disappointment."

He shook his head. "I am glad to have found you."

Rosa pushed on, and felt the reckless motion of it as if she was falling.

"I left them because they could not leave nineteen forty-five," she said. "I thought that they were cowardly, and foolish. I thought that I needed more."

Harding blinked.

"They grieved for me as though I'd died. Then I returned when I had nowhere else to go, and showed them little but scorn. I have always thought of my own wishes. I have never been truly curious." The litany was complete. She laid down her head opposite his, exhausted. "So you see, I do not know what we are, and I cannot help you."

In the next room, Tommy was snoring. Harding rubbed his eyes with the side of his thumb. Rosa watched every movement of his sober face. After a while he said, with slow consideration, "There's no one breathing who needn't be forgiven something, Rosa."

She drew back as though stung.

"Don't be good to me. Don't be kind. I can't bear it."

Each morning he combed the peak of his dark hair flat to his head until not a strand was out of place. He tied the laces of each boot with deep concentration. There were many tasks which seemed to capture him like this, drawing him down into a loop until someone intervened with a hand on his shoulder, a tug at the elbow. Loud noises made him sweat and tremble. How he had managed to move independently through the world for so long, so bewildered, was a mystery.

The question of what was to be done with him weighed more heavily on Rosa each day. While Chiyoko sent him on errands to distract him from re-aligning every object in her home, and Tommy took him to see the city, she paced the rooms of the apartment. When Chiyoko was at the labs and Rosa was left alone there, she stole into the bedroom and lay on the unmade bed.

The small space was dark and almost too untidy to move through, scattered with pill packets and food cartons and discarded clothes, the bed-covers thrown half-off. The mustiness of a place not cleaned for far too long, an old note of sandalwood perfume. Rosa raised both hands fancifully to frame a section of ceiling, as Harding had once done beneath the Sicilian constellations.

It had been some time since she thought to count her years. But now she calculated that she must be approaching twenty-seven. A decade, in her own time, since first running from that Hyde home. It did not feel possible. A decade should have been long enough to assemble something, to give a coherent account of herself. Instead she felt diminished.

It dawned on her that she could not stay much longer in Chiyoko Hira's tiny apartment, fifteen floors up from the world and on the brink of a hole in history. And neither could Harding, who was even more poorly equipped for the building of a future. There would surely be more journeys soon, another stream of unfamiliar places and faces, and she did not have the strength to meet them.

She heard the balcony door slide back and had no time to move. She sat up quickly, embarrassed, as Chiyoko came into the room and put down her bags.

"No trials today," she said.

"I'm sorry, Chiyoko, I'll get out…"

"It is very cold outside. I bought eel for *donburi*."

"Chiyoko," said Rosa. She had never found a way to speak to the other woman that was not uncomfortable, and it seemed best to cut straight to the matter. "You must want us gone, soon."

Chiyoko did not answer, and Rosa wondered whether she had even heard. But then she said, apropos of nothing, "I know this place you spoke about."

"What?"

"When I met Tommy, I learned everything I could. I searched. I read everything."

It took Rosa a moment to catch on. It was a reply to the conversation she had tried to begin days before, at the market. "The Museum? It's still standing?"

"I read about it." Chiyoko turned to her, expressionless. "Tommy is not interested."

The possibility set her mind suddenly racing, and the questions would not wait. Rosa stood up. "Have you been there, Chiyoko? Is it near here?"

"Not near. It's across the sea. I have seen it, on a map. But I have not been there." Chiyoko encircled her long hair with her hands and knotted it on top of her head. She made to leave the room, but Rosa took hold of her arm. The other woman looked at her hand as though she had been grabbed by something underwater.

"I shouldn't have run from there so quickly. I was scared, but I think... I think that might be all that's left. They knew something, they must know something. If I went back, if I took Harding..."

Chiyoko said with complete clarity, "Yes. You should go."

"Would you come too?"

For the first time, Chiyoko looked taken aback. She moved out of Rosa's grip and stared at her.

"I could not. He will not want to."

"Then leave him."

Her face closed again. And Rosa remembered Amber at the candlelit table in the studio in Montparnasse, arching her eyebrows suggestively. *Some have been more foolish.*

Chiyoko moved into the doorway, leaning momentarily against the frame as she looked over her shoulder. The silhouette of the deer curved around her bare calf. "Tommy will not like it. Don't tell him I suggested it to you." Then without any change in tone, she added, "Do you think he knows that he's dying?"

A lurching pause, in which Rosa was certain that she had misheard.

"*What?*"

"They will be back soon. I bought eel. For *donburi*."

*

We are going on a journey, Harding. In search of my answers, because I cannot deceive myself any longer; and of yours too, since I can offer you nothing. You are strong enough to travel, though you may not look it. It will be a long way, across land and sea. Perhaps by train, by boat and plane, and on our own feet. If we are lucky enough, determined enough, we might even reach our destination together.

It may be that there are stones best left unturned. But we are going to the Museum, for better or worse. I would tell you to pack your belongings, but you have none, except the uniform you brought here on your back. As for me, everything I once owned is left behind in nineteen forty-five. Look: even my pockets are empty. We must travel the way our kind have always done, lightly, thinking only of the next step along the road.

No, they will not be coming with us. They are too in love with Hiroshima. This is where they have chosen to be, entwined as I first saw them beneath the wheeling lights on a crowded dance-floor.

Do not make much of your goodbyes. Thank them for their hospitality. Shake Chiyoko's hand, but do not embrace her. She has never invited such affection. Tommy will be puzzled, a little angry, and though he barely knows this it will show in his eyes. In the shadow which seems to be creeping in around the corners of his grin.

*

On the last night before they left for the Museum, when Harding was asleep and Chiyoko in the shower, Rosa slid back the door to the balcony. He was perched in his usual spot on the railing, legs dangling in the air above the far-below street, cigarette hanging between his fingers. He did not look round, and she approached him slowly. The air of the city was glittering and cold, breeze bringing in the smell of the sea.

"We'll be going early," she said. "Before you're awake, I would think."

Tommy did not respond, hunching his back more steeply and blowing out a thin stream of smoke. She leaned her elbows on the railing beside him.

"We'll take trains, all the way up to Hokkaido. There are cargo ships which go from there to the mainland. I'm worried I might lose him along the way, Tom. He's hardly here at all."

"I think his fighting days might be over," said Tommy.

"Perhaps. But the tides might not agree."

They were silent for a while. Rosa's eyes searched the water beyond the islands, where she had seen those tentacled creatures pulsing through the dark. Primal and luminous and strange. She might have swum away with them, disappeared forever into the deep.

"Are you bored here?" he asked. "Is that what it is? Because I was thinking, it's been too long. They say there's a tide all the way back to the sixteenth, flowing from Hirado, where the trade-ships came into the port and pirates smuggled silver out to China. Can you imagine it, Rosa?"

She almost smiled, despite herself.

"We will drink spiced wine, and wear silk. We will stand on the deck of some Goan boat and watch fireworks light the sky."

He turned towards her. She rested her head on her arms, and they looked at one another in the dark over the blurred neon skyscape.

"Gypsy girl." Quietly, with a sudden tremor that made his voice seem barely his own. He finished his cigarette and dropped the stub over the ledge. "We're still friends, aren't we?"

A rupture, a gut-deep wrench of surprise. So I bleed, after all. She reached across and held on to his cold hand.

20

Almonds

At the edge of the desert, Rosa covered her hair and mouth with a red scarf. Twisted the edges, tucked them in carefully. A hot wind blew from between the dunes, coating everything in dust. Men pulled sand-goggles over their eyes. Music blasted from a tinny player which looked as though it was about to melt in the sunshine. In the belly of the boat which had brought them to this vast country, she had dreamed of light glinting from distant golden domes.

Shielding her eyes, she looked across the sands that stretched endlessly away from the ramshackle town. This appeared to be the last outpost before the wilderness. Anticipation fluttered in her stomach. On the device she had bought in Tokyo she traced the miles that were still to be traversed. The signal seemed faint. They had slipped forward seven years or so during the journey from Hiroshima, and she wondered whether the same satellites were still transmitting.

Three months to cross ground and sea; seven years forward. It had never seemed especially important, until now, to know the numbers for certain. All the way, Rosa had crossed off each day in a pocket notebook. She was no longer sure that she could remember unaided.

She turned and saw Harding heading back towards her, face muffled like her own. They had each exchanged their cold-climate clothing weeks back, though he had kept his soldier's boots. Even sunburned, he was still pale, his angular shock of hair still combed painstakingly into place. He joined her on the ridge, adjusting his sunglasses against the midday glare.

"It's no good," he said. "Nobody will take a car out there at this time of year, not for money."

"No 'copters either?"

"Not even camels."

She thought hard. It was maddening to be so close, and yet not quite within reach. "The Museum must take in supplies somehow. If there's anybody still living there."

"One of the guards at the military compound told me that a plane goes out three, four times a year, in the later months when the air's clearest." Harding was rocking himself distractedly from toes to heels. "It's a good sign, no doubt. But we can't wait here for that."

There was no good reason why they could not hold out here until the cooler season – find some ruin to shelter in, steal food from the backs of trucks. The Museum, golden domes and high towers of solid stone, was not going anywhere. But Rosa did not contradict him. The nervous urgency that he could not contain ran through her own body, too.

In need of water, they walked back down the dusty road into the town. Even the shade was scorching. Soldiers milled about in the doorways of derelict apartment blocks, old Kalashnikovs over their shoulders, roll-ups turning their fingers black. Children threw stones at a cat. Rosa looked at the boarded-up shop fronts, the scattered stalls selling bits and pieces to those who were passing through. Odd domestic items, engine parts, tyres, the cracked plastic hull of a rowboat, a folding tent. Her interest caught, she looked more closely, and spotted large plastic water-pouches, solar torches. A couple of threadbare backpacks.

Rosa looked sideways at her travelling companion.

"Harding," she said, "how much can you carry?"

*

The two of them so small, so exposed in the burning heart of the sands. Lone creatures with their backs bent under the weight of the water which will keep them alive. Exiles without a country, nomads without a tribe. Trudging step after step, gasp after gasp into the cloud of dust.

Each morning Harding unzipped the tent and emerged to stare into the haze ahead, shielding his eyes with his hand. The heat was already rippling inches above the ground. The sky was mustard-gas yellow. Still curled in her sleeping bag, Rosa saw him in silhouette, doing up his boots once, twice, three times.

"And this is the right direction?" he asked. "You're certain?"

"As far as I can be. East, towards the sunrise."

"I can't see the sun today. It's all in a fog."

When they had broken camp and shouldered their packs, preparing to walk in the direction where the horizon looked brightest, he said, "Rosa. Our food supplies will not last many days. Water even fewer. We should have an agreement."

She considered. She shifted the weight of her bag until it was a little less painful. "If we don't see this place on the horizon by the time our supplies are half-gone, we turn back."

All day they repeated it to each other like a creed, and Rosa knew in her heart that neither of them believed. This was what they had given themselves to when they left Hiroshima. They had nowhere else to go. They would continue to walk onward and outward until the last drop and the last crumb were gone, and beyond that, until their eyes darkened and their feet failed.

This was desperation. Not a flurry of hurried movements and raised voices, but a long steady march in a direction that might lead nowhere. On the map, its screen now scratched with sand, the pulsing red point grew dimmer. Rosa shook the device and held it up towards the sun to charge, but to no avail. *Until our food and water are gone. Then we turn back.*

When the sun dropped rapidly from the sky, leaving the dunes steaming in the suddenly chill air, she sat with a blanket about her shoulders and burst the blisters on her feet. Tan-coloured lizards emerged from below rocks, tongues flickering. Harding warmed packet-rations on a solar plate, set up dew-catchers and checked the perimeter for snakes. Rosa watched him as they unfolded the canvas together in silence, his entire attention on the task, fighting yet another campaign. In the mornings he rose with military discipline before sunrise and shook her shoulder until she woke, crack-lipped and cursing in the heat. They both grew sluggish on a few careful sips of water, sweat still stiffening yesterday's clothes.

"At El-Alamein," he told her, "we dug our positions by night, and lay in the sand all day with a can of beef and a packet of biscuits. The boredom was so terrible that some of the men began to give names to the flies."

She wondered whether every battle was distinct to him, or whether they flowed one into another, like the endless dunes. "You remember it all?"

"Not always. But it comes back in sharp pieces. Isn't it the same for you?"

He knew from the smell of the air when a sandstorm was coming, and the two of them became practised at pitching the tent with a minute's notice, goggles fixed over their eyes and scarves bound tightly across their mouths. They crouched breathlessly inside as the wind whipped at the fragile structure, shrieking and howling and flinging the whole surface of the desert about in the air. The weight of their bodies and their bags held the tent to the ground. Rosa shielded her head with her arms until the worst of it had passed, surprised each time to find herself unbruised, able to stand and pack up and walk on after the violent interval.

In the wake of each storm, the wide stretch of sands lay innocuously still. And all of this was once ocean. All of this was once deep quiet sea where fish flickered silver and monsters bigger than airships stirred near the surface. The passing ages collided in her mind like continents. We are bound to be burdened with this, our kind, with eyes that cannot stop seeing the world as it once was. As it will be. We can never simply look and see what is.

For Harding, it must all be noise and fury. To him the past and future of every land was the blood shed to shape it, and the battlefields where bones were buried. She thought of him caught in the centre of it all, holding down the fragile tent of his body while history raged on around him.

It pleased her somehow to imagine that he might once have come across Lance Corporal Frank Hyde: that the two of them, unknown to one another, could have shared a cigarette at the edge of a rainy parade-ground, or exchanged a weary nod as two trucks passed by on a muddy foreign road. One man strapping and fair-haired, the other dark and slight. She wished more fervently than ever that she had not sold her grandfather's watch that day in the twenty-first. Its weight around her neck, cool metal on her skin below her loose shirt, would have felt comforting now.

*

After five days and nights the water in their pouches had dipped below the halfway mark, and their remaining ration-packs could be counted on one hand. Rosa followed Harding out of the tent at first light and they looked together towards the far horizon. The sun had not yet risen, but the sky was clear lilac in expectation.

They could see for miles. No silhouette. No white stone and golden domes rising up out of the sand.

Unspeaking, they packed up the tent and continued to walk east. Dawn coloured everything deep scarlet. Rosa's mouth had been paper-dry for days now, but when they stopped in the shade of a boulder at noon, she allowed herself only a few gulps of water. Harding watched her, then followed suit. He leaned back into the thin shade and closed his eyes.

"Tell me again," he muttered, "about the Museum."

"I don't…"

"Please," he said.

She rubbed a hand across her flaking lips. Conversation seemed like a frivolous expenditure of strength. He had asked for the same thing five, six times in the course of their journey, and she always used the same words. "I was there… five years ago. In my time. Nearly a hundred years ago, in theirs." She could see him drinking it in again, hands trembling in anticipation as she struggled to form each short sentence.

"I saw the place before they even began it, and when it was almost complete. They built it taller than a temple. Grander than a palace." It felt like a fiction she was spinning to keep him sane. "They built it as far as they could from anywhere. This was when they thought the world was about to be blown apart."

"Tell me again about the treasures." He had opened his bloodshot eyes, squinting sideways at her. A fly landed on his forehead, but he barely seemed to notice. In the baking heat, Rosa tried to conjure cool stone spaces, trickling fountains and curiosities behind glass.

"They brought treasures there from every civilization which had ever been. They were afraid of what might be lost. Our people left precious things in their keeping."

"The Historians," murmured Harding.

Rosa looked out towards the horizon. "They discovered us when they were digging in the corners of history. They knew all about me." Here, she usually stopped. She hoped that Harding could not detect her fear, her frustration with the Rosa who had sat across the table from them and never quite been curious enough. "I think they could have told me... if I'd have asked..."

He let out a careful breath, flattening his hair to his head. He intoned, more to himself than to her, "They will tell us. They know what we are."

She lay awake with her face close to the wind-battered canvas, feet cold as ice in the bottom of her thin sleeping bag. Harding's sharp elbows and spine dug into her back as he stirred continually. What if, came the thought in the long bleak hours when he was asleep and she was alone with herself, what if Chiyoko had been wrong, and they had been deceived at the edge of the desert? What if the Museum had been demolished years before and lay now in ruins, its remaining stones vanished beneath the expansive sands?

She turned over to look at Harding's peak of hair, the only part of him visible outside of his sleeping bag. She had brought him this far, and it seemed to her now that his need was more raw, more stinging than her own. For his sake she did not voice the worst possibility: that the Museum stood yet, but held no truth or consolation for them within its walls.

*

You were this weak once before, Rosa. Do you not remember? On the shore of the frozen sea, where you barely kept yourself alive in the hollow between the rocks. Only Tommy Rust's disembodied grin for company. Your mind began to wander as your body lost its strength. Now there are two of you, your steps staggering, breath torn out of your searing throats. There is perhaps one more day's journey left in you.

We might quickly test, she thought, whether we are indeed undying. We might drink our canteens dry and march onward under the scorching sun. Either way, the answer we are searching for is close at hand.

"Rosa. Do you see them?" Harding's hand upon her elbow. He pulled her to a halt at the dizzying apex of midday. He was pointing into the sky, and for a moment she feared that he had run mad as poor, lost Harris Black. But then she noticed a circle of wheeling birds, wing-feathers barely fluttering as they hung on the haze.

The two travellers stumbled and gasped between scattered rocks, up the side of a sharp ridge. The birds were further away than they appeared, the dunes steeper. It was then that the sound of running water became audible. By the time Rosa and Harding had topped the rise, a feast of inexplicable green had unfolded below them.

A clear stream trickled along the bottom of the valley, which was lined with a thick growth of grass and - wonder of wonders - pink-blossomed almond trees. Clouds of bright flowers were reflected in the water. It had been so many days since they had seen anything but sand. Rosa stood sore-eyed and blinked in disbelief. Beside her, Harding dropped his pack to the ground. It was as though they had walked out of the world.

They could not descend quickly enough. They tore away their shoes as stones gave way to soft grass underfoot, shedding their belongings as they went, and waded fully-clothed into the water. It was waist-deep and flowing cool from under the earth. Rosa sunk below the surface and felt her skin wash clean. The stream wrapped itself around her limbs, light as silk.

She stood up and drank, cupping her hands and raising water

to her lips. The dust that had lined her throat for days was washed away. She pulled at the scarf which was tied around her head and dipped underwater again, running fingers through her tangled hair. It drifted across her vision, still streaked with faded cobalt blue.

The sun shone dappled through the trees into the heart of the valley, and Rosa and Harding remained half-submerged, leaning back in the water beneath the bright sky. She watched him as he took care over the washing of his face and neck, the bones of his spine and shoulder blades protruding through his sodden shirt. He stood and rested his hands upon the surface, lost in thought. There was a small stillness at the centre of him.

Rosa looked away, to where the stream trickled between tree-roots on its way out of the ground. The water itself, she realised, smelled sweet. It smelled of almonds.

*

They didn't put up their tent, but spread the canvas on the grass above the water when the light began to fade. They hung their wet things from the branches. The cool of the desert evening was gentler here. The valley seemed to hold them in its open palms.

Rosa tucked her arms behind her head and watched the bird that was rustling in the tree above. She felt ready to curl up and sleep. Harding came back from the river with the pan in which they'd heated the last of their rations. He sat down on the canvas and rested his arms on his knees, slapped absently at an insect on his wrist as he looked out into the darkening distance. In his sunburned face, washed of sand, his eyes looked light and clear.

"Rosa," he said after a while. "Let's go on."

She sat up slowly. Her muscles were aching, feet throbbing and swollen. "The map's dead."

"We'll be hungry again in the morning. There's still some daylight left. I feel as though if we go now, we might make it."

Rosa gave him a thin smile. Since Hiroshima, she had felt the need to shield him from the worst. It was odd, given how much of the worst he had already seen. "I'm sorry I led you nowhere."

"I believe that we're close."

"Listen," she said, but then found she had nothing to warn him with. She rubbed a thumb over the sore soles of her feet, still smiling slightly. Why not? Better to perish sooner, in the hard and ugly wilderness, if he believes.

She realised that he was watching her. Turn away, Soldier, she willed. Put your faith elsewhere. "I'm afraid," she said, as gently as she knew how, "that even if we get there, it won't be all you've hoped."

Harding did not turn. "It was like a light lit in me," he said. "After I saw you that second time, after I realised what you were. I carried you with me all those years, and I hoped. It didn't matter so much to me what you knew, or did not know. It mattered that I was not alone."

*

At last, when they had walked just a few more miles east in the cool of the evening, the Museum. They caught sight of it first by starlight, in the strange hour when the sun had just vacated the sky and left unearthly colours in its wake. Vapour rising from the cooling sands. Rosa's heart faltered, amazement and relief and terror washing over her all at once. Her clothes and hair were still damp from the stream. That place had been real, and so was this.

Her companion's head was bowed, the exhaustion of the long journey finally overcoming him. Rosa touched his shoulder. "Ready?" she asked.

He adjusted the weight of his pack. He nodded.

The makeshift town of tents and cabins that had once surrounded the Museum was gone. The building stood alone upon a low hill, the bottom half of its long staircase now buried under the sand. Gilt paint was peeling from the golden domes, and as they drew near a chattering flock of bats or black birds rose from the highest tower. Gardens had been planted between some of the nearby dunes, young shoots showing through the sand, a wriggling hose rigged to spray water unevenly in all directions.

As she faced the climb to the main doorway, Rosa was weakened by the momentary fear that the old building had been abandoned. But then she saw a light at one of the high windows.

At the top of the staircase she pounded her fists against the great oak door, and Harding joined her, the two of them raising a deafening clamour. She had a foolish thought of the Historians descending to answer the noise in their immaculate suits, exactly as she had known them nearly a hundred years before. Their eyes full and empty both at once, unsmiling. She wondered what had passed in this place in the time between.

Echoing footsteps in the hall beyond. Harding fell back, tense with expectation. Rosa lowered her scarf. She steeled herself to meet whatever lay within.

Heavy bolts rattled, and the door swung inward with a creaking groan. Before them stood a solitary young woman, small in stature, with spikes of white-bleached hair and metal hoops through her lips and nose. She regarded the two of them, her obvious delight mingled with shrewd interest, like a naturalist looking on a species familiar from long study.

"Travellers," she said. "Come inside."

21

The Most Beautiful Place

In the high-ceilinged space, something pale and enormous hung dimly overhead. A mountain of a beast, a thing nature could surely not have made. Out of place, out of time in this dry cool hall above the burning desert. The bones were bleached grey. The ribs might have contained a house, two, its long prehistoric jaw curved like a beak, its spine tapering to a narrow tail. Fingered fins sprouted from its shoulder-plates like wings. It was suspended from the peak of the ceiling with ropes.

Rosa could not tear her eyes from it, turning on the spot as Harding and the woman crossed the hall ahead of her. It dwarfed her to nothingness. She thought that she heard the creaking of ancient joints.

"Are you coming?"

"Yes, yes..."

Through a door at the far end of the hall, into a familiar sloping, low-ceilinged chamber. The spears hanging along the wall had gathered years of dust. Masks leered and gaped. Rosa and Harding trailed sand behind them as they followed the woman into a circular second-floor gallery, hung with gleaming white guns made from an unfamiliar metal. Rosa supposed that walls must have been demolished and rebuilt in new places since her last visit, new corners and cabinets created to house the growing collection of exhibits.

"Has much changed?" asked the women, whom Rosa realised had paused and turned, hand on her hip. She wore ragged jeans and moccasins and a short T-shirt. There was another metal hoop in her belly.

"Some things."

The woman flashed a grin. "It must have been incredible to see it at the start. Before they'd even laid the last bricks."

Rosa didn't reply. So far there had been nothing threatening in the welcome, but she was still wary. The light from the windows had almost faded, and the three of them cast long, meandering shadows across the flagstones. Tall wooden idols loomed out of alcoves. They passed through a room full of shelves of black boxes, each one emitting inexplicable beeps at a different pitch.

"Rosa, you were here at the height of the Cold War, weren't you? That's when our predecessors were really getting started."

She barely registered any surprise at the use of her name. Her weariness must have shown, as the woman checked herself, pausing in a doorway and extending a hand.

"I'm sorry. I'm Sola Emin, research fellow."

Harding shook the hand first, and Rosa cautiously followed.

Sola bobbed her head, not without awkwardness. "Well... You must be exhausted. I'll show you where you can wash and sleep."

"Just sleep, for now," said Harding. "If that's all right."

"Yes, of course." Their host looked at them. "Will you be wanting one room or two?"

"Two," said Rosa. "Please."

They were led around a corner and down another flight of stairs. Though the corridor outside was now narrower and the space had been re-purposed as a series of partitioned rooms, Rosa knew that this had once been the medical bay. She had spent weeks here recovering from her time on the frozen beach. Sola Emin unlocked two doors and motioned them each inside, flicking on the electric lights as she did so. "I'll bring you bed-sheets and something to eat. There's a bathroom at the end of the hall."

"Are you alone here?" asked Rosa.

"My colleague's up in the library. She's Alexis Haforth, Lex. She won't have heard you arrive. She'll be so excited, I should go and tell her." Sola seemed reluctant to drag her eyes from the two of them. She stood in the centre of the corridor, passing her bunch of keys from one hand to the other. "Will you be all right?"

"We'll last until morning," said Rosa. Sola pocketed the keys, still lingering. She seemed to be waiting for requests or questions which did not come.

"We'll sit down with you tomorrow, we'll talk. Take some rest. And don't mind the noises the Museum makes by night."

*

Awake in the muggy hours past midnight, Rosa threw off her blankets and walked barefoot along the Egyptian gallery, past the silent lines of mummies. Their long eyes gazed serenely back at her through the glass. How can you look out with such authority, still, pharaohs and priests, upon a world that has changed beyond your wildest imaginings? What secrets have you kept these long dusty decades?

Pausing before the sandstone sphinx which took pride of place at the head of the room, she heard movement from below. She descended the back stairs, and spied a lanky, greying woman through the open door of the little kitchen. She was humming to herself as she filled the kettle.

As though sensing that she was being watched, the woman looked around. A wide smile spread across her lined face. She beckoned Rosa into the kitchen.

"Sal told me you were both asleep. You must be Rosa Hyde."

Her voice had a slight Scots inflection. Rosa came cautiously down the steps. The woman, whom she assumed to be Lex, dried her hands on a tea towel. She was wearing a frayed dressing gown over her linen shirt and trousers, and her feet were bare.

"Now," said Lex, "I can do you a coffee if you're wanting to stay up, or something else if you'll be going back to bed. I grow my own mint and camomile and ginger in the dune-gardens."

"Coffee, please," said Rosa. "Black." She leaned against the work surface, which was strewn with empty milk cartons and unwashed mugs. Apparently the present inhabitants of the museum were not concerned with orderliness.

Steam rose from the filter, and Lex handed Rosa a chipped cup of dark liquid. It smelled musty, as though it had been too long in a cupboard. It was a wonderfully ordinary taste. She drank slowly, feeling the fuzziness at the edges of her mind retreat. Lex looked on with ravenous curiosity. "You come far?" she asked.

"In time? Or in miles?"

"Either."

"We came from Hiroshima. I hardly thought we'd make it. Does nobody else ever come out here? There are no roads, no towns for miles."

"It's true," said Lex. "We don't get a lot of visitors."

"You should build roads," said Rosa. The blisters on her feet stung against the cool floor. She rubbed the sunburn on the back of her neck. The journey already felt a lifetime ago.

"I have to say —" Lex's voice burst from her. Aware of having startled Rosa she cleared her throat. "I don't think you know what this means to us. I don't think you can understand."

"I'm sorry?"

"Sal and I are three and a half years into our four-year posting. We thought we might never get a chance to meet one of you. It's what everyone hopes for when they come out here."

"I'm nobody," said Rosa.

"No..." Lex put down her drink, and Rosa felt an ominous burning sensation begin at the back of her throat. "Listen to me.

261

Do you, do *any* of you, understand what you mean to us? What each of us would give, for five minutes with you? You are..." She shook her head. "You are the stuff of legends."

In Lex's soft tones this sentiment was not sinister, as it had once seemed in a smoke-filled tent among the first of the Historians. But since it was both undeserved and kindly meant, it cut all the deeper. "Look," said Rosa roughly. "You can say what you like to me. I've had time to think, to take all this apart. But be careful with him. I'll make it my business, to see that you only speak the truth."

"Of course. But I meant it, Rosa Hyde." Lex peered seriously over her spectacles. "It's not flattery."

"I'm afraid I'll be a terrible disappointment to you."

"No," said Lex. "No you won't."

*

They slept late, and it was afternoon before Sola called them up to a shaded roof terrace on the third floor, overlooking Lex's irrigated gardens. Rosa took time to shower and brush her hair, to put on the clean clothes that had been left at the end of her bed. This felt to her like a grave occasion. On the terrace, she and Harding took low seats opposite Lex and Sola at a table spread with files. The two women were fanning themselves, and Rosa saw them exchange a glance.

"Is it too hot up here?" asked Sola. "We can go inside."

Harding shook his head. "It's fine," said Rosa.

Lex pushed a jug of water and two glasses towards them. "Did you sleep?" she asked.

"Quite well," said Harding. "Thank you." Rosa looked past him, to the deep blue bowl of the sky. A bird hovered motionless, high above the domes and towers of the Museum. She remembered leaving this place by biplane, borne away above the patchwork of sun-scorched fields. In the corner of her vision the desert blurred, as though a gust of wind was stirring up the sand. She felt a tug in her ribcage behind her heart, and steadied herself. Hold on here. Find the courage now that you did not have then.

Sola continued. "I know you have questions, and we have some for you, too. But this can wait, if you want it to. Look around the Museum, take some rest. Whenever you're ready."

"We're here now," said Rosa at once. The bird's wings dipped, and it faltered, dropping lower. She turned back to the table, pouring herself a glass of water with a steady hand. "What's the use in delaying? Either of us could be taken away, at any time."

Sola and Lex both drew back imperceptibly. "If you're going anywhere," said Lex, "it isn't back. You haven't been seen here since the sixties. And your friend – this is the first the Museum has seen of him."

"We know you, Rosa Beatrice Hyde," said Sola. "And you know us. We're representatives of the movement who once called themselves the Historians. Our remit is the study and preservation of civilized memory. They were once... well, you met some of our early predecessors. They were scattered, disorganised, just a few believers swapping stories of sightings. You in particular left them a clear trail."

"Believers," said Rosa.

"Do you know what they called you?" Lex broke in breathlessly. "Those who first discovered your existence?"

A flash of gut-deep terror jolted Rosa's body. She was relieved when Sola broke in. "It must have been alarming for you, to meet them."

Lex met Rosa's gaze. "You showed them something more than what they'd imagined in their own philosophy. That's... I'm sure it's not the same, for your kind. But for us... well. Of course we're so much poorer, but we've painted caves, too, and dreamed of lives that don't end with these bodies." She laughed apologetically. "I'm no poet."

263

Sola shuffled her papers. Her eyes flickered uneasily sideways. Rosa remembered hands that had reached out to touch her hair and forehead, soft chanting. Their blissful expressions. Until now she had never felt much for them but alarm and contempt.

"The Historians were so different, when I journeyed forward." She dug a thumbnail into her palm. "They looked at me differently. Why was that?"

Sola opened the file at her right hand. Their gaze shifted to the man sat quietly in the other chair.

"Marcus James Harding," said Sola. "We hoped that you would come here. Even amongst your kind, your life has been strange."

A ripple passed through Harding's body. Rosa saw him clasp his hands together below the table in a bone-breaking grip.

"Do you remember much of your childhood?"

"I have something which I most urgently need to ask you," said Harding. Rosa felt her own heart begin to hammer faster. It was unbearable, and it was all that she had journeyed for. To *know*, once and for all. To be certain of that which she had carried in her heart like a black seed since the frozen beach.

"I have fought for a thousand years," said Harding hoarsely. "I have walked away unscathed from too many battlefields. You have my life there, don't you? What do you make of it? Is there any explanation but one?"

"Marcus —"

"*Am I to live forever?*" he asked. He seemed on the point of buckling.

"Marcus," said Sola Emin. "Listen to me." She reached across the table and took his forearm. "You were born to parents who were travellers, like you. As a young child you lived in many places, in many ages. You don't remember, do you? Your mother and father had a taste for treasures."

Sola showed a page in the file to Harding. It was a torn sepia photograph, carefully taped back together, of a man and a woman holding a small, dark-haired boy. Harding's father was heavily bespectacled, to all appearances as serious as his son would one day be. The woman had a clever, impish face and wore an opulent dress. Harding stared down at the portrait with a look of raw longing.

"In the early days, before there was any Museum, their collecting habits caught the attention of our predecessors. These were the Historians as you first met them, Rosa, before they'd given themselves any such title. They had little in the way of knowledge, nothing but impossible photographs, an inexplicable trail of objects found in the wrong decades. They were hungry for answers."

Lex opened another file to show a collection of maps and diagrams, charts with notes scribbled furiously in the margins. "Max and Elsa Harding were the first whose location they were able to track and pinpoint in their own time. These people..." she faltered. "How can I explain? How that kind of obsession, it becomes reckless with its object."

Their eyes had been full and empty both at once. Their hearts had been consumed with desire. Harding looked up from the picture of his parents.

"Their question was the same as yours," said Sola. "Whether these men and women, whose footprints could be found across the ages...whether they were beyond destruction."

"They believed with such passion that these beings wouldn't be touched by anything so ordinary as bullets," said Lex. "They believed that your mother and father would simply stand up and brush themselves off. It would have made no sense, otherwise, to shoot both."

"But both died," said Sola, "and the question was settled."

"We're sorry," said Lex. "It was a long time ago."

Rosa did not dare look sideways at Harding. He was silent. A wave of fury swept over her, dissipating into helplessness as quickly as it had come. It was all so very long ago. And yet it was happening still, again and again, the shots which continued to ring through time just a hair's breadth away, like the explosion at Hiroshima.

So it is conclusively answered. It was not that she had not known. She had known since the frozen beach, at least, perhaps even longer ago than that. But isn't there a way that we have, of making for ourselves a place where things are and are not?

"If we can be killed," she asked faintly, "how has he come unscarred through so many wars?"

Sola and Lex glanced at one another. Neither seemed to want to reply.

"We don't have any answer that will satisfy you," said Sola. "It can only be... coincidence. Or divine providence. Whatever you wish to call it. Perhaps even that his own belief has carried him safely through."

"The things that are certain – they're already enough for you to bear," said Lex quietly. "Let there be a little room for wonder."

Rosa hardly heard her. She rubbed her dry eyes. "I suppose we can die like civilians too, if nobody puts a bullet in our brains. I suppose we age and wither like anybody else?"

Sola seemed to be steeling herself. She laid down Harding's file carefully. "They performed post-mortem examinations on Max and Elsa Harding. They were sure they would find something different about the bodies, something new. But they only found flesh and blood. Two thirty-three-year-olds who were... too aged on the inside." She looked up. "I'm sorry. I think our predecessors asked you this, when you were here before. But how old were your parents, when you last saw them?"

"I'm not sure." It was dawning on Rosa why this mattered. Horror marched towards her with steady steps. "They must have been... in their fifties..."

Sola and Lex glanced at one another. "The theory is that the Hydes are a special case," Sola said. Her voice was even, but she toyed nervously with the ring in her lip. "Robert and Harriet never travelled any distance. They will last longer before their bodies begin to pay the penalty for their journeys. Do you see?"

There was a cavernous pause. Rosa lowered her gaze, covered her eyes with her hand. She wanted to tell Harding to shield his own eyes too, to avoid looking directly into what was now being revealed.

"We have yet to find any, with the exception of Robert and Harriet Hyde, who have lived past thirty-five."

"We don't know how you came to be what you are," said Sola. "But we can tell you what is going to happen to you. We should tell you, as a kindness." The words had clearly been rehearsed. This is half of why they're here, thought Rosa. To break this over us, and do it as kindly as they can. "It seems that no human body was made to endure passage through time. Perhaps you have noticed signs already..."

"So they're all dead, then," Rosa broke in. She felt the heat rising in her cheeks. "Or at least, they will be dead, before I can see them again as I knew them. My parents. Amber Lakshmi, the Brothers Black." A catch in her throat — she could not utter the final name.

"Rosa, I'm sorry, but... we believe there should be limitations. When it comes to giving out specifics." Sola's face barely concealed the strain. "About your family and friends, or the portion of your own lives which is still to come. But perhaps we can offer some advice..."

"I don't care about your advice." Rosa's voice had become stone-hard. "What do you know of them? Have they been here?"

The young curator did not hold for long under Rosa's fierce gaze, looking to Lex, who gave her a nod of assent. Sola spoke in a rush, as though the words might wreak less havoc this way. "In brief, then. Your father never left nineteen forty-five. Your mother did make it beyond that year, but not by much. As for Amara Lakshmi, the woman you call Amber, she is well known to the Museum. She helped put together some of the collections, and was in reasonable health at her last visit thirteen years ago. Harris Black was lost to our records not long after you yourself parted from him."

With grim resolution, Rosa asked, "Nate?"

"I'm sorry," said Lex. The afternoon's umpteenth apology tolled like a bell. They truly are, thought Rosa in dim surprise, they truly feel something for our fate. It's more than we've ever offered them. "He visited around six years ago. He was alone. Our predecessors spent many hours speaking with him, but he seemed beyond consolation. His mind was not... there was nothing they could have done." Her gaze flicked inadvertently out beyond the dune gardens, to a shaded spot marked by a series of stones. "He is buried beneath the sands."

Sola closed the file and drew it back towards her chest. A few thin plates of cloud hung in the desert sky, bright around the edges. The breeze stirred up yellow dust.

"Is there a cure?" asked Harding suddenly.

He had been silent for so long that Lex and Sola started. He was perfectly still, his back ramrod-straight and his palms flat on the table.

"What –?" began Lex.

"A *cure.*"

Sola and Lex did not reply. Rosa watched Harding flatten his hair convulsively to his head, and felt a strange sense of pride. They might think he was simple, for holding such a hope – and the truth of it was plain. But she knew that the question had been whispered too in some childish part of her heart. She was glad he had asked.

*

Later, when the Museum was quiet and the four walls of her room closing in airlessly around her, Rosa heard her name being called from the end of the corridor. She wrapped her scarf about her shoulders and ventured cautiously out, rubbing at the sore rims of her eyes. No tears. Just a hot red itch, a pressing pain in her temples.

"Rosa. *Rosa*."

Harding's door was ajar. He was seated on his bed, staring at the ceiling. His possessions, such as they were, had been lined up meticulously against the wall. His military boots. Water-pouch. Spare shirt, folded into a perfect square. Penknife, bowl and cup. There was something touching about this small patch of order, wrenched with such stubbornness from the chaos.

"They should put you in charge of the collections," Rosa said. "Nothing would ever be out of its place." He was wringing his hands together, over and over again. She sat down beside him. She didn't try to touch him, but after a while, he grew still of his own accord. "What is it?"

"I shan't sleep unless I have…something brighter to rest my mind on. But there's nothing within my reach. Can you tell me, what is the most beautiful place you have ever been?"

Unguarded, he turned to look at her. Rosa thought of all the wonders which had passed before her eyes. She did not expect to hear the words which left her.

"It was a home. In the London that has been and gone. Red and cream flowers on the curtains, photographs on the wall. A table where they ate together. Children were born and grew older there. I think… I almost think that if I had laid down in those sheets and slept just one night, I might have woken in a different life."

He closed his eyes. "Photographs on the wall. Red and cream flowers."

"Yes. And sunlight came through the windows in the late afternoon."

22

'Til Death

Why not stay a while, since you have travelled so far to be here. Why not shower each morning, with the bathroom window wide open to the dunes, the hot air billowing inwards to meet the cool water as it streams down your skin. The unforgiving azure desert sky. Why not help Lex as she goes about planting a mango grove on the south-facing slope behind the Museum, irrigated from below the earth by the same river that washed you at the green oasis.

Sit for an hour in that shaded spot where the stones are laid, where Nate and many nameless others are at rest. Pour a glass of the whisky you found in a dusty kitchen cupboard, drink to him there. Spill a little into the sand. Tell him aloud what you are thinking. You should have lived out your years, Nate Black, growing grey in that smoke-smelling cabin where you were born, never riding more than thirty miles west, where there might have been a tiny town with a baker and a blacksmith and your favourite saloon.

A place such as this one should never have entered into your wildest imaginings, man from continents away, centuries before. You should have been buried by the sons you might have had, beside the father and mother you might have cared for in their last years, in the high pasture where the steers run. Laid down deep roots, returned to the same earth that fed you. But these things cannot be, for us. Our time is all out of joint.

Outside the stone walls the sun pulses white-hot, but inside all is cool and dark and quiet. There are worse places, Rosa, in which to digest grief. The Museum seems almost made for it. Here amongst the dusty trappings of lives lived long ago, of civilisations laid below the ground, there is space to die.

Because that is what is now left to you. The long slow surrender of the tender hopeful things you have carried in secret. You always knew that it was foolish to hold them too hard. The Museum makes you ready. You almost feel that you might unpackage yourself and lay the pieces down in cabinets and cases, behind glass, to endure long after you are gone.

*

She did not ask Harding to share his own sorrow. He had, she noticed, moved his things out of the small basement bedroom, and taken to sleeping elsewhere. There were many galleries and staircases, halls and hidden little rooms; it would have been possible to disappear for days without discovery. He emerged for meals, and the four of them sat around the table in the untidy kitchen, digging into rehydrated sachets and cans from the endless cupboards, the sweet beans and succulent grasses that Lex grew in the dunes.

"The first year we were here, we had nothing fresh. The secondment before us, I think the supply planes used to come out more often. I had to start the garden from scratch."

"I told you," said Rosa. "Build a road."

Sola laughed. "With what money? We barely make a salary. It's only eccentrics and academics like us who care about the Museum now."

"We're here for love, not money." Lex dug in her fork and took a large mouthful. *I don't think you know what this means to us,* she had said. *It's what everyone hopes for, when they come here.* Rosa looked

271

between the two curators and felt that she would not much mind giving them what they wanted. What reason was there to take it all to her grave, other than some proud sense of possession. Every living piece of history would be a pearl to these people.

She found them both later in Sola's study, a red-draped room adjoining the South American gallery. There was a spreading fern in a pot propping open the door, and abstract pictures of bodies in motion adorned the walls, sketched in strong charcoal lines. Rosa wondered whether Sola had drawn them herself. The two women were leaning on the desk, talking in low voices. They looked up when she came in.

"Are you all right? Are you still hungry?"

"There's no one else who remembers," said Rosa. She leaned against the door-frame. "Is there? Who *really* remembers. You've got your statues and your fossils and your pieces of parchment, but they're not history." You know that, curators of dry bones. They're not the taste and the touch and the smell of it. The past is a land from which you are forever exiled. "We're all you've got, and we're disappearing."

Lex's face registered surprise at her directness. "Will you talk with us?" she asked.

Rosa nodded. "There's so much that I've seen. I don't want…" She scratched awkwardly at the back of her neck, realising how sentimental it would sound. All those people and all those places — they ought not to be taken to the grave. Not yet, if they could live on a little longer.

Once she had worn an embroidered gown and painted her face white and called herself the Fabulist. She had walked into golden halls and told the mighty and the wise of things still to come. Now, in Sola's old jeans and a patched shirt, she sat at a table in a small twilit room and waited while the curators placed a recording device before her. She searched for words to speak of things gone by.

It became a daily routine. Sola and Lex teased out texture and detail, taking notes on their hand-held screens. Rosa recalled as best she could the manner of dress of the court at Seysair; the feast at Mell-Supper, the flags and bells on the bridles of the horses when the ladies went hunting. There was a girl named Heloise, with a forbidding frown that vanished when she rode after her hawk. There was a lord with a fat belly who wanted to hear about flying machines.

Another place, another age. The songs that spilt from tavern windows in the London of the mid-nineteenth. Boats on the misty Thames bringing in cargo from the empire where the sun never set. Then there were Milanese painters with pointed shoes in the fifteenth; perfumes for sale in a Roman market; the famous faces glimpsed in the music-halls of Montparnasse, at the time when that quarter of the city seemed the centre of the whole universe.

As Rosa spoke, the sights she was describing flashed across her lids. Flared, faded, died. Memory after memory lost its weight and lustre, settling in her mind like leaf-matter. She felt lighter, looser in her limbs. The telling of her journeys was the exhalation of a long sigh.

A handful of things, she kept for herself. The sound of Tommy's laughter beneath the canal bridge while the masquers danced above. The sheets in that London home that had smelled of a life beyond her reach.

*

Her mind meandered, needle-sharp one minute, vague the next. Sometimes it seemed that a bank of fog had risen to shroud the shapes of the things which had made her. The answers to simple questions died on the tip of her tongue. She stared at the two faces across the table, forgetting for the terrifying space of a breath what she was doing in this chair in this room.

"Take your time," said Sola, as the curators exchanged the look which had grown familiar to Rosa, the mutual acknowledgement of the need to be cautious. "This can't be easy."

They had said, *we can tell you what is going to happen to you.* Rosa did not need them to. The aches and chills in her body told their own story. She wondered if she would journey again soon; even whether, despite their reassurances, there was a chance she would be swept back to that ancient age of sea-beasts and snow. A cold sweat covered her palms at the prospect. She clenched her fists as though she was trying to cling to the present with the strength of her hands.

"How many of your predecessors found our beds suddenly empty?" she asked. "I wouldn't want to leave that way."

"Fewer than you'd think," said Sola. "We think there are so many small waves here, in so many directions, that they all but cancel each other out."

Nate Black had said, *the tides are conscious of us. They are savage with us.* Rosa was not sure whether he was right; but some things, at least, were now clear. It has never been possible to walk upon the waves. Our journeys possess us, far more than we ever possessed them.

"I don't suppose the Historians completed their map of the tides?" she asked. "They were working on it, I remember."

"They tried for many years, with some success," said Sola. "But I think you know better than we do, why you go, where you go."

Rosa smiled slightly, wistfully. "Amber told me once that she could choose."

"It's probably true that she had – has – more control than most. But Rosa –" Sola was looking at her, pity no longer hidden. "You people... there's a way you have, of telling stories to yourselves. You seem given to a particular sort of unwitting deceit."

*

But there is one of us who never learnt the trick of it, because we never taught him. If his conclusions were wrong, they were at least honest. He stared death in the face for a thousand years. There was nobody to tell him he ought to cover his eyes and look away.

Harding, too, talked with Sola and Lex. Rosa sat down in the cool corridor outside the study as fragments of his tales slipped out through the crack under the closed door. She pressed her back against the wall and wrapped her arms around her knees. Sunlight poured in through a slit window overhead but she closed her eyes against its brightness, scenes forming on her darkened lids. Flanders fields at dawn, the night's mist lifting over the filthy burrow-holes and endless coils of wire. Troupes spilling out of 'copters like ants from a nest onto the industrial wastes of North China in the pelting black rain.

*

Like Harding, she could no longer bear to sleep underground. In the middle of the night she carried her blankets to the Greek gallery and laid them down among crumbling stone pillars and pensive statues. The enormous moon hung beyond the window. Rosa curled by the feet of a woman who was bending to fill the water-jug upon her shoulder, antique features soft in the half-light.

Restless still, she rose and wandered just as she had done in the time of the Historians, feet bare and scarf wrapped around her chilly shoulders. She discovered new doorways and staircases and entire wings, parts of the Museum that had not existed at her last visit. In the library, spiders spun webs between countless tomes. Shelves towered as high as the vaulted ceiling, catalogued by continent and century, creaking beneath the weight of words and the worlds they held. There were sliding ladders which the curators presumably used to reach the uppermost heights. Rosa blew dust from pages inscribed with long-dead tongues, ran her fingertips over cracked leather spines.

She resisted the urge to descend into the basement, to rummage through the locked cabinets and stand before the wall of photographs. Weren't the things that were already certain enough to bear? But she was drawn to the light spilling from the half-open door of a room on the landing, Lex's study: empty. The desk, lit by a funny wooden lamp in the shape of a giraffe, was covered in books and stained coffee mugs, untidy heaps of documents. Rosa glanced over her shoulder and slipped inside, her hands moving across the files with a will of their own.

At the very moment when she spotted a name she recognised, a name which shook her suddenly wide awake, came the noise of a throat being cleared behind her.

"Old friends of yours?" Lex was standing in the doorway, wearing her dressing-gown and carrying a cup of coffee. She moved forward to turn up the brightness of the lamp, and regarded Rosa benignly, taking a sip from her steaming drink. Her frizz of greying hair was tied up in a net. "I've been reading back through those records, all the visits your kind have made to the Museum. The stories they told! The true ones are enough, but some of them are completely invented. Instead of the lives the Historians knew they'd had, they spoke about homes they couldn't possibly have known. As though they'd made these places in their own minds, and lived there."

Rosa felt her hand trembling on the open page of the file. "Chiyoko Hira was here."

"Hira? Yes. She was the last to come here, actually, before you. She arrived alone and barely on her feet. This was before me and Sal. She wasn't forthcoming with her answers, they said, but asked her questions, then left. I was right, to think that you knew her?"

"I met her." An ugly thought made Rosa turn her face away from Lex. If Chiyoko was here, it meant that she left him. Something passed between them to make her leave him; or perhaps there was not enough left of him to make her stay.

Look into the mouth of it now, gypsy girl. You will not see him again; and if you did, he would not know you.

"Rosa?" She realised that she had lowered herself to the floor and that Lex had crouched down beside her. She looked at the curator, who had laid an uncertain hand upon her arm, and the kindness in the gesture cut too deep.

"How am I to live?" The corners of her eyes began bleeding tears. She looked down, surprised, as though the droplets might be coming from somewhere else. Tears splashed onto the backs of her hands and onto the threadbare carpet. "Where am I to go?"

"Rosa…"

"I can't hold on, not in any time, not in any place. I'll only fall again, and every fall will only bring the end more quickly."

You see it now. You see what is waiting for you through the collapsing telescope of the years; you saw it when the red glow of the skyscraper lit the side of Tommy Rust's face, and he was unfamiliar. You saw it so long before that, for the first time as you fled through the fields from Seysair, and your feet beat out that rhythm upon the ground.

"Don't cry," said Lex. "Please. Here…" She fished out a handkerchief from her pocket, and the gesture was so timeless in its banality that Rosa almost laughed. "I won't pretend I can understand. I'll go and make tea for you, give you a little time."

"No," said Rosa. "Don't go." She dried her eyes in two rough movements, gave back the handkerchief. Still huddled on the floor, she took hold of Lex's wrist, suddenly entranced by the fine web of lines that crossed the back of the curator's hands, fanned out from her eyes and mouth. Rosa had never looked at one of the other kind with so much attention. Their skin, it stretches and mends and ages so patiently.

"I want you to tell me what's going to happen," she said. "How it ends for us."

"I'm not supposed to…"

"I don't mean specifics. I mean for all of us. I'm tired already, Lex. Please tell me what I should be prepared for."

She still had hold of the curator's wrist. The older woman shuffled closer. They sat together on the carpet in the middle of the untidy room, darkness outside the door.

"The further and faster you travel, the quicker the decline," said Lex. "If you want to last longer you must find places where you don't feel the tides. Live as quietly as you can. I can tell you how to get back to nineteen forty-five from here, if you think that would be best." Rosa felt herself rock forward a little, back again. Each word that followed, so gently spoken, was a bruising blow. "Your body will turn against you. Your mind will fail you. The day will come when you can no longer recall who you are, or where you've come from. But maybe that won't be so distressing." Seeing Rosa's expression, she added, "I mean to say… perhaps you won't remember any longer, that you can't remember. Perhaps it's like being a child again. "

A creature that is conscious of nothing but now. When Rosa tightened her grip, Lex prised her fingers open. "I hold to what I said, the night you arrived here. We've waited so long to meet you." The curator's cheeks were flushed with sincerity, her eyes bright. "Please. See yourselves as we do. Keep the name the Historians gave you."

Rosa was hardly listening any more. She lurched to her feet, meaning to leave and find her way back to the Greek gallery, where she could curl among her blankets at the base of the statue. Close her eyes and drift and sleep without dreaming. She was so tired. But now Lex was holding on to her. "There is something..." the curator began uncertainly.

"I don't need any talk of a cure."

"Not a cure." Lex's hand had moved to her shoulder. She drew Rosa round to look at her. "Listen to me. We're so ignorant, still, of everything that you are. And I'm sorry for that. But there's something I've always observed, about your kind. Two are heavier than one. Two travel less often, more slowly, sustain less damage on the way. Nate Black might have outlived you all, had he kept hold of his brother..."

There was a long pause.

"I know that you've left your family far behind, and lost all friends save this man Harding. But if he's all you have, then bind yourself to him as closely as you can bear. In whatever manner you can bear. And perhaps, just perhaps, the world will hold steadier beneath your feet."

*

She found him at last in the observatory, at the top of the tallest tower. Telescopes pointed star-ward below the domed roof, which opened at the top to reveal a space of sky. He had arranged his pillows and bed-sheets on the tilted chair directly beneath, and lay there flat on his back. Rosa took off her sandals and moved between an array of curious copper instruments whose names and purposes she could not guess, models of the planets which spun at her touch as she passed. Saturn with its frozen skirts, the many moons of Jupiter, the small smooth sphere of the earth.

As she drew level with the chair he sat up and looked around. She seated herself at the end, beside his feet, her own soles brushing the cool stone floor. He drew his knees towards his chest, watching her intently through the dark.

Silence, again; and it was not emptiness but somehow living, breathing. Germinating. She followed the direction of its growth, found patience in herself. The earth turns so slowly. We might live our whole lives and never know that we are spinning through space. The silence stretched and settled between them.

"Would you stay here?" asked Rosa, at last.

"Perhaps. I don't want any more wars. It is peaceful here."

"But you will travel again," she said. "And you do not know where the tides will take you."

She felt the night breeze lift her hair. Harding rested his chin on his hands. His eyes were ringed by shadow. "What will you do?" he asked.

"I've spoken with Lex. She can show me how I might get back to nineteen forty-five, and find my family, as I last left them. It would be good to go —" She stopped herself. She could not say *home*.

"You said that they had already grieved you."

"Yes. But now I'm sick and sorry over not saying goodbye." Rosa closed her eyes. Bella blinking in the doorway. Harriet's hand laid against her cheek, that awful and wonderful look. Robert silhouetted at the top of the stairs, his dazed descent. A hundred years ago she had gone from the Museum back to the green corner of England where the Hydes were living their circular lives. Now she would do it again, as everything happened again, as everything had happened before.

When she opened her eyes, all she could see was his face in the starlight, sober and steady and unscarred. "Listen," she said. "You might think this strange. But I have a proposal for you."

*

She married Marcus Harding in nineteen forty-five, before a puzzled churchman in a little chapel which had been half-destroyed by the bombs. Creepers from the outside walls had begun to claim the inside of the space, bindweed pushing its tendrils between the stones and flowering white above the altar. Night was nearing, and candles guttered on sills where the windows had once been.

The pews were empty save for Robert and Harriet Hyde, and Bella, who had grown tall and wide-shouldered. She sat with her long straw-coloured hair hanging down over her sullen face, biting the nail of her thumb. Harriet seemed to comprehend no more than she had done that afternoon, when Rosa had knocked at their door with Harding at her shoulder. One hand was pressed to her lips as though silencing protests, while the other held firmly to Bella's elbow. Only Robert's face showed any delight. Cataracts had turned his eyes milky, but nonetheless he leaned eagerly forward, beaming up at his daughter.

Rosa wore the dress which had once been her mother's, threadbare from too many years in too many attics. She owned no jewels. The Soldier had combed his hair carefully back from his face and buttoned his shirt to the top. She held onto his hands and calmly echoed the old words; *from this day on, for better or worse, 'til death do us part.*

Part Four

23

No City of That Name

What it means to stay, even for a short while. What it means to wake in the same bed in the same arms with the same pear-tree just beyond the window, speckled with blossom and noisy with sparrows. How it slows the heart and quiets the mind.

In that year, that time around, the Hydes were living in a rambling old house on the outskirts of a south-coast city. There were too many rooms by far, and a garden which stretched on and on through a little woodland. From the window beside the bed, Rosa watched her sister stomping out each morning towards the trees with an axe in her hand, swinging the blade ferociously until new branches and saplings were felled. Bella returned to the house with firewood over-spilling her arms, dragging the axe along the ground behind her.

"She used to climb under my covers when the planes were too loud overhead," Rosa told Harding. "She used to pull her bear by the ear like that, along the landing between her room and mine. For a while, she was afraid of everything."

"And you? Were you afraid?"

She traced a finger down the underside of his wrist, until her palm found his. The room filled with clear morning light. Hard to remember. Those two little girls, the one's ice-cold feet against the other's knees below the covers. The red head and the fair, side by side on the pillow.

"I would tell myself that nothing could hurt me, so long as I lived to the fourth hour past midnight. Then I could bear it until the sun came up."

Breeze breathed through the half-drawn curtains. "Yes," he said distantly. "Yes, until the sun came up."

Bella vanished into the woods for hours at a time, returning past dusk with her hair tangled and her face smudged with dirt. She hunched at the long table in the kitchen and ate with her head down, answering questions in monosyllables. Rosa could not stop looking at her, hardly able to comprehend that there was now a tall body where the small one had been. Bella's room, glimpsed through the half-open door, was an angry chaos of scratched charcoal drawings, jars filled with stones and insects, plants sprouting on the windowsill.

In the rare moments when she was able to look her sister in the eye, Rosa recoiled. This had been poured into the mould of her long absence. This, she herself could so easily have become.

Bella passed Harding by without a glance, left rooms whenever he entered them. When he addressed her, she stared over his shoulder as though she had heard a dog barking in the distance. "Don't you like my husband?" Rosa asked her pointedly, cornering her outside by the wood-chopping stump.

"No reason I ought."

"Can't you at least be civil?"

Her glare, forceful as a shove in the chest. Don't you recognise it? You were every bit as fierce. Your temper might have split tree-trunks, too.

"I brought him here, Bella. That makes him a part of the family."

"No more than you are."

*

Harriet was harder to read. She was almost entirely grey; older, it was very clear now, than her fifty-odd years ought to make her.

When she looked at the daughter who had died to her a decade before, Rosa thought – hoped – there was a kind of acceptance in her face. I am resigned to it, said Harriet's level gaze when Rosa came down to the kitchen in the mornings, attempted a smile, put eggs to boil on the stove. I am beyond bitterness, said her mother's hands as they shaped lumps of grey dough on the counter. Look: I have pressed and kneaded through the bitter things in my life until they changed their substance.

Rosa's collection of trinkets had been retained in the baggage which the Hydes carried with them at the turn of each year, along with Harriet's wedding dress and Robert's bundles of photographs. A month or so after their arrival, her mother unpacked them and brought them upstairs for her, standing in the doorway to watch as Rosa turned them over in her hands. The snake-shaped dagger of Seysair, the coral-coloured conch from the frozen shore. Old friends. The magpie mask, the fossilised wing.

"I have told myself," said Harriet, "that if you had left deliberately, you would have taken them with you." Rosa looked up from fiddling the buttons on the long-dead watch. "To have vanished so suddenly, without your belongings… without so much as a word to your father…no. I have told myself, you treasured these things. You carried them all this way. You would have taken them with you."

"Mother…"

Harriet said curtly, "If I have been wrong, I'd rather not know."

"That red letter day, if I could have chosen," said Rosa, surprised by the sincerity in her own voice, "I would have stayed."

She saw her mother's tired features lit for a moment, and was transfixed. Bella's hatred she could just about stomach, but Harriet's heavy love broke her open. For so long this love had made her furious, sent her wriggling and scratching from its painful embrace. To hold still in the face of it was something entirely against her nature, entirely new.

"I think I'd stopped wishing you to stay, Rosa. Even then. Perhaps from when I saw you looking so wild at our door, not like any daughter we could ever have had." Harriet's smile was small and tight. "I began to imagine where you might have escaped to, those countries and centuries I'll only see in books."

"There's so much of it you would have loved," said Rosa.

"And maybe one day, you'll tell me about it."

Rosa nodded. Harriet's hands tucked in the strings of her apron. She did not move from the doorway, and they looked at one another. Perhaps, thought Rosa, this is what truce feels like. Raising our flags after the long weary war.

"How many Decembers have there been, Mother?" she asked quietly. *They will last longer*, Sola had said, *before their bodies begin to pay the penalty.* "How many more do you think there will be?"

Harriet Hyde laughed. "Have I once asked you why you married this man, or even who he is? That's between yourselves, as far as I'm concerned." Her face softened a little. "That number would be for me and Robert, and us alone. But if you mean to see it through, my dearest one, you'll soon learn to stop counting such things."

*

In the evenings, she watched Harding play her father at chess, the two bent over the board in agreeable silence. Bella's fire crackled in the grate. Robert adjusted his glasses on his nose and pushed a piece here, a piece there, darting quick looks at his opponent. Harding arched his fingers in a sharp steeple, giving every move his painstaking concentration.

"A true tactician," murmured Robert.

"Careful, father," said Rosa. "He's fought a few campaigns, in his time."

"Is that so?"

"It is, sir." Harding made his move — knight capturing queen. Robert rubbed his hands together, eyes roving eagerly across the board.

"This war, surely. You'll have been too young, last time around."

Harding met Rosa's eye, and she gave him a small shake of the head. He has made his world, my father, the exact shape and size he can bear it. Best not to baffle him now, with things beyond his understanding.

She made them abandon the game when it looked set to continue into the small hours after Harriet and Bella had gone to bed, and as she closed the bedroom door, heard Robert tugging down the attic ladder. The sameness of things. The little rhythms, the unchanging heartbeat of the Hyde home. Fragile with memory, she rested her elbows on the windowsill, and breathed in the sweet night air from the garden.

She felt Harding's arms around her waist, and leaned back into him. One of his hands strayed to the line of objects on the sill, the dagger, the shell, the mask, the electric watch. Straightened them carefully, aligned and realigned. Rosa slipped her fingers through his, and drew the errant hand back to herself.

"I stood like this at so many windows, you know, and watched the shadows at the end of the garden. Waiting for you to appear."

"I'm sorry to have caused you so much anxiety." He kissed her gently on the cheek, and then on the mouth, hands buried in the back of her hair. She rested her forehead against his, running a thumb down the bones of his spine beneath his nightshirt.

"It's not too quiet for you here?"

"I've ached for this quiet."

*

Rosa's body grew gradually aware of its pains, of stiffness in her joints, of a bone-deep fatigue which wouldn't dissipate with sleep. Most mornings, she wiped a sluggish stream of blood from her nose as she woke. The vagueness which had plagued her at the Museum came and went, leaving her adrift, suddenly a stranger in the midst of her own thoughts.

Harding, she noticed, would sometimes pause halfway through a task, poised over the sink with a dripping plate or leaving a book teetering as he pulled it from the shelf. Blank-eyed, he would suddenly blink, returning to himself as though nothing had happened. In bed she ran hands over the sharp blades of his shoulders, kissed the dip above his collarbone. She lay against his warm back and wondered how such a solid body might slowly become less solid, its pieces torn and scattered to the years.

But for now, Rosa, for now the summer morning is casting patches of sunlight across your covers, and your husband is whole and here with you. The pear-tree's branches are growing heavy with red fruit and the wildflowers are flourishing at the edges of the garden. For now, your father is humming benignly as he paints little model houses for his latest train-track, and your mother is reading Thomas Wolfe, absorbed and happily outside of herself. Later you will walk through the fields to the nearest town to buy bread and milk, shoes in your hand and skirt held around your knees.

For now, you can imagine all this stretching before you like a bridge across a darkly rushing river. Tread carefully, Rosa, tread lightly. Don't give too much thought to the waters below. She moved her collection of trinkets into a box and tucked it under the bed. Best, in the end, to banish the journeys from this place for as long as they could be kept away. The membrane of her skin already felt too thin.

Her heart was torn out by the simple sight of Robert Hyde creaking to-and-fro on the swing seat at the end of the garden. It was his contentment in the small pleasure of it that wounded her, the sleepy movement of his foot as it made to rock the chair as the sun went down behind the woods. She put on Harding's coat over her nightdress and made her way along the garden path, sitting cross-legged beside her father. A blackbird on a branch overhead spilt a liquid thread of song.

"How long have your eyes been bad, Daddy?"

"Oh, a little while now. Makes it harder to do close work in bad light."

"And you didn't think to see a doctor?"

"Soon," he said vaguely. "I'll go soon."

They creaked back and forth. "You know," said Robert, "I might leave it next year. The red-letter day, I mean. So much noise. And the buses, I can't always see the numbers. All those people."

"I'll come with you."

"That's all right. They play it all on the wireless. The speeches. I might... I can sit and listen in the kitchen. With tea and toast. That's celebration enough."

As the last fingers of sunlight retreated back over the horizon, Rosa watched the shadows lengthen over Robert's face. Deep lines branched from the corners of his eyes and crossed his forehead below his sparse, ash-grey hair. I will never see my husband this way, she realised. It will not be given to us, to see one another grow old.

The pity that had flooded her, because her father had become bent and withered and small, returned and did not shrink away. He leaned back in the seat and closed his clouded eyes. Oh my father, you have been so infinitely foolish, and I am made of your foolishness. She leaned her head on his shoulder. The first stars blinked into life above the whispering trees.

*

"Rosa."

Suddenly awake, bolt-upright and breathless in the tangled sheets. The window clattering in the night wind. She swung her legs over the side of the bed and sat with her head lowered, breathing hard. Blood trickled over her lips and dripped rapidly onto the floorboards.

"You feel it?"

"Yes."

She turned. Harding was white-faced and grim, clinging to the headboard with one hand as though the bed had started spinning. The surface of the room seemed to come apart from itself. Rosa groaned aloud. For a moment the wave of it threatened to wash over them both, but then it receded, and the darkness was still once again. She blotted her nose with a corner of the sheet, fighting the nausea which rose in her throat.

Harding slumped back against the pillows. They looked at one another in dreadful agreement. "I'm sorry," he said. "But I think it will be soon."

The days seemed to grow brittle, too thin to breathe. Summer burned brightly for another month and then died all at once, giving in to fractious September winds and heavy skies. Rosa felt as though the weight of her presence in nineteen forty-five was bobbing uncertainly up and down, like a buoy on a troubled sea, pulling gradually free of its mooring.

A lifetime ago, back at the Museum, she had told Harding that she regretted not saying goodbye. But now that it came to it, now that time grew short and the Hydes were here before her, she knew that it could not be done. Bella would barely hear it, and she couldn't entertain the thought of sitting Robert and Harriet down for it, of laying out earnest words for them to swallow. *If you were better, Rosa. If you were more entirely human, you would do it. But you know, by now, how much less you are than all you ought to be.*

Remember this, wherever you go. Fix it in your mind for the coming time, so that you might carry it with you. Remember your mother stood straight-backed beside the fire, your tall sister cross-legged on her bed with a stick of charcoal in her fist. Your father with the paper held too close to his face, lips moving as he reads the day's familiar stories. Remember them as they are now and as they once were, because you might never see them again.

She kept Robert company in his attic, curled quietly on a chair as he preoccupied himself with gluing new pieces to the model village beside the track. The room at the top of this house was high-ceilinged and spacious, a swift's nest tucked into the eaves below the skylight. For the most part, the two of them did not speak, and the birds flitted in and out through the open window. In the kitchen downstairs the wireless was playing a familiar tune, a plaintive trumpet. *How strange, the change from major to minor...*

"There was something," began Robert, before dropping the sentence like a ball of string. Rosa waited for him to pick it up, but when he did not, prompted him.

"Something?"

"Yes. Something I've been meaning to ask you." He secured a tiny tree to the felt hillside with great care. "My father's... you know that I always used to keep... my father's pocket watch. On my bedside table."

The years came full circle, and for a moment Rosa was seventeen again, tearful and trembling with fury, cramming possessions into her satchel in a blind rush. Past her parents' bedroom doorway with their voices still in hushed conflict downstairs, and there it was on the table, glinting gold. The watch which came back from the front in a brown envelope in place of Frank Hyde, who had tumbled in flames from the sky over Arnhem.

"You needn't forgive me," she said emptily. "I sold it in the twenty-first for a coat and a few weeks' worth of food. I didn't think you could feel anything that mattered."

"Did it keep you warm?" asked Robert.

"What?"

"The coat. Did it keep you warm?"

*

Rosa. Wake up, because the world is changing. The bricks of this house are melting like wax. Take your husband by the hand and flee with him down the stairs even as they crack beneath your feet, as the clock in the hallway calls out the early hour and its chimes diminish into the distance. Fall to your knees. Know only that he is still with you; that all else is gone but he is still with you, ragged and gasping from the strain of the journey.

Do not let go. Do not dare to think of the resigned quiet in the Hyde house when they wake to find you gone. That daughter of theirs who returns and then leaves again, always changed, always the same, like grief itself. They will forge forward into their hours and weeks and years without you. Rosa, as they always have. You are not the beginning and the end of them.

This man by your side, do not let go. Walk with him through the new future with your faces set forward, with your backs unburdened by belongings. Tread lightly. Eat the food of each place you pass through, drink the wine, glance through the lit windows of the lives that are lived there. But don't lay your head too long on the same pillow. Don't hold too hard to what you cannot keep.

*

They tumbled past the middle of the twenty-first, and the thin pain in her head became a loud howl which would not be silenced. They clung on for months at a time in cities powered by the shrinking sun, lashed by bitter northern winds; encroached by rising tides, like Venice as she had once known it in a year not so far from here. They left the island as its shores crumbled ever more rapidly into the greedy sea, and made for brighter climates.

"Away from the tides, Rosa," he said. "Remember? We have to be careful."

Away from the quiet of that house in nineteen forty-five, his terrors returned. He cried out in his sleep, as he had done in Hiroshima, and woke whimpering. Beneath the flicker of his eyelids, bombs fell out of the sky. Rosa let him shake himself into stillness. She waited while he went through the rituals that returned him to the world: the hair combed flat, the boots tied, the shirt buttoned, over and over again. Do what you need to do. Just come back to me.

They stayed in doorways and outbuildings and narrow hostel beds. At the first breath of movement below the surface of the air, at the first sign of dissolving streets, the sound of a dull distant roar, they would leave. Not always fast enough. Treading between the tides like children jumping pavement cracks. They were snatched years forward, crawled shocked and sore to their feet.

"The wars," she asked him, "are they near? Do you feel them?"

"They're always near." A derelict park on a dark evening, a city dead in time. Another year. Her arm wrapped tight about his waist below his coat, his head bent close to hers. "I worry... I worry that it can't be over. The tides know me too well."

There was not enough sound in the city. This far forward the whine of ambulances and police cars ceased. The silence said: you are on your own. The two travellers moved quickly around a hooded figure who hissed at them as they passed.

"I'd have hoped," she said, "that history would be tired of tearing itself apart, by now."

He shook his head. "There's something coming, I think. Not quite yet, but around the corner. The war at the end."

His voice was steady, but he quivered involuntarily. A sharp wind skipped leaves across the concrete before their feet. She looked sideways at him, picked at the frayed thread of his coat pocket between finger and thumb. She said, "Let's go somewhere with sunshine."

*

A scorching land where the rooftops were red and the rivers dried to dust, and Rosa recognised for a moment the shape of a face stamped onto a copper coin. She turned it until it caught the light and then laughed, half delighted, entirely unsurprised. Flipped the coin in the air and caught it on her palm, bit it between her teeth like careful merchants she had once seen in the fifteenth. In the dappled shade of the lodging she had taken with Harding in the lower part of the city, she showed him the coin, and told him what she remembered. "If that's the case," he said, "we should pay her a visit."

"Describe me to her," she insisted to the guards at the gates of the city's grandest hall. They wore loose robes and narrow blades across their backs, looking upon her with suspicion. "Tell her that a friend is here, who she once knew in Paris at the turn of the twentieth. She'll see me, I know it."

When the doors gaped open she took Harding's hand and they walked together into a long chamber. Their eyes were drawn upwards. Every inch of the ceiling's high arches had been gilded with images of stars and sheaves, bulls and fishes, spinning sunbursts and swooping birds. The windows were twinned crescent slits. Light poured in from above, so dazzling that the figure on the winged seat on the dais at the end was nothing but a stone-still silhouette until they had drawn close.

The great lady who held power in that place was all in gold. Sleek black hair framed a face which had been painted with shimmering powder, lips and eyelids and all, resembling cast metal more than flesh. Her hands rested regally upon the arms of her seat. A heavy golden band had been set across her forehead, wrought in a single coiled line.

At their approach she raised her head a little, lids slowly lifting until they could see her long, dark eyes. Rosa and Harding drew to a halt below the dais. The woman raised two fingers, and a figure darted from the shadows to fan her with a palm-frond.

"Tell me your petition," said the woman on the golden seat. There was a hard, distant edge to her voice, which echoed in the empty spaces of the chamber.

"Your pardon," said Rosa. "We're passing through your city. I saw your image on a coin, I thought —"

"I do not grant favours to any vagrant."

"But you know me. We were in Montparnasse together, a long time ago."

Silence. Harding was completely still at her shoulder.

"I know no city of that name."

"Just a small quarter in the city, full of music and candlelight. Perhaps it no longer stands."

The woman murmured something to the servant at her side.

The figure withdrew and returned almost at once with a shallow bowl, into which she dipped her fingertips before dabbing them across her cheeks. The duller patches of her shining mask were replenished. She pressed her lips together. "Do you have a name, traveller?"

"When you knew me, I was Rosa Hyde. We met you in the marketplace. You lived with the Brothers Black, in a loft apartment filled with your treasures."

For the first time, she saw something flicker across the inscrutable face. The woman on the chair stared unblinkingly down at her. "My treasures," she said slowly. "The paintings of Picasso. Worth beyond measure in years to come."

"That's right. You found a drawing of his, pinned to a café wall."

"Who is your companion?" And before Rosa could reply, with sudden force: "I have Seen You Before. You are the lover of Tommy Rust, and you came with him to that city fresh from your first wanderings."

She stood abruptly from the chair. The alarmed servant almost dropped his bowl. Harding took a step back, and Rosa, caught off her guard, let go of his hand. The woman turned, her voice lowered again.

"Prepare refreshments for us in the anteroom. No further audiences today."

The little chamber at the back of the hall was dim and cool. Water cascaded from a fountain set into the wall, splashing into a pool planted with lotus-flowers. A bowl overflowing with figs, grapes and pomegranates had been placed on the table, along with a pitcher of wine. The servant pulled the door closed behind them, and the woman faced away from Rosa and Harding as she leaned on the tabletop. Even with her back turned, the change in her was clear. Her shoulders sloped, the elegant height of her bent like a reed.

When Amber turned at last, Rosa saw that the whites of her eyes were shot with red. Close-to, the powder on her face looked thick and uneven.

"You've come a long way, traveller," said Rosa.

"As have you."

"I've seen the Museum, since we last met. I hear that you had a hand in assembling its collections. Treasures from every continent and every age. I know they're grateful to you."

Another flicker of recognition, stronger than the last. Amber passed a hand across her face. She paced to one end of the room and then returned, the back of her robe sweeping along the stone floor. The golden garment was gossamer silk, printed with a scarlet pattern around the hem. It billowed like waves beneath a sheet of rain. "Have I forgotten you as well?" she asked Harding.

"We have not met," he said quietly. "My journeys rarely crossed the paths of others."

Amber's long fingers picked a fig from the bowl and began to peel it absently. Rosa saw that her hands were shaking. After a pause she said, "Did you come to request something from me?"

Rosa shook her head. It was far simpler than that. "Only to be reminded of a time I still remember fondly. And to know whether it has been everything you wanted?"

A shaft of light from the small window caught the spray from the fountain, filling the room momentarily with shimmering mist. Amber stood in the centre of it, seemingly lost for all reply. "Your years, Rosa," she said at last. "I hope that they have been kind."

"Kinder than I deserve. But surely, you must know..."

"Have you seen any of them, since Montparnasse?" Amber interrupted. "Nate, Harris? My boys, have they kept well?"

Rosa felt Harding's hand on the small of her back. In pity, and in grief, she could only speak briefly.

"Nate is dead. I'm sorry. And Harris is lost."

Amber held her robe to her body. "Tommy Rust?"

"I'm sorry," said Rosa again, and meant it. "I didn't come here to bear bad news. But you must know by now..."

"Yes. I know." Amber turned away again and lifted the heavy gold band from her head, pausing for a long moment as she placed it on a cushion. She gave a small, wry laugh. "It had to end someday. This business of striding about the world as though we were ever-living gods."

24

The Allotment

So has it been everything that you wanted?

Do you even remember, now, the shape of the things you dreamed of when you danced before a window overlooking the London skyline, arms in the air, abandoned suddenly to hope? How your heart turned over in your chest with thrilled envy when you saw what the mayflies owned. All dim, now, thin and threadbare as the clothes you have worn to traverse the centuries.

It has been something besides what you wanted – somehow more, somehow less. This is what you might whisper to her, Rosa-at-seventeen with her fists clenched and her face full of freckles. Do not dread. What would be the use? But keep a leash on your hunger. Know that the world does not turn for you and you alone.

So, gypsy girl, you have come to count on one hand the things you have left to lose. You feel calmer than you have ever done, though the absence of the Hydes is a deep wound. That pain comes as a surprise, a call awake. You feel stripped of your skin and bare to the winds that blow in between the years, smaller than you once were, more laughable. A relief. No more need to stride about the world and insist all the while that you are not weary.

And Marcus Harding too is more, is less. Is no kind of cure, no kind of long-sought home at the end of the road. He is fading too. There are days when he feels like everything, days when his face hardly looks familiar, and the truth is somewhere in between. For this time, you are glad that you have him to hold to. Do not dwell on what comes after.

*

Their journeys took them slowly forward, sliding imperceptibly on a decade at a time until they ceased even to notice their own passing. Under the southern sun not fifty years from where they had encountered Amber Lakshmi on her golden throne, they came across a city below a cliff with a thundering waterfall plunging through its heart. The refracting light encased the whole habitation in a shimmering rainbow.

Further south still, where the ground had cracked and blackened after years of drought, a city raised on towering steel spindles into the cooler air above. Its own climate of clouds puffing out of pipes, its green fields suspended below like children's swings. At the coast, mile upon mile of floating islands like the *Suiren* at Hiroshima, tethered to one another with criss-crossing cables and narrow bridges. A bobbing, dipping mesh of towers and streets and cultivated forests. Turbines sprouting out of the waves, their blades hissing round in unceasing circles.

A city sheltered below tunnels of arching white fabric, like giant crop-covers. A city entirely abandoned, wind howling through its crumbling tower-tops, locusts the size of hands swarming across every inch of its ground. Cities under quarantine, encircled by military encampments, the ominous rumbling of waste transports rolling out by cover of night. The two travellers no longer thought to change their clothing for each new place, to walk as the people of that age walked, to speak as they spoke. They did not look up, as visitors look up, or stop to stare at sights which ought to have been cause for wonder. Strangers in strange lands, they grew ragged and lean.

They huddled on a transport out of the drought zone, crushed among a squirming mass of people. The air hot and thick and full of flies, pungent with the smell of sweating bodies. Shouting in foreign tongues. The *bump, bump* of the uneven road beneath the wheels. Harding craned his neck around, on edge, trying to breathe through a gap in the slats. In the cramped darkness Rosa had the sudden sense of being outside of herself.

The eerie premonition of standing over her own grave, as she had stood over Nate Black's. What are you doing here, child of another time? What possessed you, to stray so far?

It is not as though any of us is born wise, she told the voice. I have had choices, and I have not always made them well: but who truly knows what to make of what they're given? Harding's hand clutched Rosa's, and she willed his panic away, touched his face to find that his skin was cold. Perhaps somewhere there is mercy for what we've wasted, for what we've lost.

*

They saw in her thirtieth year with noodles and melon beer at a street-market in a drenched metropolis to the east, perched on stools beneath the canvas cover and watching the rain turn pavements into rivers. They got soaked as they ran back to the high-rise hostel, and stood laughing in the doorway beneath the neon light. The shutters in their rented room did not fully close, casting streaks of shifting blue and green across the bed.

They took off their dripping coats, hung them on the bedstead. He fetched a towel from the bathroom and scrubbed at his hair until it stood on end. Rosa twisted her scarf between her hands and wrung out a handful of droplets onto the covers. They sat close, cross-legged on the mildewed mattress.

"It'll flood, won't it? Good job we're so high up."

She reached across, combed the still-sodden hair back from his forehead with her fingertips. "We could wake up," she said teasingly, "and find ourselves adrift."

"We could wake up," he said, "and be a hundred years apart."

The floor rattled as a train passed by on sky-rails. "Not yet. We've still time."

They dozed through the humid night in fits and starts. She went to the bathroom in the early hours as she usually did, to stem a trickle of dark blood from her nose, glancing at her reflection in the filthy mirror. The cheekbones sharp, the skin dry and cracked around the mouth. Is it time, asked the eyes of the woman in the glass, to prepare yourself? When she climbed back into bed he was awake, staring at the ceiling. She rested her head in the crook of his arm. "How far do you think it goes, Rosa? What happens if we journey forwards past the end of everything?"

"You're so certain of an end? A bang, not a whimper?"

"I'm certain of it." The floor shook again, and while the walls shuddered around them Rosa watched his face in the flickering darkness. If he is right, she thought, and it is only a matter of whether our bodies or this world can last longer, then he will be the one who endures until the end. The soldier who fought for a millennium and gained not a scar to show for it.

*

And now, as your bones groan with each morning's rising, do not forget what is coming. Do not think that you can fall head-over-heels into this life again. Even though the tides pass you by, something in you is drifting now, is coming slowly to pieces. You are journeying from yourself.

Listen. Attend to each new pain, as though laying an ear to the wall of a house where a stranger lives. You have neglected this too long.

Her body felt like wreckage. On bad days the small acts of washing, walking, eating were no longer instinctive, but a source of bafflement. Hair came out in her hands. Food had lost its flavour, and a few mouthfuls were as much as she could swallow at any meal.

The fog which had seeped into her mind at the Museum spread. Only nineteen forty-five remained clear. Each new room she woke in was an impossible frontier.

"Where were we?" she found herself asking, twice, three times a day. Searching fingertips touched door-posts, bricks, warm bedclothes, as though trying to read the answers there. "Where are we?" When she realised how much this distressed him, she stopped. He was not yet so far along.

It dawned on Rosa that Harding had become entangled in all that she was; that her tenderness towards him, never simply the fleeting stuff of feeling, had put down roots. The last warm blaze in the sky, before the sun went down. There will never be children, she thought, who share our features. Pale, slight in stature, with hair bright as fire. Freckles on their shoulders.

She could not bring herself to speak of this with him. But she began to imagine that he knew, nonetheless – that he made love with a new kind of urgency, as though afraid that the space between their bodies might suddenly be torn open. Despite herself she recalled Nate Black, hunched alone at a bar with a drink in his hand, pitiful with grief. *How is it that we find each other so easily, and fall apart the same?* A flash of white lightning from beyond the window. *You see, the harder I tried to hold him, the faster he fell away.*

"Rosa," he whispered in her ear in the dead of night. "Rosa. I'm sorry. But I think it will be soon."

They lurched forward again, and there was something uneasy in the world, the smell of a storm about to break. Cities built high walls and guarded them closely. Every screen babbled of continents in the grip of sickness, of a contagion which killed in mere hours

305

and leapt across oceans. Of countries grown reckless with might. Rosa and Harding darted between smaller settlements like mice from hole to hole, taking food and shelter where they could. Out in the mountains, men and women who scratched their living from the dirt raised stone statues of old gods. They bowed and begged these half-remembered beings to save them from the coming dark.

The world was so changed that it began to feel familiar again. Perhaps it brings them comfort to build with stone and sew with cloth, as they once did. Perhaps they are reassured by the solid weight of books in their hands, the hush of ancient places which hide deep springs of the sacred and the solemn, now that everything real has grown invisible as air. So we return, so we are drawn back, wherever we have journeyed.

"Marcus," she said, in the vague place between sleeping and waking, which gave shape to shapeless thoughts, "I left something behind."

"What?"

"I'm sure I left something, maybe in... Montparnasse. Or Hiroshima. Maybe at the Museum. Do you remember what it was?"

She lost him when a jolt from within herself pulled her out of time. She was cast back into whirling nothingness with a howl still forming in her throat, with her hand still snatching at empty space.

*

So we return. It was no tide which sent her towards that year, falling faster without Harding, falling further. She spun around nineteen forty-five like a planet around a dying sun, and missed it only by degrees. It was a flash of hesitant fear in her heart which threw her off, a last-second refusal of her own will. Her body arched off-course, and she landed on her knees towards the end of the decade.

Where else to go but England, to the last place she had known them? The south-coast house with its mossy roof-tiles and its rambling garden. It was the bare month before winter. She stood before the peeling front door and wondered who lived here now, where the Hydes had gone next. The wistful thought came that they might have left some token here for her: perhaps a note in a yellowing envelope under the porch, her trinkets in a box in the attic or buried in the garden. They were so close here, a few years behind. She laid a hand against the dirty glass of one of the windows, and tried to peer inside.

Then, from the corner of her eye, she caught sight of a thin line of smoke rising into the sky behind the house. She scaled the fence and sat perched like a cat, surveying the overgrown garden. The pear tree which had blossomed outside their bedroom had been cut down. It was clear from here that the house was unoccupied, creepers clinging to the windows and encircling the handle of the back door.

The smoke was coming from beyond the woods. Rosa dropped down over the fence and traipsed across the garden, through the trees towards it. Its scent was bitter and sweet at once, the dusk air turned dim silver. On the other side of the small copse, in a dip between two hills, a woman was working an allotment in the last of the light. She was casting weeds and debris onto a bonfire which rose higher and higher, sparks and ashes flung into the sky. Behind the flames and the rows of dug earth was a small dwelling, more than a shed and less than a cottage, its plasterboard and timber frames held together by nails and rust.

Rosa drew close and stood just beyond the edge of the firelight, watching the woman as she threw an armful of uprooted bindweed onto the fire. She was tall and heavily built with broad hips and shoulders, dirty blonde hair which hung long and unwashed. Her laden arms were thick and strong. She was older than she ought to be, and she ought not to be here at all. Bella Hyde caught sight of Rosa through the flames, and for a while said nothing, continuing to hack apart roots with an axe-blade while Rosa raised a hand to cover her eyes.

"Been here long?" asked Bella.

"Can I look at you?"

"Oh, don't worry. It's been quite some time, for me. But I haven't seen you since you were last here." She glanced at Rosa. "You look awful."

Rosa said nothing. Bella wiped a muddy forearm across her face.

"Did you lose your lover, then?"

"My husband."

Bella laughed. Rosa's grief, distant and unreal to her, expanded in her chest until she could barely breathe. In the firelight her sister's face was too lined, too changed. Four years or so had passed in this place, but Bella had aged fifteen; she was older, now, than Rosa.

"Don't stand there gaping. You may as well sit a while, if you're not going to help me."

Rosa's knees felt weak. Her weariness overwhelmed her. She drew nearer and lowered herself onto a tree-stump, close to the turned earth. Bella seemed to loom huge as she strode back and forth behind the fire.

"You got out," said Rosa wonderingly.

"How do you think, big sister?"

The most likely conclusion took a moment to arrive. Rosa held her coat more closely about her shoulders. Bella paused in her work, wiping her hands on her overalls. "Father died soon after you and your lover left us. Without Robert, Mother and I made it past the end of the year. Nineteen forty-six! Land of milk and honey!" She laughed again. Her voice was hard and hoarse, like Rosa's own.

"Did Harriet… is she…"

"Oh, Mother's still here." Bella pointed her thumb over her shoulder to indicate the building behind. "She turns in early, these days."

Only when the last of the debris had been fed into the flames did Bella herself sit, crouching a little distance from where Rosa was and poking at the black ashes with a stick. The picture still did not make sense, but in the light of Robert's passing it hardly seemed to matter. How can we yet be in the world, when he is not? The thing that made us is gone, and we are cut from the root.

"He must have lived through…forty times," said Rosa thickly. "More. Did he forget there was anything outside of it, do you think? Could he ever have-"

"Him and his preoccupations had sixteen years of my time," said Bella abruptly, cutting across her. "I won't give any more to talking about them."

Shocked, half-understanding, Rosa fell quiet again. In the small space of her mind left intact she found the memory she had laid there, Robert Hyde settled in his fireside chair, reading the newspaper. She could see him stood at the joyful heart of the press of people on his red-letter day, head tilted back as confetti drifted down from the sky. All the lines of the years and his grief gone from his face.

"I tried your way," said Bella.

The fire crackled, and a blackened branch broke in two, sending the smoking greenery at the top sliding down the pile.

"After he died, I tried to go away. But Mother was left here alone, so I was careful with coming back. Months for her, each time, and years for me. By the time it showed, she was past noticing."

Rosa stared at her sister. What Bella was describing must have taken a control, a precision, far beyond anything that even Amber had ever possessed. But perhaps it was not so strange. If anybody could journey on the tide of their own will, could grasp onto the very year and month of their choosing by the strength of their own hands, it had to be the woman here before her. Nobody had ever told this solid, stubborn traveller that it was not possible.

"I didn't think so much of it," said Bella dismissively, of the entire world beyond.

Rosa remembered walking with her through the fields to the graveyard, the small yellow head bobbing beside her as Bella wheeled her bike. *Sometimes*, that peculiar child had said, *I imagine what it's like to be under the ground.* "You grow all you need here, then?" she asked quietly.

"Potatoes, onions, turnips, carrots, cabbages. Climbing beans, over there, and tomatoes on the vine when it's warmer. It's the *only* thing, you know," she added. "Keeping a garden. Everything coming to fruit, everything dying at its right time."

The pile of ash had turned from black to white. The flames retreated, leaving a smoking heap, split by fiery cracks and fissures. Thick clouds rolled across the dawning stars overhead. Rosa saw a movement at the edge of the allotment and turned her head sharply, glimpsing a yearling fox as it paused in the gathering darkness, one paw lifted, golden eyes aglow.

Bella stood to sweep the stray ashes inward with her foot, and the creature fled into the night. Rosa looked round at the ramshackle little house where their mother was sleeping, and wondered whether Harriet's endless succession of small journeys had at last washed her away; year by year, inch by inch, as rivers rise and cover all trace of human habitation.

"When I was small," said Bella, "I used to lie awake and wonder. Even when I got out and saw all you had left us for, I still wasn't sure. But I think I might know, now." There was no warmth in her grin, but there was little judgement either. "Why did you run, except as a kind of test? Why else do children run, except to see whether anybody will follow after?"

Inside was dark and chilly. Bella gave Rosa a woollen jumper and lit Harriet's bedside lamp, leaning over the sleeping figure in the bed to murmur something in her ear. When she left the room and pulled the door to, Rosa sat and watched her mother, whose silver hair had turned fine and wispy as dandelion-seed. Time had accelerated for Harriet Hyde, taking its vengeance at last for her long defiance of its course. Her skin was parchment-thin and covered in peach-coloured bruises.

You asked if I would tell you about it, one day, bring back to you all of those places you would never go. I wish that I could, but they are all but gone from me. Though if you want me to I can speak to you about Frank Sinatra and knee-socks and chocolate drops in the back row of the pictures. About children who are enfolded like fledglings under feathered wings on the last night of December, and swept backwards in time.

The lamp guttered and hissed. Rosa bent over the frail figure beneath the patchwork quilt, and pressed her lips silently to her mother's forehead. I see now that you are not this small. You are not laid so low. You are that vivid girl with Hemingway in your hands, glasses halfway down your nose in the quiet of the library, adventuring in a far-off world.

*

So has it been....?

But what do you know.

*

What can be known for certain. Because the day comes when you are far gone, far forward at the hot and dusty edge of history, that strong-armed woman and her allotment lost long ago. How many centuries you have journeyed, since then. How hard the soles of your feet have become. In this place on the brink of the downward spiral of the decade you warily guard the gold in your pockets and step past the dung in the streets. The name and the life you once had dispersing into the air, like a puff of dust from a shaken rug. Your body is a bag of bones blown by the wind. In the marketplace the rag-man pushes his cart in a rattling circle and wails his wares. The hot red orb of the sun hangs in the sky amid a humid haze. Flags flutter over the orange-carts, a fog of incense rising from low-pitched tents.

You move through the heat and the noise dressed in a dull caftan, arms and ankles red with patterned dye, the talismans of five different ages rattling around your neck. You like the shine that these things have, the way they glitter in the light. You do not know why the man at the heart of the crowd catches your eye. He is talking animatedly with the group of stallholders bunched around him, his eyes flashing, hands gesticulating freely.

You pause a moment in the midst of the bustle and noise. Bodies press and jostle on every side. He is young, barely more than a boy, dressed in a strange assortment of clothes. His hair is strawberry-blond. He breaks suddenly into laughter and it seems to you that the whole square rings with it. That in some act of graciousness he has gifted himself to the world.

His face is turned towards the sun. Towards the journeys he has yet to make.

And what do you know. What did you ever know, gypsy girl. That disembodied grin which was once bright with golden promise, wide as a never-ending lifetime.

25

Marble Halls

O utside the garden walls, the war raged on.

*

The Gardener grew tired of hearing of it. No man had been permitted to pass the gates in a hundred years, but white-armoured women came and went, bringing news of the latest victories and defeats. They were bruised and bloodstained, and they all wore the same grim look. Their tidings were delivered in a few sparse words.

The Sisters, huddled in their high round reception chamber, thrilled and shuddered and cooed over every rumour. The pair of frost-haired women, identical in every detail of manner and of dress, liked to have their fires stoked until the windows of the tower blazed. They plied each stern and battle-torn visitor with steaming tea and sweetmeats, hands fluttering, voices cajoling. Their eyes bulged at the prospect of danger. They collected stories of bloodshed, arranged them like dried flowers. *The Black Army, it is said, burn everything in their path. They sew the skins of the vanquished as trophies into their coats.*

It seemed to the Gardener that the nearer the Black Army drew, the more fondly her mistresses fussed over the order of small things: the health of the carp in the moon-pond, the pruning of the roses on the old cloister arch. Soon, she thought, looking out across the grounds on a calm day, this will all burn. Ash will rain down upon us, and we will be put to the sword.

Inside the walls, all was quiet. Water trickled gently out of the ornamental fountains, down onto a pillow of green moss. Peacocks picked their way between the trimmed conifer trees and yew hedges, feathers shivering, cries high and eerie. The Gardener coaxed five varieties of roses to climb the stone, planted silvery onopordum and heart-shaped dicentra, snowgoose flowers and spreading anemones. Grey clumps of foliage were pierced with tall white flowers. She worked until late into the evenings, until at last her body ached so thoroughly and deeply that she knew she would sleep.

She did not have much strength left. Hard hands pierced with many thorns and thistles, back bent from wheeling the barrow, dirt deep beneath her fingernails. She lived in the same hut where her tools were hung and the frail seedlings sprouted in their pots. A low bed, a stove in the corner, her muddy boots on the floor. At twilight she sat cross-legged on the groundsheet with the door open, and watched a barn owl sweep silently across her pale garden, ghostly wings spread wide.

The Sisters had her bathe fortnightly in the chamber by the kitchens, in the copper tub which the servants used. By the time she was done, the water was dark with filth. Her body was all diminished, shrivelled and sunk into itself like old fruit. Her hair had been clipped from her head and shaved close to the scalp with a rough blade. She ran her fingertips absently over the bare skin, which was warm and uneven, prickly with new growth. In the back of her throat hummed a few notes of a song she had once heard. Sometimes in the steaming heat of the bath, her nose would begin to bleed.

*

She could not recall her name, or how she had come to be here. It seemed barely to matter, buried beneath the daily weight of stones and soil, overgrown by the geometric lines of the hedgerow maze. Her name was in the ground. Its absence occasionally filled by a powerful rush of feeling which flared like a solar storm, then died.

The world had once been different.

Something had happened. Blindingly bright and thunderously loud, dust-making and earth-shaking. An expanding cloud in the sky. Smudging, wiping over the lines of history like an eraser over a page. All that had been built afterwards was salvaged from the jumbled pieces, the brutal and the beautiful, the ancient and the new. Strange wars raged. The Black Army which crawled over the faces of continents was held back only by small victories, resisted in pockets by those who left their own lives and homes to do battle. To the Gardener, who saw weary soldiers pass in and out through the gates bringing news, smoke rising far in the distance beyond the walls, it seemed futile.

Let them come – for they will come, in the end. Let it be lost. She plunged her hands into damp soil, found the tender edges of new shoots. These halls are peaceful for this short time.

The slow circular rhythms of growing, blooming, dying. The Gardener breathed in the turned earth, the greenery and the new-fallen rain. She wandered among the white arches, beneath the canopy of creepers and weeping trees. The spire of the tower rising beyond. Digging deep in the flower-beds she sometimes turned up relics of forgotten times – twisted metal and cracked glass, pieces of bewildering circuitry. Half-melted coins and faded images printed on card. The best of these she kept and lined up along the shelf in her hut. Now and then she would rearrange them, casting out those which no longer interested her and placing others at the fore.

The Sisters came to walk in their gardens only when the weather was fine and the noise from the nearest battles dim. Arm in arm, feet shuffling beneath their long gowns, murmuring to one another in incomprehensible low tones. Airy bursts of laughter which came from nowhere. They liked to stand over the moon-pond and throw pieces of bread to the fish, cooing and clicking their tongues. They had the Gardener cut the most flawless of the roses and bring them into the halls, blood-red and white and velvet-black. She stood awkwardly amid the dusty grandeur, thorny stems clasped by her gloved hand, boots leaving mud-trails across the hearth.

And then the season turned too cold, the roses growing ragged around their edges, the pond's waters clogging with fallen leaves. Inside her hut the Gardener burned dead wood and dead greenery, and barely kept warm. The messengers of the White Army had long since stopped coming. Beyond the walls the sky darkened, the horizon glowing red with battle-fires. The rain which fell was soured by smoke.

It was one such bitter, drenched night, with the Sisters shut in their high tower, that there came a call and a hammering at the gates.

The persistence of the sound finally sent the Gardener out to answer it, reluctant and huddled in a cloak. Beyond the barred gate stood a man of the White Army, drenched to the skin and streaked with mud, shielding his eyes as she held up her lantern.

"Will you not let me in?" he called, above the sound of the rain. "I have been sent out with an urgent message from my commander, to all who have not yet fled these lands."

"No man has passed these gates in a hundred years," said the Gardener.

"Then I fear I must be the first."

"The Sisters will not receive you," she said.

"Then you must receive me yourself! Please, I am weary. At least allow me some brief respite before I go on my way."

She looked over her shoulder, up at the firelight which blazed in the tower's high windows. In the late hour and the weather, there was no chance of them venturing from their warmest chamber. Furtively, she unbarred the gate and beckoned the man behind her as she hurried back through the gardens to her hut.

It was once they were both inside the small space, the lantern hung on its hook and illuminating the soldier's muddied features, that she discovered her hand had risen of its own accord to cover her eyes. The door, which he had not closed behind him, swung to and fro in the wind. Rainwater streamed from their clothes to the groundsheet on the floor.

"Do not spare me," she said. "I know that the Black Army is almost upon us. I know that your garrisons have failed. Tell me how soon they will be here."

In a puzzled voice, he asked, "Do you know me?"

She shook her head rapidly, her hand still held over her eyes. And she realised that at the sound of his voice her body quaked and weakened, like ground softened by rain.

"I think," he began. "I think…"

Her hand was trembling so violently that she could no longer hold it in front of her face. Against her will she saw him standing before her, staring at her with terrific intensity. He was lean and ashen, the white plates of his armour dull and dented. His greying hair was brushed neatly back, flat to his skull. Straight down his right cheek, still pink and raw-looking, was a long scar.

"Finally," she said, without knowing why. "It has left its mark." She heard herself give a small, bitter laugh.

His fingertips traced the length of the line along his face.

"I have Seen You Before," he said simply, in realisation.

The stillness of him was alarming to her. And she began to grow aware of how she must appear. The same tunic had hung for days upon her bony frame. She crossed her arms over her chest. The air was cold upon the skin of her closely shaved head.

"Please," she said. "Please. Do not look at me."

The soldier did not turn his gaze. The scar cut through one eyebrow and twisted the corner of his mouth downward.

"Might I drink with you?" he asked. "It has been a thirsty journey. I shall not remain long."

She brewed steaming green tea on the stove and poured it into little glasses. With the flame from the stove, she lit a bundle of dead branches in the grate. The wind rose again in the dark outside the hut, buffeting the clipped hedges of the maze and the trellis around which her roses wound. Through the gloom, the halls loomed over the rolling lawns.

He removed his armour carefully, plate by plate, until he wore only the thin base layer, close to his skin. He did not seem conscious of himself. He seated himself opposite her, an upturned box between them, and cupped a glass in the palm of his hand. The end of his nose was pink with cold. She watched him drink, and did likewise, the smoky liquid scalding her throat.

I have Seen You Before, she tried to say, but could not. She wanted to reach out and smooth back a stray strand of hair which had fallen across his forehead, but did not. The sight of the scar on his cheek brought up a choking tenderness in her throat. She placed her glass back on the table. Her cheeks glowed with sudden warmth as the fire took hold.

They drank.

"You are the keeper of these gardens?" he asked.

She nodded.

"You have a great talent," he said.

She wrapped her hands around her tea-glass and looked out through the doorway into the rain-streaked night. "You have come in the wrong season," she said. "Everything is dying. The frost has taken my best blooms and there is little to see."

"I have not seen anything green in a very long time."

"I know it is a trivial occupation," she said, "in wartime."

By the time they had drunk the pot to its dregs, the light at the hall's high window had been extinguished. The rain continued to pound at the moor beyond the walls. The fire sputtered, and steam rose from the plates of his armour, which were stacked along the wall.

"Might I take off my boots?"

She made a gesture of permission.

"I do not wish to trespass too long on your hospitality."

"You must stay at least until the worst of the rain is past."

He placed the boots beside the door, straightening her own as he did so. He peeled the damp socks from his feet carefully, methodically. Watching him, she began to feel restless and faintly panicked once again. She rose to her feet and cleared the tea things, carrying them over to the water-pipe in the wall. She rubbed her hand convulsively against the back of her neck.

Then she turned suddenly to him with a thousand things on her tongue, and gave voice to the one that was most bearable. "I understand that we are to die here, and soon. You have come to tell us that we must flee the land, but the Sisters will not leave. They would rather be slaughtered in their beds than go running through the open country, in the mud, and the rain, and the cold."

"And you?" asked the soldier. "What will you do?"

"I do not know," she said. In her mind's eye, the image of the tower shrouded in smoke, flames billowing at its windows. Her gardens uprooted, the earth sown with salt. "Only that...I have no will to run, any more."

"You have never thought to join us?"

The Gardener laughed softly. "You will forgive me, man of the White Army. But it will pass, this cause that is so dear to you. It will be swallowed up."

He listened.

319

"The world will pass, and everything in it. Nothing has ever stood that has not been under this curse. And you are fools with buckets, trying to hold back the tide."

He stood barefoot, silhouetted against the dull night outside her door.

"You will think me all the more foolish," he said. "But I do not believe that the world belongs to the curse. There is enduring, and there is being remade."

A deep silence. The fire devoured the dried stems that had fed it. He hesitated, and then moved closer to the source of warmth, holding out his hands.

The back of her throat ached. Slowly she moved to stand before the grate with him. Close-to, she saw the deep shadows beneath his eyes.

"Where is your home, soldier?" she managed to ask. "What did you leave behind?"

He blinked. "I think that there were red and cream flowers growing outside a window. My wife and I, we were there twenty years. There were children, there were models of the planets in the universe. Sunlight shone through in the late afternoon, and…"

He broke off, as though these were secrets too holy to speak aloud. There was a pause. Then he repeated, "I cannot remain long."

"No," she said. "No, nor I."

She moved towards him. He slipped one arm about her back and another beneath her knees, and lifted her entirely from the ground. Her weary body leaned into him, and she inhaled his rain-soaked smell. The room felt thin and unsteady. She held to it, winding her arms around his neck.

And as he lowered her onto the cold bed, his hand cupping the back of her shaven head and his scarred face laid against hers, she whispered something into the shell of his ear.

Epilogue

Meet me at the Museum.

*

In the burning heart of the desert, she catches on the wind the sudden scent of almonds.

She turns her head. The level sands stretch to the horizon in every direction, wet with haze. Dry dust in her nose and throat. There is nothing for the eye to fix upon: but then, even as she lifts her face to the breeze, it reaches her from the far distance. The glint of sunlight from a burnished dome.

The traveller lifts the fine red veil which blows across her face. White grains coat her freckled skin, her lips, her lashes. As she stares at the structure which shimmers against the western sky, a thin line of blood trickles from her nose. It curves around the corner of her mouth and drips down her chin. Thoughtlessly, she wipes it away with the back of her hand.

Grit settling between her teeth, she makes to lower the veil over her face again. But that breeze, that distracting breeze, lifts it from her grasp. It rises like a scarlet flag above the dunes, undulating eerily on scorching currents of air. It blows towards the west, and the branding-disk sun follows slowly, colour deepening as it sinks.

Now the unending sky is tangerine and indigo. Her shadow lengthens as she presses onward, her shorn head bowed. Her shadow seeps across the dunes. The sandal on her right foot snaps, at long last, and she tugs it away. The other is discarded too, the battered pair left in her wake, as though their wearer has evaporated to nowhere. She barely notices the blistering of her soles. Ahead, it looks as though the haze has thickened. But as she draws nearer to that great building with its peeling golden domes, she sees, with faint surprise, true water. The sea shimmers with the day's last light. The desert ends abruptly, interrupted by a thin band of green, a garden in the dunes. The Museum sits between the boundaries of sand and sea, a single diamond star alight above the observatory tower. The horizon is bruised with night blue.

She stumbles on. Thirst has nearly defeated her, and as her vision blurs she recalls the cleanness of a stream lapping at her waist. Droplets soaking her hair, trickling onto her swollen tongue. Now in the last mile before the Museum she is on her knees, on her belly, hands scrabbling in the cooling sand. The last of her strength brings her to the base of the dune garden.

The roots of mango trees are coiled around stones, fleshy fruit hanging from the branches. Each is larger than her fist. She stumbles to her feet and pulls herself up through the grasses, grasping at the nearest tree trunk until she is able to reach overhead. She tugs weakly at a fruit until it drops, and then falls upon it. Her teeth sink through the skin to the moisture below, and she swallows everything, sucking the stone dry. Another, and another, until her stomach begins to cramp and she is sated.

A hundred steps rise above the dune. The ancient stones have been cracked by the sun and the centuries. The eastern side of the observatory tower is crumbling. Bats flit out from fissures in the brick, calling shrilly. Three golden domes have begun to turn copper and moss-green.

She passes her tongue across her lips. Sharp sweetness. Grains of

322

sand. She sees, fluttering down onto the top of the steps as though carefully arranged there, her red veil.

*

On her way in she picks it up, draping it lightly about her neck. The tall oak doors, riddled through with woodworm, swing open with a puff of dust. Within it is cool and so dark that her sun-dazed eyes cannot accustom themselves. Her blisters sting on the flagstones.

Breathless from the climb, the traveller leans against the wall. As her vision returns she becomes aware that she is in a high-ceilinged space, something pale and enormous hanging dimly above her. In the bare chamber of her mind, all shadows and closed doorways, unease stirs.

It is the skeleton of a great fish. She is dwarfed to nothingness beneath it. Awed, she moves to the centre of the entrance hall, pulling the veil back over her ragged hair as though she is in a sacred place. Hush lies heavy over everything. The evening light passes through the crack between the doors, the only illumination in the huge space, splintering in the dust-thick air.

She hears, or perhaps imagines, the creaking of its ancient joints in the stillness. Her lungs hardly dare expel breath. This creature has come here from long ago. It must have swum in the deepest waters, before the world was old.

There is a door at the far end of the hall, and pushing through it she finds herself in another chamber, this time sloping, low-ceilinged. For a moment she thinks that this hall is lined by gaping sentinels. Spears in their hands, their eyes empty as pits. Then she realises that what she sees are masks hung along the wall, staring indifferently outward. Some are carved from wood or jade, others cast in brass, some intricately patterned with mosaic tiles or

323

coloured paints. Scattered between them are feathered spears and curved scimitars.

She tiptoes between these blank-eyed watchers and emerges into a circular gallery. She finds that she is now on the second floor, with many more spiralling above her, topped by the concave underside of a dome and arranged around a hexagonal ground space. Now she is surrounded by suits of armour, now delicate china displayed in glass cases, now dull and rusted electronic parts, an enormous glass sphere covered in unreadable symbols. The light from outside is fading fast, but she is sure that the galleries across from her and on the floors above must be similarly crowded with exhibits.

She moves slowly along, brushing her fingertips over the dusty rail which guards against the drop to the ground floor. When she glimpses movement, close at hand in the deepening gloom, she does not start in fear but stands and stares.

A mirror with an ornate gold border has fallen from the wall and now stands propped against it, a solitary crack crossing its length. Her split reflection stares back at her, the eyes washed of their colour. She finds that she is a smallish woman, gaunt with journeying, the skin of her freckled face stretched tightly over the bones. She cannot discern her own age, as her hair is whitened by threads of silver and by sand. Her features are as hard as the skin of her calloused hands.

A storm rages in the cavern of her head, then dies as though it had never been. The embers of images brighten and die. Snow on a man's eyelashes, geese rising from a glimmering pool, a girl alone upon a stage. Memory dissipates like smoke.

She finds that she has raised a trembling hand, thumb pointing upwards, to cover her eyes. She sinks to the ground before the dark glass. Outside, night comes.

Another desert day, the sudden attack of heat and brightness after dark hours. There is a basement where she finds cupboards full of shrink-wrapped food, a solar kettle caked with mineral deposits. She leaves it in the sunshine to charge, carries water up from the seashore in buckets, collects the condensation.

The sea is still. The sky above the sea appears oddly tilted. She notices that the sun has started to swell like a bee-sting. These details do not bother her unduly, but her sleep – beneath a fallen curtain, amongst the mummies – is fragmented. She dreams that the dunes encroach on one side of her, the tide on the other, and that she is caught in the sandy whirlpool where they meet. Waking she finds that she has crossed her hands over her chest like the surrounding dead.

The electric lights do not work. She comes across a stock of candles in one of the kitchen cupboards, and begins to position them along the corridors and halls which she has already explored. Moving through to light them each night helps her memory. Here are the tall Chinese vases, decorated in blue with feathered serpents. Here is the medieval tapestry which spans the whole length of a wall, its images faded now to invisibility. And here, flickering in and out of shadow as the candle flame gutters, the room of white guns.

She moves barefoot through these spaces with a lantern hanging from her hand. Masks leer and loom. The eyes of paintings seem to turn and follow. Bones settle and sigh. In need of more candles for the third floor, she descends into the basement, but takes a wrong turn after the stairs and finds herself in a room she does not recognise. It is sparsely furnished with two desks and a row of cabinets. Everything is cobwebbed. Holding her lamp aloft, she sees that the far wall is a sea of faces.

A step, another cautious step, she approaches in the pool of light. Hundreds of photographs are pinned along a huge board, connected by red thread, covered in scribbled notes and arrows. They are all faded. Men pose for formal portraits in top-hats and tails, are caught with a long lens crossing the road, between skyscrapers. Women have been snapped in the midst of crowds, their faces circled with black pen, or staring sombrely into the camera. Children on the steps of crumbling houses. She cannot tear her eyes away. The pictures are pasted to the board a hundred high, five hundred along.

There are more of them than stars in the sky, than sand upon the seashore.

"I have Seen You Before," she says aloud.

*

She doesn't go back there, but nothing is the same now. Her head no longer feels hollow, but singing with thoughts. The faces from the photographs are in her head. They are with her, lying down and rising. She is contented one moment, pottering amid the mango trees, then trembling with anticipation the next for no reason she can discern.

She takes to sitting out on the beach. Sea air calms her stomach. She skims flat pebbles across the breakers. Sometimes she catches herself watching the horizon for an approaching shape, as though awaiting a visitor who might choose to approach by boat. When the sea is too much the same for her she moves to the mango grove on the Museum's other side, and keeps the same vigil over the sands.

The appearance of the sun troubles her. She frames the shape of it between her fingers. Breathes mist on the mirror and draws a swollen circle with her fingertip. The sun does not rise now so much as heave itself to the zenith. For much of the day it is the colour of blood. The white stone of the Museum is dusk-pink. The sea deep crimson.

It is to get a better view of these unnaturally altered heavens that she climbs the tower, and finds that those who came before her had the same thought. At the top is an observatory, fitted with a domed roof which creaks back at the turn of a lever to reveal a space of sky. Telescopes point star-ward, all rusted on their stands. She places her lamp in the doorway and moves among instruments whose names and purposes she cannot guess, models of the planets which spin at her touch.

She ascends a few steps to the largest telescope, which is set on a stage on the far side of the circular room. Presses an eye to the glass.

The stars too have reddened and become inflamed. They hang low in the clear night like fires descending on the earth.

*

Fire and blood. Day spins around too fast from darkness. The colour bleeding down from out of the sky. The uncertain bulge of the ocean as it tries to follow the movements of the moon.

*

A quiet that breaks with the too-bright dawn, and then a hard deep rumbling in the ground. As the stone beneath her feet begins to shake she runs down the steps from the Museum out onto the sands, scattered in the sudden high wind.

Atop a sliding dune, she raises an arm to shield herself. The air is a whirlwind of bright particles. And who is that figure, dark and

327

imposing in silhouette, now moving out of the distance, out of the storm towards her? The ocean heaves and sinks into itself. She hears the Museum's tallest towers fall, stones crashing into the water below.

He climbs the dune and draws nearer, as a succession of scarlet comets streak trails across the sky. And you know him, traveller. You know him as he pulls back his scarf, showing the long scar that splits his cheek. Your impending end, smiling calmly upon you in the starlight.

Following far behind him, a procession of pilgrims in ragged cloaks. The dust of millennia upon their boots, lanterns hanging from their hands. This woman who is slender and sphinx-eyed, this one who is heavy and strong-limbed. This one with the image of a deer upon her calf. This little brother, found again, whose eyes once saw angels.

And so many, so many more besides. They are not old, but they have grown ancient. Some are not here, lost long before. They have seen empires rise and fall. Their bodies have been eaten by time. Their journeys now, at last, at an end.

With a thunderous, cracking roar, the Museum topples from its foundations. The soldier with the scar falls to his knees, and they all follow after, raising up their hands to cover their eyes. Sand swept up all around them, sky stretched and blazing as though it is about to burst.

The light is suddenly too bright to bear. She dares to lower her hand, to look into the dawning of the world that is to come.